Antipodes Jane

Barbara Ker Wilson

Antipodes Jane

A Novel of Jane Austen
in Australia

Viking

VIKING
Viking Penguin Inc.,
40 West 23rd Street,
New York, New York 10010, U.S.A.

Originally published in Great Britain under the title
Jane Austen in Australia.

First American edition
Published in 1985

LIBRARY OF CONGRESS CATALOGING IN PUBLICATION DATA
Wilson, Barbara Ker, 1929–
Antipodes Jane.
Originally published as: Jane Austen in Australia.
1984.
1. Austen, Jane, 1775–1817, in fiction, drama, poetry,
etc.   I. Title.
PR9619.3.W582J3   1985   823   84-48836
ISBN 0-670-80586-6

Printed in the United States of America by
The Book Press, Brattleboro, Vermont
Set in Trump Mediaeval

Antipodes Jane

Avant-Propos

IT need occasion no great surprise that the visit made by Jane Austen to the Colony of New South Wales in 1803–4 passed without significant remark at the time, and as a consequence has not been previously described. At that time she was quite unknown; her first novel to be published, *Sense and Sensibility*, did not appear until 1811, almost a decade later.

There is in fact very little evidence of the events of Jane Austen's life between May 1801 and September 1804, when she is known to have visited Lyme Regis with her parents, her sister, Cassandra, and her brother Henry and his wife. None of her letters for that period survive. There is, however, a well-founded tradition that sometime in 1801, probably while on another family holiday, at Sidmouth, she formed a romantic attachment, and that after the Austens returned home to Bath, they received a letter with the news that the gentleman in question, the hero of her romance, had died.

Sir Francis H. Doyle, in his *Reminiscences*, quotes an apocryphal story that this romance took place in 1802, following the Peace of Amiens, when – according to this account – Mr Austen took his two daughters, Cassandra and Jane, on a tour of Switzerland. Here, Jane is supposed to have fallen in love with a young naval officer who joined their party. *En route* to Chamonix, he elected to journey across the mountains, while the Austens took the easier way by the high road. The young man never arrived: he overtired himself and died of brain fever on the way. It seems clear enough that this is mere fabrication, and that Jane Austen's suggested trip to the Continent has somehow grown out of the visit undoubtedly made to France at this time by her brother Henry and his wife, Eliza.

In the narrative which follows, the details concerning the imprisonment and trial of Jane Austen's aunt, Mrs Leigh Perrot, are factual, and the quotations from letters she wrote while seeking bail in London, and from the Gaoler's Lodgings at Ilchester, are authentic; as are the extracts quoted later from the *Sydney Gazette*. Other events described both in England and New South Wales may be verified . . . for example, the Austen's house-hunting at Bath (related by Jane Austen in her letters); the proposal of marriage made to Jane by Harrison Bigg-Withers; the visit made by Governor King and his lady to the Cow Pastures in December 1803; Surgeon Savage's unsuccessful attempt to introduce inoculation for the smallpox to the Colony; and the curious episode concerning the deportation in His Majesty's ship *Calcutta* of a French pedlar believed to have been implicated in the Castle Hill revolt. And there are records of D'Arcy Wentworth's appearances at the 1787 and 1789 sessions at the Old Bailey, London. The martial air 'The Bold Fusilier' was much later adapted for the tune of 'Waltzing Matilda'. A specimen of the butterfly which escaped from James Leigh Perrot was later collected by Alexander Macleay, first president of the Australian Museum, in the 1840's. It is the Regent Skipper (*Euschemon rafflesia rafflesia*.) The male, but not the female, possesses the frenulum characteristic of a moth. It would have been outside its usual habitat, if observed in Parramatta.

For the rest, the author presents this account of Jane Austen's visit to the Antipodes without prejudice, trusting it may be received with indulgence and an appreciation of the humble spirit in which it was conceived.

One

Upon an unlucky Thursday, the 8th August 1799, in the city of Bath, a certain lady went shopping for a quantity of black lace with which to trim a gauze evening cloak, and as a consequence suffered a grave and astonishing misfortune. So grave, so astonishing, in fact, so dismaying to her family and true friends, so titillating to the scandalmongers, and so far-flung in its final effect, that it was to provide a chief topic of the season in the public and private meeting places of that famous English spa. For Mrs Leigh Perrot, the lady in question, was so respectable a citizen, with, moreover, such a keen awareness of her own respectability, that it seemed the wildest flight of fancy she should ever be apprehended as – a common thief!

'Poor lady': such, after the event, was the universal soubriquet coupled with her name ... and yet, before that fateful day, it was unlikely in the extreme that anyone should have thought to speak thus of Jane Leigh Perrot. On the con- trary, her acquaintance would have been much more likely to couple her name with envious, rather than sympathetic adjectives.

There were a number of reasons why Jane Leigh Perrot might arouse envy in the nubile, ample or withered bosoms of other ladies. It was not so much her affluent circumstances: most of those other ladies lived in similar comfort, in well ordered households with polished furniture, Turkey rugs, gleaming silver and a liveried footman to answer the front door. Nor was it very likely to be her family connexions, though to be sure she was in the habit of making frequent reference to the fact that on

7

the maternal side, she was directly descended from Lord Willoughby of Parham. Such overt social pride was apt to draw forth an indulgent smile, rather than a sneer.

More likely, perhaps, to arouse the bile of envy was Jane Leigh Perrot's handsome appearance. Now in middle age (she was known to be in her early fifties), she showed a singular lack of such unpleasing traits as a plural chin, stoutness, stooped gait, fallen teeth, grey hair, a lacklustre eye, wrinkled complexion — in short, the whole dismal catalogue only too familiar to most of her contemporaries. She was a handsome woman of middle height, whose upright carriage gave the impression of her being somewhat taller than she was in fact. Her features were perhaps a little too clearly defined; she herself took great pride in her high-bridged patrician nose. Her complexion was still fine and smooth, her eye bright, and her hair retained its pleasing chestnut hue.

Wealth, position and good looks apart, the single circumstance most likely to encourage the wistful envy of Jane Leigh Perrot's female acquaintance was this: she enjoyed an exceptionally contented marriage. There was simply no gainsaying it, no chink in her marital life where gossip or calumny might worm their way. She and her husband, Mr James Leigh Perrot of Scarlets, Hare Hatch, in the county of Berkshire (an estate which boasted a pleasant modern house set in a parkland of oaks and beeches planted in Tudor days), were quite devoted to each other, and had shared their lives in civilized amity for seven and thirty years. The cynic who, in conversation relating to *mariage à la mode*, might exclaim: 'Give me one instance of truly happy wedlock!' was apt to be refuted by the prompt example of the Leigh Perrots' domestic bliss. She steadfastly doted on her James; he never ceased to count himself the most fortunate of men when, as plain Mr Leigh, he had met his Jane. He had later followed the usual custom, upon inheriting an estate and fortune from a great-uncle Perrot, of taking the latter's name and arms and adding them to his own.

There were no children of the union. It was rather doubtful whether Jane Leigh Perrot herself had any pronounced maternal yearnings; more likely it was her mild-mannered husband who regretted the absence of sons and daughters and the busyness of family life. He would, indeed, have made an admirable, kindly father; instead, he had always proved himself a favourite uncle to his nieces and nephews.

On the part of the Leigh Perrots' nearest relatives, the lack of a direct heir to their joint fortune caused considerable speculation, particularly within the family circle of a certain country clergyman, the Reverend George Austen of Steventon, in Hampshire. He had married James Leigh Perrot's sister Cassandra, and their eldest son, prudently christened James, had quite confident expectations from his uncle's estate. The Austens visited Bath from time to time; it was even now but two months since Mrs George Austen and her younger daughter, Jane, had spent some weeks there. They had shared lodgings in Queen Square with Mrs Austen's second son, Edward, his wife, Elizabeth, and their two eldest children, all come from Kent. During that visit they had seen a good deal of their relations, exchanging calls between Queen Square and the Leigh Perrot house in the Paragon, and accompanying them to a ceremony in Royal Crescent, where Jane Leigh Perrot's illustrious connexion, the present Lady Willoughby, presented colours to a Corps of Yeomanry. They had also enjoyed the fireworks and illuminations in Sydney Gardens, gazed in all the shop windows, and Fanny and little Edward had vied with their Aunt Jane Austen in their capacity for Bath buns. The main object of the visit, however, had been for Edward to take a cure; he had been in poor health, and had greatly benefited from taking the spa waters, and trying the new electricity treatment. The Austens had departed for Hampshire and Kent respectively, well satisfied with their visit, and with no idea in the world that their next intelligence respecting the Leigh Perrots was to prove extraordinary in the extreme.

But now we are arrived at that unlucky Thursday, that August morning with the sun shining down upon the pale Ionic columns of the royal spa, striking the bright new pavements and dappling the surface of the River Avon as it flowed beneath Pulteney Bridge. The Leigh Perrots lived at Number One, the Paragon – a curving terrace near the mail coach terminus, and not far from the church of St Swithin Walcot. To this town house they came regularly from Scarlets so that James might seek relief for his frequent attacks of gout, while his wife enjoyed the social hubbub of the city.

Together with a host of fellow sufferers, James followed in the halting footsteps of those administrators of the Roman Empire who, forever grumbling about the climate of their far northern colony, had evoked the healing power of Sul Minerva and built the city of Aquae Sulis two thousand years ago. The Great Bath they had used now lay forgotten, silted up beneath the ground; nowadays, a single open-air bath remained, and here one might observe the mundane modern spectacle of men and women, clad in long calico gowns and oilskin caps, trudging purposefully through the steaming thermal water from one side to the other – the quest for health become a conscientious duty rather than a sybaritic Roman ritual.

And yet the graceful new Palladian city of this century, with its colonnaded streets, its squares and crescents, Theatre Royal, shops and Assembly Rooms, was surely a worthy successor to that ancient Aquae Sulis. Until a few years ago, the city had been surpassed only by London itself as the gathering place of the Beau Monde, but in recent times the Beau Monde had inclined towards the new seaside resorts and the vaunted efficacy of sea-bathing. Though still very lively and fashionable, Bath was gradually becoming more of an elegant centre for retired gentlefolk: Herculaneum rather than Pompeii. Which suited the Leigh Perrots and their style of living very well.

From Number One, the Paragon, that summer morning, while Frank the footman held wide the door, out stepped that fortunate couple, Jane Leigh Perrot and her husband James. The weather was too warm for a pelisse; she wore a cream dress of fine cashmere and a brown Leghorn bonnet lined with ruched silk of a pinker hue, achieving an effect not unlike the crinkled underside of a vast mushroom. Happily this comparison had not occurred to the wearer of the bonnet; she was confident it became her well. Mrs Leigh Perrot took exceptional pains with her attire, aided by her maid Evans, who had been in her service many years. – It was, indeed, nothing more nor less than vanity, vanity of person coupled with the season's whim that no lady could possibly appear at the Upper Rooms, the Theatre or any other social gathering without black lace upon her evening cloak, which encouraged Mrs Leigh Perrot to set out this day upon her shopping expedition.

Already the world was abroad in the streets: in the main

thoroughfares the dash of carriages, the heavy rumble of carts and drays, and the bawling of newsmen, muffin-men and milk-men provided a noisy background to private and public occasions. In harmonious counterpart, frivolous young ladies pattered along the pavements in flimsy slippers; philosophers and politicians plodded past deep in thought; liveried footmen bore those invitations and notes of assignment that kept the social intercourse of Bath revolving in its concentric circles; and militia men, naval officers and bang-up Oxonians on vacation strolled by, ogling those same frivolous young ladies, who, giddy as butterflies in their sprigged and spotted muslin gowns, made a very good pretence of ignoring such attention – every now and then betraying their real interest with backward glances and sidelong looks. Mrs Leigh Perrot might appear to have spawned a mushroom upon her head, but other bonnets, it seemed, had sprouted fruit this summer. Bunches of fat strawberries and glistening grapes, clusters of little plums and apricots, all with realistic leaves fashioned from green silk and wire, were to be seen bobbing jauntily along each thoroughfare. Lady Fust swept by with a veritable fruit salad upon her straw poke, and there went pale Miss Mapleton, sporting enough shiny cherries to make a sizeable pie.

After a while James left his wife and went off in the direction of the Cross Bath. He limped as he crossed the cobbled carriageway, wincing from the intolerable pressure of his silver-buckled shoe upon an inflamed great toe. His wife, who until now had slowed her walk to accommodate his lameness, stepped out jauntily on her own, continuing towards Bath Street and Smith's the haberdasher. On the way she exchanged the time of day with a pale young lady she knew by sight, a Miss Langley, her bosom much exposed as usual, and nodded briefly to old Mrs Fitzgibbon, notorious gossip and carnivore of reputations. Turning into Bath Street, she caught sight of a clergyman dressed in unrelieved and gloomy black; it was Dr Hall, who had delivered such a very direful sermon at the Abbey two weeks ago. He raised his hat with a mournful smile, as though he knew that an unhappy fate awaited her this morning.

And now Jane Leigh Perrot swept confidently into the haberdasher's, and at once the shopkeeper, a Miss Gregory, who had lately taken over the establishment on the demise of her elder sister, came forward to assist her. Miss Gregory pulled out a chair and, at Mrs Leigh Perrot's request, produced several cards of black lace. She knew this well-dressed lady to be one of her late sister's best customers and assumed a deferential air towards her, washing her hands in air in a nervous manner as she addressed her. This irritated the forthright Jane Leigh Perrot, who observed with distaste that the woman's hands were distinctly grubby. The elder Miss Gregory, she thought regretfully, had been a woman of clean fingernails and earnest dedication to the world of pins and needles, embroidery twist, stay tapes, whalebone and Petersham ribands. This younger sister – though one would scarcely call her *young* – knew little of her trade, she suspected. She had a blowsy, untidy look.

Mrs Leigh Perrot peered at the different patterns of lace before her, finding none absolutely to her liking. She flicked one card disdainfully. 'This,' she pronounced, 'is cobbled work.' Passed over another – 'I do not care for that at all.' Considered a third – 'A clumsy pattern' – and finally, with a sigh of resignation at having to choose the best out of an inferior selection, made her decision: 'I daresay this will do.'

'An excellent choice, ma'am!' Miss Gregory declared, clasping her dingy hands in a positive ecstasy and asserting that the lace in question was not inferior to the French patterns her late lamented sister used to stock before the War made such purchases impossible.

'Bonaparte has much to answer for,' Mrs Leigh Perrot remarked sarcastically, 'of that we are all aware. But he is not, I think, responsible for such a decline in the quality of English lace. The War is no excuse for cobbled work such as you first showed me. The lacemakers of Devon did not win their reputation with such trash. – Make haste to put this up for me, if you please, I am in a hurry.' Her gaze was cold, her tone arrogant; she quite failed to observe the quick flush of offence upon the shopwoman's face. If she had, she would not have cared.

'At once, ma'am,' Miss Gregory murmured obsequiously, masking her resentment. She summoned the man who helped her in the shop, a pasty, lank-haired individual with shifty eyes. He had been shopboy to the elder sister, who had suspected him of stealing small change but had never found the proof. Now Sam Filby stood in a different, intimate relationship to the younger sister. She, weary of spinsterhood and lacking a respectable suitor, was not particular to distinguish between a man's liking and his lust – and was inclined to graft her own hopeless affection merely upon the baser instinct.

'Put up this lace, Filby,' Miss Gregory said now. 'Pray make haste.'

'At once, Miss Gregory.'

Was there not something odd about this brief exchange, a scarcely discernible accentuating of the *Miss* in his response which verged on impudence? It was as though a vulgar wink had passed between the pair of them.

Mrs Leigh Perrot opened her reticule and handed the shopman two sovereigns. The price of vanity was high: the lace she had chosen cost something over twenty shillings. She felt it was overpriced, but did not care to pursue the matter; the whole transaction had become disagreeable to her: the indifferent goods, Miss Gregory's fawning manner, and now the appearance of this shifty-looking shopman. She earnestly desired to leave and be on her way.

Miss Gregory followed the shopman to the back of the establishment, and Mrs Leigh Perrot heard them whispering together as the lace was wrapped and her change counted out. What an age they were taking! Impatiently she drummed on the counter top with her gloved fingers, then went to the shop door to look into the street through thick whorls of glass that distorted the scene outside.

In the back room, Sam Filby was whispering villainy to Susan Gregory.

'Oh Sam, we durst not do it – not to her. It is too bold. She is called Lady Parrot, or some such name, and has great friends among the gentry.'

'All the better.' Sam laid one finger along his long, thin nose. 'The higher they be, the greater the reputation at stake, and *presto*! the more willingly they fall in with our little schemes. Think of the trick we played on Mrs Chalmers – how we fooled the Hon'able Miss Tempest, and Lady Fortescue . . . *they* paid up meek as lambs, every one.' He smiled slyly. 'We'll succeed just the same with this Lady High-and-Mighty, Mrs Make-Haste, Bring-Me-My-Change-Directly, you'll see! We'll make this Lady Parrot squawk!'

13

'Ssh, Sam, she'll hear us' – but Susan's apprehension was lessened by his persuasion. 'Pr'aps you know best,' she conceded. 'It's you has the hardest part to carry out. Mine is all polite and easy.' Her face darkened. 'I'll give her "cobbled work", "trash" – and all that gallipot talk about old Boney!' She was determined now. 'Quick, while she's gawping out of the door. Look – there's this card of white driz to go along with the other –'

Deftly Samuel Filby tied the parcel, scooped up six half-sovereigns and a handful of small change, and returned to the front of the shop.

'At last!' Their customer took her change and the parcel, nodded curtly, and hurried into the street. The jangle of the doorbell seemed to echo her irritation with the whole business; and now, as if to acquiesce with her changed mood, she found the sky had clouded over; the clear golden morning had dissipated.

Alone in the shop, Susan Gregory and Sam Filby gaped at each other in vulgar glee at the plot they had set in motion, the wicked mischief they had perpetrated upon their customer.

'You're a bold, sly cove, Sam Filby,' Susan told him, with a suggestive glance. 'You've led me into wicked ways, you have.'

He smirked, then without ceremony began to propel her urgently towards the back room once again, past a display of tangled ribbons and a tall post that displayed a bonnet trimmed with dusty flowers, like a head tumbled by the Frenchies' guillotine and flaunted on a pole. A plot well laid stirred Sam to sexual need; he began to breathe heavily, and there was a congested look upon his face which Susan knew well. He pushed his *sans-culotte*, his easy-come Susan, against a cupboard, using one hand to fumble her skirts up, while with the other he unbuttoned. She gasped lasciviously and rubbed herself wantonly against him as he thrust into her moistness greedily, his eyes closed tightly, lids jerking as in his fantasy he violated Mrs Leigh Perrot and all rich, powerful women on whom it was his lot to dance attendance behind a haberdashery counter.

Two

JANE LEIGH PERROT stopped and waited at the corner as she spied her husband limping downhill on the way from the Cross Bath. His gout was worse today, she saw, and felt a soft surge of sympathy. The cursed affliction never seemed to make him bad-tempered, as it did other gentlemen of their acquaintance, particularly when they were forbidden their customary comforts of claret, Madeira and port, and allowed only a meagre ration of Constantia wine. Mr Rowlandson made gout a subject of much ribald merriment in his cartoons, but in truth there was nothing merry about it.

'Perrot,' she greeted him affectionately, 'well met.' And rested her arm lightly on his as they continued together along the pavement.

James smiled at her fondly above the agony of pinching shoe and throbbing foot, and told her he was intending to visit the apothecary's in Milsom Street, to settle an account.

'Be sure he itemizes everything, my love,' his wife advised. 'There is no one so adept as an apothecary at overcharging, 'tis well known.'

They made a slow passage to that handsome street of fashionable shops, where, in the apothecary's window, tall glass jars — red, blue, green — were struck by the sudden reappearance of a single shaft of sunshine into ruby, lapis, emerald. Inside, the shop smelled pleasantly of medications and bay rum amid a cool, tranquil atmosphere. Mrs Leigh Perrot purchased a fresh supply of the curiously strong peppermints to which she was addicted, and a jar of rosewater for her complexion.

Mr Powys, the apothecary, greeted the Leigh Perrots courteously and, their business settled, the two men entered into an earnest conversation upon the subject of diurnal Lepidoptera. The landed gentleman and the busy apothecary shared a passion for natural history, and eagerly James described his recent sighting of a butterfly unknown to him, in a meadow starred with daisies and studded with buttercups, at Scarlets.

'*Brown* markings, the wings fringed in bronze?' Mr Powys repeated James' description in his lilting Welsh voice. 'My dear sir, I would venture to suggest one of the fritillaries – yes, indeed, a fritillary, depend upon it.'

But now their discussion was interrupted by Jane Leigh Perrot, who recollected that she was carrying in her reticule a letter she wished to post. She plucked her husband by the sleeve. 'Let us go home by way of the post-office, Perrot,' she said. 'What a pity I did not remember the letter when I was at the haberdasher's – 'tis but a step to the post-office from there.' She frowned, recalling the annoyance she had felt upon leaving that shop – it must have driven all thought of the letter from her mind. 'If we make haste,' she went on, moving towards the door, ' – that is, as much haste as you are able to make, my love, it will catch the midday coach.'

They left Milsom Street and retraced their steps to Bath Street, where the post-office was situated, then turned homeward towards the Paragon.

It happened that Sam Filby was standing in the doorway of Smith's, taking a breath of air, when he spied the Leigh Perrots slowly advancing along the other side of the road. He at once retreated into the shop and urged Susan to enact the first scene of the villainous pantomime they had devised.

'Now's our chance, girl! I did not think 'twould come so soon. Play your part well – I'll take myself off to wait where our two gulls are bound to pass on their way home.' And without waiting for her answer – indeed, his speech was a command – he went out through the back door of the shop.

Nervously Susan stepped forth and crossed the street, intercepting the Leigh Perrots as they came opposite the shop. She bobbed a curtsey and said: 'I beg pardon, ma'am, but was there by mistake a card of white lace put up with the black you bought?'

Jane Leigh Perrot looked at her in surprise and frowned beneath the pink ruching of her bonnet. 'A card of *white* lace? I really cannot tell, since I have not been home since I was in your shop. The parcel has never left my hand. If you wish, you may open it and satisfy yourself on the matter. Any mistake is entirely the fault of your shopman and yourself.'

'Thank you, ma'am, I *will* open it.' And, somewhat to Mrs Leigh Perrot's discomfiture, for several people passed by while this interchange took place – among them, she observed with vague annoyance, that insatiable gossip Mrs Fitzgibbon – Susan Gregory took the parcel and opened it.

James, meanwhile, long-suffering, had turned to regard the snuff mixtures in a tobacconist's window. 'Twas but an idle gesture to fill the moment; he had forsworn snuff along with his port, Madeira and claret. There was nothing like a hearty sneeze to jolt a gouty limb into agony.

'Oh, here it is!' Susan exclaimed in a well simulated cry of discovery. 'I am sorry to have troubled you, ma'am.' And she took the card of white lace that had been parcelled up with the black, and, sketching another curtsey, scurried back to the shop.

'How tiresome,' Jane Leigh Perrot remarked to her husband as they continued on their way. 'But I cannot say I am surprised at such negligence, after visiting the shop this morning. Smith's is not what it was. I shall take my custom elsewhere in future.'

They had almost reached the Abbey churchyard when they were accosted by Sam Filby, who appeared to be labouring under a sense of great injustice.

'I must speak to you, ma'am,' he said boldly. 'I desire to know your name and place of abode; *I* never put that white lace into your parcel, and no one shall accuse me of it! Why, 'twas worth twenty shilling, and 'tis no light matter to say I made such a mistake!'

As she listened to this outpouring, Jane Leigh Perrot felt a faint stirring of alarm: the shifty-eyed shopman seemed so very agitated, the whole extraordinary incident was so very peculiar. She looked to her husband, extreme exasperation apparent on her face.

'I suppose it can do no harm to acquaint this fellow with our name and the whereabouts of our dwelling,' James said reluctantly; if his uppermost thought had not been to get home and release his foot from its infernal shoe, he might well have shown more caution at this juncture. As it was, he proceeded to spell out his name and street to Sam Filby, who promptly noted them down.

Irritated beyond measure, Jane Leigh Perrot addressed the shopman firmly. 'I neither asked for white lace, nor was I shown any all the time I was in the shop,' she said; 'it is nothing to do with me. Be on your way, and do not trouble us again. – Come, Perrot.'

Had she looked back she would have beheld Sam, triumphant with the information he had sought, thumbing his nose after her as she walked on beside her limping spouse.

The next day, and over the weekend, the inflammation in James' foot worsened, so that he was forced to take to his bed, where he rested in embroidered nightshirt and tasselled cap, reduced to a light diet of calves'-foot jelly and Dr Oliver's biscuits. Jane Leigh Perrot, solicitous as ever where her husband's welfare was concerned, sat in his bedchamber and read aloud from the newspaper, carefully avoiding those items which she judged might serve to depress or aggravate him. Thus, while skimming over details of the detested Bonaparte's ever increasing popularity within France, she read out in full an account of how some French soldiers, digging trenches in Egypt during their campaign against the Turks, had unearthed a curious stone which scholars surmised might hold the key to ancient hieroglyphics. – This was just the sort of thing that James found interesting. She was especially careful not to mention the iniquitous Income Tax which Mr Pitt had just introduced to help ease the burden of paying for the War – a temporary measure, he had assured the nation. Even to the easygoing James, the notion of paying two shillings in the pound out of his income in a direct tax to the Government was like a red rag to a bull. Moreover, since they had no children, they were not eligible for abatement upon that score. (There was a sliding scale . . . those whose quivers overflowed with ten children or more were allowed to keep a quarter of their income tax-free . . .) The news from India was most satisfactory: the British had captured Seringapatam, and that horrid Tippoo Sahib of Mysore was dead.

They shared an agreeably scandalous interest in a paragraph concerning Lady Conyngham's ascent into the affections of the Prince Regent. 'To think she was a mere shopkeeper's daughter,' Jane Leigh Perrot remarked, 'before she captured her Irish earl – and now she aims highest of all!' The word 'shopkeeper' reminded her of recent unpleasantness, and she turned hastily to another item.

'It says here that Sir Humphry Davy has used a substance called – er – nitrous oxide – as a palliative to ease the pain of tooth-drawing.' She looked up from the printed page, eyebrows raised to seek James' thoughts on this development.

'A pity it cannot be used to ease this confounded gout,' he growled; and the tassel on his cap swung from one side to the other as he eased himself into a slightly more comfortable position.

In another room, the maid Evans sat diligently plying her needle, sewing the black lace edging to her mistress' gauze evening cloak. She was a small, pale, dark-haired woman of indeterminate age, stooped and diminished by years of service to a demanding and often unsympathetic employer, to whom, in the way of faithful servants cowed by habit, she yet harboured a sense of loyalty. If you had asked her opinion of Mrs Leigh Perrot, she would very likely have answered, quite simply: 'She is my lady.'

As she bent to her task, peering at the line of fine stitching, she could not know that her mistress would never wear her cloak with its new trimming; that an undreamed-of calamity was about to overtake that proud ruler of the household, so secure in her position within a world where some were born to give orders, others to obey.

Because of James' indisposition, the Leigh Perrots cancelled a visit to the theatre, where *A Cure for Heartache* was playing ('twas said to be vastly amusing), and also one or two private parties. Jane Leigh Perrot had looked forward to wearing her refurbished cloak on all three outings, but consoled herself with the thought that there would be plenty of other occasions on which to show off her lace . . .

On Monday it rained, and the glistening pavements echoed to

the clack of pattens. James averred the bad weather made him feel more poorly, even though he was warmly tucked up in bed. Jane sent Evans with an umbrella to the Circulating Library to exchange her book – there was really no need to waste money on a sedan chair and go herself. She handed Evans a list. 'Ask for any of the titles written here,' she told her. 'I should particularly like the latest novel by Mrs Edgecliffe – or is it Edgebury? Edge-something, I know. And be very careful to keep the book dry. And have a look inside the book, to see that it is clean. I had to use my embroidery scissors to turn the pages of *The Memoirs of Lady Woodward*, so soiled and dog's eared they were. The book was not fit for a Christian to read!'

Whether this last assertion referred solely to the state of that book, or to its contents, or perhaps both, Evans could not be sure. She tramped off through the rain, and though her feet and shoulders were soaked by the time she returned, she dutifully made sure that *Castle Rackrent* kept dry.

As for James, he was assured of delightful reading matter, for the latest issue of *The Naturalist's Miscellany* arrived by the morning post, and he cheered up amazingly. He was not only a subscriber to this journal but an occasional contributor upon the subject of Lepidoptera.

The evening post, however, brought the shadow of imminent disaster into the tranquil parlour at the Paragon, where Jane Leigh Perrot sat at her tapestry in the soft lamplight, serene in the knowledge that her husband rested peacefully upstairs. She was seeking a fresh skein of wool when Evans entered the room with a letter, just delivered.

'What's this?' her mistress demanded, turning it in her hand and peering at the inscription. Her eyesight was not as good as it used to be, but she was too vain to resort to eye-glasses. 'What a curious form of address,' she exclaimed, deciphering the crude handwriting. 'Mrs Leigh Perrot, Lace dealer.' She opened the letter and was astonished to discover the following lines, written without salutation or signature:

Your many visiting Acquaintance, before they again admit you into their houses, will think it right to know how you came by the piece of Lace stolen from Bath St:, a few days ago. Your husband is said to be privy to it.

'Ma'am, are you unwell?' Evans asked; for her mistress, on reading the letter, had lost her colour and put one hand to her brow as though overcome by dizziness.

'It – it is of no account,' Jane Leigh Perrot replied faintly. But she shivered in spite of her words, as though some vile intruder had entered her snug parlour. Then, her mouth drawn in a firm line, she deliberately folded the offensive paper and put it in her pocket. 'That wretched lace,' she muttered, half to herself. 'Will I never hear the end of it? What it is all about, heaven only knows!' She could only imagine that she was being made sport of in some senseless jest. She would simply ignore it – no one should have the satisfaction of knowing they had upset her.

Evans, hearing those half-spoken thoughts, did not know what was troubling her mistress. She had not received a full account of the shopping expedition; she had merely been informed that the shop people at the haberdashers had been negligent and impertinent and (several times) that her mistress would never, on any account, patronize the shop again. She went over to a decanter that stood on a side table and poured a glass of brandy. 'Here, ma'am, this will help you overcome the disagreeableness of that letter.'

Mrs Leigh Perrot sipped the brandy; colour was restored to her complexion, calmness to her mind. 'Now, Evans,' she said warningly, 'on no account must your master know anything of this letter. I would not have him disturbed by it for the world. It is not in the least important.'

Three

SAMUEL FILBY WAS in an ugly temper. In the living room above the shop, seated at a table bearing the remains of supper, he slammed his fist down so that the crockery rattled and Susan Gregory jumped in her chair.

'How dare they dangle us like this?' he shouted. 'That letter should've brought Mrs High-and-Mighty with her parrot's beak running here as fast as a dose of salts would send her running to the privy.' He glowered into his mug of ale.

'There's no one else has held out on us, only her,' Susan remarked miserably. Sam was apt to cuff her when his temper turned sour. 'What shall us do, then?'

Sam's eyes gleamed with fresh cunning. 'If she won't play our game, we'll take it a step further – that's what we'll do. We'll call their bluff. We'll go to the Mayor and Magistrates, my girl, and lay charges as to how a certain gentlewoman, name of Leigh Perrot, stole a quantity of driz, to the value of twenty shilling; to which wicked thieving act we both was witnesses.'

'Oh Sam, would you go that far?' Susan exclaimed, feeling a thrill of terror. 'A theft of twenty shilling – why, that's –'

'A hanging matter!' Sam shouted. 'Aye, so it is – and there's many a one of my condition knows it, what has been took to gaol and hanged by the neck for lifting no more than a quartern loaf when he was starving.' He reached clumsily for Susan's hand across the table. 'But don't fret, it won't come to that. We won't see Lady Parrot dancing on air. – Anyway, they send 'em off to Botany Bay these days instead of the gallows, often as not. Soon as we lay charges, they'll be on our doorstep, you'll see, begging and pleading with us to withdraw 'em. For the doing of which we shall demand our fee, as is only right and proper. And that fee, my doxy, will amount to *twice* as many of those golden guineas, those sweet canary birds, as we was intending to ask before!'

'Oh Sam, you're right!' Susan exclaimed. She gazed at him admiringly. How bold he was! In her poor mind she mistook his low scheming for a high resolution. 'They must come running to us now – they'll have no choice!'

On Wednesday, James announced his intention of leaving his bed later in the day. He possessed a large shoe, specially made for victims of the gout by a Bath bootmaker, and thought that if he wore this and used two sticks for support, he should be able to get about tolerably well.

Meanwhile, he was still absorbed in *The Naturalist's Miscellany*, and as Jane sat in his bedchamber that morning, he regaled her with an account of the curious water mole which had been observed in the distant Colony of New South Wales, half a world away.

New South Wales – that Botany Bay of the street ballads, whither Mother England swept the dregs and undesirables of her society, such as were reprieved from the gallows: Jacobins and other agitators; abductors of heiresses; bigamists; counterfeiters; confidence tricksters; poachers; plain common-or-garden thieves; suspected murderers, every other sort of criminal known to man or woman. New South Wales . . . surely the last place on earth where anyone of true refinement and sensibility would wish to find himself! – Well, it appeared that the Governor of that salubrious Colony, a Captain John Hunter (as keen a naturalist, it would seem, as James Leigh Perrot himself), had sent a specimen of this water mole, a most unusual creature, to Sir Joseph Banks, President of the Royal Society, along with a drawing made from life, which had been copied in the *Miscellany*, and which James now showed to his wife.

'Most peculiar,' was her observation as she inspected the drawing. 'It appears to be covered in fur, with a duck's bill and webbed feet –' She shook her head in instinctive disapproval of such an unlikely creation.

'Sir Joseph has named the creature *Ornithorhynchus*

Paradoxus,' James said. 'He describes it as part quadruped, part bird, part lizard – a paradox indeed! But,' he added, 'it seems certain scientists believe the creature to be a fake, assembled by some artful Chinee.'

His wife nodded. 'I should not be at all surprised.'

It was at this moment that Evans entered the room. 'Beg pardon, Ma'am, but there is a – a person downstairs who wishes to speak to you without delay. Frank has shown him into the parlour.'

'A *person?* The *parlour?* Without delay?' Jane Leigh Perrot raised her eyebrows. 'It was quite unnecessary to show a *person* into the parlour, Evans; that courtesy is for gentlefolk, as Frank well knows.'

'Oh, ma'am' – Evans twisted a corner of her apron in fierce distress – 'I am afraid *this* person cannot be put off; he insists most particularly that he must speak to you directly.' She could not bring herself to tell her mistress exactly what manner of person it was who waited in the room downstairs. – Besides, had not her mistress warned her against causing alarm to the master?

With a sigh Mrs Leigh Perrot rose from her chair. 'It seems I am *commanded* to go down to deal with this importunate person,' she told her husband wryly.

James, whose attention was now held by a description of *Heteronympha banksi* in that same article concerning the natural wonders of New South Wales, looked up briefly and nodded incuriously. The following few moments, while he perused the notes on the first sighting of that antipodean butterfly, were to provide his last peace of mind for many a long day.

Mrs Leigh Perrot, most consciously and evidently the mistress of this household, went briskly down the stairs, followed by Evans, and marched straight into the parlour, prepared to quell this uninvited visitor, whoever he might be. But she stopped short upon the threshold of the room, quite taken aback to discover, standing in the centre of the Turkey carpet before the fireplace, a burly, bearded constable of the city watch.

'You are Mrs Leigh Perrot and this is your residence?' the constable demanded in a grave tone. He was a stern-featured man of middle-age. His truncheon, symbol of office, was tucked under one arm.

24

She inclined her head, registering with surprise his direct address to her, the lack of courtesy. 'I am Mrs Leigh Perrot. Did you wish to speak to my husband? I fear he is indisposed at present.'

The constable drew forth a sheet of paper and proceeded to intone the formula he was accustomed to recite on such occasion: 'Mrs Leigh Perrot, I have here a warrant from the Mayor and Magistrates of this city, requiring your immediate appearance before them to answer charges that have been laid against you this day, the fourteenth of August, *Anno Domini* 1799.'

Evans, standing behind her mistress, uttered a strange sound, somewhere between a gasp and a smothered shriek. Two red spots glowed in her usually pale cheeks. Jane Leigh Perrot laid both hands upon the back of an upright chair to support herself while she absorbed the shock she had sustained. Frank, hovering within earshot in the hall, found his fantastic speculation dragged headlong into the realm of reality; he stood stock-still in disbelief.

'Pray, what form do these charges take?' Mrs Leigh Perrot inquired, endeavouring to keep her voice steady while her soul shook.

'Larceny,' was the constable's unexpectedly laconic reply; and then, elaborating: 'You are charged with larceny above the value of five shillings. Grand larceny, Mrs Leigh Perrot.'

Above the value of five shillings ... Well might the two servants quake inwardly at those dread words: to steal above the value of five shillings was punishable by death.

When Evans was a small child, known within her family as 'our little Gwyn', her mother had taken her for a walk one day in the countryside, and they had passed by a gibbet, where the blackened figure of what had been a living, breathing man swung twisting in the wind. A sheep stealer, the mother told the child . . . and now the man twisted there, riding a horse foaled by an acorn, as the saying went, while the fat Welsh sheep in safety grazed the green pasture all around. Young Gwynneth did not forget that sinister object lesson. Nowadays, of course, the penalty for theft was most often commuted to transportation, but that was scarcely a case for consolation.

'It is the lace, it can only be the lace,' Jane Leigh Perrot

25

thought bitterly. Who would have imagined those two wretches at the haberdasher's would carry their imposture so far? For now it was quite clear to her what nasty business was afoot. A sort of blackmail ... to play a trick upon honest citizens by unscrupulous shopkeepers for their own gain. It was all so very undignified, an unconscionable affront: of course there was not, there could not be, the slightest doubt in the world that the whole sorry affair would be speedily resolved. But there was evidently a great deal of tedious official rigmarole to be got through first. She drew herself upright and told the constable as calmly as she was able: 'I must acquaint my husband with this news.'

'Very well,' the constable said sternly, 'but make haste, Missus. His Worship the Mayor and other gentlemen await you now.'

What gall lay in his plain address to her! She did not ever recall anyone speaking to her in such a manner.

Mr Leigh Perrot's consternation, when his wife returned in distress and agitation to his bedchamber, may be easily imagined. His immediate impulse was to leap out of bed: he tossed his tasselled nightcap from his head, flung back the bedclothes – but alas, such impetuosity was arrested as soon as his gouty foot touched the floor. 'Fetch me my large shoe, my love,' he groaned, adjusting his movements to his condition. 'I must and will accompany you to the Mayor and Magistrates.'

Forthwith Frank was sent to fetch a sedan chair; and, having dressed in uncommon haste, and with the aid of his two sticks, James shortly hobbled out of the house with his wife, accompanied by the constable, while Evans and Frank both stood holding the front door ajar, their mouths likewise agape, their world turned topsy-turvy.

What passed before the Mayor and Magistrates was solely ordained by the due process of law. That bold couple, Samuel Filby and Susan Gregory, swore solemnly and with vindictive resolution that *he* had seen the lady take the lace; that *she* had found that selfsame article, to the value of twenty shillings, in the possession of the said lady. And, whatever the private opinion of the Mayor and Magistrates might be, they were obliged upon the oaths of those two conspirators to perform their duty, to indict the lady of this capital charge and commit her to the County Gaol at Ilchester to await trial. However harsh the antiquated English law might be, at least this might be said for it: that it applied impartially to each division of society. Once charged, a suspect must prove innocence, whatever his degree.

The Leigh Perrots' lawyer, Mr Watts, had been hastily summoned, and he immediately advised that an application for bail would be made; this, however, would necessitate a journey to London on the part of the accused, to appear there before a Judge.

'You will in due course be escorted to London by the Governor of Ilchester Gaol, Mrs Leigh Perrot,' the Chief Magistrate told the unfortunate lady before him. The kindliness of his tone was in strange juxtaposition to the words he uttered.

'And I shall be with you, my dear – never fear!' James Leigh Perrot averred stoutly.

And now, as Jane Leigh Perrot, that respectable middle-aged lady, that well loved spouse, that mistress of two households, that descendant of the Willoughbys of Parham, realized that all this was indeed happening to her, that she was not merely fallen into a vivid nightmare, that she was here and now to be taken directly to the County Gaol, the utmost dismay settled upon her proud features, and with anguished gaze, in mute appeal, she besought her husband to . . . to do what? For there was nothing he could do. The loving husband, landed gentleman, upright citizen, amateur naturalist was equally helpless before the implacable machinery of the law.

'Tell – tell Evans to bring my warmest cloak,' his wife said finally, her voice quavering. 'It will be cold in – in that place where I am going.'

Cold, cold . . . iron and stone, gloom and the clank of fetters from prisoners who had done with their trials and been found guilty: already she seemed to hear the clang of the spiked prison gate that would separate her from all the busy, bustling, fashionable, happy world she knew. Oh, that life should be so changed in an instant of time! That one should drink hot chocolate at breakfast out of a china cup, with no more immediate concern in mind than the choice of which pelisse to wear that day, and that same evening lie on a prison pallet, wrapped in an old frieze cloak!

And yet, as she left that room and walked past her two accusers, she managed to hold her head high; at the sight of that blowsy woman, Susan Gregory, and her sly companion, a surge of sheer righteous anger seemed to explode in her inmost being, stronger far than any craven dismay.

Four

THERE COULD BE few sights more peaceful, in this seventh
year of England's war with France, than a Hampshire village
upon a Sunday afternoon in high summer. Chestnut and elm
trees stood in full greenery; children played about cottage
doorways; cows and sheep grazed the meadows and distant,
gentle hillside: everyone and everything was redolent of the
restful Sabbath, with church duty done and the best dinner of
the week to look forward to.

Such was the scene, upon the Sunday following Jane Leigh
Perrot's arrest, at the small village of Steventon, near Basingstoke, where the Reverend George Austen held his living. The
grey stone church with its grassy graveyard and ancient yew
tree, where he christened, married and buried his parishioners
and delivered his pleasing, somewhat literary sermons, stood a
little aside from the main part of the village, upon a rise crowned
by a grove of beeches. And below the church stood Steventon
Rectory, an attractive, rambling house with a pretty garden that
boasted a lawn, elm walk and ornamental shrubbery, in addition
to its own glebe land.

This was the house to which George Austen had brought his
bride, five and thirty years ago. It had remained their family
home ever since. Here their eight children had been born, and
although their sons were now either married or pursuing their
careers elsewhere (with the exception of poor young George,
who was mentally defective, and cared for by a kindly nurse in
another part of the country), the Rectory was home still to their
spinster daughters, Cassandra and Jane, aged twenty-six and

twenty-four respectively.

For those two sisters the old Rectory held the happiest memories, with the laughter of a large, jolly family echoing down the years. Cassandra and Jane were devoted to one another; few sisters could ever have enjoyed so completely each other's confidence. 'If Cassandra were going to have her head cut off, Jane would insist on sharing her fate,' their mother had once declared. But that had been long before the reign of Madame Guillotine which had followed the Revolution in France . . . Mrs Austen would never have expressed such a sentiment nowadays. In the light of latter-day events it would have sounded crass and heartless . . . particularly as Jane and Cassandra's cousin Eliza had been widowed in '94, when her French husband, the Comte de Feuillide, had lost his head to that busy, ruthless blade in the Place de la Révolution.

Inside the Rectory on this summer afternoon, in the sunny sitting room with its straight-backed chairs and the tall pier glass that reflected a flowery garden view, Mrs George Austen sat dozing on the sofa, a lace cap set upon her snowy hair, while Cassandra wrote a letter to her brother Charles, a Lieutenant in the Navy. He had just been appointed to the frigate *Endymion*, and was now in London, staying with Henry, another brother, while awaiting orders to sail. (Henry, it so happened, had recently married that same engaging widow Eliza de Feuillide, even though she was a good ten years his senior.) A third brother, Francis, was also a naval officer, Commander of His Majesty's sloop *Petterel*, presently on duty off Cadiz. The family's latest news of Frank had told of his delivery of dispatches to Admiral Nelson himself, on guard against the French at Palermo – dispatches which had conveyed to Nelson the vital intelligence that the French Admiral Bruix had made his escape from Brest, where the British blockade had kept him at bay, and entered the Mediterranean with a considerable fleet. Cassandra's pen scratched the paper as she crossed her letter a second time, squeezing in as many words and as much family news as possible.

Upon the sofa, her mother emitted the gentle, purring snorelets of an afternoon snooze. She had recently recovered from a protracted illness, and any unusual excitement or exertion was apt to set her nerves askew. On such occasions, twelve drops of laudanum were her 'composer', as she liked to call it. For several months now, Cassandra had been in charge of the housekeeping at the Rectory; even as she wrote her letter, thoughts of the pease soup, spare rib and treacle pudding she had planned for dinner occupied part of her mind. As soon as her letter was folded, she would go to the kitchen to make sure all was well. *The summer weather is extremely fine, and my Father expects an excellent crop of hay at the glebe harvest. My bees are busy as ever . . .*

The Rector himself, with James, his eldest son, who was also a clergyman – that same James Austen who had been named for his uncle Leigh Perrot – were sitting together in the library, both relishing the satisfaction of having delivered their Sunday sermons, with only the brief homily of Evensong yet to come. James had ridden over to Steventon for the afternoon from his house at Deane, the neighbouring parish. Steventon and Deane had formerly comprised a joint living, but when James married, his father had handed over to him the emolument and duties of the latter parish.

James had actually married twice; his first wife had died suddenly when their daughter, Anna, was but two years old. Mary, his new wife, had recently given birth to a son. Mary and her sister Martha – 'the Lloyd girls', as they had always been known to the neighbourhood – had been close to the Austens for many years. Martha was the particular friend of Jane Austen.

The Rectory study, that quiet room overlooking the shrubbery, with its book-lined walls and revolving terrestrial globe, was where the Austen sons had received their initiation into the mysteries of Latin, Greek and holy scripture, together with other pupils sent to their father from time to time. His very first pupil, even before James was born, had been young George Hastings, son of the renowned Warren Hastings of India. Another was Thomas Fowle, whose connexion with the family had led to a romance.

Four years ago, Tom Fowle and Cassandra Austen had fallen in love and become engaged. Tom, who had been ordained when he came down from Oxford, had been promised a rich living in Shropshire by Lord Craven, a distant relative. This would enable him to marry and provide a comfortable style of life for Cassandra, and their future seemed secure. While he waited for the living to fall vacant, Tom had gone off to the West Indies as Regimental Chaplain to that same Lord Craven, and Cassandra had waited at home and sewed her trousseau. Then, in February '97, news came from San Domingo that Tom Fowle had died of yellow fever. Quietly Cassandra folded away her dream of a happy marriage together with the cambric and muslin and linen she had so diligently seamed and hemmed and embroidered. As in every trousseau, there were tiny baby garments, and these she gave away to the deserving poor in the village, steadfastly refusing to succumb to maudlin sentiment.

It was of Cassandra and Jane and their yet unmarried state that father and son were speaking as they took their ease in the library; or, rather, the son was speaking while his white-haired father listened indulgently. James was very fond of expressing his views.

'. . . she must have got over Tom Fowle's death by this time,' James was saying with a hint of impatience in his voice, seeming almost to reduce Cassandra's tragedy from the finality of death to a mere passing affliction. (But, after all, had not *he* known widowerhood, and ordered his life anew?) 'It is high time both my sisters were spoken for,' he continued. 'Do you not think so, sir? I fear my Mother's indisposition has made her less active in such affairs –'

George Austen drew on his pipe as he answered mildly: 'I do not believe Cassandra has any strong inclination towards marriage. Certainly not for the mere sake of becoming a married lady. She gave her heart to poor Tom, and he, alas, is dead. She is, besides, kept very busy here – she runs our little establishment now, you know. Your dear mother quite depends upon her.'

James nodded sagely. An eldest daughter to look after his ageing parents: that was a sound enough notion. Besides, that good fellow Tom Fowle, God rest his soul, had left Cassandra an annuity of a thousand pounds. Yes, he could accept Cassandra's single state with a degree of equanimity. 'But what of Jane?' he persisted. 'That young Fellow from Cambridge she met at the Lefroys last summer – what has become of him?'

His father smiled. 'Ah, you must mean Mr Blackall. He did intend to return to Hampshire for Christmas, I understand, but wrote to cancel the arrangement. Our good neighbour Madam Lefroy tells me his prospects really are not good enough to allow him to marry yet. I believe Jane was relieved to know this, rather than otherwise: she told me that she had nothing to say against Mr Blackall's moral character, but found him all too fond of instructing young women at great length and in a loud voice.'

James frowned. 'That is exactly the sort of remark Jane would make!' he exclaimed. 'How will she ever find a husband if she does not learn to curb her tongue?'

His father raised a sardonic eyebrow. 'Jane's intelligence and wit may well be to her disadvantage where marriageable young men are concerned. She will need to find a suitor of rare discernment. I trust, James, you do not regard a husband-hunt for your younger sister in the same light as – what shall we say – finding a home for a stray kitten. It will be a lucky man who finds himself in possession of her hand – and, more importantly, her companionship.'

'Yes, yes, that goes without saying, sir. But there are practical considerations. Jane is past her first bloom of youth, one cannot deny it. The marriage portion you are able to provide cannot be large. She has already spurned the attentions of a number of promising suitors.' James shook his head sadly. 'I fear she is too nice in her consideration of what a husband should be. There are precious few ideal husbands . . . or wives.'

Was there a slight tinge of bitterness in the addendum to this last remark? George Austen felt a surge of compassion for his worthy first-born son. James' second marriage, he reflected, did seem to lack a certain joyousness.

'Well, if Jane cannot find a suitable husband, perhaps she had best keep her single state,' her father said after a moment's pause. 'She has strong principles and is not fond of compromise.'

But James would not allow the subject to lapse here. 'We are not talking about a ball at Basingstoke and sitting out a cotillion for lack of a dancing partner,' he protested. 'It is Jane's whole future life at stake. What is to become of her? It is a sad thing to see a spinster lady wearying herself through the years with whist and watercolours, and little acts of charity. Jane is so – so lively, and so warm-hearted beneath her cleverness.' His voice softened. 'My little Anna is her devoted slave.'

Little Anna had spent several months at Steventon after her mother's death, and had only returned to her father's house when he remarried. Her preference for her aunts at the Rectory was a matter of some resentment for her stepmother.

George Austen smiled in fond reminiscence. 'The child used to follow her Aunt Jane around all day long while she was staying here, always asking for another story. – Jane, you know, used to tell her about the doings of an imaginary family, inventing instalment after instalment; Anna could never hear enough of it.'

'Well,' James said at last, 'Mary and I propose to give some dinners this autumn and winter, and we will see what table companions we are able to provide for my two sisters. And I daresay Edward and Elizabeth will invite them to visit at Godmersham before long. It will be a pity if we cannot find at least one husband between us.'

Glimpsing a new and preferable topic of conversation, the Rector pounced upon it eagerly and talked at some length of his son Edward's improved health since his cure at Bath, and of his plan to enlarge the deer park at Godmersham.

James allowed his thoughts to wander from his father's monologue. Indeed, it was his habit to draw aside from his parents' very obvious pleasure in his brother Edward's worldly good fortune. 'Lucky Edward' . . . that was how his younger brother had always been designated within the family circle for as long as he could remember. And with good reason. When Edward was still a boy, he had become the clear favourite of George Austen's patron and distant cousin, the wealthy Mr Thomas Knight and his wife, who had no children of their own. They lived in great style at Godmersham Park, in Kent. Young Neddy's visits to Godmersham became more and more frequent and of increasing duration, until at last the Knights decided they could not bear to part with him at all. Whereupon Mr and Mrs Austen had prudently consented to Edward's formal adoption by Mr Knight, who made him his heir. Edward, for his part, had added the name of Knight to his own: he was now Edward Austen Knight. He had subsequently been sent on the Grand Tour and had later married his Elizabeth, an heiress in her own right. Two years ago, Mr Knight had died, and Edward now lived in the great house at Godmersham Park, and had become a landed gentleman of large fortune.

Listening with half an ear to his father's description of the fallow deer at Godmersham, James glanced about the library and smiled wryly as he recalled how Neddy used to frown and sigh over his Latin grammar. Yet James himself could take comfort in contemplating his own considerable expectations. Was he not the virtual heir to the Leigh Perrot fortune?

While the voices of father and son droned on within the library, while Mrs Austen snored upon the sofa and Cassandra's pen scratched upon her paper, what of that younger daughter, Jane? She was upstairs in the dressing room that led off the bedroom the sisters shared. This little room served also as a quiet place to sit; it was furnished with Jane's square piano, a table, and some chairs.

She had drawn one of the chairs up to the table, provided herself with ink and paper, and was busy writing. She was, in fact, writing a novel. It was called *Susan* – the name of its heroine. A good deal of the narrative so far was concerned with the whole subject of novels and their readers, especially those delightful, horrid tales of terror such as *The Mysteries of Udolpho*. But Susan's story was mainly that of a young girl coming out at her first season, attending her first ball, receiving her first compliments – and experiencing the first pangs of heartache. Jane had already introduced into the story the young man whom Susan was destined to marry. He was called Henry, after her favourite brother; she liked to give her characters names that belonged to her family and friends. But Susan and Henry's happiness would not be assured until a series of imprudent adventures, misapprehensions and misunderstandings had taken place, and been satisfactorily resolved. All of which would arise from the follies and foibles of human nature, such as Jane herself had observed when, not so very long ago, she had first visited the Assembly Rooms at Bath, and attended her first ball at Basingstoke.

She had assuaged a passing doubt that novel writing was not, perhaps, the most suitable occupation for the Sabbath day; but she had done her duty at church that morning, and the quiet afternoon offered a rare opportunity to finish the episode where Susan first met Henry's snobbish, money-conscious father . . .

This was not her first attempt at a novel; locked in her writing desk were the manuscripts of three other stories, neatly titled, respectively, *Lady Susan, First Impressions* and *Elinor and*

Marianne. She had first begun to write for her own amusement and to entertain the family. When the tales were read aloud before the fire on winter evenings, their reception had been extremely gratifying to their creator. Appreciative smiles had greeted her more telling descriptions of characters whom her family often recognized from their own acquaintance; quite often outright hoots of laughter would punctuate the narrator's flow.

Jane herself was not entirely satisfied with any of these manuscripts. On the whole, she felt that *First Impressions* was probably her best attempt; she had, indeed, been known to refer to that work as her 'darling child'. *Lady Susan* and *Elinor and Marianne* were both told in the form of letters, but she did not feel she had succeeded very well with this device. In *Lady Susan* she had attempted to portray an unscrupulous adventuress against a background of the *haut ton*; and, in her own opinion, had failed dismally. She had first been tempted to portray this lady – one could scarcely think of her as a heroine – as a result of listening to Martha and Mary Lloyd describe the notorious career of a member of their own family, 'the beautiful, gay and fascinating Lady Craven', as Dr Johnson had described her, yet known to others as 'the wicked Lady Craven'.

Jane's father had enjoyed *First Impressions* so much that, two years ago, he had obtained his daughter's permission to write to a London publisher, to ask if he would be interested to view the manuscript, and how much it would cost to publish it at the author's expense. He had informed the publisher that the novel was about the same length as Miss Fanny Burney's *Evelina*. The publisher had replied promptly: he was *not* interested to view *First Impressions*. Whereupon Jane had put the manuscript away . . . but one day she intended to take it up and work over it again.

She dipped her pen in the inkwell and began a new paragraph, but at that moment the Sunday calm of village and Rectory was shattered by the approach of a postchaise being driven in a headlong rush from the direction of Andover. The village curs, dozing in the sun, leapt up and began an uproar of frenzied barking; children were called from the road by shrill, anxious voices as the vehicle swept through the narrow lanes, raising a cloud of dust.

Who could possibly be travelling on a Sunday? No one ever journeyed on a Sunday – it was unheard of. The driver, in caped cloak and cockaded hat, guided the horses up the main street towards the church; at last the chaise came to rest at the Rectory gate, where the two steaming horses stood blowing and tossing their heads in the shade of a great chestnut tree.

The commotion clearly penetrated the open windows of the Rectory. Mrs Austen woke suddenly in the middle of a snore; Cassandra, on her way to the kitchen, paused in the stone-flagged hall; James and his father broke off their conversation; and Jane's train of thought was quite distracted: she laid down her pen and left poor Susan stranded with General Tilney.

'Who can it be? Travelling on a Sunday! Can anything have happened to Edward – Henry – Charles – Francis – or even to poor George?' – Such were the sentiments expressed by those within the Rectory. Whoever it might be was taking an unconscionable time to get from the chaise to the front door; at last the bell pealed; Jemima went to answer it, and ushered the unexpected visitor into the sitting room, where Cassandra had rejoined her mother.

'Mr Leigh Perrot.'

Incredulity was superseded by curiosity and concern.

'Brother! What brings you here?' Mrs Austen looked beyond her visitor into the hall, as though expecting to see her formidable sister-in-law advancing in her husband's wake. Instinctively she put up her hands to adjust her cap. 'Jane is not with you?' she asked.

'Alas, no; would that she were! Oh, my dear Cassie, I have such a tale to relate –' And James Leigh Perrot hobbled forward into his sister's embrace.

'Oh, your poor foot, James. Pray sit down. – Cassandra, fetch a footstool for your Uncle to rest his poor foot on. And ask Jemima to prepare some refreshment. – And tell your father and James that my brother is here. – Oh, and Jane too, of course: she is upstairs, I think.' Mrs Austen had already grown flustered in anticipation of her brother's news. Sudden death, a dangerous illness, a carriage accident – at the very least a tumble downstairs: all these flashed through her mind.

Her brother, meanwhile, settled himself on the sofa with his gouty limb stretched out upon a footstool. 'Ah, my nephew

James is here — that is good. My poor dear wife was especially anxious that he should know what has befallen us; she has much faith in his prudence and good judgement.'

At last they were all assembled in the drawing room; a tray of cold mutton, bread and home-brewed ale was set before their visitor; and he, ignoring these offerings, embarked upon his tale. Its beginning appeared utterly fantastic to his listeners.

'I have come to inform you, my dearest sister — brother-in-law — nephew — nieces — that my beloved wife, your esteemed sister-in-law and aunt, is now residing in the Gaol at Ilchester, having been charged with grand larceny.'

Mrs Austen's amazement was such that she felt her palpitations coming on. She placed one hand outspread upon her chest. Her elegant, superior sister-in-law apprehended as a *thief*? Surely pigs might fly sooner than such an astounding circumstance be believed! 'Cassandra,' she murmured faintly, 'a few drops of my composer, I think —'

As Cassandra went to fetch a glass of water and the laudanum drops, she caught her sister's glance. They exchanged wordless astonishment. Haughty Aunt Perrot in gaol? A moment later, looking towards her uncle, Jane's expression softened to compassion. His distress was pitiful to see, and his affliction seemed to compound his anguish.

Mr Austen had assumed his gravest expression, one usually reserved for that occasion of final solemnity, the burial service. As for James Austen, he was quite overcome. How could his aunt possibly have allowed herself to fall into such a case? She, of all people, a woman of such poise and refinement! He realized that as the Leigh Perrot heir-apparent, he would be expected to play a highly supportive role in this unhappy affair. It was, of course, flattering and reassuring to realize that his aunt had such a high regard for him, but . . . It was at this point that, sidling its way insidiously into an unsalubrious corner of his mind, there came to him an unwelcome and unworthy speculation.

The dramatic tale of lace and larceny was told at length, and was received with gasps of incredulity, indignant or sympathetic exclamations, whichever was most pertinent to the moment, and much sorrowful head-shaking. After he had given a graphic description of his wife being led off to the

County Gaol, James Leigh Perrot concluded regretfully: 'I have since learned that such perfidy is not uncommon. It seems that an acquaintance of ours, Lady Fortescue, had a similar trick played upon her: it is evidently all too simple for deceitful shopkeepers to extort money from their victims. The law, made in the first instance to protect honest folk, is turned upside-down to become the tool of the dishonest.' He paused, and when he resumed a new note of resolution had entered his voice. 'Filby, the rogue who instigated this nasty business, had the temerity to approach me again after my poor wife had been taken off to Ilchester. He offered to withdraw the charge in consideration of a certain payment. But it is a matter of principle upon which Mrs Leigh Perrot and I are steadfast: we will never acquiesce to such demands, never compromise our principles for the sake of mere expediency.' He drew himself into a more upright position upon the sofa. 'The victim must and will be vindicated, the true guilt revealed, and my dear Jane's innocence proven beyond all doubt.'

'Bravo, brother! If only everyone in a similar case were to act as you, there would surely be an end to such attempts.' Mrs Austen was all in favour of principle being adhered to.

James Austen agreed. 'It will prove an uncomfortable and protracted business, I fear. But you are quite right, Uncle: there is no other way, no possible alternative.' *Unless*, came that unworthy speculation squirming in his mind, *unless* . . .

It occurred to Jane that her Aunt Perrot was displaying far more courage than she, for one, would have credited her with. There must surely have been some temptation to pay off the extortionists and avoid the County Gaol; she did not doubt that most well-bred, wealthy women in a like circumstance would have settled for the compromise. Presumably Lady Fortescue had done so. She must applaud her aunt for her firm stance; but still she felt that she could never harbour a really warm regard for her. Aunt Perrot was so very haughty and unbending, and held such a prejudiced attitude towards the world in general. Then there was her passionate inclination towards thrift, which she held to be a cardinal virtue. However, Jane reflected, it was not absolutely necessary to *like* someone in order to admire them . . .

'Bail is to be applied for, you say?' George Austen inquired of his brother-in-law.

James Leigh Perrot nodded. 'We travel to London shortly for that purpose – in the company of the Ilchester Gaoler.' He sighed. 'High summer is the worst time of the year for such business: no judges are available at present – we must await their pleasure.' He turned to his sister. 'My dearest Cassy, you cannot imagine what a boon it is to be able to share my anxiety with you and your family. Already the burden seems lightened by your sympathy.'

'Families should draw close on such occasions,' Mrs Austen replied equably. The laudanum drops had achieved their effect; her palpitations had died away.

'Be assured I am at my aunt's service at all times,' James Austen said stiffly, with a little bow.

'There is little we can call upon you to perform at present, nephew,' his uncle replied. 'Later, however, I know that your presence at the Assizes for the trial will be of the utmost comfort to your aunt.'

James' spirits sank; the extent of his duty was all too plain, related as it was to the size of his expectations.

Mr Leigh Perrot then coughed self-consciously, looked down at the worn and faded carpet for an instant, and glanced up again in a manner that seemed to portend some new disclosure. 'If,' he began hesitantly, 'by some tragic chance, my dear wife should fail to be acquitted of the charge laid against her –'

'Do not think of it!' Mrs Austen broke in impetuously.

'I must think of it, dear Cassy. – As I was about to say, in such an event, so my lawyer informs me, it is almost certain she would be given a sentence of transportation to the penal colony of New South Wales, most probably for a term of seven years.' He paused. 'It seems redundant to remark that such a sentence would represent a complete travesty of justice.'

It was even more redundant to remind them that according to the strictest application of the law, the Judge could place upon his head the black cap of the death sentence. Everyone within that comfortable, sunny drawing room was aware of it. Only last week, they each recalled, a poacher from Deane had swung from the gallows . . .

Cassandra shivered. 'Seven years . . . and so far away,' she murmured. *So far away* . . . that had been her first thought when she received the news that Tom Fowle had died at San Domingo.

40

New South Wales was farther still – at the opposite end of the earth!

'Should such a miscarriage of justice occur,' James Leigh Perrot continued, 'I have of course resolved to accompany my dear wife to that place, to sell up my properties here and make a new life out there for the years that are left to us.'

James Austen, hearing this, paled visibly. Scarlets, that pleasant country seat, and the elegant town house in Bath – sold up! All his uncle's assets transferred to the other side of the world! This, he reflected bitterly, was just his luck . . . the very reverse of his brother Edward's! Godmersham and the Knight fortune had simply dropped into Edward's lap like a ripe plum.

'Come, my dear sir, do not dwell on such a possibility,' George Austen told his brother-in-law in a hearty tone. 'We must all pray that the wrongdoers will be confounded and that true justice will prevail.'

'Amen to that,' James Leigh Perrot and James Austen uttered fervently and in unison.

The postchaise which Mr Leigh Perrot had hired at great expense for his precipitate journey into Hampshire still waited at the Rectory gate; by now, the day's shadows were lengthening; the golden glow of the afternoon had declined. Nothing Mrs Austen could say would deflect her brother from his intention of returning at once to Bath. And so, with a package of pork pie and some strawberries from the garden to sustain him on the journey (for he had left the bread and mutton untouched), he drove off the way he had come, and for the second time that day all the dogs in Steventon gave tongue as the postchaise retraced its passage through the village, leaving another cloud of dust in its wake and, in the Rectory upon the hill, a family singularly bemused by the drama which had been delivered to them.

'There will be gossip, whatever happens,' Mrs Austen predicted gloomily. 'Bath is a terrible place for gossip. I have heard reputations ruined in a moment – why, your true scandalmonger can wreak havoc with a mere knowing expression, or the raising of an eyebrow. "No smoke without a fire" – that's what they will say.'

James Austen, upon the point of riding back to Deane, saw the opportunity to mention that uncomfortable notion that still lay in his mind. 'I have heard,' he said with unaccustomed diffidence – it was, after all, a delicate subject – 'that sometimes, in middle age, well-to-do ladies have been known to develop a curious habit, when they go shopping, of – er – *purloining* items that take their fancy. As I understand it, such behaviour does not exactly fall into the category of *stealing*. It is more to be regarded, I suppose, as a peculiar, uncharacteristic and – ah – purely temporary falling away from moral standards . . .'

'That is a most unworthy and disloyal speculation, James – from you, of all people, in whom our aunt places so much faith!' Cassandra exclaimed indignantly.

Mrs Austen pursed her lips. 'I agree. And I am bound to remark, James, that there is something distasteful in your reference to ladies of – of a certain age.'

Jane offered a cogent point. 'My dear suspicious brother, you are forgetting the details of our uncle's account of the fateful shopping expedition. He absolutely testified, you may recall, that the parcel of lace remained unopened from the time our aunt made her purchase until the shopwoman accosted her in Bath Street. A person suffering from – what was your unfelicitous expression? – "a peculiar and uncharacteristic falling away from moral standards" – would surely have concealed the purloined goods upon her person.'

James' face cleared. 'Ah yes – of course. You are perspicacious, Jane.' The irony of his sister's tone had quite escaped him.

'It is a bad business,' Mr Austen remarked gravely. 'A time for all the family to prove its loyalty, one to the other.'

They watched James mount his horse and ride off to Deane. He was a keen horseman and rode to hounds with the local hunt. Now, quite unnecessarily, he put his mare over the gate instead of dismounting to open it, and cantered off in showy style.

At dinner that evening, over the pease soup, spare rib and treacle pudding, all of which, to Cassandra's satisfaction, had turned out well, Jane Leigh Perrot's arrest and incarceration still formed the main topic of conversation. As the meal drew to its close, it was Jane Austen who neatly epiloguized their discussion. 'To think,' she remarked finally, dabbing at her lips with her napkin following her second helping of treacle pudding, 'that a mere insubstantial cobweb of lace should have enmeshed us in such misfortune. It seems a paradox, does it not?'

Five

IN LONDON ONE month later, at The Angel Inn behind the church of St Clement Dane, Jane Leigh Perrot sat down to write a letter to her cousin, Mountague Cholmeley. Their relationship was close and their correspondence frequent. This was hardly surprising, for she had spent most of her growing years at her cousins' house in Lincolnshire, being sent there at the age of six from Barbados, where her father had been appointed to the Governor's service. Mountague and his sister Penelope had been her constant companions.

Dimly in infant memory, Jane Leigh Perrot could recall a brilliant tropic sun; a blue sea creaming in gentle waves along a white-sanded beach; gigantic, broad-leafed palms and glowing scarlet flowers; and herself, a little, chubby, dimpled Jane upon the lap of a dark-skinned nursemaid with a soft, singing voice . . . memories long since overlaid by England's rain and mists, chilblain winters and lowering skies.

This September morning she sat over her paper beside the open window of their private sitting room, while James reclined upon a horsehair couch, his gouty leg stretched out along its length. To underscore his avowed intent to accompany his wife to New South Wales should she by mischance receive a sentence of transportation, he had embarked upon a scheme to improve his knowledge of that distant Colony. A scheme distinctly distasteful to his wife, who had prayed him to refrain from speaking of it. He had procured a copy of the *Journal* of James Cook, in which that famous navigator described his first circling of the world in the bark *Endeavour*, when he had solved that geographical conundrum which had teased men's minds for generations – was there or was there not a Great Southern Continent? There was: he had discovered it, and had charted a significant amount of coastline. Whether he was in fact the first navigator to do so was open to some doubt. James was aware that the Dutch strongly disputed such a claim. They had, indeed, accused the British of removing brass plaques formerly affixed to certain trees and rocks by their own seamen, when they took possession of the Great South Land in the name of His Majesty King George III. The French, too, seemed still to entertain vague designs upon the great continent, even though the Colony of New South Wales had been established now for over a decade. The first fleet of convict transports had arrived there in 1788. The discovery of the Great Southern Continent had, indeed, been made at a most convenient moment: it had provided a new penal settlement just as the American colonies were lost to British rule and British convicts.

Of special interest to James Leigh Perrot, amateur naturalist, were those passages of Cook's *Journal* concerning Sir Joseph Banks, that passionate gentleman botanist, who had accompanied Lieutenant Cook (as he was then) as an observer of fauna and flora. James, sofa-traveller, had this very hour, in company with Cook and Banks, reached Tierra del Fuego, where two negroes in the party which landed from the ship to collect plants had become separated from the rest, and, without the means to make a fire, froze to death during the night. In recent days, James had learned to desist from his wonted habit of imparting to his wife such choice morsels of his reading. She had responded to his last attempt by placing both hands over her ears. 'I beg you, Perrot, do not tell me of *anything* pertaining to that place,' she implored him. So now James merely allowed himself a 'tchk tchk' of compassion, a private margin-note upon the fate of the two negroes.

Mrs Leigh Perrot found it difficult to decide whether it was preferable to keep the window of their chamber open or closed, and which was the worse to endure: the musty smell of an airless room, or the sour odour of the street, wafted indoors by every tired breeze. This very moment, that selfsame breeze ruffled the paper on the table as she began her letter; a ripe stench of open drains, fishbones and rotten cabbage permeated the apartment.

It was certainly not by the Leigh Perrot's choice that they had taken up residence at The Angel; it was the hostelry where Mr Scadding, the Ilchester Gaoler, was accustomed to stay whenever he was obliged to visit London. This same Mr Scadding, a stout, bacon-faced man, had become their daily companion ever since Jane Leigh Perrot's incarceration at Ilchester. In the event, she had escaped a dank cell and a straw pallet in the Gaol itself, and had instead found accommodation in the Gaoler's Lodging, reserved for prisoners able to afford such exclusive treatment. Not only was she obliged to pay a large sum for this concession, she had to suffer the inconvenience of living almost as a member of the large and noisy Scadding family. The Gaoler's features habitually wore a calculating expression; Jane Leigh Perrot had felt his gaze quickly assess the value of the pearls, rings and brooch she wore. His attitude towards both the Leigh Perrots was one of obsequious and sickening respect.

In one respect, however, The Angel was a welcome choice: the Leigh Perrots were unlikely, in this part of the city, to meet by chance any of their London acquaintance, and be forced into tedious explanation of their circumstances. Several Cholmeley and Leigh Perrot connexions lived in the more salubrious districts of the capital. Had this been a normal social visit, the Leigh Perrots would certainly have called, for example, upon James' nephew Henry — Jane Austen's favourite brother. Henry, a Captain Adjutant in the Army, had recently caused a stir within his family when he married Eliza de Feuillide. The Henry Austens were living in some syle in Upper Berkeley Street. In happier circumstances, Jane Leigh Perrot would certainly have taken the opportunity to satisfy her curiosity concerning that ménage.

Compressing her nostrils against the malodorous fragrance of the street, she resolutely continued her letter to Mountague Cholmeley.

You never imagined your Cousin would have addressed you from a Gaol, and altho' I do not absolutely do that *now* — being in London in order to give Bail for my appearance at the Spring

Assizes, yet my dearest Husband is not now my *only Protector*, as I have the *Ilchester Jailer* in my suite – though to do him justice he has such a reliance on my honour that I scarcely ever see him, and since I have had the *Honour* of his acquaintance nothing can have been more respectful than his behaviour . . .

There was no point, she thought, in revealing her deeper thoughts concerning Mr Scadding's character. She resumed:

Indeed we have every alleviation to our Misfortune that People can experience from the Kindest Sympathy of friends, and from the universal detestation the Authors of my troubles are held in by all ranks . . .

She paused here, reading over what she had penned so far. She realized that by now her Cousin Mountague would be agog to know what such an opening might portend. Sighing, she continued:

It is now five Weeks since I went into *Smith's*, a Haberdasher in Bath St; to buy some black Lace to trim a Cloak . . .

She proceeded to relate everything that had befallen her, and so full was her account that she ended by crossing the letter several times to fit in her final words:

We shall be detained here till after Monday as that is the first day the Judge can settle our business. Accept our love and believe me dear Couz:, Your affectionate J. L. P.

It was undeniable that the finished letter made dramatic reading.

In spite of every trying circumstance and each attending indignity, Jane Leigh Perrot's spirits at this juncture remained undaunted. She had absorbed her initial shock and dismay, and was sanguine that by the following Monday, bail would have been granted and she and James would be able to return together to Scarlets or Bath, to await in the comfort of their own home her eventual trial at Taunton Assizes.

But as a warm September gave way to the first wintry chill of

October, the change of weather seemed symbolic of a downturn in her fortunes. To the Leigh Perrots' astonishment and bitter disappointment, the application for bail was refused and *the accused* (as Jane Leigh Perrot was learning to know herself) was returned to Ilchester, to be remanded at the Gaoler's Lodging until the next Assizes, in seven months' time.

Seven long months! Her sole consolation was that her beloved husband would be allowed to share the discomfort of her residence within the Scadding household.

When Jane Leigh Perrot once more took up her pen to acquaint her Cousin Mountague with the latest developments, she sounded far less sanguine. Even her handwriting had lost some of its customary flourish.

> Ilchester,
> October 10th, 1799
>
> I should have written to you long ago, to have given you every information concerning my cruel disappointment after having like a School Girl anticipated the intervening days between my imprisonment and my return to the Comforts of a home, which I have not now been at *for 7 weeks*. I was flattered with the Idea of being only ten days here; and God knows, I am so far from feeling inured to all I see and hear that, had the choice of *Death* or such a 7 weeks as the last been left to me (and had there been no *dearer Object* in view to stimulate my wish to live) I should not have hesitated one moment in determining the first.

She paused here to rub her hands and pop a peppermint into her mouth. Even though she was wearing fine woollen mittens, her fingers were cramped with cold. The slatternly maid of all work who looked after the two rooms set aside for their use had put damp wood upon the fire, so that it gave off prodigious quantities of smoke and very little heat. She glanced towards the fireplace despairingly. James Leigh Perrot, that *dearest Object* to whom she had referred so touchingly, sat by the cheerless hearth absorbed in the book he had been reading ever since their London sojourn began. What a husband he was! Never once wavering in his support for the stance she had taken against those *villains*. A sudden rush of affection towards him

47

seemed to warm her whole being. She bent to her letter again
and wrote:

> When I look upon the Man who seems to me from his
> *Fortitude*, his sweet serenity, and his *Affectionate behaviour*
> to have been sent as my Guardian Angel, my true Support
> under every Affliction, I am all Gratitute to the Almighty . . .

James turned another page of Cook's *Journal*. He had by now
travelled as far as Stingray Harbour, which the *Endeavour* had
entered for the first time just nine and twenty years ago . . . that
same Harbour subsequently renamed Botany Bay, on account of
the rich variety of plants discovered there. Smoothing the new
page, he glanced up at his wife, busy with her letter. The very
mention of Botany Bay would, he knew, cause her to shudder
alarmingly; how he wished he could share with her his idle
thought that all those street ballads that sang of convicts, crime
and punishment would not sound half as jolly without the
alliteration of that name.

Jane Leigh Perrot's quill scratched upon the paper. Sucking
her peppermint, she frowned as she continued:

> To be the wanton Sport of Malice and Villainy in every shape
> is too much to endure – and although the Newspapers have
> only reached as yet the *Initials* of my Name, they consider me
> now as fair game, and I shall travel for the future at full length
> I daresay. Oh, my good Cousin, it may be to answer some wise
> purpose that such an Atrocious Act has gone so far, and I hope
> the Merciful disposer of Events will enable me to bear up in
> spight of such Affliction, but indeed I am not so far a good
> Christian as to refrain from wishing the Villains of this piece
> may suffer all the horrors of a worse situation even than mine:
> Worse indeed it must be now, for their Consciences must be
> their most terrible accusers . . .

At this point, feelings of self-pity arose so poignantly within
her bosom that she was obliged to relinquish her pen and hold a
handkerchief to her eyes – refraining, however, from allowing
any melancholy sound to escape her lips. She was determined,
in spite of everything, to play the Philosopher and maintain her

48

fortitude. She had never been one of those feeble creatures of her sex, all muslin and ringlets, who would weep upon a male shoulder at the slightest excuse. An image of simpering Miss Tebbit, of pale Miss Mapleton, floated into her mind's eye . . . dear God, how long ago it seemed since she had passed those two young women in the street upon that fateful shopping expedition!

She gave a forthright sniff and continued:

I must keep very fair with my Jailor, because I hear, and indeed sometimes from his own Mouth, that he has a Number of Relatives and dependents who are always on the petty *Jury* and may do me favour or otherwise if he pleases. Good God! and am I to depend on so many People's good Opinion!

She looked across to where James sat reading.

One of my greatest Miseries here is the seeing what my dearest Husband is daily going through – Vulgarity, Dirt, Noise from Morning till Night.

Reading this last sentence, she decided she had complained enough.

What a letter I have written, and all about this *sad self*. We are much better in health than I expected – anxiety of Mind is not good for Bowels naturally tender, and a *Head Ache* plagues me frequently, but my Heart aches so much oftener that I must not mention these lesser ills.

– And, having done so, she concluded her epistle with a sense of regret. Letter writing was now their only form of communication with friends and relatives. Quite the worst aspect of their confinement was the complete absence of social intercourse. The Leigh Perrots had discovered, through their trouble, just who their true friends were. In addition, some of their Bath correspondents spoke of the admirable loyalty displayed by the Leigh Perrot servants, Frank and Evans. Frank had apparently become involved in fisticuffs at a tavern upon taking exception to a remark made about his mistress by someone else's footman;

and Evans was no longer on speaking terms with Mrs Fitzgibbon's personal maid, who had repeated some biting comments to Mrs Leigh Perrot's detriment made by her loose-tongued lady.

And James Leigh Perrot had received a touching letter from one of their former servants, whose sentiments, however inelegantly expressed, brought a tear to his eye:

Honored Sir, – You may have forgot your old postillon Ben Dunford but I shall never forget yours and my mistresses great goodness to me when I was taken with the small pox in your service. You sent me very careful to mothers, and paid a nurse and my doctor, and my board for a long time as I was bad, and when I was too bad with biles all over my head so as I could not go to sarvice for a many weeks you maintained me. the famaly as I lives with be a going thro' Bath into Devonshire and we stops two days at the Inn and there I heard of the bad trick as those bad shopkeepers had sarved my mistress and I took the libarty of going to your house to enquire how you both do and the housekeeper said she sent a pasel to you every week and if I had anything to say she could send a letter. I hope Honored Sir you will forgive my taking such a libarty to write but I wish anybody could tell me how to do you and mistress any good. I would travel night and day to serve you both. I be at all times with my humble duty to mistress and you Honored Sir your dutifull servant . . .

'Oh yes, I recall Ben Dunford,' Mrs Leigh Perrot remarked when she read this. 'Always falling prey to one sickness or another . . . but 'twas good of him to write.'

The Austen family wrote regularly from Hampshire – James Austen was especially dutiful towards his aunt, assuring her in every letter that he would be present at her trial.

Whenever Jane Leigh Perrot thought of that public court of justice where she must appear, her heart sickened. Her foremost fear was this: that because she had been refused bail and imprisoned so long, the jury might be hopelessly prejudiced against her. *Why*, she asked herself for the hundredth time, had that London judge refused bail? Was it from some wise consideration beyond ordinary comprehension – or merely because he had been suffering from dyspepsia that day? She tried to find comfort in the thought that three eminent lawyers, Messrs Dallas, Jekyll and Bond, were retained as her counsel. In her thoughts, if not her prayers, this legal triptych assumed almost the significance of the Holy Trinity.

James, for his part, had set about quietly arranging his affairs so that in the event of the dreaded miscarriage of justice, he might accompany his wife to New South Wales.

Meanwhile, they must endure this Gaoler's Lodging until next March! The months of imprisonment seemed to stretch ahead endlessly. It was as though they had been shipwrecked upon some foreign shore, so different was the way of life of their Gaoler and his family to their own comfortable existence. Meal times were the most trying experience of all, for the Leigh Perrots were expected to sit at the family table.

'Give the gen'leman some toast,' Mistress Scadding would order one of her many infants – whereupon grubby Liza, or carrot-pated Tommy, or little Sarah with her squint eye would seize a slice of greasy toast in unwashed fingers and lay it, in the absence of a plate, upon James Leigh Perrot's knees, as often as not knocking over a mug of small beer in the process, which would meander across the table and trickle into Jane Leigh Perrot's lap. All this James accepted with a sweet composure, while his wife with difficulty repressed her utter revulsion and disgust. The main dish at dinner time was best described, in Mrs Leigh Perrot's apt phrase, as 'a mess of pottage'. Her own share, after she had been helped by Mrs Scadding, who used a knife 'well licked to clean it of the taint of fried onions', as she informed her Cousin Mountague, usually ended up beneath the table, to be eagerly pounced upon by the flea-ridden dogs and three cats lying in wait.

As for the perpetual household din – 'Not Bedlam itself can be half so noisy,' Jane Leigh Perrot declared, as the shrieks and quarrels of the children joined with the loud profanities of Gaoler Scadding and his vulgar cronies to set her head aching yet again.

The Scaddings did have one pretence to gentility – a cottage piano which they had accepted from some other unfortunate in lieu of payment for his enforced habitation in their midst. To perform upon this instrument, now sadly out of tune, there were two spotty Scadding daughters in their teens, who were often urged to perform 'for the lady an' gen'leman' the few pieces they had been taught. Mrs Leigh Perrot suffered these recitals by simply closing her eyes, the better to banish from her consciousness this travesty of gentle manners.

'I always knows you are delighting in the music of my girls, ma'am, by the way you shuts your peepers when they play,' Mistress Scadding told her. To which there really was no possible answer. In truth, Jane Leigh Perrot had evolved a certain compassion for poor, overworked, exhausted Mistress Scadding, with her loud-mouthed husband and brood of unruly children. So she said nothing and endured everything, reminding herself very frequently that this time would pass.

Six

A BAD CONSCIENCE was never likely to trouble the villainous Sam Filby; and as for Susan Gregory, though she had once followed the example of her pious elder sister and knelt by her bed each night to say her prayers to the Almighty Adjudicator of good and evil, she was now so completely subservient to Sam that she had all but forgotten the very notion of right and wrongdoing. And so the hope expressed by their victim languishing at Ilchester, that 'their Consciences must be their most terrible accusers', went unfulfilled. And though it might well be true, as Jane Leigh Perrot had assured her cousin Mountague, that the authors of her troubles were held in 'universal detestation', this, strangely enough, had not caused them to suffer materially. Indeed, Smith's haberdashery business had increased amazingly.

This was due quite simply to the fact that the quality of the goods for sale had improved dramatically. Smith's was now the only place in Bath where one might obtain the finest French lace, the richest cut-velvet and satin ribands, the most subtle shades of tapestry silks. Cards of cobbled home-grown lace such as Jane Leigh Perrot had scorned were a thing of the past. Samuel Filby had gone into the importing business. He had become a dealer in contraband goods. In simple parlance, he was a smuggler, at the receiving end of the game. At The White Hart one evening he had met the leader of one of the most successful gangs operating off the Cornish coast, and had seized the opportunity offered him to invest in the enterprise. – That is to say, he invested Susan's money in regular deliveries of contraband, carelessly demanding her acquiescence. He had by this time quite abandoned any show of courtesy towards her, and maintained his domination by his bullying manner, and by encouraging the lustful habits she had fallen into under his tuition. These dulled her poor mind as effectively as any drug. She had learned as much of lust and as little of love as any doxy in a whorehouse.

Sam did not see himself staying long in this new game: once the trial of Milady Parrot was over (at which he and Susan, as her accusers, were obliged to be present), he would give turnips to the smuggling lay and his dull mistress both, and take himself off to London. He had a small fortune stashed away by now – he added a hefty percentage for himself to the payments made to the smugglers, and had always milked the shop takings, 'weeding the lob' as he expressed it, at his pleasure. He would skip straight off to London as soon as the trial finished.

A pity that little ploy had gone awry: who would have thought the old Parrot would show such spunk? 'Twould be a rum joke if she were sent to Botany Bay! 'Twould almost make the whole episode worthwhile, even though they had got nix out of it . . . It afforded Sam some wry amusement to see how the so-called friends of Milady Parrot sent their maids to the shop to choose from the tempting goods. No doubt they thought to save face by sending their Abigails instead of coming to the shop themselves. Hypocrites! They reminded him of those false witnesses at a trial who kissed their thumbs instead of the Holy Book.

There was no doubt about it – London was the place for richer pickings, and a woman more to his liking, some young Cyprian with a bright eye and a tight muff. God, he was sick to death of his lacklustre Susan, with her foxy smell and her pitiable eagerness to please. She was stale – he had got all he wanted from her.

The contraband was always delivered by night; they would leave the back door of the shop ajar and wait in the dark until a cart with well-oiled wheels stole by, and a soft-footed, shadowy figure placed a box of goods just inside the threshold. Then, using a single candle, they would unpack the lustrous silks and exquisite laces and stow them safely. There was a certain spice of excitement in this clandestine activity, an echo of dangers already braved under the noses of the Excise men along the rocky Cornish coast.

One morning early in November, following such a night, Susan was waiting behind the counter (Sam having taken himself off to the tavern for a hearty breakfast), when a well-dressed young man entered the shop and, smiling pleasantly, asked to see some lace suitable for shirt frills. It was not unusual to serve gentlemen customers; Bath was filled with swells and fops who vied with each other to achieve the latest fashion as eagerly as any of the fairer sex. Susan, swallowing a yawn, and tucking a stray strand of hair beneath her cap, pulled out some of her finest stock, exquisite bobbin work from the lacemakers of Valenciennes in a *maille ronde* pattern suitable for his purpose.

' 'Pon my word,' her customer remarked, 'it is unusual to find such fine quality nowadays. I see you have a pretty taste in merchandise to match your pretty face.' And he looked upon her tired, pasty features with feigned admiration.

'We choose our suppliers carefully, sir,' Susan answered coyly, flattered by his compliment. She noticed his fine-boned hands and filbert fingernails as he examined the lace carefully.

'So it would appear,' he answered somewhat enigmatically. 'You say "we" . . . have you a partner in the business?'

'This is my own shop, sir,' Susan replied, surprised both by his question and by the vestige of pride that lay behind her answer. 'But – yes, I have a . . . partner who helps me.'

Her customer nodded. His information was correct: the woman owned the shop, but was herself owned by the rogue Filby, who had been observed closing a deal in The White Hart with a certain notorious Cornishman. Badly used by him, too, from the looks of the drab. Doubtless Filby was the prime villain of the piece: yet, as owner of the shop, she would stand as receiver of the contraband and he as her accessory when the time came to charge them. Well, let them play their game for a while longer. It was the capture of that Cornish ringleader he wanted, not merely these small fry. Their time would come . . . he could afford to wait. Eventually, after looking with considerable interest through almost the entire stock of lace, he purchased a length of the Valenciennes and departed.

Shortly afterwards Sam returned, replete with ale and mutton pie.

'There was a cove came in for lace,' she said.

'Was he a man – or a Miss Molly?' Sam sneered.

'He was a proper man, Sam Filby,' Susan retorted. She looked at him sideways. 'He told me I had a pretty face.'

Sam's response was a cruel guffaw. 'In that case he must have been blind cupid, my Blowsabella.'

Susan bridled. 'It's been a long time since *you* give me a kind word. You used to pretty-talk me in the beginning, but I daresay that was just to get your paws on my inheritance. – I been a bleedin' cully to you, an't I, Sam Filby?' Appalled at her own boldness, she clapped a hand to her mouth and cowered as though before a blow.

Strangely, Sam did not bawl at her, nor clip her head. Instead, he put a clumsy arm around her shoulders. 'Come, you goose-cap, that ain't a pretty thing to say to *me* – now is it?'

'I – I s'pose not.' Her flash of self-knowledge dissipated, her spurt of resentment against him evaporated.

'We mustn't quarrel, you and me,' Sam told her. 'We're playing in a dangerous game and need to keep our wits about us.' He sighed inwardly, longing for the time when he would be rid of her. 'Don't you get rumbunctious with me on account of some flash cove and his fine words. There's the trial of that old bird to think of, too, where we must play our part together. We can't afford to spar, my mopsy.'

Christmas that year, with its happy reunions and celebrations, seemed to bring a fresh realization of the Leigh Perrot's plight to their friends and relations. Mountague Cholmeley was especially persuasive in urging his cousin Jane to allow him to visit her at Ilchester. She sighed as she read his letter:

Why will you persist in wishing me not to come to you? You tell me that your good sister Austen has offered you one, or both, of her Daughters to continue with you during your stay at that vile Place, but you decline the kind offer, as you cannot let those Elegant young Women be your Inmates in a Prison, nor be subject to the Inconveniences which you are obliged to put up with – I grant that in declining this offer you act with propriety, but this will not hold good with me – a Man may be lodged in the town. Pray therefore permit me to come to you . . .

But Jane Leigh Perrot was adamant in her decision to refuse all such kindly offers. Husband and wife spent Christmas amid the uncomfortable Scadding family bosom, and afterwards Mrs Leigh Perrot wrote to Mrs Austen:

A fine roast Alderman supplied our festive dinner. Did you every hear this quaint expression? – 'Twas a plump Turkey encircled with a string of sausages – his chain of office! For the rest, we were regaled by *our gracious Host* relating the pretty details of a Hanging at Tyburn last sennight, and watched the Children stuff themselves with Sugar-Plums and play the old game of Snapdragon, snatching their raisins from a dish of burning Brandy-wine. The two Accomplished Daughters of the house played Christmas Airs with little grace upon the pianoforte. Snow fell last week, and I fear we are full of Christmas Compliments in the form of coughs and cold (which we freely exchange with one another) and chilblains . . .

Snow lay on the fields and hedgetops at Steventon, where the Rectory family spent their usual convivial Christmas. They were especially cheered by the news that Frank, still in the Mediterranean, had been promoted to Post-Captain as a result of his distinguished action in taking a French brig. Jane's birthday had fallen upon the fifteenth of December. Twenty-five and still unmarried, and no prospect in sight . . . this lamentable fact still gave her brother James more anxiety than it seemed to cause Jane herself. The James Austens had duly gone ahead with their plan to give a number of dinner parties, to which Jane and Cassandra were invited to meet a number of eligible men of various ages, but nothing had evolved from these encounters.

'Jane is altogether too apt to laugh . . . she is not serious enough,' James complained to his father. 'It is discomfiting for a gentleman who wishes to converse earnestly upon some important topic, to find he is not being accorded proper attention by his interlocutor.'

'Indubitably it must be so,' Mr Austen replied solemnly.

It was James Austen, ever mindful of his duty to his uncle, who had prompted his mother to offer her sister-in-law the consolation of her daughters' company at Ilchester. She had penned the offer with the somewhat reluctant consent of Cassandra and Jane, who, though they earnestly deplored their aunt's unhappy situation, did not feel it incumbent upon themselves to share it with her. They had not really supposed she would accept it – and this was the very reason why Jane, in particular, had been opposed to making it.

'It was not made entirely in good faith,' she told her mother when, to their relief, the offer was declined. 'There was something of the *syllabub* about it.'

They were in the warm, busy kitchen, stirring plum puddings to be distributed among the cottagers. A spicy aroma redolent of Christmas filled the cosy room. Mrs Austen sighed as she wielded her wooden spoon. In meeting her son's wishes, it seemed she must reap her daughter's censure.

'James will be at the trial to support our aunt,' Cassandra said soothingly. 'Family honour will be served.'

December brought not only Jane's twenty-sixth year, but the last days of the century. 'Eighteen hundred! How unfamiliar that sounds, to be sure,' Mrs Austen exclaimed at dinner one afternoon.

'Twill be the eighth year of this wretched War,' her husband added, carving a plump chicken. 'Pray God it may end soon.'

'Amen to that!' Mrs Austen uttered devoutly. In proper order she thought first of her two sailor sons, and then of the exorbitant cost of imported goods. 'The price of tea is beyond anything,' she declared. 'A *pound* a pound!'

Six weeks ago, Napoleon Bonaparte had accomplished a *coup d'état* over the French Assembly, whereupon that volatile nation across the Channel had voted to accept a new Constitution, and elected their Corsican hero as First Consul. His armies, still on the rampage in Europe, had launched a fresh onslaught against Austria, the only ally that remained to England now that Russia had defected. – To England, however, Bonaparte had expressed his desire for peace. But George III, with an insolent hauteur worthy of the Stuarts whose throne he occupied, had effectively repulsed his overture; he told Bonaparte that the best earnest France could give of her desire for reconciliation would be the restoration of her King. This dusty answer had goaded the First Consul into attempting a continental blockade designed to fell the detested nation of shopkeepers to the ground . . . and so the War dragged on.

Spring arrived at last: in the Rectory garden the daffodils tossed palely beneath the elms; cowslips shone in the glebe pastures and yellow kingcups flowered beside the stream. It was March, month of blustering winds, of the first lambs, of the rooks' untidy nest-building . . . March, the month so anxiously awaited by the weary prisoner at Ilchester. And then, just one week before he had planned to travel to his aunt's side to be present at her trial, James Austen's horse fell under him while he was cantering across a field, and he was thrown with one leg caught in the stirrup.

'A damned rabbit hole,' he swore as the glebe bailiff came running to his aid. His leg was broken; the bone-setter at Basingstoke shook his head: no question now of going to Taunton. A lowly rabbit had foiled the gallant gesture he had intended.

What now? Tossing upon his bed, James feverishly considered possibilities. His father . . . no, he could not leave his parish duties, which would now embrace his own, at Deane, during the next few weeks. – 'You could go, Mother,' he suggested eagerly when Mrs Austen came over to the Vicarage to offer sympathy and a jar of cowslip wine. ' – No, perhaps not,' he muttered a trifle shamefacedly, in answer to his mother's reproachful stare. 'But Cassandra . . . Jane – could *they* not attend the trial? Just to be there, to show that we *care* . . .'

'James has a commendable solicitude for his Aunt Perrot,' George Austen remarked dryly when he heard of this latest proposal. 'Make the offer, by all means, my dear,' he told his wife, 'but do not be surprised if it is refused, for the same good reasons as before.'

'And Jane, I daresay, will tell me there is something of the *syllabub* about it,' said Mrs Austen, sighing.

Seven

FATE WAS NOT proving kind to Jane Leigh Perrot: at this penultimate moment before her trial, she received a double blow. On 21st February, Mountague Cholmeley wrote to her:

> I am punished for the presumptuous Promise I made you, that *nothing* should prevent my being with you at that cursed Trial. I am laid hold of by Lord Chief Justice Gout, and so tight does he have me that my Legs, Knees and Hips are useless and I am lifted in and out of Bed like an Infant – and though I suffer so much pain, yet the uneasiness I feel at this disappointment is to the full as distressing to me . . .

There was some consolation in the letter, however: he wrote that his two sons and his sister Penelope would be coming to Taunton to lend support.

James Austen's involuntary defection came on top of this. Oh, that she should be deprived of the two champions upon whom she had most depended! Her sister Austen again urged her daughters' company upon her . . . but not, she noticed, her own. Was there not something a little empty and puffed-up about this offer, Mrs Leigh Perrot asked herself. Surely they must know she would never accept it. She wrote back to her Cousin Mountague:

> I have been disappointed in another quarter. In a letter from my dear Affectionate Sister Austen, I had the pain to hear of her Valuable Son *James* having had his Horse fall with him by which his leg was broken. This is a loss indeed because he had

been a perfect Son to me in Affection and his firm Friendship all through this trying Business had taught me to look to him to have come to us at the Assizes. Now I can ask neither Mother nor Wife to leave him, nor could I accept the Offer of my Nieces. To have two Young Creatures gazed at in a public Court would cut one to the very heart.

Meanwhile, after months of inactivity, all the busy preparations for the trial were now upon them. There were frequent meetings with kindly Mr Watts, their solicitor from Bath, who also attended consultations with that legal trinity, Messrs Dallas, Jekyll and Bond, in their London Chambers. All three would be coming to Taunton, together with Mr Pell, a fourth partner. They had now prepared their brief, which was delivered for the Leigh Perrots' perusal. The Accused was also preparing her own speech which she must deliver to the Judge and jury. Her eager pen spilled out a torrent of words, protesting her innocence and the villainy of her accusers. It was left to her legal advisers to fashion it into a less emotional and more cogent plea.

There was no time now for James Leigh Perrot to pursue his investigations concerning New South Wales. He had lately begun the *Narrative of an Expedition to Botany Bay*, written by Captain Watkin Tench of the Marines, who had sailed with the twelve transports of the First Fleet to found the settlement at Port Jackson. But this was laid aside as husband and wife pored over their counsels' brief, acquainting themselves with every fine point it contained.

Four of their Berkshire neighbours and four acquaintances from Bath were to appear on her behalf as witnesses. Mrs Leigh Perrot wrote again to her cousin Mountague:

Mr Watts says that fresh People come forward every day to offer their services to me as Witnesses. The ruinous Expense is what we shall long feel – but we are not expensive People and believe me, *Lace* is not necessary to my happiness . . .

The cost of the whole sorry affair weighed heavily upon her. Besides the expense of their present lodging, there were the lawyers' fees – and now the business of conveying all those witnesses to Taunton and providing their accommodation for

two whole days. Doubtless they would all eat their heads off . . .
it really did not bear thinking about. Her sister Austen had
written recently about the scandalous price of tea . . . standing
as witness would doubtless prove thirsty work.

Wartime inflation had affected much more than the price of
tea, however, as Mr Watts tried to explain to his client when she
asked him why she had had to wait so long for her trial to take
place.

'There is urgent need for sensible revision of our criminal
code,' he told her. 'The gaols are crammed with prisoners whose
petty offences have been blown up out of all proportion by the
fact that a shilling no longer holds the value it once had. Yet the
definition of grand larceny is still the theft of goods over the
value of five shillings . . . which today will purchase just four
ounces of tea leaves! All those prisoners must come to trial –
and so our legal system is slowed down, and you, dear lady, have
had to wait seven months to prove your innocence.'

'I daresay there is a good deal of wisdom in what you say, Mr
Watts,' Mrs Leigh Perrot commented. 'But even though a shilling may no longer be a shilling, a thief is still a thief!'

Wisely, Mr Watts desisted from pressing his point, realizing
that his client was too occupied with her own case to extend her
interest to the wider question of revision of the legal system.

In spite of the confident assurances of Mr Watts and her other
legal advisers, Jane Leigh Perrot was by no means entirely
hopeful of the outcome of her trial. She wrote gloomily to
Mountague Cholmeley:

So very black a Character as the Villain bears who is the
witness against me, one can only wonder at his Courage in
exposing himself to examination in a public Court and yet
there seems to be so great a Combination of deep laid
schemes, that I can only think with additional horror of what
Art may do against *Innocence*. That he has been thoroughly
disappointed in not having a Sum of Money offer'd is most
certain . . .

Her months of imprisonment were succeeded, on a rainy,
windy March day, by a trial that lasted six hours. The Assize
Court sat in Old Castle Hall, and was presided over by Mr

Justice Lawrence, who had a reputation for leniency. Castle Hall was packed for the occasion. While the case to be heard was commonplace enough – trials of shoplifters were two a penny – the circumstances were pleasantly titillating, and folk arrived early to make certain of a good place. It was a great lark for the local peasantry and the riffraff of the town to gawp at a lady in the dock. Their numbers swelled the body of the court, making the Judge's nosegay a rather necessary adjunct to his office, for the wet weather caused their garments to steam odoriferously in the close atmosphere. Also present were certain of the neighbourhood gentry and respectable yeoman families, for whom the trial provided an agreeable diversion, and an opportunity to lay bets upon the outcome; besides friends of the Leigh Perrots from Bath and elsewhere. In the end, no fewer than twenty-three witnesses had arrived to support the accused: they, of course, remained outside the court until they should be called.

Heads turned, mouths gaped, elbows nudged neighbours' sides as Mrs Leigh Perrot arrived at Castle Hall, dressed in a handsome black gown and supported by her husband on one side, by her cousin Penelope Cholmeley on the other, and with Mountague Cholmeley's two sons following behind. As she descended from her carriage, she had stepped in a puddle, and as if the ordeal before her were not enough, she had in consequence to suffer the discomfort of wet feet for the remainder of the day.

As for the prosecutrix, Miss Susan Gregory, she and Mr Samuel Filby had arrived in Taunton the previous day, together with a third accomplice, Mary Raines – a cribbage-faced girl more than willing to accept a bribe, who used to help at Smith's occasionally. These three arrived neatly dressed and solemn-faced, masquerading as a chorus of honest shopkeepers. They had also brought with them, as additional witnesses for their prosecution, a number of those creatures who made a living by such means, being paid by the word for their false speeches.

Susan was even paler than usual; she hoped she would not again 'cast up her accounts', as the saying went; for she had soon parted company with her good breakfast at The White Lion that morning. She feared the reason for such indisposition lay curled within her belly: Sam Filby's bastard. When she told him, would he marry her, she wondered. He seemed to have changed so much – ever since he had joined the smuggling game . . . or was it before that? He never gave her his cheeky grin now, scarcely a civil word, though now he was looking sideways at her and honouring her with an unnatural smile – for appearance' sake, she supposed. He *must* marry her, if only for her money – though, mysteriously, there seemed to be less and less of that, in spite of their increased trade.

Mr Filby was to appear as chief witness for the prosecution, Miss Raines as second witness. The three, aided and abetted by a rascally lawyer, had rehearsed their story well. Sam and Mary (who was to swear that she had been in the shop at the same time as the accused) were to swear that they had seen the latter secrete the card of white lace beneath her cloak; whereupon Susan was to relate how she had accosted the lady in the street and accused her of stealing it; which accusation, she was to vow, had 'made the lady turn scarlet' with guilt. Their lawyer, in shabby black and a moth-eaten wig, had taken up his place near the nauseated prosecutrix, his brief of lies and slander spread before him. The card of white lace, sole item of evidence for the prosecution, lay on the table beneath the Judge's bench, and very grubby it was to become by the end of that day, after it had been passed from hand to hand by the petty jury of twelve good men and true.

'Pray silence for His Honour! The Court shall be upstanding!'

The Judge appeared, stately in scarlet robes and fresh-powdered wig, his nosegay of sweet-smelling violets held to his nostrils; and so the trial began.

During the next six hours, prosecution and defence put their cases, called witnesses, examined and cross-examined, made their summings-up, and finally let their cases rest before the Judge and jury. After retiring for less than fifteen minutes, that jury returned their verdict: *Not Guilty*.

Three days later, Mrs Leigh Perrot, now restored to her proper superiority as a respected gentlewoman, sat down in her own house to write a final letter concerning her ordeal to her cousin Mountague. She and her husband had sped to Bath as soon as her innocence was proven. *Not guilty!* What a welcome they had received from Evans and Frank at their front door! And what bliss it was for Jane Leigh Perrot to sit again at her own little satinwood desk, to pen the familiar superscription of her own address, to be beside a bright, smokeless fire, amid the fragrance of beeswax, pot-pourri and vases of spring flowers! The sole circumstance to detract from this satisfaction was the fact that as a result of having sat throughout the trial with sodden shoes, she was now suffering from a heavy cold. She took up her pen:

Once more I address you unprison'd, but oh! how I have been wrung! – to the very quick I believe. You will rejoice to hear that I was most honourably acquitted – but you will grieve with me that we cannot punish my *pretty pair of Lovers* – my Solicitor says nothing can be done. But now a public Court and an honourable Acquittal is satisfactory to the whole World – and how can *we* blacken those People more than they have blacken'd themselves – *the Man is off* and the Shop I hear must be ruin'd . . .

Here she let her pen rest while she blew her nose. Her gaze fell upon a vase of daffodils . . . she frowned: how stiffly Evans had arranged them – reaching across, she pulled the flowers upwards and allowed them to splay out. There would be daffodils now beneath the trees at Scarlets, under the elms at Steventon . . . She began to write again:

I felt greatly Obliged to your dear Sister for her kind Appearance at the Trial. Indeed *She* well proved her Friendship. Others talked, and wrote of it, perhaps felt it – but it was a distant Glow, or rather a little spark which required more trouble to blow up than the thing was worth . . .

She wondered if these remarks were quite fair to her Sister Austen; and decided, with a little *moue* of bitterness, that they were. Why had she offered companionship which she must have known would be refused? It had been a mere empty gesture.

Mr Justice Lawrence behaved handsomely, he wished me seated and several times sent Mr Jekyll to repeat certain of my Observations in a louder Voice than my Agitation would allow. But I must at the same time confess that in my opinion he did not let enough be said of Filby's Villainy – he thought enough had been said to fully clear me, and was pretty sure that the winding up of his Charge to the Jury would put every doubt respecting my Innocence out of the Question; but I think it was a dangerous Experiment . . .

At this point she noticed the the inkwell needed replenishing. She frowned again. Could Frank have been neglecting his duty? Or had Evans failed to make a fresh supply of ink? Really, it was too bad. The pair of them had had little enough to do for the past half year. She rose to pull the bell, and did not resume her letter until a suitably chastened Frank had taken away the inkwell, refilled it, and restored it to the desk. 'The Mistress is her old self again,' he informed Evans without rancour.

I confess that when I came into Court and found that not only the Prosecutrix and Filby but a *Shop Girl* was in the same Story, I was struck with horror to see how far Wickedness might proceed. The Prosecutrix swore that, on her seeing me pass on the opposite side of the Street, she went out, and upon my giving her the Parcel and saying, if there was white Lace put up with the black I had bought, it must be through the Negligence of her Shop Man, She answered: ' 'Tis no such thing: you stole it.' Could anyone believe that all this could have been said to me in one of the most public streets in Bath, when everybody was passing, and that no one should have heard it? Could anyone believe that if She had dared to have said this to me, my Husband would not have taken some legal steps against such defamation of a Wife's Character? Her words were so very different to what *She swore*, that I could not even suppose it an Accusation – tho' She said it made me *turn Scarlet*. – When the Man came after me to know our Name, I own then a presentiment of intended Villainy flashed on me, and *then* I should not have wonder'd at turning Scarlet or any Colour of the rainbow.

She sat back in her chair to peruse what she had written, and then a fit of coughing assailed her, and obliged her to get up and pour herself a small glass of Ipecacuanha wine, so soothing to the bronchial tract. On the table beside the wine carafe she noticed one of James' books, *Journal of a Voyage to New South*

Wales. She shuddered; why he should still be engrossed by reading about that place she could not understand. Idly she turned a few pages. Ah well, her dearest Perrot would soon forget these outlandish *kangarus*, duckmoles and the rest when he was once again pursuing summer butterflies at Scarlets, she reflected comfortably, and went back to her letter:

> *Three* out of three and twenty Witnesses we had brought to Taunton were examined, and were sufficient to prove *Mr Filby* Rogue enough in all conscience . . .

She thought regretfully of all those superfluous dishes of tea her witnesses must have consumed.

> His witnesses were nearly as bad as himself; swearing *black* was *white* seem'd nothing to them. Why Judge Lawrence should stop my Advocate when he was shewing to the whole Court that Filby was the greatest Villain that ever existed I know not – but this I do know, that if I had been allowed to speak at that point, I should have proposed a few questions which would have been, I think, unanswerable. For example – why, if the Man saw Lace secreted under my Cloak, did he let me quit the Shop? (That I had no Cloak on was to affirm what I could bring only my Husband to prove, and this, alas, is not possible between *Man* and *Wife*.)

She really must not run on too far – the cost of sending this letter to Lincolnshire would be ruinous! Trying to make her handwriting smaller, she went on to the summing up.

> The Judge, after he had said everything respecting Filby's Deposition as well as the others, added: 'And now you have heard all this, if you can believe Filby's Evidence, if you should be inclined to believe his Evidence, I have only to desire you to consider the Attestations of those Gentlemen who have attended on behalf of Mrs Leigh Perrot's Character.' He then repeated each kind Friend's testimony, which were all as highly gratifying as possible. Some of the Jurymen, who seemed more enlightened than Petty Jurors generally are, took Notes and when the Jury retired were 7 *minutes and a*

half explaining those Notes to their less intelligent companions, which accounts for their being above a quarter of an hour before they brought me in 'not Guilty'. A clapping of hands to shew Approbation and Joy immediately began, which the Judge hushed as not being allowable – and so this Vile Matter rests. You can imagine nothing more gratifying than the reception we have met with in Bath. To be sure I stand some chance of being killed by Popularity – tho' I have escaped from *Villainy*. – I shall not feel quite easy till our heavy charges are *known* and *paid*. The frightful Expense I cannot Estimate. I am told it will be nearer *two* than one thousand pounds . . .

The Leigh Perrots' misadventures continued to provide gossip for Bath (that Infernal Bath, that Den of Villains, Harbour for swindlers, as Mountague Cholmeley had condemned it in one of his letters to Ilchester) for some time to come. The *Bath Chronicle* gave a full and accurate account of the trial, and interest in the case was spread farther afield; upon picking up the *Chronicle* for the last week in April, James Leigh Perrot noticed the following advertisement: 'This day is published The Trial of Mrs Leigh Perrot, Sold by Crosbie, Stationer's Court, Paternoster Row, London.' He resolved to obtain a few copies of this pamphlet to present to some of their friends and relatives . . . the Cholmeleys, for example, and his sister Austen at Steventon.

No sooner had the verdict been received than Sam Filby, pushing Susan and Mary before him, left the court with all speed, ignoring the scornful, despising and even threatening glances cast upon them, and travelled back to Bath post-haste. Among those who came to the shop next day was that same fair-spoken young man who had bought lace for shirt frills upon a previous occasion. He did not linger . . . he had merely looked in to ascertain that the woman Gregory and Sam Filby had indeed returned from Taunton.

Mary Raines, paid off with a mere half-crown for her services, complained bitterly that Sam had promised her a guinea; he, however, avowed that was only if the verdict had gone their way.

'Then you'll never see me in your shop no more,' Mary told him, her pock-marked face ablaze with anger. ' 'Twas a guinea you promised me, I swear it, and now I'm fobbed off with half a bull. Next time you wants a false witness you can find some other booby.'

Susan was dismayed to hear the slander Sam smeared across the counter, swearing, for instance, that the jury had been bribed by the defendant. ' 'Tis only making more mischief for no purpose to spread such wrinkles abroad,' she said wearily. 'Cannot you leave a bad halfpenny alone?'

It was the end of the day; they were busy shutting up shop.

'And who's to say the jury was not bribed?' Sam retorted. 'Maybe 'tis not all wrinkles – there's one law for the poor and another for the rich, as is often said, and I for one believe it. Such gentlefolk as our fine Lady Parrot are able to get away with all manner of Mischief.'

Perhaps it was a newly hatched maternal instinct to protect her unborn child against all the manifold wickednesses of this world which now enabled Susan to see her Lover (but no, he had never been truly that) in a new, cold light. Appalled at such evidence of Sam's genius for self-deception, quite apart from his proven ability to deceive others, she shook her head in a final negation of all he stood for and said with quiet conviction: 'You're a bad lot, Sam Filby.'

Sam looked at her with undisguised dislike. 'And you're a drab, Susan Gregory, and no better than you should be. If it hadn't been for *your* shop and *your* money in the till, I'd never have looked twice at you.'

Stung to the quick, Susan let out more than she meant to at this moment. 'Then your child will have a rogue for its father and a drab for its mother,' she spat out, and burst into tears.

Sam stared at her, and knew suddenly the reason for her peaky looks and vomiting behind the back door.

Susan, her mouth working, looked at him blearily. 'Will you g-give it your name, Sam?' she quavered.

Sam took a step backwards from her. 'No, by God, I'll not! There'll be no parson's mousetrap for me, no wedding and no christening!'

Susan looked full on him with a gaze of agony, but Sam ignored her. Here was a fine to-do! High time he dinked the woman and made himself scarce. There was only one reason to delay his going until tomorrow: this evening he had a final appointment at The White Hart with the Cornishman (Sam had never learned the man's real name – he was too fly a cove to divulge it) to hand over payment for the last lot of goods. There was no getting out of it – there would be a knife in his ribs if he failed to turn up with the money. – That payment, by the bye, would empty the shop of every farthing: it was a shame, but there would be nothing left for Susan. 'Twas her own fault – she should have kept a better head for business. At any rate, he would be on tomorrow's coach for London, and what befell the slut was no concern of his.

'I'm off now for my supper and some cheerful company,' he told her callously. 'I'll doss down in the shop when I get back . . . sweet dreams, my mopsy!' And with a mocking jangle of the doorbell he was gone.

Susan did dream that night; worn out with weeping, she crept beneath her fusty blanket and slept straight away. Her dream began sweetly: she was floating in the sky, oh, it was fresh and clear up there. Then some little fleecy clouds came bowling along, soft, frothy clouds like a feather bed . . . but no, 'twas not clouds at all, but a pile of heaped-up lace, like frost-spangled cobwebs . . . and now she was all entangled in it. Faugh! 'Twas a gigantic spider's web! The more she struggled, the faster she was held by those soft filaments. She could not breathe, there was a caul of cobwebs upon her face –

Sweating, she awoke with a cry upon her lips, her arms flailing, and realized it was a hammering upon the door below which had awakened her, and the sound of deep, authoritative voices commanding her to open up. Shivering, apprehensive, she lit her candle, pulled on a dingy wrapper and crept downstairs, then struggled to pull back the heavy bolt. There upon the pavement stood two thickset officers of the watch, with Sam pinioned between them. A third person stood behind them; he moved forward and held high the lantern he carried, and Susan gasped as she recognized the fair-spoken customer who had purchased some of her best Valenciennes lace.

'Susan Gregory?' he demanded, his voice icy now, his stare relentless.

She nodded, not trusting herself to speak.

70

'Do you know this man?'

She nodded again, unable to meet Sam's eyes. *She knew that man*. And she knew it was all up with them both. This was the end of their sorry game – of all their games and deceits.

'Susan Gregory, you are charged as a receiver of contraband merchandise –' the excise officer's voice was toneless. 'Samuel Filby is charged as an accessory after the fact.'

So the trap closed. The woman Gregory and the man Filby were taken into custody to await trial, together with John Trennock of Polzeath, the black-bearded Cornishman. The law officers had sprung upon Trennock and Filby as they sat at The White Hart. Forthwith all goods upon the premises were seized, and the shop itself closed down.

It was generally agreed that Divine Providence had brought retribution to as pretty a pair of villains as had flourished for many a day. And how should Sam and Susan escape hanging now? It seemed they were indeed upon the highway to the gallows.

Eight

A T STEVENTON ONE evening in May, the Rectory family dined on beefsteaks with oyster sauce, accompanied by peas and new potatoes from the garden, a homely meal shared by James and Mary Austen, who had driven over from Deane. James and his father very soon followed the ladies into the sitting room. To stay long at table after dinner was a confinement Mr Austen could not endure; gladly did he move to those with whom he was always comfortable.

They found their womenfolk discussing changes to be made in furnishing the dining room: an extending table had been ordered – a gift from Edward – and the Pembroke table was to be placed by the sideboard.

'But where shall we put the little table that stands there now?' Mrs Austen asked distractedly.

'It may conveniently take itself off to the best bedroom,' Jane pronounced gaily, rising to help Cassandra pass round the coffee.

'The only thing *I* crave just now is a new mangle,' Mary Austen declared in her downright way. 'My old one is quite worn out.'

'Then you must give it a decent burial – James can attend to the proper obsequies,' Jane told her sister-in-law lightly. ' 'Twould rest well beneath the mulberry tree, I think.'

'Really, Jane, you are too absurd.' Mary was never sure whether she was being laughed at or not where her husband's sisters were concerned. 'A mangle,' she continued solemnly, 'is a very necessary item in any household.'

Upon which Jane's face fell into a very serious expression, and she and Cassandra carefully avoided each other's glance.

'Ah,' said Mrs Austen, 'here are our menfolk come to join us.'

James sat on the sofa beside his mother, his long legs stretched out before him. The broken bone had not quite healed; he could not yet ride, and walked with a stick. He held a paper in his hand. 'My father was telling me that he had received this pamphlet about our aunt's trial from my Uncle Perrot,' he remarked.

'Why yes, we have all read it,' Mrs Austen said.

Mary said petulantly: 'It is surprising James did not receive a copy too – do you not think so, dear?' She turned to her husband.

He shrugged. 'I daresay my uncle thought it unnecessary to go to the expense of sending two copies when he knew my father would share his with us.'

Cassandra, replacing the coffee pot, gave Mary an oblique glance. Her sister-in-law had such a complaining manner . . . Not for the first time, Cassandra speculated whether it was the small pocks Mary had suffered as a child and its legacy of a pockmarked face that had made her ultra-sensitive, so quick to take needless offence.

Jane's hazel eyes sparkled above the rim of her coffee cup. 'Surely it would be *Aunt* Perrot who would think of the unnecessary expense?'

Her mother shook her head, intending mild reproof, but could not help a faint smile. Her sister-in-law was – thrifty, there was no gainsaying it.

'And yet,' continued Jane irrepressibly, 'you will read in the pamphlet my aunt's own confession of enjoying riches beyond the dreams of avarice! – It is contained in her own speech to the Judge and jury.'

'Is that a suitable tone to adopt when speaking of our unfortunate aunt?' James inquired with raised eyebrows. Intrigued in spite of his admonition, he opened the pamphlet and riffled through it until he found the speech in question. 'I suppose these are the lines to which you allude,' he said loftily, and proceeded to read them aloud in the sermonizing voice he used in church.

' "Place in a Situation in every respect the most Enviable – blessed with a Tender and most Affectionate Husband who is

73

ever anxious to indulge my Wants and anticipate my Wishes and whose Supply of Money is so ample as to leave me rich even after every desire is gratified, what inducement could I have to commit this offence? Depraved indeed must have been my Mind if with these Comforts I could have been tempted to this Crime . . ." '

He raised his eyes from the page and smiled at Jane. 'I take your point, dear sister,' he confessed. And a glance of rare and delightful understanding passed between them – to be intercepted by Mary's asking resentfully: 'And pray, what is so amusing about *that*?'

Cassandra hastily suggested a game of cards, and Jane fetched a green baize cloth for the table. Mrs Austen excused herself from the game and got out her sewing. She was dressing a doll for Anna.

'You spoil the child,' Mary told her mother-in-law, admiring the miniature garments.

'That is my prerogative as a grandmamma,' Mrs Austen replied with her sweet smile, and then inquired after little James, Mary's infant son.

'He is teething still,' Mary sighed.

Mrs Austen glanced at her and decided to risk making a delicate suggestion. 'I expect you know that Madame Lefroy has undertaken to vaccinate the village children from the cow,' she said casually. 'Jane is to help her, you know. She says it would be so helpful if you would consent to have James done. – As an example, you know, to the cottagers . . . It is a quite painless procedure, Jane assures me.'

'Really,' replied the unpredictable Mary, 'I find it quite extraordinary that Madame Lefroy could not ask me about this herself. I suppose,' she went on with disconcerting candour, touching her pitted face, 'it is because of *this*. But I am not such a sensitive ninny! Of course James shall go to the cow.'

As daylight faded the lamps were brought in, and with card-playing and sewing and conversation the evening passed quietly and pleasantly, until tea was served at ten o'clock, and the baked apples and cheese-cakes left over from dinner reappeared.

In truth, Jane had little heart for cards this evening; all day she had been thinking regretfully of what little time she seemed to have for novel writing these days. At least she now had the satisfaction of having completed *Susan* . . . although she might well go back to it sometime in the future to revise some passages: there always seemed to be scope for improvement whenever she re-read anything she had written.

The remainder of that year was so very occupied that it was as much as Jane could do to keep up with her correspondence, let alone begin a new novel, or return to *First Impressions* to carry out her long-term plan to revise that manuscript. Edward Austen Knight spent a month at Steventon, and Cassandra returned to Godmersham with him for a long visit: Elizabeth was expecting yet another child, and as usual relied upon Cassandra to stay until after her confinement. This meant that Jane was left to supervise the Rectory housekeeping. Their brother Charles paid several visits on leave from Portsmouth, and Jane undertook to sew the three dozen shirts he needed to fit him out for his service on HMS *Endymion*. His ship was under orders to sail, and she sent off the shirts by half-dozens as they were finished; she grew heartily tired of white cambric, and seemed to be forever plying her needle to start a fresh seam.

Cassandra and Edward, on their way to Kent, stopped in London to carry out various shopping commissions, all of which Jane acknowledged promptly. 'My Cloak came on tuesday,' she wrote to Cassandra, 'it is too handsome to be worn, almost too handsome to be looked at.' (Nevertheless, she did wear it to the very next ball she attended.) 'The Glass is all safely arrived also . . . Mary is delighted about the Mangle . . . You will thank Edward for it on their behalf, & as you know how much it was wished for, will not feel that you are inventing Gratitude.'

November came in with a tremendous storm which felled three elms in the Rectory garden, and at the end of the month Jane went to Ibthorp to visit Martha Lloyd. Martha sent a note to ask Jane to bring some books with her, whereupon Jane pretended to take umbrage: 'You distress me cruelly by your request about Books; I cannot think of any to bring with me, nor have I any idea of our wanting them. I come to you to be talked to, not to read or hear reading. I can do *that* at home; & indeed I am now laying in a stock of intelligence to pour out on you as *my* share of Conversation . . .'

Talk they did, especially as the weather kept them indoors

most of the time. The three Miss Debaries, who lived in Ibthorp Parsonage, called the day after Jane arrived – but, as Jane told Cassandra in her next letter; 'I have not yet been able to return their civility; – You know it is not an uncommon circumstance in this parish to have the road from Ibthorp to the Parsonage much dirtier and more impractical for walking than the road from the Parsonage to Ibthorp.' Cassandra smiled as she read this: the company of the Debaries was never sought with eagerness.

Jane had left her mother very well, and given her strict orders to continue so; she enjoyed her visit to Ibthorp without the smallest notion that within a few days the pleasant country world she had known all her life would come crashing down as suddenly as those elm trees in the garden. She and Martha planned to return to Steventon together, walking as far as the village of Whitechurch, 'and there throw ourselves into a postchaise,' Jane scribbled to Cassandra, 'our heads hanging out at one door, & our feet at the opposite'. And so they arrived at Steventon one December afternoon – not quite in the manner described, but in high spirits, holding on to their bonnets as they tripped up the path to the Rectory porch, in case the wind should seize them and whirl them across the fields into the next county.

Did neither Jane nor Martha perceive the solemn faces which met this exuberant homecoming? While Jane was away, her parents, alone in the big, rambling house, had arrived at a momentous decision. George Austen, now nearly seventy, had decided to retire, and hand the living of Steventon and its Rectory to James and Mary. Thoughts of retiring had been in his mind for some time; just as his wife, with her delicate health, now found the running of the house too much for her, so he found it difficult to manage the parish and glebe. His bailiff was grown old too, and the farm had returned scarcely three hundred pounds this year.

It was in the dear familiar sitting room, with a cheerful fire blazing in the hearth, to which Jane and Martha drew near to warm themselves, that Mrs Austen suddenly blurted out with no preamble: 'Well, girls, it is all settled. We have decided to leave Steventon . . . and go to live at Bath.'

Jane fainted dead away. Being a healthy, well nourished young woman who inhaled plenty of fresh country air, she was not given to the vapours, but the shock of this abrupt announcement simply numbed every faculty, including her ability to stand upright and remain conscious. In a moment or two she came round, and was supported to the sofa by Martha and her anxious parents.

'Oh, I did not know *how* to tell you – knew you would take it badly – lived here all your life – seemed best simply to break the news straight away . . . I daresay I should have beaten about the bush, softened the surprise –' Mrs Austen's kind face was creased with remorse.

Martha, almost one of the family herself, shared Jane's shock and dismay at the unexpected news. 'To *Bath*?' she said unbelievingly.

'But,' said Jane weakly, 'why did you not consult all of us?' Oh, it was too hard, too cruel a blow! *Bath*, of all places! 'All our friends are here! In Bath we have mere acquaintances –'

Her father took one of her limp, cold hands in both of his. 'Our family is grown up now, Jane – grown up long since. We cannot stay here for ever. James and Edward have families of their own, Henry is married – I daresay it will not be long before Frank takes a wife, and eventually Charles, too.'

'And my girls,' Mrs Austen broke in.

Martha had turned towards the fire to conceal the colour mantling her cheek; she had always harboured especially tender feelings for Francis Austen.

'Oh, marriage!' Jane sat up and made a supreme effort to overcome her indescribable feeling of despair. 'Why,' she asked with a tremulous attempt at gaiety, 'is the world so bent on the idea of marriage? I would rather be a – a teacher at a school – I can think of nothing worse – than marry merely for the sake of situation! I rather think, dear parents, that *this* spinster daughter at least will remain in her present perfectly agreeable single state . . . unless . . . unless by an extraordinary chance she should happen to fall in love!' She actually managed a shaky laugh. 'Well, if adventures such as falling in love will not befall a young lady in her own village, I suppose she must seek them elsewhere – I daresay Bath is as suitable a place as any for finding them.'

'We have been talking about making a visit to the sea,

somewhere in the West Country, after we are settled in Bath,' Mrs Austen said soothingly; 'Lyme or Dawlish, or perhaps Sidmouth – we might try sea-bathing, Jane dear – they say it is most beneficial and quite the ton.'

'One thing at least is certain,' Jane declared; 'we shall never be at a loss for a topic of conversation for the rest of this winter. Whereabouts in Bath we shall reside – what furniture we should take with us – how many servants we shall need – oh, there will be no end to it!'

'So James and Mary will come to Steventon?' Martha said.

Mr Austen nodded. 'And there will be a new incumbent at Deane. What a pity our son Henry abandoned his first idea of taking orders: the living could have been his, I daresay.'

Henry, the most brilliant and – so far – the least successful of Jane's elder brothers, had thought of entering the Church when he came down from university, but instead had joined the Army.

'I cannot imagine dear Eliza as a country clergyman's wife,' Mrs Austen murmured. 'Their London town house is much more her style.'

Still feeling decidedly shaky, Jane got to her feet and went upstairs. She paused for a moment at the open door of the little room where her manuscripts lay locked in her writing-desk. At that moment it seemed that another woman must have sat there dreaming her plots and characters so lightheartedly . . . as for herself at this instant, why, she had never felt less inclined to write an amusing novel in her life.

In bleak November, Susan Gregory gave birth to a lusty, howl-ing male child – howling, no doubt, for the sins of his parents and the fact that he was able to obtain little nourishment from his mother's breast, after her months of semi-starvation in gaol. This noisy, red-faced scrap of humanity who had squirmed and wriggled his way into the world after hours of labour upon a pallet in the prison infirmary meant everything in the world to Susan. And had he not saved her life? She and Sam Filby had been brought to trial some three months before the child was born. Both were found guilty of the capital crimes of which they stood accused. They stood together in the dock but were as strangers to each other. Susan was stony-eyed, and Sam averted his gaze from her. He had fared well enough in prison, having money in his pocket to secure the relative comfort of a cell shared with only one other inmate.

The case of the Crown *vs* Gregory was not concluded on the gallows. Susan had learned a great deal while languishing in the cell she shared with a half dozen other females awaiting trial, including the fact that a woman with child could not be hanged – so long as her pregnancy was proven. It seemed that many condemned women bribed the turnkey to impregnate them, so that the hoped for issue of a few moments up against the cell wall might save their necks. 'The belly plea', they called it. In Susan's case, there was no need for a jury of matrons to pronounce whether she was carrying a child or not: the learned Judge was very well able to see for himself how her tattered gown was stretched across her belly, extended by the presence of a seven-month babe. In this manner did Susan Gregory's son justify his existence even before he was born; his mother's sentence was transmuted to transportation for seven years to Botany Bay.

There had been some confusion over the perfunctory christening carried out a few hours after the child was born (such haste was necessary: most of the infirmary brats breathed their last very soon after they had given their first feeble cry). Susan held out her babe for the holy water to be sprinkled upon his head. 'Name?' the priest demanded – to which, thinking 'twas her name he asked, she answered: 'Gregory.' So Gregory Gregory the child became – a hiccup of a name, but unforgettable. And now mother and child awaited transport in one of His Majesty's ships to that land of chain-gangs and black heathen natives, strange hopping horses and ants as large as mice ... Some said the Great South Land was joined to China ... whatever the truth of that might be, it was certainly a terrible long distance away, as far as a man might travel without falling off the very edge of the world.

As for Sam Filby, he too managed to escape a wry neck and a pissen pair of breeches upon the gallows tree. After the Judge in his wisdom had passed sentence on the woman Gregory (and upon her unborn son), he acceded to the male prisoner's request that he be permitted to enlist in the Army rather than suffer the death penalty; a procedure which, after eight years of war, and with towns and villages full of hideously maimed ex-soldiers and sailors, provided a useful supply of cannon fodder. 'Twas no wonder Wellington referred to the rank and file of the regular Army as 'the scum of the earth'. So Sam's manacles were struck off, and he was thrust into the lowest rank of a company of infantry. Here he soon learned there was little to choose between hard labour in the hulks and the daily lot of an ordinary soldier – save that the latter stood a better chance of sudden death. Let our last glimpse of Sam Filby be as he marches off in his scarlet coat, one of His Majesty's 'bloody backs'. He was to survive a further nine years, and eventually become a hero, slain in the Battle of Talavera.

Nine

SINCE THERE WAS no help for it, gradually Jane grew reconciled to the notion of living in Bath. It was true, she thought, that the best years, the real family years in her beloved Steventon, were past. And then, the prospect of spending future summers by the sea, away from the white glare of Bath, was delightful. – So, to her own surprise, she found there was considerable interest in the business of planning and packing up, all the bustle of removing.

Cassandra stayed longer at Godmersham than she had anticipated, and could take part in all that bustle only from a distance. Jane kept her closely informed about every proposal and decision. 'We plan having a steady Cook, & a young giddy Housemaid, with a sedate, middle aged Man, who is to undertake the double office of Husband to the former and sweetheart to the latter. No Children of course to be allowed on either side,' she wrote.

Both Francis and Charles Austen came home on leave, and Henry visited Steventon as well. The latter had now left the Army and had decided to attempt a career in the business world, setting up as an Army agent, with offices in Albany, off Piccadilly.

'Dear Henry, perhaps you should have taken holy orders after all,' Jane told him one afternoon as they strolled through the Elm Walk together. 'My father envisaged for you the curacy at Deane, you know.'

'That would have been rather pleasant,' Henry said wistfully. 'I do sometimes wish I had entered the Church – it was my firm intention for a while, when I was up at Oxford.'

It must often be confusing for very brilliant, clever people, Jane mused, when it came to choosing a career. (There was not the slightest doubt in her mind that Henry was both brilliant and clever, and very charming besides.) They must feel so many doors were open to them – but they were apt to spend so much time peering across the threshold of first one, then another, that there was the danger of any real achievement passing them by. Earnestly she hoped this would not be Henry's fate.

Charles' ship, *Endymion*, had taken a French vessel prisoner, and with some of his prize money he had bought his sisters gold chains and topaz crosses. Jane was delighted by the gift, but touched even more by his generous impulse. Both he and Frank were full of their exploits at sea – no need to worry that either of her two sailor brothers would ever have second thoughts about their careers!

Jane wrote to Cassandra about the distribution and sale of their furniture and other possessions at Steventon. James and Mary were really behaving in a quite rapacious manner. 'The brown mare, which as well as the black was to devolve on James at our removal, has not had patience to wait for that, and has settled herself even now at Deane,' she wrote ironically to Cassandra. 'Everything else I suppose will be seized by degrees in the same manner.'

It was beyond their means to take any but the smallest objects with them to Bath – removal costs were prohibitive – so James was buying most of their furniture, as well as his father's library, which comprised some five hundred books. Jane felt especially aggrieved about those books: she suggested that James should take them at half a guinea a volume, but he stubbornly insisted on having them valued, and in the end got the lot for seventy pounds. Her own books were sold, as well, and her cherished piano disposed of for a mere eight guineas.

'The whole world is in a conspiracy to enrich one part of our family at the expense of another,' she told Cassandra crossly. Everyone had heard stories of the greed of kith and kin, and family fallings-out when wills and testaments were read or property entailed . . . but no one had died at Steventon! It was too bad to see Mary calmly assess and appraise each piece of furniture, and actually hear her complain because the sitting room sofa was so faded ... 'But then this room is most inconveniently situated – the windows catch all the afternoon sun,' she grizzled.

But at last everything was settled, and early in May, Cassandra still being delayed in Kent, Mrs Austen and Jane went to Bath to stay with the Leigh Perrots and begin house-hunting.

'There is only one possible place for you to live – in the vicinity of Seymour Street.' Such was Mrs Leigh Perrot's pronouncement the morning following the arrival from Hampshire of her sister-in-law and niece. 'Pray, have you considered Axford Buildings? The apartments there are very genteel, so I am informed, most suitable for your situation.'

Her Aunt Perrot, Jane thought, had such a knack of making one feel both rebuffed and defensive at one and the same time. She meant well – had very kindly offered them hospitality until they should find a place to their liking – had made up a party for one of the last balls of the Season, in the Upper Rooms next Monday – and yet already Jane was experiencing that familiar sensation of suffocation generated by her aunt's dominating presence. Glancing at her mother, she noticed that she had assumed a guarded look: all the Austens were perfectly united in feeling a particular dislike of that part of the town which included the Paragon and Seymour Street.

'Seymour Street ... yes, I daresay there is much to recommend it,' Mrs Austen said vaguely. 'But,' she continued with sweet definition, 'my husband has expressed a preference for the environs of Laura Place, across the river.'

How useful a husband could be, Jane reflected, especially when he was not present to deny any preference which might be ascribed to him! Her father was in fact visiting some distant relatives, and perfectly content to relinquish his share of house-hunting.

'I would expect the houses around Laura Place to be above your price,' Mrs Leigh Perrot remarked loftily, and would have said more, had not a fit of coughing prevented her.

The cough she had brought back from Taunton still lingered; Evans was constantly mixing hot lemon and sugar for her, or providing doses of Ipecacuanha wine. Jane and her mother considered Aunt Perrot looked thinner, but otherwise unravaged by her recent unfortunate experiences. Her persistent cough meant there was no question of her venturing out to accompany them in the quest for a desirable residence, and for this they were profoundly relieved.

Curiously enough, it was their uxorious uncle who appeared the more changed of the pair; he was unusually restless, and did not seem able to settle to any occupation for long. A perpetually wistful gleam was to be discerned in his eye – wistful for what, neither Jane nor her mother could surmise.

That whole sorry episode of lace and larceny was tacitly understood to be inadmissible as a topic of conversation: in Bath, it was already superseded by newer, more fashionable scandals. Only once or twice did Jane Leigh Perrot herself refer to it. Driving out one afternoon with her sister-in-law and niece, the carriage passed along Bath Street and she saw the former haberdashery shop still shuttered and awaiting a new tenant.

'Those two vile creatures turned out a pair of slip-gibbets in the end,' she remarked acidly, employing a phrase she had heard upon the lips of Mr Gaoler Scadding. '*She* had a child, and has gone to Botany Bay. *He* opted to go for a soldier – I hope a cannon ball carries him off!'

James Leigh Perrot, though restless, was also much occupied with business, writing letters and consulting the latest reports on funds, bonds and securities.

'Perrot is rearranging our affairs to help offset the ruinous expense we have been put to,' his wife informed them carefully. 'He is hopeful that by a little judicious selling and re-investing, we shall be able to recoup what we have spent. We have also had to make household retrenchments,' she added meaningfully.

That was rather obvious: the cuts of meat at meal times were scarcely adequate for four people, and Jane was often obliged to 'disorder her stomach with Bath buns', as she expressed it, to satisfy her appetite. And if the house had been warmer, she could not help reflecting, perhaps her aunt's cough would have cleared up more quickly. There was clearly a great saving of the fuel bill by leaving fires unlit.

Their days became filled with examining the newspaper advertisements for suitable leases, then making excursions to view anything that sounded promising. They visited Westgate Buildings ('centrally situated' turned out to be far too low in the town); Charles Street ('sought after and fashionable' signified 'too expensive'); Green Park Buildings ('attractive river and rural views' denoted dampness and putrid fevers).

Mrs Austen hankered after Queen Square, but that really was beyond their means. They found a very reasonably priced place in Trim Street, but – 'Do not consider it,' Jane Leigh Perrot advised them. 'Trim Street is not what it was when General Wolfe lived there. It has gone down dreadfully.'

Their evenings were filled mostly with card parties; cassino, whist, cribbage and tedious small talk – 'a monstrous deal of stupid quizzing and commonplace nonsense' Jane told Cassandra; and the ball they attended was a rather tame, end-of-season affair, enlivened only by the presence of a certain notorious lady, reminiscent of that Lady Susan whose story Jane had related, and by the inebriation of another lady's husband. 'I am proud to say that I have a very good eye at an Adultress,' Jane wrote to her sister; 'for tho' repeatedly assured that another in the same party was *She*, I fixed upon the right one from the first . . . Mrs Badcock & two young Women were of the same party, except when Mrs Badcock thought herself obliged to leave them to run round the room after her drunken Husband.'

Jane could not help observing, as they departed for this ball, that her aunt's gauze evening cloak was now bereft of its black lace trimming. Evans, who had laboured so diligently to sew on the lace, had been equally diligent to obey her mistress' firm instruction to remove it. 'I never wish to set eyes on the wretched stuff again!' Jane Leigh Perrot had declared – and, upon Evans inquiring what she should do with the lace after she had unpicked it, her mistress had reflected, then said: 'It will do nicely for a birthday gift for one of my Cholmeley god-daughters . . . we cannot completely waste it.'

Cassandra and her father finally arrived in Bath in June. And at breakfast one morning, shortly after their arrival, James Leigh Perrot read aloud this interesting item from the *Chronicle*: ' "The lease of No. 4 Sydney Place, 3 years and a quarter of which are unexpired at Midsummer –" ' ('Gracious heaven!' Mrs Austen exclaimed, buttering a slice of toast, 'to think we are halfway through the year already.') ' "– The situation is desirable –" ' ('Imagine,' Jane observed, 'we should overlook the

Pleasure Gardens and might lose ourselves in the Labyrinth every day!') ' "– the Rent very low –" ' ('Good,' Mr Austen commented with an approving nod) ' "– and the Landlord is bound by Contract to paint the two first floors this summer –" ' ('Excellent,' Aunt Perrot commented, 'such a saving of expense.') Doggedly her husband continued in the face of all these interruptions. ' "A premium will therefore be expected –" ' ('How much, I wonder,' Cassandra mused practically) – ' "Apply Messrs Watson and Foreman, Cornwall Buildings",' he concluded triumphantly, and beamed around the breakfast table in a benevolent manner.

At an appropriate hour, Mrs Austen put on her new straw bonnet, and the Austens, accompanied by James Leigh Perrot, who considered himself solely responsible for the viewing, went off to examine the house in question. It was part of a four-storeyed terrace, lofty and elegant, not far from Pulteney Bridge. The Abbey, Pump Room, Circulating Library and Milsom Street were all within easy walking distance. Best of all, perhaps, Sydney Place comprised part of a new estate on the edge of open countryside, promising rural walks, a welcome escape from the town. In short, everything was suitable: house, surroundings, rent and premium, and the Austens promptly contracted to move in.

But first they were to take a holiday, that seaside holiday they had long planned; they were to go to Sidmouth, on the Devon coast between Exmouth and Lyme, one of those little fishing villages adapted to cater for summer visitors. They were to become initiated into the delights of sea-bathing, of health-giving fresh air laced with brine, fresh crabs and lobsters, shell collecting, rock pools and bracing clifftop walks – always assuming, of course, that the rain held off.

And it was at Sidmouth that Miss Jane Austen, aged twenty-six, was destined to lose her heart.

Ten

IT WAS HIS Majesty King George III who had set the fashion for going to the seaside when he first visited Weymouth ten years before. Soon afterwards the Prince Regent had turned the little village of Brighthelmstone, in Sussex, into a seaside echo of London; and then, pretty Lyme, in Dorset, acquired the royal accolade as well. It all began as a quest for health; sea-air and sea-bathing together were declared a match for every disorder of the stomach, lungs or blood. They were anti-spasmodic, anti-pulmonary, anti-septic, anti-bilious and anti-rheumatic. Sea air was healing, softening, relaxing – fortifying and bracing – sometimes one, sometimes the other. Sea-bathing was especially advised for the winter months and the early morning before breakfast. Every few years, one heard of some new coastal village or other starting up and growing the fashion. And, when so many visited the seaside to seek cures for their afflictions, real or imagined, it somehow became inevitable that such a venture might also involve the risk of a broken heart.

The Austens had desired to visit Lyme, but by the time they had done with their house-hunting it was too late to procure good lodgings there, and so they settled on Sidmouth, smaller and less well-known, but with the selfsame sea washing its shore.

Mrs Austen found no difficulty in switching her allegiance from Lyme to Sidmouth. 'A young and rising bathing-spot – the sure resort of the very best company – regular, steady families of thorough gentility,' she declared approvingly. 'I have heard that

Sidmouth has the purest sea breeze on the coast – deep water ten yards from the shore – no slimy rocks – yes, Sidmouth is just the place!'

A very few years since, Sidmouth had been a quiet village of no pretensions: now it had acquired Assembly Rooms, a Circulating Library (which also offered its patrons parasols, gloves, souvenir brooches made from varnished shells, decorative arrangements of dried seaweed – all the useless things in the world that could not be done without), and that unique and indispensable feature of every seaside place: an Esplanade.

'Depend upon it, a little sea-bathing will set us up,' Mrs Austen said with satisfaction, gazing out from the window of their villa onto the beach below. 'Saline air and immersion will be the very thing. My sensations tell me so already.' She had purchased a little guide book from the Circulating Library and read aloud: ' "Perfect repose of body and serenity of mind are absolutely necessary to promote the purpose of this great remedy and give it full force and efficacy." '

Upon hearing this, Jane smiled. 'It is to be hoped that the temperature of the water will not upset such repose and serenity. Many female bathers have a tendency to squeal and even shriek upon immersion, I have heard.'

On several mornings, Mrs Austen set out early with Cassandra and Jane for the Ladies' Bathing Enclosure, while Mr Austen went off somewhat unwillingly (not being entirely convinced of the efficacy of sea-bathing) to the Gentlemen's Enclosure. A bathing machine, octagonal and turret-like, set upon high wheels and pulled by a horse, took them a little distance into the sea – but not out of their depth. Driver and horse then retired discreetly to the shore, and, having disrobed inside the machine, the female bathers, clad in all-enveloping bathing dresses and caps, descended into the water, and proceeded to disport themselves. (Some of the gentlemen actually swam, Mr Austen reported.) Then, robed again and, if healthy, glowing from the invigorating experience; if not healthy, shivering and coughing, the bathers returned briskly to breakfast and the novel excursions planned for the remainder of the day.

Cassandra and Jane had brought sketching equipment, and attempted picturesque views on the cliff tops, following the strict principles of the Picturesque laid down by the Reverend

William Gilpin in his renowned sketcher's manual, *Observations relative chiefly to Picturesque Beauty*. He spoke sternly of such essential considerations as distances and perspectives, light and shades. Their equipment included the indispensable Claude glass recommended by Mr Gilpin; this was a mirror specially designed to gauge the effectiveness of a chosen view. The artist turned her back to the view, peeped into the glass over one shoulder, and thus obtained the impression of how a framed picture of the scene would look. The sisters did not in fact fare very well upon the cliffs – it was far too breezy; one gust of wind carried Cassandra's view of sea, sky and fishing boats clear across the Channel towards France.

Another day, Mr Austen hired a carriage and they drove to Bicton, close by, to view the Italian Garden and Pinetum, which were pronounced very fine. There were innumerable strolls beside the sea, the endless fascination of watching the waves break upon the shore, and the discovery of curious shells and pebbles at low tide. It was best to look out to sea and avert one's gaze from the melancholy sight of invalids too feeble to walk, borne along the beach in donkey-carriages with jingling harness to inhale the briny air.

One morning rain fell; Jane offered to go out to the Circulating Library to obtain a novel they might read aloud and enjoy together. 'Nothing *improving*, mind; it must be all for entertainment, with a great deal of nonsense in it,' Cassandra instructed her.

Jane found the Library filled with others persuaded towards literature by the inclement weather, besides shoppers examining the display of souvenirs. Out of the throng, one gentleman in particular seemed to impel her notice. She observed him covertly while she waited her turn to bespeak a volume. He was just the sort of man she considered good-looking and agreeable: he was tall, clean-shaven, dark-haired, with a somewhat saturnine, almost too pale a countenance. He had an overall air of distinction, and looked to be the sort of man who would not easily indulge in small talk, but would, if drawn out in proper conversation, reveal definite, well-informed opinions worth listening to. The cast of his features seemed not insensible to humour, and – yes, there was a certain air about him, something in his bearing and conservative style of dress, his courteous kindliness as he spoke to the proprietress of the Library, which seemed familiar to Jane, daughter of one clergyman and sister to another. Surely he was a churchman . . .

At that moment he half-turned and glanced about, as if in tacit apology for causing delay to the other patrons who waited there. Jane's face caught his eye, and he looked at her with a degree of earnest admiration, which she could not be insensible of. She was, indeed, in remarkably good looks this morning, her features having the bloom and freshness of youth restored by the fine moist wind which had been blowing on her complexion, and by the animation of eye which it had also produced. It was evident to Jane that the gentleman admired her. She dropped her gaze, and he turned back to take the volume he had chosen. She heard his voice; it had a mellifluous timbre; surely, she thought, it was a voice used to intoning the Collect, leading a congregation in prayer, reciting the Benediction . . .

She could not help wondering if he were married. Yes, depend upon it, he would have a devoted wife and six dark-haired, pale-complexioned children . . . well, perhaps not as many as six; he looked to be in his early thirties. Yet he did not have *exactly* the air of a married man. Perhaps he was a widower . . . a young widower, as James had been when he married Mary Lloyd.

He had taken his volume; he passed close to her on his way out – she felt his nearness acutely – he was leaving the shop. Sighing inwardly, she moved forward to request Miss Burney's *Camilla*; it lacked the 'nonsense' of Cassandra's prescription, but was a story they all enjoyed. Jane had, in fact, been one of the subscribers to this novel when it was first published.

A few moments later, she emerged from the Library in her turn, sheltering *Camilla* from the rain by holding it beneath her cloak with one hand, and adjusting her hood with the other. Alas! she had forgot there was a shallow step leading down from doorway to street: she stumbled, put out one hand to save herself, but collapsed on the wet pavement in a heap, still clasping *Camilla* to her bosom.

Instantly a tall presence hovered above her; a solicitous hand was supporting her elbow, assisting her to rise. 'Are you injured? Are you able to stand?' that mellifluous voice was asking anxiously.

'I – I think so, sir,' Jane answered shakily, attempting to regain her feet as gracefully as possible. Gingerly she tried her weight upon one ankle, then the other. Mercifully there was no serious sprain – she felt she would be able to walk with his assistance.

The perfect stranger offered his arm and said: 'In the circumstances, perhaps it would be permissible for me to introduce myself. My name is Fordwick – Elliot Fordwick. I beg you, pray allow me to assist you to your lodging.'

'Sir – Mr Fordwick – you are very kind,' Jane responded; and the gentleman in his turn marvelled at the extreme sweetness of her voice. She accepted his arm, and by the time they drew near the Austens' villa, she found she was no longer limping. Their walk took them the length of the Esplanade and occupied, at that slow pace, a quarter of an hour, affording a unique opportunity for a *tête à tête*. Books and reading was the obvious topic that presented itself, in view of the circumstances of their meeting; taking charge of the book Jane had been carrying, Mr Fordwick noted the title. 'Ah, *Camilla*,' he said approvingly.

'You are a reader of novels, Mr Fordwick?'

'The reader who finds no pleasure in a good novel must be intolerably dull-witted,' he replied with conviction – and could not guess what particular pleasure this utterance afforded the delightful young female clinging to his black-sleeved arm. 'The volume I have chosen is *Sir Charles Grandison*,' he continued. 'I have read it several times – I find that Richardson's delineation of the human condition, his wit and humour, his style and choice of language never cease to enthral me.'

Jane was much gratified to discover that they shared an affection for that particular novel; her own partiality for it amounted almost to a passion – Yes, that was not too strong a word: in the old, happy days at the Rectory she had even dramatized certain episodes from *Sir Charles Grandison* for their family theatricals, which they used to stage in the Rectory barn.

'I had the happy fortune to be allowed the freedom of my father's library,' she told Mr Fordwick. 'Richardson – Fielding – Sterne – they all sat upon the shelves.' Fielding and Sterne sat there still, she thought, but that well-read copy of *Sir Charles Grandison* had *not* comprised part of her brother's bargain when the library fell into his hands!

Mr Fordwick's eyebrows had risen in some surprise. A

liberally read young female indeed! 'And may I inquire your opinion of *Tristram Shandy*, Miss Austen ... and of *Tom Jones*?'

Jane's eyes sparkled as she looked up at him and answered demurely: 'Fielding has a fine perception of human weakness, does he not? His expression is –' she hesitated '– singularly robust. But I believe I share Dr Johnson's opinion, that his moral standpoint is somewhat lax.'

Mr Fordwick absorbed this viewpoint; on the whole he agreed with it. Clearly Miss Austen held high moral principles. He felt a joyous uplift of his spirits. It seemed that Fate – no surely Providence would be a word more apt – had been extraordinarily accommodating to arrange this chance encounter with just such a young woman as he had often desired to meet ... amiable of disposition, educated to a degree, fluent in expression – and pretty as well. So different from the majority of young ladies, who were apt to be very accomplished and very ignorant. Could such good fortune really be his at last?

They went on to speak of poetry – of Byron, Crabbe and Cowper, exchanging a few favourite quotations (delightful coincidence! these often proved to be the very same), and by the time they reached the villa, and Mr Fordwick had delivered his charge safely across the threshold, while Jane assured her family that she had suffered no serious consequence from her mishap, the initial attraction each felt for the other had grown into a certain desire to become better acquainted.

Mr Fordwick was quite easily prevailed upon to enter their little sitting room and take a glass of Madeira; he was formally introduced to each member of he family, and, when he addressed himself to Mr Austen, Jane found her previous surmise confirmed: Mr Fordwick was indeed a clergyman. At present, he told them, he held a curacy at Epping, in Surrey, but hoped soon to take up the living of a parish in Sussex, in the gift of Lord Eaglemont, who had in the past shown him some favour. Moreover, it was established in one brisk paragraph of conversation that he and Mr Austen upheld the established Anglican tradition, and had similar views on the noisy religion of the Evangelicals, with their distressingly emotional desire to achieve conversions of lost souls.

'I have a dear friend with whom I studied at Oxford,' Mr

Fordwick told them. 'Augustus Penberthy – a delightful fellow. He has been quite won over to the Evangelical persuasion – I confess I am unable to understand it. However,' he added with a smile, 'I am happy to say that circumstance, unfortunate though it may be, has not impaired our friendship.'

Mr Fordwick was delighted with the little family; with the genial, white-haired father; the mother's refined and pleasant manner; the quiet elder daughter – handsomer than her sister, perhaps, her features more regular, but lacking the latter's engaging liveliness and sparkle. He could not stay longer than the allowable quarter of an hour upon this first occasion, but requested permission to call the next day – 'to ensure your daughter has completely recovered from her accident' – and by the time he left, he was already halfway to having fallen in love with Jane Austen.

As for Jane herself, she was in a similar state, her sensibilities aroused to a pitch she had never experienced before. Cassandra, glancing at her glowing face, speculated that such colour, such a glow, could not be entirely due to the sea air.

'Such a charming gentleman!' Mrs Austen pronounced. 'So obliging of him to take care of Jane. And Sussex,' she continued with a leap of the imagination, 'is such an agreeable countryside.' She scarcely dared to harbour the hope that arose in her maternal bosom: had her younger daughter finally met a gentleman she could favour?

'A sensible fellow,' George Austen commented briefly, reaching for his pipe. 'Sound views on the Dissenters.'

And so the holiday at Sidmouth took on a new prospect, as neatly framed within the several minds of the Austen family as if it were a long-desired view glimpsed at last through a Claude glass.

The remaining two weeks at Sidmouth were filled with Mr Fordwick's romantic courtship of Mr Austen's younger daughter; and his honourable intention to ask for Jane's hand in marriage began to seem a safe assumption.

'We should have the ceremony at Steventon,' Mrs Austen told her husband as they lay behind the seclusion of their bed curtains one night. 'I am sure that is what dearest Jane would wish. – Though perhaps Bath might be more convenient.' A sudden thought struck her. 'Why, she could be married at the very church where our own nuptials took place, my dear – St Swithin Walcot!' And she gave a little sigh of happy remembrance . . . and then another, less happy little sigh of regret that newly wedded bliss must, inevitably, come to this: a four-poster bed shared from habit, all very comfortable and cosy, to be sure, but far from the few-found delight she had discovered as a bride.

Her husband, that once eager bridegroom, now halfway to sleep, murmured something comprehensible only to his wife.

'No, dear, but he will,' she replied confidently. 'To be sure, it would be a little – precocious for him to propose so soon; propriety demands more time. But we shall be seeing him in Bath very soon after we return there, I am sure of it. – Goodness and mercy, how busy we shall be, first moving into our new home, and then with wedding preparations . . .'

Mr Austen mumbled again.

'Of course, dear, it goes without saying we need to know much more about Mr Fordwick and his family – though as to immediate family, I understand his parents died some time ago, and he has just one brother – but everything of that sort will be made clear before long. Then there will be all the business of the marriage settlement . . . How pleased our eldest son will be to see one of his sisters wed at last! Oh! dear, dear Jane, how happy I feel for her!' And now she gave another sigh, a long, contented one this time, and drifted into slumber.

One evening Mr and Mrs Austen, Cassandra, Jane and Mr Fordwick strolled down to the beach to witness an event they had been told they should not miss on any account: the drawing of the *seine*. It was indeed a curious sight, entirely carried out by women. Jane was fascinated by these fisherfolk. Stoutly made and deeply tanned from their exposure to all weathers, they were dressed barbarously, with stays half-laced and kerchiefs about their necks. They wore a single coloured petticoat and went barefoot; and their coats were pinned in trouser shape between their legs, leaving them naked to the knee. Mr Fordwick declared he could not have imagined such a race of females existed in a civilized country; had he come to this shore by sea, he should have almost fancied he had been cast upon some newly discovered coast.

These fisherwomen proceed to draw a huge net into a boat, then rowed out to sea a little way in a rough semicircle, spreading the net all the way, one side of it being kept above water by means of corks. When this was done, they landed on the shore again and half of them returned to the beginning of the net. With amazing strength, these Amazons then hauled the net into shore by its two ends, both groups moving towards each other in the process. The fish they had caught were encircled in the middle of the net, which emerged from the water last – whereupon, joined now in one group, the women sent up a great shout and fell upon their catch, shrilly disputing their shares. They had caught above four dozen mackerel in that single haul, someone informed them.

Jane had never known such happiness as she felt now. Each day she looked forward with almost unbearable suspense to Mr Fordwick's arrival at the villa, or to joining him at some meeting-place they had arranged. That they should see each other every day was accepted, both by themselves and Jane's family, as a matter of course. Meanwhile, Jane discovered that her previous views on husbands, matrimony, households and children were becoming strangely mellowed by the simple circumstance of having fallen in love. Up to now, she had regarded these components of the double state with a certain cynicism, deploring the case of those wives whose families steadily increased year by year, until they were worn out by childbearing. Elliot Fordwick was so very much her notion of the ideal man that she could imagine no greater bliss than to be his wife, indulge in mutual companionship, arrange his household and – yes, bear his children. In her wholehearted acceptance of his attention, she grew noticeably softer in her opinions generally, and desisted a good deal from her habit of expressing herself in witty but often rather harsh pronouncements. She was content to feel simply happy. It was a curiously satisfying experience. She was especially delighted to discover that she and Mr Fordwick seemed to share a similar sense of humour, a keen appreciation of the ridiculous. 'Follies and nonsense, whims and inconsistencies *do* divert me so,' she confessed to him, her eyes gleaming mischievously.

They took long walks and drives, sometimes accompanied by Cassandra, or else as a family party. Mr Fordwick consolidated the high opinion he had achieved within her family by further converse on church matters and politics with Mr Austen (they saw eye to eye in their regard for Tory principles), and by showing Mrs Austen a very proper respect and courtesy. Cassandra found Mr Fordwick entirely agreeable and thought him most suitable as a prospective brother-in-law; she rejoiced for her sister even as Jane had rejoiced for her before poor Tom Fowle had died in the West Indies.

As the days went by, there surely could be as little doubt of Mr Fordwick's serious intention as of Miss Jane Austen's partiality for him. Any doubt on that score which might have lingered in her mind was firmly settled one afternoon as he and she walked along the deserted beach; the tall, pale gentleman and the light-footed, glowing young woman. Jane had been speaking of her sailor brothers, revealing the touching pride she felt for them both, when suddenly Mr Fordwick halted, turned, and gazed into her eyes.

'It is my earnest desire, my fondest wish, my dear Miss Austen, that before very long I shall be acquainted with the rest of your family – and you with my brother Frederick – alas, the only member of my family left to me.'

Jane coloured and turned her melting gaze seawards. Surely there could be no plainer indication of his feeling for her than this? 'I – I hope that may come to pass, Mr Fordwick, for it is my fond wish also,' she murmured.

He stooped, selected a flat pebble from the sand and with a deft flick of the wrist sent it skipping across the wavelets. 'I am forced to return home the day after tomorrow by – by an unbreakable engagement.' He paused, shook his head as if regretting his choice of words, and added: 'I would far rather stay in Sidmouth.'

To be with her – Jane knew this was his meaning.

'I shall hope, Miss Jane, to call upon your father soon after you return to Bath, once you are settled at Sydney Place. I will write to your father to announce my coming.' He paused, and a shadow seemed to cross his face. 'There is one circumstance which . . . That is to say, there is a matter that first needs to be resolved . . . But all will be well, I *know* it will.' And he threw another pebble, this time with a gesture which was almost savage, so that it sank without trace.

Jane glanced at him almost sharply. This was unlike the usual fluent expression of his thoughts. She could not bear to see the faintest shadow of anguish upon his pale brow. She touched his sleeve gently, relinquishing her hold upon her loosened bonnet strings. 'Pray do not distress yourself, sir – can you not confide in me if there is something that troubles you?' she asked tenderly.

He gazed at her, his dark eyes seeming to pierce her through. Then a sudden gust of wind seized her bonnet, which, unanchored by her grasp, flew off her head and bowled along the beach. As they ran after it, she did not hear the moan which was his response: 'If only I could! Oh, if only I could!' – And yet again he asked himself the question that had haunted his mind ever since his first meeting with this angelic, this unsurpassed young woman: should he have begun – come so far in his courtship? Until he *knew* . . . until he was sure he might proceed without impediment? Bitter, bitter fate if this happiness were to be snatched away! For a moment – until the wind blew the opportunity away together with her bonnet – he had hovered on the brink of telling her everything.

He retrieved the fugitive headgear and Jane replaced it carefully upon her glossy ringlets, tying the strings. The sprint across the beach had brought a fit of coughing upon Mr Fordwick; he pressed a hand to his side.

'It – it is nothing, only a stitch,' he told Jane; then turned the conversation back to the absorbing topic of her family. 'Pray, tell me more of your brother Henry . . . I feel we would – nay, *shall* have much in common, he and I . . .'

The move into Sydney Place was accomplished smoothly, with fresh energy engendered by the seaside holiday, and by their eager hopes for a happy event in the not too distant future. They were installed by late August, amid new wallpaper, new chintzes and the few familiar objects they had brought from Steventon. Then began the eager anticipation of the message that would announce Mr Fordwick's intention to visit Bath . . . which, as the days went by and no communication from him arrived, turned first to mild, then to acute anxiety. Jane's complexion grew pale; there were shadows beneath her hazel eyes, which were dulled with disappointment. Cassandra went about with a perpetually worried expression; Mr Austen felt much concern for his younger daughter; as for Mrs Austen, she fell into a highly nervous state and had to resort once more to her 'composer', the laudanum bottle.

The whole situation was unbearably aggravated by Mrs Leigh Perrot's constant inquiries as to whether they had yet received word . . . had they heard from Mr Fordstock . . . or was it Wickford? She was careless of remembering names – unless, of course, they were especially worthy of recollection, had perhaps some aristocratic or other significant connexion. How Mrs Austen regretted that impulse which had led her to confide to her sister-in-law the news of Jane's romantic attachment!

Then, in September, a letter came. It was black-bordered and its contents provided a very final resolution of the puzzle of Mr Fordwick's silence, replacing anxiety with anguish, speculation with a dreadful certainty. The letter was addressed to the Rev. Geo. Austen Esq.; the handwriting was unfamiliar, and Mr Austen opened it in the room set aside as his study. After he had perused the shocking contents, he sat in his chair for some time, dreading the office that he must now perform. Poor Jane! he thought compassionately; poor, wretched child!

In the event, having summoned Jane from the sitting room, where she was listlessly embroidering a cushion-cover, he felt the simplest procedure was to hand the letter over to her, first giving her a clear indication that it contained grave news. She read:

It is my most melancholy duty to communicate to you and yr family a Circumstance as necessary as painful to make to you. I wish the shock could have been lessened by a better preparation – I know my Brother would have wished it so. But the Event has been sudden, and so must be the information of it. . .

Having read so far, Jane raised her head and looked towards the window unseeingly. It was all too clear what must follow these portentous opening sentences.

My beloved and esteemed Brother, Elliot, was taken from us two days since following a recurrence of a Pulmonary infection with which he has unfortunately been afflicted for some time. It was hoped – he himself entertained the most sanguine and fervent hope – that a recent medical regime which prescribed his Visit to the Seaside might have restored him to full health and vigour; but it was not to be; he succumbed to a sudden Fever and weakened rapidly. It was all over within a few hours; he passed away steadfast in his Faith, and with his dying breath besought me to convey to Yr Family, and especially to yr daughter Miss Jane Austen, his most affectionate duty, esteem and regard . . .

The signature was *Frederick Fordwick*. – Yes, he had spoken of a brother, she recalled the name . . . oh, agony! Dead! Lost to her forever! All hope destroyed, all happy plans laid aside, never to be fulfilled . . .

And now, surely, the meaning of his cryptic, unfinished sentence during their last stroll together along the beach at Sidmouth, the shadow which had crossed his face, her feeling that something troubled him, were all explained. His illness – the pulmonary infection – *that* was the matter he had spoken of, which needed to be resolved. Alas for his sanguine conviction that all would be well!

She folded the letter with the most meticulous care, and with an unnatural composure handed it back to her father. 'I think – I shall take a walk,' she told him. 'I shall return before dusk. Pray acquaint my mother and sister with this painful news, for I – I – cannot.'

And calmly, quietly, hopelessly, she left the room.

Eleven

SPRING OF 1802 brought a truce between England and France. The Peace of Amiens, the statesmen called it, but with English ships and merchandise still excluded from French ports, the nation of shopkeepers could scarcely be blamed if they regarded it with some misgiving. The Austens of Sydney Place, Bath, learned with dismay that the Austens of Upper Berkeley Street, London, were to visit France to try to establish some claim to the estate of Eliza Austen's first husband, the Comte de Feuillide. Cousin Eliza – the Comtesse as she then was – had come to England for safety as soon as the Revolution broke out; she had actually been staying at Steventon when the news of her husband's execution was received.

The Feuillide estate lay near Gaboret, in Guyenne. The visit seemed a rash undertaking . . . supposing war broke out again and Henry and Eliza were stranded in enemy territory! The very thought was sufficient to bring on Mrs Austen's palpitations.

The fragile nature of the Peace was further underscored by the organization of the Sea-Fencibles, recruited to guard the English coast and give warning of invasion from across the Channel. Captain Frank Austen was posted to Ramsgate to take charge of a force of Kentish Fencibles. He had recently become engaged to a Miss Mary Gibson and, in July, his sister Jane visited him in Ramsgate, and met there her future sister-in-law. She pronounced her a charming girl, and Miss Gibson, for her part, found Miss Jane Austen singularly agreeable. 'But – I only wish she were not so sad,' she told Frank.

Frank shook his head. 'It is her – her disappointment: she still feels it dreadfully. She and Mr Fordwick were all but betrothed, you know.' He sighed. 'She used to be so merry, always the one who made us laugh.'

He asked Jane if she were still composing stories; upon which, with an echo of her old spirit, she replied that life in Bath was far too occupied with serious triviality for mere novel-writing.

In truth, the seascape of Ramsgate brought added heartache to Jane: strolling by the shore, hearing the seagulls cry, watching the tide ebb and flow, and moreover a daily witness to the happiness of Frank and Mary, how could she help but feel poignant regret for what might have been?

Towards the end of the year, a curious incident occurred. In November, Jane and Cassandra went to Steventon to spend a few days with James and Mary, as guests at the Rectory. This seemed strange enough; the sisters were quite often obliged to restrain themselves as Mary showed them her 'improvements' and innovations – the drawing-room sofa, Jane noticed, wore a new chintz cover. Then they went on to Manydown, just a few miles away, to visit the Bigg-Wither family. The Austen children had grown up together with the three Bigg daughters and only son – Harris, now twenty-one, and heir to his father's considerable fortune. A day or two later, James and Mary Austen were astonished to see the Bigg-Wither carriage drive up to the Rectory, and to behold Cassandra, Jane and the Bigg girls descend from it, all five of them in a clearly agitated state. Catherine and Alethea Bigg were in floods of tears, pressing their handkerchiefs to their eyes. It was almost like watching a scene from a play: the Bigg young ladies tenderly embraced the Austen sisters, then climbed into their carriage again and drove off with a scrunching of gravel.

'Cassandra! Jane! What in the world has happened?' James exclaimed, rushing out to conduct his sisters into the house.

Cassandra turned to her brother, her bearing very much that of *Miss Austen*, the elder daughter of the family, and matched by her tone of voice. 'We must return to Bath at once,' she told him. 'And you, James, must accompany us in the public coach from Winchester. We cannot, of course, travel by ourselves.'

'But,' Mary cried indignantly, 'that means James will not be back in time to conduct the Sunday services – surely nothing can be so urgent as to take precedence of your brother's Sunday duties –'

Cassandra wheeled round and swept the objection away. 'It can and it is, Mary,' was all she would say.

So they took the Bath coach from Winchester and, as they journeyed, James learned the reason for this extraordinary behaviour. At Manydown the previous evening, after a pleasant family gathering, with music, games and a little informal dancing, Harris Bigg-Wither, who had long harboured fervent admiration for Miss Jane Austen, had proposed to her – and been accepted! The evening's gaiety and happy laughter had reminded Jane so poignantly of the life she used to know at the Rectory . . . the sort of life she might lead if she chose to marry young Mr Bigg-Wither, that for a moment, for a few hours, she had deluded herself that this was all she asked of life. Everyone had been delighted when Harris announced the news, his boyish face aglow with pride . . . everyone except Cassandra; but Jane chose to ignore her sister's incredulous expression.

Then, during a sleepless night, she had repented her rash action. How could she have accepted the proposal? How could she have thought it sensible to form an alliance with this family, pleasant, respectable, well-endowed though it was, and amiable as she knew Harris himself to be? With a kind of horror, she realized she had fallen into a trap which, in her right mind, she had always been determined to avoid. The lure of worldly security, of salvation from a future as an unmarried daughter and maiden aunt, had led her to accept the proposal. Dear Harris himself, with his spaniel gaze, was the least reason for that acceptance! Besides, there was the difference in their ages . . . Tossing on her pillow, Jane imagined herself and Harris at thirty-seven and thirty-one respectively . . . forty-one and forty-seven . . . sixty-one and sixty-seven – oh, it did not bear contemplation! (But above all, there was the memory of that tall, pale clergyman; beside Elliot Fordwick, Harris Bigg-Wither and all others were mere shadows.)

At dawn, she had held a haggard conference with Cassandra; and later, descending to meet Harris for a morning stroll before breakfast, she had informed him that their engagement must be broken off. She could not become his wife.

Harris Bigg-Wither, very properly, was heart-broken; but at

one-and-twenty broken hearts may be promptly mended and high tragedy commuted into useful experience: thereby is gained that indispensable commodity, worldly wisdom. The Austen sisters proceeded to stammer their apologies, their regrets: they must leave at once. The Bigg sisters, for their part, could on no account allow their visitors to depart alone – and so the tearful, abrupt take-leave was accomplished.

James sat back in the public conveyance and heard this little history (conveyed in discreet, *sotto voce*, yet intense tones which automatically impelled the attention of the other passengers) with little comment beyond an occasional nod or grunt. He was quite seriously annoyed at having to forgo his Sunday service – his curate had been hastily delegated to take charge in his absence – and now, looking with dispassion at his younger sister's dark-circled eyes and weary features, he observed to himself that surely *this* would have been her last chance of a suitable marriage. He sighed. What would become of her?

Neither James nor Cassandra nor Jane herself could possibly have imagined what was about to happen to her: it would have seemed the wildest flight of fancy. But as the coach jolted along the wintry highway with its withered hedges and stark, leafless trees, her immediate future was even then being decided, in a confrontation between Mr and Mrs Leigh Perrot in one of the hot-houses at Scarlets, that pleasant country house in Berkshire.

A confrontation? Between such a devoted husband and loving wife? But this was no vulgar spat; rather it was the eventual blaze of a slow combustion which had been burning steadily ever since their shared unspeakable experience of imprisonment and trial and eventual return to normal life. It was today, upon this hour, as they inspected the hot-house blooms forced into unseasonal bud and flower, that the matter between them finally caught fire. It was, to be precise, the sight of the pale yellow, spiky blooms – repulsive to Jane Leigh Perrot, irresistibly attractive to her husband – of *Banksia integrifolia*, flowering so incongruously in this English setting, which sparked the flame.

James Leigh Perrot derived much satisfaction from his successful propagation of this plant from a handful of seeds given to him by none other than the great Sir Joseph Banks.

'The colonists in New South Wales call it White Honeysuckle, I believe,' Sir Joseph had informed him. 'These native plants are difficult to rear in our climate, though I have had some success at Revesby with my waratahs and Norfolk Island pines.'

The opportunity for conversation with Sir Joseph had followed a lecture he delivered at the Royal Society in London upon the flora of *Terra Australis*. James Leigh Perrot had followed with rapt attention Sir Joseph's description of the plants which he and his assistant – one Dr Solander, a former pupil of the illustrious Swedish botanist Carolus Linnaeus – had collected and classified during their voyage in the *Endeavour* with Captain Cook. Sir Joseph had brought with him several examples of flora, and it was after the lecture, while exchanging a few words with James, that he had pressed upon him the gift of *Banksia* seeds. Sir Joseph's intense interest in *Terra Australis* had never diminished; it was he, indeed, who had so strongly advocated before a House of Commons committee the establishment of a penal colony at Botany Bay, and he was constantly consulted by the Government upon matters relating to the administration of that Colony.

James Leigh Perrot and Joseph Banks were of an age (and alike afflicted by the gout), but the former was humbled to reflect how much the latter had packed into the same span of years. So many and varied were Sir Joseph's interests that he had achieved a reputation for almost universal wisdom. 'And what,' James Leigh Perrot thought dismally, 'have I achieved apart from an insignificant collection of local Lepidoptera?'

'I was extraordinarily interested to read of the part you played, Sir Joseph, in Captain Cook's first voyage to the southern continent,' he ventured to say to the great man upon that foggy evening at the Royal Society in Albemarle Street. 'I – I confess, sir, I find myself strangely drawn by everything I learn about *Terra Australis* . . . I – I long to see something of it for myself.'

This was the first time James Leigh Perrot had permitted himself to formulate his great desire in speech. He was quite startled by his boldness. At home, the slightest reference to Botany Bay or indeed any other part of the continent remained abhorrent to his beloved wife. Since the happy outcome of her unfortunate experience had done away with the necessity to plan for a possible removal to *that place*, she was quite unable to understand his continuing interest in it. So, prudently, he kept his unabated fascination to himself, while continuing to discover as much as he could about the exotic fauna and flora of that distant land. Other men kept secret mistresses; *Terra Australis* was James Leigh Perrot's clandestine passion.

And now Sir Joseph Banks, conveyor of universal wisdom, looked straight at James Leigh Perrot, amateur lepidopterist, and remarked: 'Sir, if one *longs* for something, then the obvious course is to undertake some action to assuage that longing.' And what might perhaps have seemed sarcastic in his speech was softened by a wry smile of recognition for the plight of man in middle age. 'Moreover,' continued Sir Joseph, 'if you should decide to make that journey, sir, I would be pleased to write of your intention to the Governor of New South Wales, Mr King, who is himself most interested in natural history. He has sent me some important specimens –'

Others were pressing round, anxious for the chance of a word with the great man, but James was bold enough to prolong their exchange with a question. 'Have you, sir, ever wished to return there yourself?' he asked.

Sir Joseph's fine eyes gleamed. He raised one hand, his lace cuff falling back to reveal a spiralling *moko* upon his wrist, a mark of honour engraved there by a Maori *tohunga*. 'In truth, my dear sir, could it be done by Fortunatus' wishing cap, I have no doubt that I should this day remove myself and family to *Terra Australis* and solicit a grant of lands on the banks of the Hawkesbury river.'

More than satisfied with this answer, and bearing his *Banksia* seeds with reverence, James Leigh Perrot had wandered out into the foggy street, filled with new resolution.

And now those seeds had brought forth an exotic yellow flower, and new-found resolution had turned into decision: and thus husband and wife reached this November moment of confrontation in the hot-house.

'How warm it is here!' Jane Leigh Perrot exclaimed, pinching a withered leaf from a peppermint pelargonium. Her gaze fell upon that outlandish plant of which her husband was so proud. In her opinion, the *Banksia* resembled nothing so much as a worn-out loofah, unworthy to take its place alongside her beautiful begonias and pelargoniums. She strongly suspected the fire was kept stoked so high solely for its sake.

James, invoking the inspiration of Sir Joseph Banks, at last found courage to pronounce the decision he had reached. 'Well, my love, it is my intention that we shall shortly be enjoying the naturally warm climate of the Antipodes, far from England's inclement winter weather.'

His wife gazed at him in utter astonishment. 'Perrot! Husband! You cannot mean – oh, it is impossible!'

When a mild-mannered man decides over a length of time upon a definite course of action, he is less likely to be swayed in his intent than a man of a more choleric and impetuous nature. So it was with Mr Leigh Perrot. 'We are to make a journey to New South Wales, my love,' he said quite firmly. 'I am resolved upon it. For a few months only. No longer,' he pointed out quite reasonably, 'than the time we spent at Ilchester as – ah, the guests of Mr Scadding.'

Jane Leigh Perrot, flushed by the hot-house atmosphere and rising indignation and on the brink of reproachfully condemning such an irresponsible, foolish, impractical, *selfish* scheme, was suddenly and effectively silenced. Her husband's words perforce reminded her of his staunch and uncomplaining support through all those dreadful months, never for an instant wavering in his devotion, even though his health had suffered . . . Had she not, many times, eulogized the behaviour of 'this Treasure of my Life' in her letters to her cousin Mountague? Had she not declared: 'I have a pride in letting the World see, and know the Man who thinks *me* deserving of so much affection' – and much more besides, calling him her 'Guardian Angel', her 'true Support under every Affliction' and never ceasing to offer up her gratitude to the Almighty for his presence?

She lowered her eyes, crumbling the pelargonium leaf to peppermint dust between her fingers. How could she not respond to her dearest Perrot as he had responded to her?

'I do not know exactly how it is, my dear,' he said, 'but I have such a very strong desire to see the curious creatures and plants, the Antipodean landscape and all the natural wonders of that Colony while I am still able to make the journey and return again, God willing.'

Those words, so quietly spoken, embodying as they did the awareness of approaching decrepitude and mortality, quite wrung his wife's heart. She could not oppose the scheme, she could not deny this dear, dear husband of hers the opportunity to satisfy such strongly felt desire.

Sensing her acquiescence, James offered more cogent and pragmatical persuasion. 'You are aware, my love, that I have lately rearranged some of my business affairs in order to recoup the sum we paid out in lawyer's fees and other expenses connected with that – ah, unfortunate experience. On the advice of my stock-jobber, I withdrew some monies from Government Funds and reinvested them in a commercial enterprise, helping to underwrite a spice cargo from the West Indies.'

His wife gasped and laid one hand on her heart, fearing the outcome of such a rash act. To withdraw from the Funds! That was not at all in keeping with her husband's customary caution in such matters.

Alas, he confirmed her fears. 'Unfortunately, the ship was wrecked and all her cargo lost, and with the failure of that enterprise, more losses have accrued on top of those we have already suffered. It will be to our advantage to let Scarlets for a year to some suitable tenant. I happen to know of a naval officer, an Admiral retired from active duty since peace was declared, who desires to rent a country property while he looks round for a place of his own in the district. Our town house we could leave empty in the care of Frank and Evans, as we did before; now that my sister Austen is in Bath, she could keep an eye on it for us.'

He paused, noting how stricken his wife appeared. 'Do not misunderstand me, my love – we are by no means poor, nor are we in debt. It is simply that I am anxious to restore our fortune to what it was before our trouble fell upon us.'

'It was *my* trouble, Perrot,' his wife acknowledged. 'And would that I had never brought it about!'

'Well,' James continued quite cheerfully, 'our excursion to the Antipodes may in a sense be regarded as a prudent retrenchment; we shall spare ourselves all the cost of town living, while garnering an income by letting Scarlets.'

Viewed in this light, the proposal began to assume a positively sensible, indeed a necessary aspect to Jane Leigh Perrot. And a sea voyage, though a hazardous undertaking (she repressed a shudder for the fate of that West Indian vessel), could be beneficial to one's health. Though in truth her spirit did quail when she reflected upon the vast distance of the voyage to the Antipodes. But what better cause could there be than the restoration of a fortune eroded by litigation and unlucky investment? And so at last she gave her willing consent to the plan, upon which James, relieved beyond measure by the success of his persuasion, embraced his wife so fervently that she all but fell into the prickly foliage of a monstrous *Polystichum aculeatum*. The head gardener, old Isaac, happening to pass by at that moment trundling his wheelbarrow, was quite startled by the sight. 'It be too hot in there,' he muttered to himself as he tramped along the frosty path to the vegetable garden, where Brussels sprouts clung frozen to the stalk.

Upon reflection, Jane Leigh Perrot decided that the adventure which lay ahead really could not be contemplated without a female companion. Once arrived in the Colony, Perrot would most likely be abroad observing and collecting all day long, and she suspected there would be scarcely anybody there able to provide the social intercourse to which she was accustomed.

'I have a capital idea,' she told her husband one day. – They had returned to The Paragon, where the faithful Evans was now busy dust-sheeting the furniture while her master made arrangements for sailing to New South Wales and her mistress wrote lists of necessary items to take on the voyage. 'Why should not one of those elegant young Austen nieces of ours accompany us to the Colony – Cassandra or Jane, I mean? I should prefer Cassandra, I think; I find her more – docile, more agreeable than her sister; but I very much doubt whether *she* could come. Mrs Austen Knight is sure to produce another child this year, and they utterly depend upon Cassandra for every lying-in at Godmersham.' She sighed at the very notion of being brought to childbed once a year and said regretfully: 'I daresay it will have to be Jane.'

A faint frown shadowed her brow as she thought of the younger sister's unpredictable sense of humour . . . But then she recollected that in fact poor Jane laughed very seldom these days. 'Why,' she went on more cheerfully, 'it will be just the thing for Jane, after the disappointment she suffered over Mr Wickford – or was it Fordwick? – dying so inconveniently. She has been down in the dumps ever since. Yes, now that I think of it, a sea voyage and a complete change of scene is just what a physician would advise for a touch of melancholia – which appears to be what Jane is suffering from. Nothing could be more fortunate for her than the chance to accompany us on this tour.' Another thought occurred to her. 'I do not suppose she would be likely to form any attachment in the Colony – but one can never tell. Though it is not like going to the India station; many quite respectable alliances are made there.'

Her husband was perfectly amenable to this scheme, being particularly fond of his niece Jane. And so it was laid before the Austen family during a call at Sydney Place one morning.

'It will be quite an adventure,' Mrs Leigh Perrot told her astonished sister-in-law. 'Jane and I will find our own amusements while Perrot is off examining the – the kangarus and butterflies and curious plants. My niece has not had the opportunity to travel beyond England's shores – I, of course, being born in the Barbados . . . my father . . . the Governor . . .' her voice trailed off into the stunned silence that had greeted her proposal.

'Such a very long way,' Mrs Austen murmured faintly, drawing her cashmere shawl about her for comfort. 'The voyage so perilous –'

'A large number of vessels have made the round voyage quite safely,' Mrs Leigh Perrot said with assurance. 'And now that peace has been made, there is no danger of being attacked by French privateers.'

Mr Austen cleared his throat and glanced across at his younger daughter, who sat composedly beside the fire, dressed in a plain grey gown. She seemed to favour a more sober style these days, eschewing colour. He thought it a pity – he did not wish to see her fade so soon into a resigned spinsterhood. 'Well, Jane, this is a matter for you to decide,' he said at last.

Cassandra, busying herself with spirit lamp, silver kettle and tea caddy, looked across at her sister, trying to divine her thoughts.

'Oh, I do not expect Jane to decide just at this moment,' Mrs Leigh Perrot said. 'She will require a little while to think about it. But we shall need to know by next week – Perrot is securing a passage on the *Jason* – stern cabins, of course. As for what we will take with us, I am making lists –'

Her flow was interrupted by Jane's rising and going over to her mother. She took hold of one of Mrs Austen's hands with gentle affection. 'If I were to accept this – this generous invitation from my Uncle and Aunt Perrot,' she said, 'could you manage here without me? I should be absent for more than a twelvemonth; Cassandra may be called to Godmersham; your health still gives us some cause for anxiety –'

While Mr Austen nodded approvingly at such a proper exhibition of filial concern, Mrs Austen sat bolt upright as though to display her vigour. 'Dear child, of course I should manage,' she told Jane, quelling the tremor in her voice. 'Have we not removed to Bath with the specific object of making our life as easy as possible? Reflect: I have no garden to supervise, no still-room, no parish visiting ... why, my chief occupation nowadays is to sit upon the sofa!'

Ignoring the conspicuous rattle of teacups in the background – Cassandra, dreading a similar impetuosity to that which had led Jane to accept Harris Bigg-Wither's proposal, was desperately endeavouring to attract her sister's attention – Jane smiled and turned to her Aunt Perrot. 'Then, Aunt, I think there is no need to delay my acceptance of your kind proposal. I shall take the greatest pleasure in accompanying my uncle and yourself to the Antipodes.'

Whereupon a Spode teacup slipped from Cassandra's fingers to the polished floor and smashed in smithereens.

Twelve

THE TRANSPORT *Jason* sailed from Portsmouth on a surprisingly mild February day in 1803. This dumpy-looking vessel, sitting upright upon the grey waters of the Solent, was for the next several months to be their floating world for all who sailed in her: officers, crew, cabin passengers, convicts, ship's cat, and assorted vermin. Her stout planking would preserve them from the unfathomable seas; upon her somewhat flimsy masts, sails would be rigged to catch each hastening wind; her provisions would sustain master, midshipman, privileged passenger, convicted felon, whiskered rat and lowly weevil. Her route, as laid down by the Admiralty and designed so that the sailing ships might take advantage of both the prevailing winds and revictualling ports, was by way of Tenerife and the Cape Verde Islands to Rio de Janeiro, thence across the South Atlantic ocean to Table Bay, at the Cape; and from there, following the thirty-ninth parallel of latitude, with no land mass closer than India to the north and the Antarctic (as yet undiscovered and unnamed) to the south, to landfall at Port Jackson, New South Wales. This journey of thirteen thousand nautical miles would occupy between four and six months, depending on the weather they encountered. No transport had ever reached Port Jackson in less than a hundred and twelve days.

This little universe of creaking wood and bellying canvas, rum, salt pork and ship's biscuit, sailors' oaths, convict misery and naval and military discipline, was disposed as a faithful microcosm of society as it was ordered in the land they left behind them. The upper deck accommodated the ship's officers and cabin passengers; in the fo'c'sle the seamen slung their hammocks; between decks, with hatches battened down, the convicts were officially allotted berths six feet square to accommodate four persons – providing eighteen inches width for each one; and secure in the hold lay a valuable cargo of general goods upon which a satisfactory profit would be made when it was traded in Sydney Town. Only the vermin – and the ship's cat – moved freely between each rank of this society, quite unaware of superior or inferior status. As the estimable Dr Johnson had remarked but recently, upon being asked to pronounce which was the better of two minor poets: 'Sir, there is no settling the precedence between a louse and a flea.'

Beneath the raised poop deck at the ship's stern were two large cabins with glazed windows, the best accommodation on the vessel, and six smaller cabins, all built around a drawing room with shining brass fittings, red Turkey carpet, gleaming mahogany tables and velvet-cushioned sofas. One of those two best cabins was occupied by Mr and Mrs Leigh Perrot, and one of the smaller cabins (it really would have been needlessly extravagant to have secured the other great cabin for their niece) by Miss Jane Austen. Since these three passengers did not intend to sojourn long in the Antipodes, their baggage was relatively light. Their main concern was to provide themselves with occupation and diversion for the long voyage. They had brought on board books, playing cards, sketching equipment, a chess set, sewing materials, and notebooks, goose quills and ink powder . . . and, for Jane Leigh Perrot, an ample supply of those curiously strong peppermints to which she was addicted. They also had a number of slender bamboo poles and a quantity of fine muslin, from which to manufacture butterfly nets . . . in which James Leigh Perrot hoped to capture some splendid specimens of Antipodean Lepidoptera. More: he nursed a secret ambition to be the first to document the existence of one particular species of butterfly or moth, which might bestow upon him a flutter of immortality by virtue of its name. A swallow-tail, perhaps? *Papilio perrotsia* . . . how well that sounded! Or possibly one of the browns, the forest dwellers: *Heteronympha perrotsia* . . . it was, he thought, an ambition not beyond the bounds of accomplishment.

There would, of course, be the acquaintance of their fellow passengers and the ship's officers to help the days and weeks to pass, with its commolition of conversation, speculation and gossip — besides, no doubt, unavoidable glimpses of the convicts from time to time. And to begin with, at least, the novelty of life at sea, the daily routine of an existence regulated by the ship's bell and the activities of the sailors, would afford its own considerable interest.

The other large stern cabin belonged to a Mr and Mrs Strongbow, a young couple but newly wed. As if the novelty of marriage were not sufficient, they intended to take up land in the Colony and settle there. Their cabin was crammed with a bewildering array of necessary and redundant objects, selected for practical and sentimental reasons, upon advice both wise and ignorant. They had, besides, other possessions stowed in the hold, everything needful for the conveyance of civilization, from a four-poster bed to a full set of Bristol glass. They appeared decent, genteel sort of folk.

Of the remaining two passenger cabins, one was occupied by Lieutenant Giles Watson of the New South Wales Corps, which had been established in '98 for duty in the Colony. He was the officer in charge of the small military contingent on board to guard the convicts.

The other cabin was occupied by Mr Robert Campbell, a merchant in his mid-thirties or thereabouts, who had, it appeared, established a flourishing business at Port Jackson, having previously been engaged in commerce at Calcutta. He was returning home ('How singular that he should refer to *that place* as "home",' Aunt Perrot was to observe more than once during the *Jason*'s voyage) after transacting business in England, impatient to be reunited with his young wife and first-born child. Besides a quantity of trading goods, he had brought on board one of the latest Broadwood square pianos as a surprise gift for his dearest Sophie. The piano had been carefully battened down in his cabin. And in the hold he had a brand new two-wheeled gig, which would surely be one of the smartest turn-outs in Sydney town, he thought with satisfaction.

All these privileged passengers of the upper deck were hoisted on board in the bosun's chair and received with due deference and civility; the convicts were already embarked, having been transferred from the hulks during the previous two days. Their reception had its own strictly observed ritual; in the interests of hygiene, they were stripped of their garments, which were summarily disposed of by the simple expedient of throwing them overboard; then, shivering in the winter breeze, each felon had a bucket of salt water thrown over him by seamen detailed for this courtesy. Finally, issued with rough but clean slop-clothing, and with religious tracts distributed by the Evangelist Society thrust into their hands (regardless of the fact that the majority were illiterate), they were double-ironed and sent down to their berths. Since the Peace had removed the fear of enemy attack, they would be allowed to muster and exercise on deck in the fresh air during the voyage – a welcome respite from confinement in their fetid quarters.

And so the *Jason* set out upon her journey, her rounded hull bobbing like a cork across that vast expanse of ocean, bearing her complement of some five hundred souls with all their hopes, fears, anguish, homesickness, seasickness, regrets, repentance, resentments and resolutions – and among them, three passengers whose feelings upon leaving their native shore were inevitably more lighthearted . . . for were they not to return in a little over a twelvemonth?

Miss Jane Austen looked happier than she had for many a day as she stood by the ship's rail, watching the coast recede into the distance. Her hazel eyes held almost their old sparkle as she breathed the salt air, clasping her cloak closely to her for warmth. To be at sea . . . to be embarked upon the longest voyage in the world! She shivered with a sudden feeling of undeniable excitement. Ships and the sea, the exploits of her sailor brothers, their tales of foreign ports and adventure upon the watery highway – these had always fascinated her. Now she was to experience for herself the motion of the shifting deck for weeks on end, to lie in her cabin cot each night and feel the ceaseless roll and pitch of the vessel as the *Jason* breasted every wave.

She was well aware that beneath the tender take-leave of her parents and Cassandra when she set off from Bath with her uncle and aunt, there had lain a certain mystification as to why she had accepted the Leigh Perrots' invitation with such alacrity, such a seeming lack of due consideration. The shards of a shattered teacup had registered Cassandra's instant astonishment. 'Do reflect,' she had urged Jane later, with a tinge of asperity in her tone, 'that you will be with our aunt each morning, noon and evening – there will be no escape from all that wearying worldliness, that comfortable assumption that *her* opinion is correct upon every subject. – Unless, of course, you choose to jump overboard!'

Mrs Austen had expressed simple bewilderment that her youngest daughter could so easily (it seemed) contemplate a journey to the other end of the earth, when the announcement of a mere removal from Hampshire to Bath had caused her to faint dead away. As for Jane's father, he, with compassionate intent, had sought to remind her that however far she travelled, there would be no removal from the interior landscape of her soul. 'Dear child,' he told her gently, 'your sorrow over the loss of that young clergyman will travel with you. It is a steadfast faith in Providence, and the passage of time, which heals misfortune's wounds, not the superficial traverse of distance, and unfamiliar sights.'

When Jane's family realized she was in fact quite set upon the project, that there was no possibility she would change her mind, they had cloaked their incomprehension with conventional sentiments, assuring each other that it would, after all, be a unique experience for Jane, that the change of scene would be just the thing to restore her spirits . . .

Jane did not believe she would come to regret her decision. She would miss Cassandra dreadfully – that was the worst aspect of this adventure. Up till now, whenever the sisters were apart, they had always been able to write to each other as frequently as they pleased, dashing off whatever nonsense came uppermost to their mind in delicious letters which relayed all the froth and bubble of the moment. It would be possible to send letters home from Rio, from Cape Town, and from Port Jackson when the *Jason* turned round to go back to England. And Jane knew that Cassandra would write from England by the next ship – but these would be letters of a different kind, chronicles and news bulletins to be read weeks and months after they were penned. The froth and bubble of the moment would be long dissipated.

As Jane gazed at the Isle of Wight, now no more than a smudge on the horizon, her uncle came to her side. 'Dear niece, will you go to your aunt?' he asked her, looking anxious. 'She feels the motion of the ship – she is unwell.'

Poor Aunt Perrot! Retching and wretched, she lay prostrated in her cot. Jane, slightly smug (it must be said) that she herself appeared to be what was known as 'a good sailor', recalled authoritative remarks made by her brothers upon the subject of *mal de mer*, and assured her aunt that she would soon 'find her sea-legs'.

'A singular phrase, niece,' the victim gasped, bending to the chamber-pot yet again to cast up her accounts.

But this indeed proved the case; long before the ship reached Rio, Mrs Leigh Perrot was fully restored to her somewhat formidable self.

Their shipboard routine was soon established, and they quickly got to know their fellow passengers. Lieutenant Watson conceived a boyish infatuation for Miss Jane Austen, whose clear, olive complexion, glossy ringlets and fresh garments were in wonderful contrast to the stinking, tattered females it was his duty to inspect between decks. She accepted his attention with a good grace; she seemed, she thought wryly, to hold some fatal attraction for very young gentlemen. Her uncle teased her about the sheep's eyes young Watson made at her across the Captain's table, where the passengers were usually joined by the ship's surgeon, Lieutenant Clinton, as well as two other naval officers. Aunt Perrot strongly disapproved of Mr Clinton because before they had been long out of Portsmouth, it became generally known that he was consorting with a comely female convict who was enabled to visit his cabin after dark. Aunt Perrot feared this was a forerunner of the lax moral behaviour they might expect to find in the Colony.

The *Jason*'s Master, Captain Teasdale, was a man of few words, who often chose to take his meals in his own cabin. There was a reason for this: he had a set of badly fitting porcelain teeth, which he felt obliged to wear whenever he did make an appearance at table, although they gravely impeded both speech and mastication. There were certain words he clearly found more difficult to pronounce than others; he assiduously avoided addressing the surgeon by name, and on one occasion he embarked, disastrously, upon the subject of the 'climate of the Colony'. Jane was always happy to observe the Captain on deck *sans* teeth and with his full confidence restored. It was the

Master's office to take divine service each Sabbath on the poop deck, and on these occasions, too, Mr Teasdale wore those diabolical teeth. After one memorable struggle with the third chapter of Ecclesiastes, the Bible reading was delegated to one of his officers for the remainder of the voyage.

The Strongbows turned out to be a pleasant enough young couple. Aunt Perrot declared herself puzzled by the obvious social discrepancy between husband and wife: bluff Daniel Strongbow with his ruddy, out-of-doors complexion was of yeoman stock, exactly the sort of man to take up land in the Colony. He informed them, with quiet assurance, that his family had farmed in Devon for generations. But fragile Emma Strongbow – she could not be more than eighteen or nineteen – clearly belonged to a more elevated social plane. How she would fare as the helpmeet of a pioneer farmer was more doubtful. When it shortly became evident that Emma Strongbow had fallen into an interesting condition, for Aunt Perrot at least the puzzle was solved.

'Depend upon it,' she told her husband in the privacy of their cabin, ' 'twas a marriage of necessity, and her family has provided the means for them to settle in New South Wales, far from scandalous tongues. – I daresay the child will be born before we reach our destination.'

Mr Robert Campbell afforded agreeable company, even though he was engaged in commerce. 'Very gentlemanlike,' was Aunt Perrot's verdict upon this passenger.

It was all very well for Mrs Leigh Perrot thus to speculate about the Strongbows, patronize the merchant of Sydney Cove, emanate moral disapproval towards Mr Clinton . . . She was only too well aware of the speculation and moral disapproval concerning *herself* which might arise, should the fact that she had stood trial for theft be circulated about the ship. Who could tell that one or other of the passengers or the ship's officers might not have read an account of the trial, or heard it gossiped about? People were apt to read and listen carelessly – who knew what garbled recollection the name of Leigh Perrot might stir in their minds? A trial by jury . . . something to do with stolen lace . . . Heaven forbid, it mght be surmised that she was one of those occasional privileged felons who were permitted to travel in luxury to the Colony! She was so sensitive upon the matter that already she imagined Captain Teasdale sometimes seemed to pause reflectively upon her name when he addressed her.

'What would be the best course to take, do you think?' she asked her niece anxiously. 'Pray advise me. I am not exactly desirous of calling attention to my late misfortune, yet 'twould be most uncomfortable to become the subject of false rumour.' She sighed, and resorted to a peppermint for solace. 'To be disgraced in the eye of the world,' she continued, her speech mint-flavoured and slightly indistinct, 'when in fact one's actions were all innocence, and the misconduct of another the true source of one's debasement, is a peculiarly aggravating circumstance – do you not agree? Heaven knows, I have suffered enough from that!'

Jane Austen inclined her head gravely. 'Your apprehension may be without foundation, Aunt – yet, as you say, there's no telling what people may have heard. Perhaps,' she went on demurely, 'the best notion might be to relate the account of your misfortune to one of our fellow passengers in strict confidence – then you may be sure of everyone learning the truth of the matter in the shortest possible time.'

Mrs Leigh Perrot looked at her niece sharply. 'A cynical enough suggestion,' she remarked, 'yet that might indeed prove the best way to foil mischievous speculation.'

The very next day, enjoying the sunshine on deck, Mrs Leigh Perrot related her tale of larceny and lace to Mrs Strongbow, who found the account so fascinating that she told her husband of it, whereupon he in turn regaled Mr Clinton with the story . . . and so in due course it became common knowledge. Mr Leigh Perrot's great interest in the natural wonders of the Colony soon became well known as well, and his desire to observe these for himself was perfectly understood. And what of Miss Jane Austen? It was soon rumoured (upon a hint dropped by her aunt) that *she* had suffered a disappointment in love . . .

James Leigh Perrot was delighted when his wife finally expressed her desire to know more about their destination. He produced *An Account of the English Colony in New South Wales* by Mr David Collins, who had sailed as Captain-Lieutenant of the Marines with the First Fleet, and had returned to England five years ago. Some time before the *Jason* sailed, Mr Leigh Perrot had made it his business to visit Mr Collins, whose house in London was a meeting place for those with an interest in the Colony.

'When I first arrived there,' Mr Collins had informed him, 'I thought of the place as nothing more than a convenient shore of banishment for the outcasts of our society. That, sir, was a most erroneous opinion; now I yearn to return there.' It was no secret that Mr Collins had been hoping for some time for an official appointment which would take him back to New Holland; and when James Leigh Perrot met him, he had just received his commission as Lieutenant-Governor of a proposed new settlement at Port Phillip, in the Bass Strait. He expected to set sail in April.

David Collins, in fact, might be described as one of the first people to fall into that ambiguous attitude towards the Colony, compounded of irrational proportions of liking and loathing, which was already familiar to many. During his time there, Mr Collins had alternated between feeling supremely content, and longing with all his heart to leave. When the Marines were replaced by the New South Wales Corps, he was with difficulty prevailed upon to remain by his close friend Governor Phillip – yet now, as he had told Mr Leigh Perrot, he yearned to go back. He had written his book, as he said in his Preface, to dissuade people from regarding New South Wales 'with odium and disgust'.

Aunt and niece took it in turn to read this work aloud to each other. Jane Austen was especially interested in those passages which described the native inhabitants of New Holland, the Aborigines.

'They do not appear to be so *very* savage,' Aunt Perrot observed as they sat on deck one morning with the book between them. 'It would seem, indeed, that Mr Collins considers them quite *noble* savages.'

It was doubtful, she thought, whether her aunt had actually read any of the philosopher's works. The noble savage – what a conversational cliché that phrase had become, Jane reflected, ever since Rousseau had coined it half a century before.

Mrs Leigh Perrot now recollected an instance of an Aborigine being introduced to the ways of the civilized world. 'A few years ago,' she said, 'there were accounts of one Aborigine – his name quite unpronounceable – who was brought to England by

119

Admiral Phillip when his term as Governor of the Colony expired. This native, whatever his name was, had the honour of being presented to the King, dressed up in a velvet suit and a bag wig. Can you imagine it!'

'And what became of him after that?' Jane Austen asked.

Her aunt shrugged. 'Who knows? Who cares?'

Pacing the deck was the sole exercise available. Jane Austen, known to her family and friends as 'a desperate walker', severely missed the country rambles she was used to. Wooden planking seemed a poor substitute for country paths lined with hedges of dog-rose and honeysuckle. Sometimes she took an early morning turn with her uncle, while the sailors were still busy with the holystone.

On one such morning, James Leigh Perrot recalled a detail of his visit to the Collins' house which he surmised might specially interest his niece.

'Mrs Collins, I believe, is a lady novelist,' he told Jane. 'She did not accompany her husband to the Colony, I understand, but was left on her own for some ten years – I daresay she found time hanging on her hands, poor lady.'

Jane smiled to herself. Her uncle's tone seemed to suggest that novel-writing was a mere time-filling occupation – an alternative to embroidery, perhaps, or patchwork.

During their weeks of voyaging, James had discovered an unexpected depth of character and a sharp sense of the ridiculous beneath those charming features and that candid gaze. He could not help reflecting that his niece would make an uncomfortable companion for any man less quick, less intelligent than herself. That Fordwick fellow seemed to have possessed the right requirements – a thousand pities he had turned up his toes! So James mused, until Jane, catching sight of a school of porpoises, drew his attention to them. They watched entranced as the creatures disported themselves close to the ship.

'They are just like children playing in the water!' Jane exclaimed, laughing with delight at their antics.

Besides the porpoises, they saw gambolling dolphins and elegant little flying-fish, flashing an iridescent blue, as the ship bobbed and dipped its way across the ocean. Mr Leigh Perrot, anxious to establish whether the flying fish actually *flew*, or merely leapt from the top of one wave to fall upon another, used to lean over the ship's rail, watching them keenly as a hawk. 'It has never been established whether they really do fly or not,' he told his niece.

It was her opinion that the fish certainly rose from the water and fluttered their fins rapidly – rather like a lark rising – then seemed to sail along for a little while, before turning; and finally, after staying in the air for several seconds, dipped again into the sea. 'I have often mistaken them for birds,' she told her uncle. 'But then I am rather shortsighted, you know.'

But he was very pleased with her remarks. 'Aha!' he said delightedly. 'Some of our most eminent naturalists affirm that *Exocetus volitans* can neither turn nor flutter. There is nothing to compare with first-hand observation!'

And once again he allowed his thoughts to dwell with eager anticipation upon the marvellous and manifold observations to be made within the Colony to which they journeyed.

Thirteen

PAST THE CANARY Islands, after days and weeks without any object to break the line of the horizon, another ship was sighted. All the passengers, even Emma Strongbow, grown cumbersome with the child she carried, hurried to the deck rail to watch that ship approach.

'This is the moment when we used to watch for the enemy colours to break upon the mast,' the red-bearded First Mate informed Mrs Leigh Perrot.

'Thank God we are at peace,' that lady responded fervently.

The next moment the ensign with the new and still unfamiliar Union Jack was seen spreading to the breeze.

'Ship ahoy! What ship is that?' Captain Teasdale called through a speaking-trumpet once the vessel was within hailing distance. He had assumed his teeth, to mark the significance of the occasion, and his sibilant inquiry hissed its way across the waves.

'The *Betsy* of Liverpool, homeward bound from Rio de Janeiro,' came the gruff reply, whereupon the two masters exchanged latitudes and longitudes, and the *Betsy* sent a boat across to the *Jason* to collect letters for England.

Quite unprepared for this opportunity, and vainly wishing that she had kept a daily log to send, Jane scurried to her cabin, seized a quill, and hastily tossed off a letter to Cassandra, which contained little more than an assurance of her own good health, and tender messages for the family. '... And now I must forthwith deliver this into the hands of the honest sailor from the *Betsy*. I have so many quaint matters I should like to relate, but "the tide tarrieth no woman". I shall hope to send another communication from Rio de Janeiro.'

A few more days, and at last they reached that pleasant landfall. The privileged passengers enjoyed touring the city while the ship replenished her stores. Those less fortunate ones aboard remained closely confined. Lieutenant Watson appointed himself Miss Austen's escort as they walked about the narrow streets. How much more agreeable this was, Jane thought, than being blown along Milsom Street or Lansdowne Crescent by a cold March wind!

The town was thronged with a mixture of two races: the pale, proud Portuguese and dusky West African slaves from Guinea and the Ivory Coast. Aunt Perrot remarked on the large number of churches in this devoutly Catholic country, and the many niches bearing statues of the Virgin, set in the walls of buildings. Captain Teasdale had warned the gentlemen that the townspeople expected every male visitor to show proper respect by raising his hat each time he passed a church or shrine.

'Would it not be more convenient for you to carry your hat in your hand?' Jane suggested to Lieutenant Watson, who could not quite tell whether she was teasing him or not.

'I daresay there is some policy in all this Popish superstition,' Aunt Perrot declared loftily. 'The negro slaves appear to outnumber the white inhabitants so hugely . . . all the mumbo-jumbo doubtless serves to keep their minds from thoughts of rebellion.'

The Leigh Perrots' little party attracted a good deal of polite attention; there were approving murmurs of 'Sta bon Ingles!' as they passed by.

And now the *Jason* weighed anchor and set sail for the Cape. At the Captain's table that evening (Captain Teasdale had decided to honour them with his presence, and greeted his passengers with a gleaming smile), the conversation turned to the rights and wrongs of slavery after Mr Campbell told the assembled company that he had visited the slave market at Rio.

'A most unhappy experience,' he assured them, fingering his glass of claret. 'A Guinea ship had newly landed with its cargo of human merchandise.' He paused to glance at little Mrs Strong-bow, wondering whether he should enlarge upon the misery he had witnessed. Ladies in an interesting condition, he knew, should be spared such grisly details. 'They were sold chained together like cattle,' he summarized. 'I am all for Wilberforce and his anti-slavery movement, and this visit has reinforced my feeling.' He added with some heat: 'A few unenlightened fools have had the temerity to suggest that we might enslave the Aborigines – a suggestion, I am thankful to say, which was given short shrift.'

'There are scores of felons on this ship in double-irons,' Mr Clinton commented drily, lounging back in his chair.

There was a moment of awkward silence as recollection of those below them intruded into their thoughts.

But Captain Teasdale shook his head. 'Let me assure you that compared to the conditions aboard a schl- slaver, the accommodation provided on board His Majesty's transports is humane and generous. If we have the misfortune to pass a schl- schlaver between here and Africa, and get downwind of her, you will not easily forget the exchperience, I fear.'

Jane Austen paled. The stench emanating from below decks when the convict quarters were opened up was an experience unforgettable enough. She pushed aside her helping of chicken curry.

Generations of sturdy yeoman farmers stretched behind Daniel Strongbow as he spoke up. 'For myself, I could not abide to *own* a man – 'tes against nature.' His ruddy complexion deepened, as always when he entered into a conversation. Emma Strongbow, who was merely toying with her curry, which she found exceedingly heating, smiled at her husband fondly.

Mrs Leigh Perrot cleared her throat importantly and they all looked towards her expectantly. 'I spent my early childhood in Jamaica,' she told them graciously, 'where of course slaves are used to work the plantations. My impression is that they led a happy, simple life. They delighted in wearing bright colours, they were always singing . . . If slavery is abolished, pray who will perform the menial work throughout our colonies? I fear our trading interests must suffer a fearful blow. How should we keep up the production of sugar – cotton – coffee – indigo? The disposition of these natives is well known to be indolent. Unless they are enslaved, they simply will not work at all.'

No one felt sufficiently bold to answer this formidable female viewpoint directly. However, the other naval officer who sat at table this evening – a Lieutenant Purvey, whose special interest was the science of navigation – took it upon himself to take up her challenge in an oblique manner, by steering the conversation towards his own favourite topic.

'The new *machines* will surely change our society beyond recognition,' he predicted. 'There is your new slave – the machine, at the service of mankind.'

'Machines require their own slaves to tend them, do they not?' James Leigh Perrot inquired. 'Are we then to create a new species of sub-humans – the slaves of slaves?'

'We are already doing so,' Mr Clinton broke in hotly. 'The deplorable conditions of those who toil in the mills and coal mines – '

'An unavoidable initial period,' Mr Purvey resumed blandly. 'There is no necessity for the introduction of the machine to accompany exploitation of its worker.' His eyes positively glowed as he went on: 'In due course the genius of inventors and engineers will free the world from drudgery and speed the rate of manufacture beyond our wildest dreams.'

'And will there be *machines* to pick cotton and coffee beans?' Mrs Leigh Perrot inquired sarcastically.

'It is not beyond the realm of possibility, madam,' Mr Purvey replied, oblivious of a cockroach creeping boldly towards his plate to feast on a crumbled poppadum. 'I daresay there will be machines to relieve the drudgery of housework, too – machines to sweep, to polish, to – er, er . . .' he was unable to think of any other items of housework drudgery. 'Machines to *sew*!' he added enthusiastically; then, catching sight of the cockroach at last, he killed it with a single blow and swept the carcass to the deck.

A ripple of amusement stirred the table at the idea of a sewing machine, combined with relief at the fate of the cockroach. Jane Austen sat privately cogitating the absurd but alluring notion of a machine to *write*. Lieutenant Watson, who was placed opposite her, sat silently admiring her misty gaze.

'But,' James Leigh Perrot objected, 'what would then become of the servant class? What would their occupation be, if a machine operated by one person were to take over the work of several housemaids – and every seamstress?'

'Quite right, Perrot.' His wife nodded vigorous approbation.

'We need to keep the lower orders fully occupied, otherwise who can say what notions of equality and revolution will not enter their minds?'

Mr Clinton felt the conversation was degenerating into fantasy. It was always the same when that wretch Purvey got on to his pet subject. The man was machine-mad. The surgeon stared scornfully at his fellow officer, who returned the stare with no quarter given. He heartily despised the surgeon and deplored his loose living. He was sick and tired of overhearing the frenzied moans, grunts and squeals of fornication that penetrated the flimsy partition between Mr Clinton's cabin and his own almost every night.

'Well,' Mr Purvey pronounced at last, deftly deflecting every argument that had been raised against the machine, 'we must leave the restructure of society to our politicians. But it will indeed be tragic if human error destroys the genius of human invention.'

That proved to be the last word on the subject; the general conversation broke into private pleasantries and less debatable topics, and presently the cloth was drawn and the company dispersed.

As Emma Strongbow's time approached, she grew increasingly nervous of the ordeal before her, of the awful inevitability of birth. To be in an interesting condition, to dream of cradling her own little baby in her arms – that was delightful! – Though, to be sure, the condition had grown exceedingly tiresome, and she longed to return to her old shape . . . her *own* shape. For months she had been able to tidy away to the back of her mind the thought of actually giving birth; but now she could not help dwelling upon it with some dread.

Mr Clinton tried to reassure her; he told her that several of the prisoners aboard had given birth during the voyage. In every case – he was, in truth, rather proud of this fact – mother and child had survived.

'But *they* are different!' Emma wailed – and then recalled the surgeon's regrettable association with one of the convict women, and fell into some confusion.

She said hastily, hoping to divert Mr Clinton's notice from her unfortunate remark: 'Mr Leigh Perrot was telling me about the kangaru. It – it seems the female kangaru has a pouch on her – her front, into which her young are born directly – through the nipple, it is thought.' (How strange, she reflected now, that she had felt no embarrassment when kind Mr Leigh Perrot had acquainted her with these somewhat intimate details.) 'The young kangaru is born at a very early stage – when it is no larger than a walnut, Mr Leigh Perrot told me, though I must confess I find that hard to believe. It is said to complete its development inside the pouch, sustained by milk from the nipple, and leaves it – the pouch, that is, as soon as it is able to fend for itself. – A very sensible arrangement, do you not think?' And she gazed down at her large belly, doubtless wishing it was a pouch, and that the tedious business of producing the fruit of her womb had been accomplished, in the ingenious manner of the kangaru, soon after the much more diverting process of conception.

Mr Clinton smiled sardonically. 'I fear we have no alternative to the human arrangement,' he replied. Then, to prepare her for what he suspected might be the case – she was so very large – he asked: 'Tell me, Mrs Strongbow, are there *twins* in your family?'

'Twins!' Emma clapped a hand to her mouth. 'But we have only brought one cradle!' Among their possessions stowed in the hold was an old oak cradle, which Daniel had already had brought up to their cabin. Then she recalled that her grandmother was indeed a twin; she and her sister, identical in looks, had been renowned for their high spirits and horsemanship. Emma recalled a double portrait of them both as infants, which used to hang in her mother's bedroom at Merehampton . . .

Half amused that Mrs Strongbow's first reaction should be to lament the lack of a cradle, Mr Clinton said: 'Oh, I am sure the ship's carpenter will be able to amend that situation.' (He hoped devoutly that the carpenter would indeed be called upon to construct a cradle, and not a coffin.) He went on to suggest that he should find some suitable young girl from among the prisoners to help nurse Emma and her baby – or babies. And so it was that Rebecca Ashcroft, fifteen, transported for seven years for stealing a coral brooch, was promoted to service on the poop deck. Convicted felon the girl might be, but Emma took to her at once. She was docile and soft-spoken, with gentle ways, and became quite neat and clean once she left her companions in their vermin-ridden quarters.

127

'Does it not seem a little harsh to send a young girl halfway across the world for seven years for such a little misdemeanour?' Emma asked her husband.

'Thieving is thieving,' Daniel Strongbow replied with implacable logic; but he did concede that the theft of a gimcrack brooch was a less heinous crime than poaching or sheep stealing, or cattle lifting.

Rebecca, always willing to fetch and carry, became quite a favourite among the poop deck passengers, to whom by this time a new face was a welcome diversion: even the face of a felon. Mrs Leigh Perrot favoured the girl with an occasional frosty half-smile and once even proffered her a peppermint. James Leigh Perrot was delighted when she took over the making of his butterfly nets, which neither of his own two womenfolk had yet attempted. Jane Austen discovered that the girl was able to write her own name, and undertook to enlarge her literacy, conducting reading lessons on deck, where Rebecca's etiolated pallor rapidly grew tanned.

It was in the middle of one such lesson, sitting in a shaded corner of the deck where teacher and pupil might study undisturbed, that Rebecca confided her history to Miss Jane Austen. Teacher and pupil were using the Bible as a learning instrument, and this day were reading from the twentieth chapter of Exodus; they had in fact reached the Ten Commandments.

'Honour – thy – father – and – thy – mother . . .' Stumblingly Rebecca followed Miss Austen's slowly moving finger. 'Thou – shalt – not – kill. Thou – shalt – not – com-mit – adul-adul-'

'Adultery,' Miss Austen said firmly.

'Adultery,' Rebecca repeated obediently. And then: 'Thou – shalt – not – *steal* –' At which, to Jane Austen's dismay, the girl's eyes suddenly filled with tears, she covered her face with her hands, and began to sob in a most heartrending manner.

'Rebecca! – please stop! Dear child, heaven knows there is enough salt water all around us –' and she offered her weeping pupil a fine cambric handkerchief which Cassandra had embroidered with her initials.

Rebecca took the handkerchief and mopped her eyes. 'I – I'm s-sorry, miss,' she quavered, chin quivering. 'B-but you s-see, *I did not steal that brooch*. 'Twas all a m-mistake, and the fault of M-Mistress Turnour. I'm not a thief, oh, miss, I'm not!'

'Perhaps,' Jane suggested gently, 'you had best tell me about it.' There was, she thought, that in the girl's distress which seemed to ring true. Inevitably, she recalled Aunt Perrot's predicament over that wretched card of lace. Could this be another example of a false accusation – which, in this case, had landed its victim with an unjust sentence?

Rebecca swallowed, sniffed back her tears, and began her story hesitantly. It seemed, Jane thought, far from the glib delivery of a felon seeking to excuse her crime.

Rebecca's parents, she told Miss Austen, were country folk who lived in Surrey. Her father had a smallholding with two cows and some goats. But times were hard, and Rebecca, the eldest of six children, had been sent into service in London as a dairymaid at the age of twelve.

'At the Sign of the Ass and Foal – that's where I were, miss,' she told Jane, 'just off Grosvenor Square. 'Twas a high-class dairy, we supplied the quality with asses' milk. 'Twas my duty to milk the asses twice a day and then go out delivering to houses round about.' Rebecca's dark eyes looked wistful. 'I grew quite fond of all our neddies – we had names for each of 'em . . . Violet, Clover, Buttercup, all flowers they were . . . ' Remembering, she gazed mistily at the horizon of the South Atlantic ocean. The *Jason* was drawing near the halfway mark of her long voyage; soon they would reach Table Bay.

'And your trouble, Rebecca,' Jane prompted gently. 'How did it happen?'

Rebecca recollected herself. 'Well it was like this. There was one lady we supplied regular what lived in a house in Charles Street. Mrs Turnour, she called herself – though there never was a Mister Turnour, of that you may be sure. A very painted and popular lady, she was – I believe she'd been an actress at Drury Lane. Well, one day this Mrs T got it into her head that she'd bathe herself all over in asses' milk. Quite a large lady, she was, so we had to supply a lot of milk for this lark, you can imagine. I remember my master jesting that if all the ladies in London took up this notion, we'd have to add a whole herd of neddies to our dairy! Anyway, off I set that morning with two full buckets hanging from my yoke, and then I had to go straight back to fetch two more. I had to take the milk right up to the bed-chamber and up-end my buckets into a hip bath there. All foaming it was after I'd tipped it in.'

Listening to this extraordinary tale of a Cyprian's whim, Jane Austen wondered at the mixture of artlessness and worldly awareness in Rebecca's mind.

'And then,' the girl went on, 'that Mrs T asked me to stay to help her, seeing as 'ow her maid had gone out. "My guests will be arriving soon," says she – lor', you could've knocked me down wiv a feather! She was making a reg'lar party of it – her friends was all coming round to visit while she lay there in her bath! Lucky it was foaming so much, thought I. – Well, I agreed to stay and hand round the cups of choc'late. She promised there'd be a bobstick in it for me – '

And now Rebecca's face clouded as she continued: 'Oh, miss, if only I'd beat it there and then and gone straight back to the dairy!' She stared into space, seeing again every detail of that fatal morning . . . the creamy, foaming surface of the milk in the bath, set in the middle of that large, ornate bedchamber with its gilded chairs, half-tester bed draped with rose-coloured silk, and vases of roses disposed about the room, whose perfume did not quite conceal a certain musty odour. She sighed. 'Mrs T was wearing a sprigged neggledigee with a brooch pinned on it – coral, set in gold. She didn't have nothing on underneath, and when she took her gown off she wasn't half a funny sight. She'd painted her face, you see, and the rest of her was a sort of greyish putty colour, with this pink and white face stuck on top. She could do with a bath, I can tell you!'

Jane Austen recoiled from this vision of the naked, grubby Cyprian with her painted face, but there was no stopping Rebecca now.

'Well, she gets into the bath and arranges herself so that nothing shows what shouldn't – and then, miss, she makes me pick a handful of petals from the roses in her vases, and tells me to scatter 'em all around her. Next moment we hears the sound of folk arriving downstairs . . . then all of a sudden Mrs T lets out a shriek, and I sees her looking horror-struck at something hairy what had floated up through the milk. It give me quite a turn – I thought it was a mouse at first. I was busy folding her neggledigee, and had taken off that coral brooch to put it on the dressing-table. I had it in my hand, Miss, when I heard her shriek, and as I rushed across to see what was the matter, I must 'ave stuck it in my bodice without thinking. I swear that's the truth, Miss, I swear it!'

Whereupon Rebecca placed her right hand firmly on the open page of the Bible, her palm quite covering all Ten Commandments.

'And what happened then?' her listener inquired, repelled yet fascinated by this tale.

'Well, miss, she fished that hairy thing out of the milk, all dripping, and thrust it into my hand. " 'Tis my mirkin!" she screamed. "The glue has come unstuck!" – And then I knew 'twas one of them false hair-pieces some ladies wear when they've lost their own fuzz – you know, Miss, *down there*.'

Jane Austen shuddered.

'Just then,' Rebecca went on remorselessly, 'the footman announced her guests – "Lord So-and-So!" "The Honor'ble Mr Nibs!" – I forget their real names now. In they all came, ladies and gentlemen both, and I was sent off to fetch the choc'late in a great silver jug, and I gives 'em each a cup . . . and there Mrs T sits all the while, laughing and talking, and every now and then frothing up the milk to make sure she was still covered. Well, after a while most of these people left, and only Lord So-and-So stayed on – and I could see *my* services would not be required to help Mrs T out of the bath. His Lordship – he was quite an ancient codger – was on his knees by this time, frothing up the milk for her, and 'twas plain how such playfulness would end. So then Mrs T says to 'im: "I promised this girl a shilling for her trouble" – and he fished a bobstick out of his fob pocket.'

Rebecca drew breath. 'So I went back to the Ass and Foal, and as soon as I got there one of the other girls noticed the brooch pinned to my bodice – I ask you, Miss, if I'd meant to steal it, wouldn't I 'ave hidden it away, instead of wearing it for all the world to see? "Wherever did you get that, Becky?" she asks me, an' I claps my hand to my mouth and straightway unpins it, and would 'ave run back to Charles Street then and there – but she says the master's bin asking why I've been gone so long, and that I'd best get on wiv my work, and so I resolv'd to return it later. But before I could do that, a constable comes to the dairy and says: "Which is the maid what delivered milk to Number Twenty-six Charles Street?" I steps forward, and straightway he accuses me of stealing a gold brooch set wiv coral, value two pound two shilling, the property of Mistress Turnour, and takes me off to the watch-house . . . and oh, Miss, there wasn't nothing I could say, nor anything my good master could do to help me. I was put up for trial at Newgate, and Mrs T came there wiv her painted face to give evidence I had took her brooch, and no one would believe me when I swore it 'ad all happened by mistake – and so I was give my sentence . . . and there's an end to my sorry tale.'

Whereupon Rebecca held the handkerchief to her eyes again.

'A sorry tale indeed, Rebecca,' Jane Austen said sadly. She decided to reserve her opinion as to whether the girl was guilty or innocent; though indeed she thought the tale pathetic and plausible enough, and Rebecca's distress certainly appeared genuine. 'But reflect,' she went on, 'if you work willingly and honestly in the Colony, you may well be set free before your seven years are done. I believe prisoners of good conduct may be granted some sort of conditional pardon.'

Rebecca nodded dolefully. Then she brightened somewhat. 'Mistress Strongbow has promised to keep me in her service after we reach Bot'ny Bay. 'Twas a piece of luck I was chosen to nurse her and the babe, I reckon.' – She was not yet aware there might be two babies to look after.

'I think so too,' Jane Austen agreed. 'Let us hope it proves a happy omen for your future life. – And now, Rebecca,' she said more briskly, 'we will finish reading the Ten Commandments, then turn to Numbers, Chapter Twenty-two, and read the story of Balaam and his ass, which spoke to him when he smote it. And,' she added, 'do not forget to return my handkerchief to me after you have washed it.'

Fourteen

AT TABLE BAY the ship's complement was increased by twelve large and remarkably woolly sheep, which were ushered on board with considerably more care than had been bestowed upon the convicts' embarkation. They had been purchased by Mr Campbell, who, it transpired, owned land in New South Wales as well as pursuing his trading interests. 'We are jacks of all trades in the Colony,' he said cheerfully.

'What singularly noble creatures,' Jane Austen observed – she happened to be standing at the ship's rail next to Mr Campbell as the sheep came on board. She watched their sedate contemplation of their new surroundings. 'They look rather like a committee of learned judges – especially the rams.'

'Judges whose wits have gone wool-gathering,' laughed Mr Campbell. 'They are Spanish merinos, Miss Austen,' he went on earnestly. 'Capable of producing the finest quality wool on poor pastures where there is low rainfall – the ideal breed for New South Wales, as several of us are attempting to prove.'

Jane divined a proselytizing gleam in Mr Campbell's eye. 'Then it would seem that our ship is well named,' she remarked, 'and these are golden fleeces –'

'Quite so,' Mr Campbell assented vaguely; his grasp of classical mythology was slight. 'Our Chaplain, Mr Marsden, who also happens to be one of the most knowledgeable farmers in the Colony, has a small flock of merinos ... as does Captain McArthur.'

Jane was diverted by the notion of a Chaplain who shepherded both souls and sheep. And was it her imagination, or did Mr

Campbell seem to pronounce the name of Captain McArthur with some distaste?

'Captain McArthur – of the new South Wales Corps – is at present in England,' Mr Campbell continued. 'Besides er – other business, he is championing the cause of these noble woolly-birds, and hopes to bring a substantial flock to the Colony, so that breeding may be carried out on a larger scale.'

What Robert Campbell omitted to explain was that McArthur, that prickly thorn in the side of the civil administration of the Colony, had actually been dispatched to England by Governor King for court martial, after attempting to discredit the latter. Furthermore, upon a point of honour linked to that attempt, McArthur had provoked his own commanding officer, Lieutenant-Colonel Paterson, to a duel and had wounded him quite seriously.

Mr Campbell frowned as he reflected how McArthur, arrogant arch-schemer that he was, had appeared to have got on the right side of the authorities in England, especially Lord Camden. During his stay in London, he had heard a rumour that McArthur was confidently expecting a land grant of five thousand acres, no less, at the Cow Pastures – some of the best land in the Colony – for his sheep-breeding experiment. He had taken some merino fleeces with him to England, and these, apparently, had been pronounced of a very superior quality, equal to the best which came from Spain. Everything seemed to work for McArthur's good and to conspire against the hard-pressed Governor. Robert Campbell's frown deepened as he brooded upon the grievous loss of Neil McKeller, Governor King's Adjutant, who had sailed for England last April with McArthur's sword and all the Governor's dispatches relating to the unfortunate affair of the duel – in which McKeller himself had acted as Colonel Paterson's second. Alas, his ship had gone down. If only McKeller had reached London and had been able to put forward the Governor's case, things might have worked out very differently.

But there seemed little point in acquainting this pleasant young lady by his side with the troubled politics of New South Wales. Robert Campbell sighed; soon he would be in the midst of those squabbles once again. He did his best to maintain an independent position apart from both factions, civil and military, but there was really no escaping the pervading atmosphere of dissension, mutual distrust and acrimony.

Daniel Strongbow, meanwhile, had drawn near. 'Merinos, eh?' he said, appraising the new arrivals. 'I hope to breed fat lambs myself, Mr Campbell. – For mutton chops, Miss Austen,' he added, turning towards Jane, 'or a nice roast leg with new potatoes and mint sauce – nothing better!'

Jane inclined her head; an endless procession of dishes bearing haricot mutton, a staple of dinners at Steventon, seemed to pass through her mind . . . in truth, she was beginning to find this talk of sheep somewhat indigestible.

'You'll be hard put to it to find a decent dish of roast lamb in the Colony,' Mr Campbell informed them. 'And the mutton is usually as tough as old boots. How do you fancy the thought of a succulent kangaru steak instead, Miss Jane . . . or a fricassee of waumbat . . . or perhaps a slice of parrot pie? All these are enjoyed by the colonists. I can assure you that young kangaru is delicious, quite as tender as veal.'

Jane raised her eyebrows and turned to Daniel Strongbow. 'Pray, Mr Strongbow, why do you not consider breeding young kangaru instead of fat lambs? If the meat is as delicious as Mr Campbell maintains, it would surely save you all the trouble of building up a flock of creatures which are not indigenous to the continent.'

Mr Campbell, she was amused to see, looked quite shocked, even slightly offended, at this suggestion. 'The consumption of native animals is, I assure you, but a temporary expedient,' he responded stiffly. 'In time, I have no doubt that the Colony will be able to offer the choicest cuts of lamb, beef, pork . . . Pray remember that we are but a *young country*.'

This was an admonition Jane was to hear repeated many times during her sojourn in the Colony. Now she nodded meekly, and privately determined to sample some slices of kangaru for herself.

Mr Campbell and Mr Strongbow entered into an agricultural discussion concerning the relative merits of different breeds of sheep for varying conditions, whereupon Jane made an excuse to drift to the other side of the deck.

They had not ventured ashore here. The Peace of Amiens had restored Cape Colony to the Batavian Republic, and the temper

135

of the Dutch inhabitants was thought to be uncertain. Everyone said the manners of these Dutch colonists were apt to be surly at the best of times. James Leigh Perrot thought wistfully of opportunities lost ... how splendid to have hunted *Papilio oppidicephalis*, the largest butterfly of Africa, up and down the dark, silent *kloofs* lined with maidenhair and other exotic ferns!

Past the Cape, they entered the great expanse of the Indian Ocean, and presently moved into the southern hemisphere. Gradually the night sky had assumed an unfamiliar aspect.

'I feel the loss of the North Star, niece,' Aunt Perrot complained a trifle peevishly as Ursa Minor disappeared. 'It is like saying farewell to a companion one has known all one's life.'

Soon the Great Bear, too, shambled below the horizon, a further desertion of the familiar. The stars of this southern sky seemed to shine more brilliantly than their northern counterparts, and Lieutenant Watson took the greatest delight in pointing out Crux Australis to Miss Jane Austen as they paced the deck in the warm evening. Jane could not help thinking to herself that several other groups of stars seemed to form quite as much of a Southern Cross, but she did not wish to spoil Lieutenant Watson's manifest pride in pinpointing the constellation, a process which appeared to necessitate his firm grasp of her elbow to direct her gaze in the right direction. Truth to tell, she was never absolutely sure that she *had* managed to locate the true Cross in that dark, velvet sky; her shortsightedness did not help matters as she peered upward.

James Leigh Perrot was stirred by the sight of the great white albatrosses – *Diomedea exulans* – which often soared majestically alongside the ship like silent spectres. And each time the sailors shouted: 'There she spouts!' he would scurry on deck to peer across the waves for the sounding whale that they had sighted. Regrettably, those jolly tars soon divined his passionate desire to view these Leviathans of the sea; more than once they amused themselves by proclaiming imaginary spouts, guffawing among themselves as, sure enough, the neat figure of Mr Leigh Perrot scurried on deck to gaze eagerly across the waves.

By this time, Mrs Strongbow's fellow passengers daily expected to hear news of her confinement. She kept to her cabin now, too burdened to venture out in company: however cunningly she draped her shawl, she could no longer begin to conceal her prodigious belly. The oak cradle stood waiting for its occupant, beside a second, cruder cradle fashioned by the ship's carpenter. Throughout the voyage, Emma Strongbow had sewed quantities of little garments; everything was ready; the world awaited her progeny; all she had to do was to endure the horrid, messy, painful process of parturition. Daniel Strongbow, to whom lambing and calving, foaling and whelping had always been part of everyday life, maintained a remarkably calm demeanour. Eventually it became a matter of speculation which would occur first: the sighting of the coast of the southern continent, or the arrival of the Strongbow offspring.

At last, at long, long last, a sailor perched on the masthead shouted: 'Land on the port beam!' and hurried down to claim his due bonus of a double ration of rum. It was the western tip of the great southern continent. Now they were in Australian waters, and soon were sailing across that large indentation in the coastline, the Great Bight, with its barren shores and steep cliffs, infamous for storms and rough seas. Until two years ago (as Lieutenant Watson was eager to inform Miss Jane Austen) it had been known simply as 'The Unknown Coast' – until Mr Flinders explored and charted it, upon that same voyage in which the Aborigine, Bungaree, had accompanied him.

Captain Teasdale broached his finest claret at dinner to celebrate the sighting; even as those around his table sipped their wine appreciatively, the wind was gathering strength, soon to rise to gale force . . . and Emma Strongbow, ensconced in her cabin with Rebecca to keep her company, felt her waters break, and the first contractions come upon her.

Rebecca, looking a little frightened, suddenly appeared in the dining saloon, whereupon Daniel Strongbow, guessing her mission before she announced it, rose from the table, as did the surgeon. Bowing to the company, both left – Daniel to comfort his wife, Mr Clinton to fetch his forceps. The Captain, swishing a final mouthful of claret around his china teeth, took his leave also; the ship was now heaving quite alarmingly as she rode the mounting waves; a pile of plates slid from the dining table and crashed in smithereens, together with a large bowl of sherry trifle.

'Come, niece,' Aunt Perrot commanded urgently – she had not felt seasick since the beginning of the voyage, but she found the present motion of the vessel, combined with the pungent aroma of sherry wine, distinctly upsetting.

With some difficulty they made their way on to the deck; and both recoiled at the scene before them. Aunt Perrot clutched her niece's arm in dismay. As for Jane herself – how often, she thought, had she read of seas *mountains high* and thought it a trite, exaggerated phrase! Now she knew it for a true description indeed. The *Jason*, rigged with a close-reefed mainsail, was scudding through an immense valley of water. Mountainous waves indeed circled the ship: and even as aunt and niece clutched tightly to the nearest rail as well as to each other, slowly the vessel began to climb the steep ascent until she was poised on the summit of the rolling height, from which a dark, dreary waste of ocean heaving with giant billows was spread before them. Then down she plunged into the next terrible abyss . . . slowly to rise and mount another wave, in a ceaseless pitching motion. Extraordinary to relate, beside the vessel two of those wraith-like albatrosses sailed serenely above the towering waves, and dived alongside her into the yawning gulf. Small wonder that the superstitious sailors regarded the albatross with awe and reverence, Jane thought in the midst of her terror. For she was terrified. But somehow, reminding herself firmly how often her seafaring brothers must have experienced storms far worse than this, she managed to quell her fear and propelled her quaking aunt along to her cabin.

Even as the storm increased and tossed the little wooden ship from one sea-valley to the next, so, as Emma Strongbow's labour progressed, her unborn children took utter possession of her body, irresistibly pressing their way into the world at this wild hour. Dismissed from the cabin, Daniel came on deck to stand stolidly contemplating the awful seascape, while at Emma's bedside the surgeon, gripping the serrated handle of his forceps, his shirt and forearms spattered and smeared with blood, shouted orders to Rebecca above the howling of the weather and Emma's desperate shrieks. Eventually, as wind and waves at last abated around midnight, he thrust first one, and then, after a pause, another mewling morsel of humanity into Rebecca's charge. The first child arrived a few minutes before midnight, the second a few minutes after, with the singular result that the birthdays of these twins fell upon two different dates. And so

Emma Strongbow was safely – if somewhat brutally – delivered of two living children, both male.

'My sons!' Daniel marvelled, called into the cabin at last to view the twins with their creased red faces and tiny clenched fists.

'*Our* sons,' amended Emma in an exhausted whisper.

'The little darlings,' Rebecca declared lovingly.

'Two healthy boys,' Mr Clinton said with satisfaction, wiping his forceps.

Next evening it was Mr Strongbow's turn to provide some choice burgundy for the dinner table, and once again Captain Teasdale honoured them with his presence. He was obliged to offer the new father his *congratulations*, which, though enunciated with difficulty, were nonetheless heartfelt.

' 'Twas a mercy we were not pooped last night,' he observed. ' 'Twould have been a most unfortunate circumstance for Mrs Strongbow.'

The Captain intended this as a mere pleasantry, but Mrs Leigh Perrot pounced upon his words. '*Pooped*, Captain Teasdale? Pray, what is the meaning of that extraordinary expression?'

'Pooped, madam? Why, 'tis when a huge strong wave crashes above the ship's stern, breaks the windows of the two cabins there, bursts upon the doors and washes the whole length of the poop deck!'

'And was there a danger that we might have been – er, that such a thing might have occurred last evening?' she inquired.

The tableau it conjured up, of mother and babies being helplessly swept overboard, was not to be dwelled upon.

'Lor' bless you, madam, it takes a real storm at sea to poop a vessel,' Captain Teasdale told her.

Aunt Perrot shuddered, recalling those appalling mountains and valleys of the ocean. That had been storm enough for her!

Mr Campbell was appraising the burgundy, holding his wineglass to catch its ruby glow in the lamplight. 'I am confident that in time, we shall produce our own wines in the Colony,' he was saying to Mr Clinton. 'The grape vine has grown readily wherever it has been planted.'

'Not as readily as home-grown spirits, so I hear,' riposted the surgeon. 'The Colony is said to be awash with illegal poteen –

besides the rum imported by the gentlemen of the militia.'

'Has not the New South Wales Corps been dubbed the Rum Corps?' Mr Purvey said tactlessly, and broke into a braying laugh.

Opposite him, Lieutenant Watson raised his head sharply above his soup, and the surgeon directed a contemptuous glance at his fellow officer.

Mr Campbell's expression darkened. 'Many of the colonists, myself included, deplore the monopoly which the officers of the Corps held until recently upon the importing and selling of spirituous liquors,' he said gravely. 'Governor King, I am happy to say, has enforced an order that no military officer is to carry on this trade in future.' – And what a furore *that* had caused among the scarlet-coated officers, he thought to himself. He sipped his burgundy thoughtfully. 'As a merchant,' he said, 'I am concerned about another monopoly, that of the East India Company. John Company owns the sole right to export our goods in their ships to England. One day soon, the House of Campbell will have to challenge that right by sending one of our own vessels to England with a cargo of goods produced in the Colony – whale oil and fleeces, for instance,' he added, almost as though he were actually detailing the bill of lading for such an enterprise.

Mrs Leigh Perrot regarded Robert Campbell shrewdly. For such a relatively youthful man, he certainly appeared to hold considerable assets. During the voyage it had emerged that besides his importing business and his farming interests, he was also engaged in shipbuilding and whaling. An astute man of business could soon garner a fortune in New South Wales, it would appear . . . in rather the same manner that the Nabobs had prospered under the East India Company. All the same, she wondered if Mr Campbell was not overreaching himself in planning to flout John Company.

'Do you have any idea of what you will call your sons, Mr Strongbow?' Jane Austen ventured to ask the proud new father, as a dish of pickled pork was brought in.

Daniel Strongbow grinned boyishly, not yet accustomed to hearing 'his sons' referred to. 'Not yet, Miss Austen. 'Twas always the Strongbow custom to name each child from the Bible. 'Tis how I came to be Daniel. My elder brother is Ezra, and

my father's name is Micah. But Em– that is, Mrs Strongbow –
has different ideas. It seems we shall most likely give one of the
boys her family name –'

Aunt Perrot leaned forward, hoping to catch that name,
whatever it might be. But Daniel's flow was interrupted by
Captain Teasdale, who had been reminded of his duty by this
talk of naming the newborn bairns. 'We will have the christening tomorrow morning, Mr Strongbow,' he said. It was wisest to
christen a newborn babe, whether healthy or sickly, without
delay, in his opinion.

'In that case we must make up our minds,' Daniel responded.

'Why, they will be – New Hollanders!' Mr Purvey exclaimed.
'Born within sight of the southern shore.'

Mr Campbell spared a tender thought for his own native-born
infant. 'The first generation of colonial-born children is almost
grown now – 'tis full fifteen years since Admiral Phillip brought
the First Fleet to Botany Bay,' he remarked.

A whimsical notion occurred to James Leigh Perrot. His
thoughts had strayed to those other New Hollanders who
already inhabited the land when the First Fleet arrived.
'Perhaps, Mr Strongbow, you might choose Aboriginal names
for your sons?'

'Mr Perrot!' his wife expostulated. 'These are Christian
children!'

Mr Campbell, having made short work of his helping of
pickled pork, laid down his knife and fork. 'As a matter of fact,
Mr Leigh Perrot, our senior Chaplain in the Colony, Mr Johnson, chose to give one of his daughters an Aboriginal name – he
called her Milbah.'

'Hmph,' Aunt Perrot commented.

The next morning, the two babies were named, respectively,
Ezekiel Courteney and Joseph John, to be known familiarly
throughout their lives as Zeke and Jos.

'Courteney . . .' Aunt Perrot murmured musingly when she
heard that name. 'I believe there was a well-connected family of
that name living in the West Country . . .'

She was quite correct, as it happened: Emma Strongbow was
indeed the former Miss Courteney, of Merehampton Abbey; and
it was Emma herself who told her own story to Mrs Leigh Perrot
and Miss Jane Austen when they visited that other large stern

cabin to pay their respects to the young mother and her twins. Rebecca, instantly a doting nursemaid, sat between the two cradles, contriving to rock them both at the same time. Having peered dutifully into each one and paid the usual admiring tribute, the two ladies turned their attention to the mother, who lay against her pillows looking pale but charming.

'How I wish,' she told her visitors, 'that my dear parents could have lived to see their grandchildren.' She gave a sad, wistful smile, and then and there, in nostalgic mood, proceeded to relate her poignant history.

The sole offspring of her parents' marriage, she had, she told them, spent a happy childhood with an indulgent father – the squire of Merehampton – who doted on his daughter, and a loving but delicate mamma. Alas, Emma admitted ruefully, her father was the sort of man, charming, indiscriminate in his generosity, who could never resist either an appeal to his charity or a wager. By the time she reached her eighteenth year, his fortune was entirely dissipated, and in a continuing attempt to meet his debts, Merehampton Abbey was gradually stripped of its fine furniture and paintings. The gardens fell into neglect; her mother's jewels were sold; and only two or three faithful retainers remained in the service of the family. Then, two winters since, her father had succumbed to an inflammation of the lungs as a result of following the Merehampton hunt on a day of rain and bitter wind. Shortly afterward her mother died as well, her naturally delicate constitution worn out by anxiety and grief. Emma, now nineteen, was left a penniless orphan; a bleak future seemed to stretch before her, as companion to a great aunt who offered her a home out of a cold and reluctant sense of family duty.

Throughout this affecting narrative, Emma's two visitors punctuated her tale of changing fortunes by raising their eyebrows or shaking their heads appropriately and emitting soft murmurs now and then to express their sympathy with her plight. – At the same time, however, Mrs Leigh Perrot, in her worldly wisdom, was recalling similar examples of reckless gambling; and Jane Austen, mindful that every story should have a plot, was awaiting the inevitable appearance of the hero.

They learned that Daniel Strongbow had in fact already entered Emma's life, when she was sixteen, at the last Christmas ball to be held at Merehampton Abbey. Daniel, some years older, had danced with Emma – the Courteney heiress, as she was then known – and both young people had felt an instant attraction to each other. *Then* it had seemed impossible that an attachment could ever be formed between them: Daniel was not even the eldest son of that stalwart yeoman farmer, Micah Strongbow; he would not inherit Merecombe Farm and its lush acres. Nevertheless, during the difficult months that followed, Emma's thoughts often turned to Daniel Strongbow – whilst *his* thoughts dwelt upon Emma constantly, as he told her afterwards. And later, when Emma Courteney was an heiress no longer, but orphaned and fortuneless – why, the impossible became the possible, and she had received Daniel's courtship with full reciprocation of the affection he felt for her.

It was Daniel Strongbow's determination to gain a farm and acres of his own, younger son though he might be, which had spurred him on to investigate settling in New South Wales. The first months of their marriage, Emma said, had been spent in the rambling Merecombe farmhouse, where Daniel's mother, kindly and capable (surely, thought Mrs Leigh Perrot, she must have harboured some misgivings concerning Emma's role as pioneer helpmeet), had taught her gently nurtured daughter-in-law to spin, make bread, milk a cow, churn butter, brew ale, and care for the vegetable garden, besides sundry other household tasks. So the young couple had embarked upon their great adventure – and here they were, Emma concluded, smiling happily, their little family already doubled in size, about to set foot upon the southern shore.

'I daresay you are quite astonished to hear that I am able to milk a cow and grow cabbages,' she said, 'but I assure you, I intend to become a proper farmer's wife in the Colony.' She gave a little sigh, philosophic rather than regretful. 'All that is left of my former way of life is contained within this ship: a four-poster bed, a few family portraits, odd pieces of glass and china . . . items saved from my father's creditors.'

Mrs Leigh Perrot reflected charitably that Emma Strongbow was quite an astonishing young woman: it seemed clear that unexpected reserves of strength and determination lay beneath her fragile appearance. To have experienced such a reversal of worldly fortune; to have survived the ordeal of giving birth to twins in the midst of that dreadful storm (whatever Captain Teasdale might say, Mrs Leigh Perrot knew it had been a dreadful storm) was surely no mean achievement.

Jane Austen, too, felt admiration for this heroine of her own narrative. As for the tale itself, she felt that cows and cabbages nicely counterbalanced love at first meeting at a Christmas ball. Emma Courteney, she thought, was a lucky young woman to have been snatched from misfortune. Fate – or Providence – was not often so benign. And her thoughts turned fleetingly to that future she had envisaged for herself, and to the tall clergyman she had walked beside so briefly two summers since, at Sidmouth.

At this moment the twins set up a hungry wailing in perfect unison, and Rebecca picked Zeke out of his oak cradle and placed him in his mother's arms. Emma gazed at her firstborn adoringly, then cast a distressed glance towards her second son, in his rough-hewn cot.

'It is time for that dreadful woman to feed Jos,' she said resentfully. 'I am able to provide sufficient nourishment for Zeke, but must allow Joseph to be wet-nursed. Mr Clinton has found a convict woman who herself gave birth a short time ago – she overflows with milk.' She sighed. ' 'Tis not that I object to the notion of a wet-nurse, but this woman – Hawker is her name – is so – so very uncongenial. Yet I cannot allow one of my babies to starve.'

Jane nodded sympathetically. She herself, as well as Cassandra and all her brothers, had been wet-nursed by a comfortable cottage woman in Steventon, a good and trustworthy soul. It was the usual practice. But to have to relinquish one's babe on to the bosom of a female felon was a quite different proposition.

Rebeccca, meanwhile, turned to the other cradle and lifted Jos out to await his nourishment. She positively resented having to hand him over to Bet Hawker. When she had lived between decks, she had learned various unsavoury details concerning the latter's career in a doss house at Portsmouth. Wisely she kept her knowledge to herself; 'twould only serve to distress her young mistress further to know, for instance, how Bet had boasted that her speciality was to satisfy two sailors at one time, and to rob both before they left her tumbled bed. Her own babe, down below, was a queer mite with a dusky skin and something of the Chinese in its appearance . . . 'twas as though more than one father had contributed to its conception in her womb.

Fifteen

THE ARRIVAL AT Port Jackson of a ship, any ship from any port in the wide world, but especially from England, was an event to stir the inhabitants of Sydney Cove to a frenzy of anticipation. What news would she bring, that seaworn vessel, of events abroad: of families, business affairs, war and revolution, peace treaties and politics, royalty, domestic scandal, murder and mayhem, the latest fashions (albeit of several months ago) and the price of bread thirteen thousand miles away? No sooner was a sail spied from the semaphore lookout at South Head and the signal sent to Flagstaff Hill than a motley crowd drawn from every corner of the settlement began to flow down the slopes that led to the waterside: soldiers, free men, convicts – male and female; labourers and idlers – drunk or sober . . . exiles all, save for the children, who alone had never seen a different shore.

And gazing eagerly from the ship's rail, the far travellers arriving at their destination saw a large village ingenuously laid out before them, every building plainly revealed in the clear, sparkling air beneath the high blue sky. For, though the settlement might have the aspirations, the pretensions, the vices and temptations of a little world complete unto itself, it had yet the mere dimension of a village.

The *Jason* sailed past the bay where rushes were cut for thatching roofs – so Mr Campbell, revelling in these harbour scenes so familiar to himself, informed them with a proprietorial air – and there, beyond the wharf, they saw rows of little houses, single-storeyed, stretching up the slopes away from the water's edge, most with a paling fence and square of garden. A clock-tower (one hundred and fifty feet high, Mr Campbell announced with pride) was the tallest building in sight, there being as yet no church spire to dispute its dominance. Jane Austen, for whom this near-distant scene was enveloped in a charming shortsighted haze, smiled a little to herself when she discerned that clock-tower: it seemed to signify that here, too, man was ruled relentlessly by moments, days and hours, the span of his mortality.

'The new windmill –' Mr Campbell said, gesturing towards a hill in the near distance. The wooden arms flailed in the breeze.

'Yes, one can tell it is a windmill,' Mrs Leigh Perrot remarked tartly. She was finding her first glimpse of the Colony somewhat dismaying. And yet . . . the day was sunny, the sky cloudless. It seemed an agreeable climate. She sucked upon a peppermint and decided to reserve her judgement.

'A very fine windmill, sir, very fine indeed,' Mr Leigh Perrot responded heartily, noticing the wry look Mr Campbell directed towards his wife.

'Government House!' Mr Campbell went on importantly, pointing towards a simple, whitewashed dwelling of two storeys, with a shingled roof and a verandah, upon which the scarlet and white figure of a sentinel could be observed . . . a toy soldier guarding a toy house. Close by, the river that meandered through the settlement – the Tank Stream, Mr Campbell called it – ran beneath a bridge and down to the mud flats of the harbour.

Beyond Government House and the other buildings nearby lay a steep hill dotted with patches of smoke and deep man-made pits. 'Brickfield Hill,' Mr Campbell proclaimed. 'You can see the smoke from the kilns, and those are the clay-pits.' He cleared his throat. 'The lower slopes of Brickfield Hill are, alas, a most unsalubrious area.'

The excitement of arrival had penetrated between decks: the dim, stinking quarters of the felons buzzed with noise and speculation and false rumour. They would remain aboard until they were mustered, inspected and assigned over the next few days. Two of their number, however, were luckier: Rebecca Ashcroft and Bet Hawker were permitted to disembark with the Strongbows.

147

And now a ragged cheer went up as His Majesty's transport *Jason*, one hundred and forty-two days out of Portsmouth, dropped anchor this June morning, this blue and golden day of winter sunshine. There was a press of traffic upon the harbour waters: barges, coracles, an American brigantine, an East India-man, several whalers, native canoes ... and presently two rowboats set out towards the ship. As the slung chair was hoisted to transfer the cabin passengers from ship to boat, Robert Campbell, shading his eyes with his hand, at last located his Sophie in the crowd upon the wharf, and waved his kerchief in boyish exuberance. He was home at last!

There was someone else amid the jostling elbows, the clumsy feet, the pickpocket fingers of that crowd upon the wharf: a convict woman, young-old, old-young, like so many of her kind, who held a small boy close to her skirts. Now she watched idly as one by one the slung chair plucked each passenger from the ship's deck. Into the first rowboat went a sturdy, youngish man, then a lady holding a baby in her arms, whom he supported with tender care as she was lowered into her place; next a young servant girl, by the look of her shabby dress, who also held a baby; and finally a fat, blowsy woman, obviously a felon. The second boat made ready to receive its passengers. Here came a gentleman of business in the Colony – the woman on the wharf knew him by sight ... next, an officer in the uniform of the Corps ... and then, suddenly, that watching convict stiffened in shocked amazement, drew in her breath with a hiss of incredulity and tightened her grasp on her infant son so that he cried out protestingly.

' 'Tis never!' Susan Gregory exclaimed aloud. 'It cannot be!'

But as the slung chair lowered its latest occupant to the boat, she saw that she was not mistaken in her startled recognition of that well-remembered figure, especially that beaky nose ... that lady who now sat bolt upright in the boat, her head held high ... just as she had looked in the courtroom at Taunton Assizes upon a rainy day in March, two years ago. Amazing, unbeliev-able, astonishing as it might seem, here, half a world away from her natural habitat, Susan Gregory recognized the old Parrot herself!

Her instinct, though there was only the remotest chance that she herself might be observed, was to draw the hood of her cloak close to her face. And now she saw two other passengers hoisted over the ship's side to join the merchant and *that lady* in the boat: a soberly dressed gentleman whom she knew to be the old Parrot's husband, and a young lady she had never seen before. Her thoughts seemed to whirl in her head. *Why* had that Mr and Mrs of such high and mighty principles – why had they, of all people, come to Botany Bay, of all places? They did not belong – should not be here – were part of that far-off land of pavements and palaces, shops and sedan chairs, Assembly Rooms and Abbey, and perpetual grey skies. It was not right! Susan felt as though the whole world had suddenly turned topsy-turvy. What in heaven or earth could have brought them here?

The child pressed against his mother's skirts, Gregory Gregory, offspring of a lustful, loveless coupling (but a bright -eyed, healthy boy withal), cried out again as he felt his mother's fierce astonishment. She relaxed her hold on him at once.

'I did not mean to hurt you, my bub,' she murmured unsteadily, stooping to kiss him in quick repentance. 'Come, we have seen the ship; 'tis time to go back.'

It had been a half-guilty indulgence to bring Gregory down to the wharf to see the transport arrive: Susan had been sent out on an errand and should by rights have returned straight back to the big brick house near the Tank Stream bridge, where she was assigned to teach plain needlework and help with the daily chores. Mrs King's Orphanage was home for a hundred girls, most of whom were illegitimate as well as orphaned. Under the strict supervision of a formidable matron, they were given lessons in spinning, plain cooking and elementary reading, writing and numbering as well as needlework. Gregory, though a boy, was permitted to live there with his mother. He had the run of the garden, planted with fruit trees, where he vied with the opossums for fallen peaches and apricots. His double name, accident of his hasty christening, had a curiously Aboriginal sound; a few years later, the cruel little orphan girls would tease him to distraction, claiming his father was a wild naked bushman and chanting 'Gregory-Gregory, Gregory-Gregory!' as they chased him round those fruit trees.

His mother had come to realize that here, at the end of the earth, her son would have a chance to make something of his life – which was more than a pauper's son would have back home. Whatever Susan's own remorse and regret, however fallen and despised she felt herself to be, at least her son gave her the promise of a future. She lived now for him, and strenuously maintained her reputation within the vicious world of Sydney Cove as a 'decent' convict woman . . . which reputation had won her a position at the Orphanage. She wanted no more truck with men . . . just to be left in peace to bring up her son and carry out her duties in hours filled with housework and plain stitching – hemming, seaming, patching, darning and button-holing . . .

The Leigh Perrots and Miss Austen bade farewell to their companions of the voyage, exchanging mutual protestations of the absolute necessity to meet again as soon as possible. Mr Campbell was joyfully reunited with his Sophie, and the Strongbows and their entourage made ready for their journey on to Parramatta, some fifteen miles from Sydney. Meanwhile, James Leigh Perrot was respectfully greeted by a very civil and smiling young man who introduced himself as William Chapman, Secretary to His Excellency the Governor. Straightway he conducted the Leigh Perrots and Miss Austen up a steeply sloping path, slowing his pace to allow their sea legs to become used to the strange sensation of walking upon dry land once more, and halted in front of a little whitewashed house, one of a row of officers' dwellings close to the military parade ground.

At the open door of this dwelling stood a coarse-looking convict woman wearing a clean apron, evidently awaiting their arrival. She sketched a clumsy curtsey, favouring the travellers with a lopsided grimace which did duty as a smile.

'His Excellency has placed this house at your disposal, sir, until you decide exactly whereabouts you wish to reside for the duration of your stay in the Colony,' Mr Chapman informed Mr Leigh Perrot. 'His Excellency did not consider that the hostelries of Sydney would be – ah, suitable for the ladies of your party.' He bowed to Mrs Leigh Perrot and Miss Jane Austen. 'Ellen Bowden is assigned as your servant,' he went on, indicating the female at the door. As he spoke, he could not help remarking the striking contrast between the crude convict woman and the elegant young lady in her straw bonnet – Miss Austen was the Leigh Perrots' niece, he understood. 'I – ah –

believe, sir, that you intend to remain here for the space of a few months?'

There had been considerable speculation at Government House concerning the advent of these somewhat unusual travellers who had chosen to visit the Colony. Sir Joseph Banks himself had written of their impending arrival; his note had arrived in a whaling ship which had dropped anchor at Port Jackson a month ago.

'That is indeed our intention, Mr Chapgood,' Mrs Leigh Perrot responded firmly. 'Mr Perrot is quite fascinated to observe the natural wonders of the Colony; that is the object of our visit.'

'My special interest lies in the study of Lepidoptera,' her husband added, speaking for himself. 'Both diurnal and nocturnal – that is to say, butterflies and moths.'

'So we are led to understand by Sir Joseph Banks,' William Chapman said. 'We must ensure you have the opportunity to meet the many other gentlemen here who share your interests. His Excellency himself is, of course, most interested in the native fauna and flora. It was he who sent the first specimen of the platypus to England . . . along with the head of an Aborigine –' He turned to the straw-bonneted young lady, wondering if his reference to that pickled native head were indelicate. 'I trust that you, Miss Austen, will find your sojourn here a pleasant one. We enjoy our picnics and balls, you know, and there is a host of agreeable prospects for the sketchbook – I know how fond young ladies are of sketching! My sister Fanny . . . alas, so far away . . .' His words tailed off as Jane Austen favoured him with a polite yet rather remote look which he found a little disconcerting. She was not, he realized, such a very young lady after all. His first glance had misled him; there was some experience of life lightly but unmistakably etched upon her smooth olive complexion. A spinster lady leaving youth behind her . . . hmn, perhaps she was hoping to find a husband during her travels? Well, there were certainly a number of lonely gentlemen here, though most managed to console themselves quite adequately with the dual comfort of convict concubines and liberal draughts of spirits.

Jane, meanwhile, had coolly stepped past the uncouth servant into the little parlour of the house, and now they heard her exclamation of pleasure at seeing a vase of flowers upon the round polished table. Such unusual flowers: red, spiky blooms with stiff, serrated leaves, strangely effective in that unpretentious room . . . as welcoming as a glowing fire in winter. (But, Jane recollected, it *was* winter here . . . winter in June!)

'Ah – *Telopea speciossima*, if I am not mistaken,' her uncle murmured, entering the room.

Mr Chapman beamed. 'Her Excellency – Mrs King herself arranged those flowers to welcome you,' he said. 'She is the kindest lady in the world, and greatly looks forward to making your acquaintance.'

William Chapman was almost one of the vice-regal family himself; indeed, he had been godfather to Utricia, one of the Kings' daughters – she, alas, had died in infancy. This close association had begun years ago. William had first come to the Colony and been appointed as a civil officer to Norfolk Island when Philip Gidley King was appointed Lieutenant-Governor there. Mr King had brought his bride with him from England – and William, homesick for his own family, had come to regard Mrs King as a beloved elder sister. It had been her very first experience of colonial life as well, though not her husband's; he had sailed to Botany Bay with the First Fleet, and at that time had been sent to establish the Norfolk settlement, which lay some days' sail from Port Jackson.

In truth, Mr Chapman was delighted that these two ladies, Mrs Leigh Perrot and Miss Austen, should have arrived in Sydney just at this time, for poor Mrs King was sorely in need of diverting female company. Her long-standing friendship with both Mrs Paterson and Mrs McArthur had been sadly disrupted by that unlucky duel between the husbands of those two ladies, and the Governor's subsequent intervention. The three ladies were now scarcely on speaking terms, whereas before they had intimately enjoyed each other's company. It was a sad business.

Aunt Perrot inclined her head, acknowledging the kind expectation of the Governor's lady. 'We shall be delighted to call at Government House at whatever time is considered most suitable,' she told Mr Chapman.

'Tomorrow morning, then, ma'am,' Mr Chapman said promptly. 'It is but a brief stroll to the seat of government.' – Then, as two sailors appeared, toiling uphill with the Leigh Perrots' portmanteaux, he took his leave, eager to bear tidings of these travellers to that two-storied house just across the bridge, where Josepha King sat enjoying the winter sunshine on the wide verandah.

Mrs Leigh Perrot and Miss Jane Austen were conscious of their crumpled gowns when they called at Government House the next morning. Six months of being folded away in a sea trunk amid last year's lavender spikes had not been beneficial to either Aunt Perrot's fine blue cashmere, or her niece's cream merino. But they soon discovered that the Governor's lady did not stand upon ceremony, and crumples and creases were put out of mind as they exchanged the first overtures of what promised to become an agreeable acquaintance. Sipping China tea from Mrs King's blue-sprigged Spode dishes, they sat in a sunny little parlour with a wide view of the harbour. It led off the long, formal drawing room with its twin portraits of King George and Queen Charlotte in their coronation robes, set in heavy gilt frames. Conversation in the drawing room, Jane Austen reflected, would surely have been constrained with those two august presences looking down upon them.

Mrs King was not a handsome woman; her features were irregular, but she had a most kindly and vivacious expression. She was tall, and on occasion could assume a proper vice-regal air. Her dark, curly hair was held back with a bandeau that matched her gown – a most outdated fashion, Aunt Perrot observed to herself. – Why, one had not seen a bandeau in Bath for above two years!

'I am particularly fond of my Souchong brew,' Mrs King informed them, sipping her tea appreciatively. 'My housekeeper told me yesterday we had almost run out of it – and now, thank heaven, the *Jason* has brought a new supply, as well as my regular order for a guinea's worth of dressmaking pins. Such trivial yet important details! We had quite run out of pins at the Orphanage, and the poor girls can scarcely be expected to seam or hem without pins. – The Orphanage is a very particular interest of Governor King and myself,' she went on. 'The numbers of neglected children in the Colony are scandalous – almost a thousand when we arrived, and their number increases all the time.' She gave a wry little smile. 'There is no heeding Mr Malthus' advice concerning the advantage to society of moral restraint here, I fear!'

'Mr Malthus?' Aunt Perrot did not believe she had heard the name before.

'A clergyman philosopher, Aunt,' Jane enlightened her. 'I have heard my brother James speak of him.' (Her aunt nodded; if James Austen spoke of this Mr Malthus, he must be worth remarking.) 'As I recall,' Jane said carefully, 'Mr Malthus has addressed himself to the problem of society becoming the constant prey of misery and vice because it tends to populate faster than its means of subsistence. – There is, I believe, considerable controversy about his conclusions.' She did not care to say more, feeling the population question to be scarcely a suitable subject for a first formal call at Government House.

Josepha King glanced at the younger woman approvingly. Clearly, she was no flibbertigibbet. She might prove quite an asset to their little society were she to remain here . . . At the back of her mind, the Governor's lady began to review the eligible bachelors and widowers in the Colony . . . 'We hope to start another girls' Orphanage at Parramatta soon, and then do something for the boys,' she told her two visitors. 'It seemed necessary to begin with the girls – we aim to train them for virtuous wifehood.' She shook her head sadly. 'Do you know, Mrs Leigh Perrot, Miss Austen, out of nine thousand souls in New South Wales, there are but three hundred and fifty married couples? There is, alas, but the smallest respect for the institution of family life.'

'I suppose,' Aunt Perrot remarked, 'that is hardly to be wondered at, when one considers the type of female who is transported here.' She was a little surprised by Mrs King's choice of conversational topic, especially in the presence of a young unmarried lady.

Were the male convicts to share none of the blame for this unhappy state of affairs, Jane wondered to herself. – Alas, the fable of Adam tempted by Eve was altogether too deeply ingrained.

'But how I do run on about the Orphanage!' Mrs King exclaimed. 'I vow it occupies my thoughts so much, I am in danger of neglecting my own children!'

They spoke then of the vice-regal family – the Kings, it transpired, had three children. 'Phillip, our son, was born when

154

we lived on Norfolk, during our former residency in the Colony,' Mrs King informed them. 'He was named for Governor Phillip, whom my husband holds in the highest regard. We left Phillip in England when we came here this last time – he is to follow in his father's footsteps, and enter the Navy. Our daughter Maria is also with friends in England, but Elizabeth, I am happy to say, is here with us. She is just seven years old.'

Josepha King did not mention Utricia, nor did she speak of her husband's other two sons, Norfolk and Sydney, both grown now, and also following careers in the Navy. She had helped to bring them up alongside her own family. There was no need to speak of them: it would not take long within this little community for the new arrivals to learn that when Mr King was first sent to colonize Norfolk Island in '88, he had fathered those two sons upon the convict woman Ann Inett. *She* was still in the Colony, living at Parramatta, and had been married for some years now to a convict transported for life – though she herself had received her pardon long ago.

Glancing out of the window, Jane Austen saw a little girl playing in the green garden which sloped down to the water's edge: an almost tropic garden of great ferns, flowers of astonishing size, and shady trees – here, though ruthlessly hewn down elsewhere in the settlement, the trees had been allowed to stand. An idyllic place, she thought, for childhood games.

Aunt Perrot was curious about Parramatta, which was so oftened mentioned. 'Such a strange name,' she observed. 'Is it a native word?'

Mrs King nodded. 'There is some doubt about its meaning; some maintain it means "head of the river", others "the place where eels lie down". Indeed the settlement does lie at the head of the creek which joins an estuary of Sydney Harbour – we call it the Parramatta river. And certainly there are plenty of eels in it! It lies some fifteen miles from here – an agreeable place. Until a few years ago, it was thought that Parramatta, rather than Sydney, might be the seat of government, and for a time there were more people there than here. But now that the Hawkesbury district is being developed, there seems no good reason to have the capital of the Colony situated between those farmlands and the port. – We are, of course, anxious to develop an export trade in due course.' She smiled happily. 'I always enjoy our visits to Parramatta; I trust I may have the pleasure of showing you our residence there before long. And our very first stone-built church is at Parramatta – St John's. We held the first service there at the beginning of this year.'

'There is no church in Sydney?' Aunt Perrot exclaimed.

Mrs King shook her head almost apologetically. 'That was the everlasting complaint of Mr Johnson, our first Chaplain. Poor, long-suffering Mr Johnson! In the end, he quite despaired of any official action, and put up a little place for worship at his own expense.' She smiled again, gently. 'He never wearied of telling everyone precisely what it cost him: the amount is quite engraved upon my heart, as Queen Mary said of Calais: sixty-seven pounds, twelve shilling and eleven pence halfpenny! Governor Hunter, Mr King's predecessor, finally recompensed him for the outlay, even to the halfpenny. It was a very modest structure, as you may imagine, wooden, with wattle-and-daub walls –'

'And I gather it is no longer standing, ma'am?' Jane said.

'Alas, no. Governor Hunter was extremely concerned at the lack of observance of the Sabbath Day in the Colony, and he issued an order that all convicts and military officers were to attend Divine Service each Sunday without fail – an order which, I may say, Mr King enforces most rigorously. Well, shortly after that order was given, Mr Johnson's little church was burnt down.'

By the convicts . . . or the military gentlemen, Jane wondered.

'And so,' Mrs King continued, 'that is why our services here are held in a storehouse – properly consecrated for the purpose, of course. I fear Mr Johnson returned to England a disappointed man. He went three years ago, and we are still awaiting his replacement. Matters spiritual are apt to lie fallow at the Colonial Office. Meanwhile, each Sunday, our very able Assistant Chaplain, Mr Marsden, takes Divine Service here in the morning and at Parramatta in the evening.'

'We have heard of Mr Marsden,' Aunt Perrot remarked. 'He is an Evangelist, I understand.' Mr Campbell had spoken of him.

'I am glad to say that Mr Marsden is shortly to receive a curate to assist him – I just forget his name for the moment. Oh, we shall have a church in Sydney before too long, Mrs Leigh Perrot, and it will be named St Philip's. The plans are all drawn up, but their execution will take time.' She sighed. 'My poor husband is not exactly an enthusiastic churchgoer himself at the moment, being scarcely able to kneel at the communion rail. He is sorely afflicted with the gout, which I could almost believe to be brought on by anxiety: he has so many difficulties to contend with.'

'Gout! That wretched enemy!' Aunt Perrot declared. 'Mr Perrot suffers it too, though he has kept remarkably well during our voyage here – he has had scarcely a twinge for months.'

The Governor's lady felt an upsurge of empathy with Mrs Leigh Perrot. 'We have been married for twelve years,' she said, 'and I do not believe one twelvemonth has gone by without that wretched enemy, as you rightly call it, launching an attack upon Mr King. One of the first actions I took soon after we married was to cancel Mr King's annual order of thirty-six dozen of port wine –'

The discussion of ill-health has an undeniable way of super-seding every other topic of conversation, and while the two older ladies fell to discussing causes, symptoms and treatments, Jane Austen fell into a reverie, from which she emerged to hear Mrs King saying: ' . . . a poultice of seaweed, most beneficial.'

From gout those two ladies turned to the high price of housekeeping in the Colony. 'Sugar two shillings and sixpence a pound; if you can believe it, butter *four* shillings . . .' And this time, as Jane collected her straying thoughts, it was to hear her aunt repeating in a deeply shocked voice: 'Tea *four pounds* the pound! No wonder you import your Souchong yourself, ma'am.'

'Possibly prices will become more stable now that we have the Peace,' Mrs King said optimistically.

'If the Peace lasts,' Aunt Perrot added gloomily.

'Oh, do you consider it may not? – well, I am afraid Mr King is rather of that opinion, too. He thinks that Bonaparte is so clearly intent upon further conquest –' Then the Governor's lady smiled and added in a determinedly lighthearted tone: 'You will be surprised, I think, to hear that we have recently harboured here some of our former enemies. The French have been upon our very doorstep!'

Her raillery created the little sensation she intended, and she proceeded to enlighten her visitors. 'Almost a year ago, two French vessels arrived here, engaged upon a surveying and scientific voyage. They had had a hard time of it: their sailors were so stricken with the scurvy and starvation they did not have sufficient strength to sail inside the harbour. Mr King sent a boatload of Mr Flinders' men from the *Investigator* to bring in the Frenchies. Many were taken straight to the hospital. Some died, but most recovered. The leader of the expedition was Monsieur Baudin, a most agreeable gentleman; he and his officers frequently attended gatherings here at Government house. *Cher* Monsieur Baudin!' Mrs King smiled in reminiscence. 'He paid Mr King the most exquisite compliment. He said: "Governor King" (he spoke English with the most delightful accent) "has given the whole of Europe the example of magnificent benevolence." '

'And what happened, ma'am?' Jane Austen asked. 'Did Monsieur Baudin return to France?'

'They stayed in Sydney for several months,' Mrs King replied, 'then, last November, Monsieur Baudin set off to resume his survey. Before he sailed, the dear man presented me with the sum of fifty pounds, no less, for the Orphanage – such a thoughtful gesture! – Then, after all that had passed, and in spite of the very real *amitié* which had been established between us, you may perhaps appreciate Mr King's feelings when he heard, soon after Monsieur Baudin had sailed, that it had been common talk amongst the French, while they were here, that they intended to hoist their flag over a settlement in Van Diemen's Land! We really did not know quite what to do; we had formed such an *entente cordiale*, we felt this must be a more than unpleasant rumour. But Mr King thought it prudent to send a small ship after the French, bearing a British flag on board . . . he gave instructions it was to be planted on Van Diemen's Land, to make our prior claim quite explicit. Better safe than sorry, as he said.'

'A wise move,' Aunt Perrot commented. 'You simply cannot trust the French.'

Mrs King smiled a trifle enigmatically. 'In the event, it was left to a foolish young midshipman to carry out Mr King's order regarding the flag. This young man found Monsieur Baudin at King Island (named after the Governor, you know), and, after handing him a very diplomatic communication from Mr King, he proceeded to plant our flag right on top of the French tents, in the most provoking manner possible!'

'And did the French claim Van Diemen's Land?' Aunt Perrot was all prepared for patriotic indignation.

'No, they did not; Monsieur Baudin denied any knowledge of French plans for a settlement. In fact, he sent Mr King a somewhat philosophic letter on the subject of whether any Europeans have the right to seize in the name of their governments a land seen for the first time.'

'He would have put forward a different philosophy if the French had been the first to settle here!' Aunt Perrot declared stoutly.

Mrs King shook her head gently. 'Monsieur Baudin maintained that neither the British nor his own countrymen have any moral claim to Van Diemen's Land . . . an original point of view which I confess I found interesting. 'Twas a most courteous letter, with an amusing if somewhat embarrassing postscript . . . for Monsieur Baudin happened to mention that in his zeal, that young midshipman had planted the Union Jack upside-down!'

Aunt Perrot pursed her mouth; she found it strange, to say the least, that the Governor's lady should find such anti-colonial sentiments 'interesting'.

Jane Austen reflected that Monsieur Baudin appeared to have made a favourable impression indeed upon Mrs King. 'And where is Monsieur Baudin now, ma'am?' she inquired.

'Oh, he is continuing his survey – he sailed from King Island, intending to go on to Timor, I believe . . . I daresay we shall have word from him before long.' She added casually: 'He promised to send me a Sèvres dessert service . . . he was always so complimentary about our peaches.'

A little clock on a side table chimed the hour, reminding Mrs Leigh Perrot that their take-leave was overdue. As aunt and niece departed, Mrs King invited them to accompany her one morning to the Orphanage.

'The other official visitors, besides myself, are Mrs Paterson and Mrs McArthur,' she said, in a slightly forced tone which concealed the pain of disrupted friendship. 'But Mrs McArthur is kept very busy at her farm in Parramatta just now, since her husband is in England. I am sure you will find Mrs Paterson most – agreeable.'

Her departing visitors murmured their willingness to make such a visit, then strolled back towards their modest dwelling, picking their way carefully over the tree stumps on the rough road. A brisk wind had sprung up, blowing gritty particles of fine white dust into their faces. Heads bent, they reached their cottage at last, where the servant Ellen, who had evidently been on the lookout for their return, almost dragged them inside, then banged the door shut. Jane noticed she had closed all the windows.

' 'Tis a brickfielder on the rampage,' she told them. ' 'Tis terrible, the dust from them brickworks when the wind blows. Worse nor the flies in summer, and that's saying summat!' Suddenly she advanced upon Aunt Perrot, who instinctively cringed, imagining for one incredulous instant that she was about to be attacked. But all Ellen did was to brush the dust from her pelisse, with a surprisingly gentle touch – surprising, that is, to Mrs Leigh Perrot, who was unaware that Ellen Bowden had been one of the most lightfingered pickpockets in Cheapside, a queen of the clouting lay. When a clerk from the Commissary, delegated by Mr Chapman, had called to take Mr Leigh Perrot on a tour of the town, soon after the ladies had set off for Government House, Ellen had seized the opportunity to sift expertly through her new employers' belongings. But she had found nothing of sufficient value to risk a spell of hard labour at the Female Factory.

'Just look at yer hopper-dockers, Miss!' she exclaimed now.

'Hopper-dockers?' Jane echoed, following Ellen's gaze and finding that it rested upon her dusty shoes. 'Oh yes, I see –' Mentally she reserved the phrase for that letter to Cassandra which she was continually composing in her mind.

At that moment, James entered from the street, his black beaver translated into a light grey by the prevailing dust.

' 'Ere, sir, give me that,' Ellen said with a quaint lack of ceremony; indeed, her whole attitude could not have been further removed from the deference shown by the Leigh Perrots' servants at home. Forthwith she departed for the back regions bearing the hat and with the ladies' pelisses – or *togs*, as she called them – looped over one arm.

'She has an original turn of phrase,' Jane Austen remarked.

'She speaks *cant*, my dear – the language of the criminal

classes,' Aunt Perrot said loftily, recollecting the echoes of that foreign tongue which used to drift about the Scaddings' dinner table at Ilchester. 'If we were to eavesdrop upon any of these convicts, I daresay we would not comprehend a quarter of what they said.'

Her husband fell into a chair, thankfully resting his weary legs, and proceeded in tones which were slightly slurred to regale them with his morning's adventure. His tour of the settlement had been extensive, his guide enthusiastic: towards the end of the morning, both men had agreed that sightseeing was thirsty work, and the clerk had contrived a homeward route by way of his favourite tavern, in Pitt's Row.

'The main impresh – impression I received in the course of my ramble,' James concluded, 'was that this is very much a garrish – garrison town. I rather feel we would be well advised to remove to Parramatta, where I believe there would be much more opportunity to observe the natural wonders of the Colony. There is a good deal that strikes me as – undesirable – in this place.' He thought of some of the unnatural wonders he had witnessed during the morning: a chain-gang clinking by . . . the unspeakable slatterns lounging outside certain shacks in Pitt's Row . . . The drunkards sprawled on the ground outside the worst of the numerous grog shops.

'Whatever you think best, Perrot,' his wife responded, wrinkling her high-bridged nose and detecting a distinct whiff of spirits. She wondered uneasily whether that record of scarcely a twinge of gout could be maintained here for very long – Mrs King's recipe for a seaweed poultice might, alas, be called for.

And now, as though to underline James' assertion that Sydney was first and foremost a garrison, there came the call of drum and bugle. The new arrivals had woken that morning to the sound of reveille; soon they would become used to hearing the retreat each evening, and the sonorous, clanging bell that summoned off-duty redcoats before the Barrack gates were closed each night. Surrounded by a thick stone wall ten feet high, with four gates, one on each side of the rectangle that enclosed the Barracks, this grim fort was indeed the very heart of Sydney town.

Sixteen

M RS LEIGH PERROT had run out (as Mrs King might have expressed it) of peppermints, a circumstance which made her feel distinctly irritable. Peppermints, she had long since discovered, were a soothing influence upon her disposition. She had given her very last peppermint (she had not realized it at the time) to one of the Orphanage children when she and Jane had visited there with Mrs King and Mrs Paterson. The wretched child had popped the sweetmeat in her mouth, then made a face and promptly spat it out again.

Jane Leigh Perrot never realized what perturbation her advent caused to one member of the Orphanage as they inspected those hundred girls in their clean pinafores, so diligently spinning, weaving, sewing. Susan Gregory sat with head bent as the lady visitors were shown round by the matron in her rustling black dress. Mrs Leigh Perrot knew, of course, that her female persecutor had been transported to Botany Bay, but it simply did not occur to her to associate Susan Gregory with Mrs King's Orphanage. Besides, Susan herself did not fully realize how much she had changed in appearance; she was no longer the dough-faced slattern who had fallen in so easily with Sam Filby's wiles. Curiously, her later experiences had refined her, sharpening her features, turning her figure gaunt, greying her hair. And so an encounter which might have aroused bitter feeling in both protagonists did not occur. And, having escaped notice, Susan's curiosity concerning the astonishing appearance of that old Parrot in Sydney town evaporated as quickly as morning dew beneath the Antipodean sun. Who cared what had brought that Mrs High-and-Mighty here? Just so long as she and Gregory were left in peace – that was all she asked.

And so the single untoward outcome of that visit was the dearth of peppermints.

'Surely it must be possible to procure peppermints of some description here,' Aunt Perrot complained fretfully to her niece. 'Do try to find out if there are any to be had, Jane. I do not expect them to be up to Mr Powys' standard, of course –' She sighed as she thought of the apothecary in far-off Milsom Street, with his never-failing supply of the curiously strong peppermints she craved.

Jane Austen dutifully inquired of Ellen Bowden, who in turn undertook to ask about. But the striped humbugs Ellen produced, confected alongside vats of toffee and fudge in a dubious establishment at the foot of Brickfield Hill ('As prime a gob-stopper as you'd find in the Old Country, missus,' she averred), were summarily rejected by Aunt Perrot.

'Too sweet – and soft in the middle,' that lady complained, removing the sticky little cushion from her mouth. Upon which, unobserved, Ellen retrieved the humbug, popped it into her own mouth, and took no further interest in her employer's quest.

The following week, the Leigh Perrots and Miss Jane Austen were invited to dine at Government House: a formal dinner to be followed by a ball. They were bidden for three-thirty – evidently the colonists retained the old-fashioned custom of dining early – and by four o'clock on the appointed day, the company was all assembled around the long dining table, which was profusely decorated with lilies and ferns.

James Leigh Perrot had already paid his formal respects to His Excellency, but for Mrs Leigh Perrot and Jane Austen it was their first encounter with Philip Gidley King, representative of His Majesty King George III in the Antipodes. To Jane, Mr King appeared as very much the bluff naval officer, middle-aged, balding, with a rather abrupt manner of speaking and a habit of repeating his words and phrases. He was quite portly, and every now and then seemed in danger of losing his breath. Jane, with her predilection for the Navy and all who served in it, thought she detected a kind, well-meaning soul beneath that bluff exterior. Governor King, she thought, seemed to have the embattled air of one who has struggled long against adversity and false report: . . . although, as she acknowledged to herself, he might merely be suffering from dyspepsia.

As for Aunt Perrot's first impression – 'Not *quite* a gentleman,' she observed to herself; and, to support her intuition, she learned from Mr King himself during the course of the evening (they were speaking of the West Country at the time) that his father had been a linen draper in Cornwall. He seemed a conscientious sort of man, she decided, with sound enough convictions; doubtless he was well suited to administer this penal colony at the end of the earth.

They were fourteen sitting down to dinner; a number of other guests had been invited at a later hour for the ball. The gentlemen at table outnumbered the ladies, who were judiciously sprinkled amongst them by Mrs King's thoughtful placing. Mrs Leigh Perrot was seated at the Governor's right; a Captain Eber Bunker, a bulky individual, was on her right. He and the Governor appeared to be on the most cordial terms. Mr Leigh Perrot was at Mrs King's right hand, and on his right sat Mrs Robert Campbell, still glowing from the happy circumstance of her husband's safe return. Miss Jane Austen was seated halfway down the table; to one side of her sat Mr Flinders, the young naval officer whose name so often came to the fore in colonial conversation – always, it seemed, in terms of admiration. He was very thin, and sallow of complexion. A Mr Wentworth, a Mr D'Arcy Wentworth, was on her other side, a gentleman in early middle age. Jane was immediately struck by his handsome appearance, attractive presence and penetrating blue-eyed glance.

Looking down the table, she noticed Mr Chapman talking to Mrs Paterson, who caught her eye and smiled. Jane had quite taken to Elizabeth Paterson, with her soft Scottish voice and clear, direct gaze, on the occasion of their visit to the Orphanage. Tonight, Mrs Paterson was attending the dinner without her husband, who had been in indifferent health ever since he was wounded in that infamous duel with Captain McArthur. Colonel Paterson had, in fact, temporarily retired from his public duties. Mrs King's invitation to join this dinner party was by way of being an olive-branch held out to Elizabeth Paterson . . . yet, as William Chapman sadly observed, the two ladies still appeared very stiff and formal with each other.

Apart from Mr Flinders, there were two other naval officers present, and, towards the far end of the table, a single military gentleman. The absence of any other army officers was surely remarkable, Jane thought; she could only suppose it must demonstrate the friction that existed between the Governor and the military, about which they heard so much. Indeed, that was the chief topic of discussion, gossip and tittle-tattle within the Colony, sending out ceaseless waves of conjecture, speculation and rumour, and even promoting doggerel verses which mocked and ridiculed Mr King.

In spite of the sad shade of the late lamented Mr Fordwick, forever hovering at the periphery of her soul, Jane was quite able to appreciate the agreeable sensation of being seated between two amiable gentlemen; of knowing she was in good looks; of being aware that her blue taffeta was quite in fashion compared to most of the other ladies' attire (though Mrs Campbell out-shone them all in her crimson moiré gown, ordered by her husband from a London dressmaker); and with, moreover, the prospect of dancing to follow the dinner-party. She was, in fact, entirely prepared to enjoy herself, and quite easily fell into the mildly flirtatious mood which Mr Wentworth's flattering gaze and lighthearted conversation seemed to induce. His voice had a rich, seductive timbre, with a slight Irish accent.

The convict servants – who, if one had cared to think about it, provided the *raison d'être* for this genteel assembly – flitted about their duties dexterously, handing dishes, removing plates, pouring wine, their felonious hands neatly encased in white cotton gloves, their faces inscrutable.

At the head of the table, His Excellency was relating an anecdote which had taken his fancy. Last Sunday afternoon, it seemed, an illegal cockfight had been set up in one of the notorious dens on Brickfield Hill, the opposing champions being a part-coloured bird named Bone-a-part and a ginger of true English breed, Sir Sidney. But the outcome of their battle was never settled – for, as Mr King informed them, chuckling and wheezing, a posse of constables and troopers had shortly arrived upon the scene: whereupon the sole desire of all the gamesters had been to escape arrest.

The Governor wagged a forefinger over his corned beef and

buttered parsnips. 'In an instant the two champions were left to their own devices,' he said. 'The *heelers* took to their heels; the owners disclaimed their property; and all who had laid bets decamped without adjusting their accounts! But the best part of all,' he went on, 'the best part of all, I say, was that in their haste to escape, most of those rogues and rascals ran directly into Blackwattle Swamp, where Mr Surgeon Harris keeps his herd of deer' – here he nodded and waved in the direction of that sole military gentleman at the far end of the table – 'Yes, directly into the Swamp! Well, that fixed 'em. There they stuck, still as statues, until the constables and troopers came to their rescue and escorted 'em to gaol. As for those two famous champions, as for Bone-a-part and Sir Sidney, why, *they* were sent straight to the Orphanage to be turned into cock-a-leekie soup. Yes, cock-a-leekie soup!'

This tale was much appreciated by Captain Bunker, who gave a hearty guffaw. Mrs Leigh Perrot had ascertained that the Captain was engaged in the whaling trade – had, indeed, been the very first of the Colonists to engage in it. He told her that during his voyaging in the South Seas, he had acted as an emissary between the Governor of New South Wales and the King of Tahiti, who supplied pork to the Colony from time to time.

Now, as a fricassee of rabbit replaced the dish of corned beef, the good Captain sat back in his chair and cudgelled his brains to think of something else to say to the somewhat formidable lady at his side. 'Ahem – if you were to settle in the Colony, ma'am,' he said at last, 'what should you miss most of your former way of life?'

Much to his surprise, Mrs Leigh Perrot answered promptly: 'Peppermints, Captain Bunker. There are simply none to be found here. It is most provoking.'

Upon which the Captain, who was more used to sighting a whale upon the horizon than taking on board a lady's problem, pondered a moment, then said helpfully: 'Perhaps you would permit me, ma'am, to offer you a humble *substitute* which I believe you may find has much in common with the peppermint? 'Twas introduced to me by an American, a seaman who joined my whaling fleet last year.'

Aunt Perrot was intrigued. 'By all means, Captain; I will try anything. I am quite desperate for peppermints. But I very much doubt whether any – er – *substitute* could adequately replace them.'

Captain Bunker's eyes twinkled. 'Once you have tried this,' he said persuasively, 'I am bold enough to predict you may change your opinion. I shall send you a supply first thing tomorrow. Why, some of my sailors have even abandoned their tobacco quids in favour of it.'

'I do not chew tobacco, Captain,' Mrs Leigh Perrot told him repressively. She did not appreciate being lumped together with rough seafaring men.

'Why no, of course not, ma'am. But I would venture to suggest that your partiality for peppermints lies not only on their taste, but in the fact that you are accustomed to sucking them –'

'If you are suggesting, Captain Bunker, that I am *addicted* to peppermints,' Aunt Perrot said drily, 'then I daresay truth is on your side. They are – a comfort to me.'

'Just as the tobacco quid is a comfort to my men,' Captain Bunker said. 'Or was, until they tried this substitute.'

'Well, Captain, I shall let you know in due course whether I become addicted to his mysterious *substitute*,' the lady told him good-humouredly; then turned to her other side as Mr King began at this point to speak nostalgically of Cornwall . . .

James Leigh Perrot, meanwhile, had been attending to the Governor's lady and hearing about the many difficulties which beset her husband. 'Just imagine, Mr Perrot, what it is like to administer this little world of nine thousand souls – give and take a few – so isolated from any other civilized part of the globe; to have to settle every decision, from the granting of lands to the care and discipline of the convict population and the most judicious way to treat the Aborigines . . . and, as if all this were not enough, to be forced to carry out the task in the face of –' she lowered her voice, anxious not to endanger her fragile olive-branch, '– in the face of the most wilful and determined provocation from *certain quarters*.'

She gazed down the length of the table, through lilies and ferns, to the distant figure of her husband, who happened at that moment to have reached the climax of his cockpit anecdote, and consequently appeared anything but careworn. 'It delights my heart to see Mr King able to enjoy himself for a change,' the

Governor's lady said then. '– Oh, Mr Perrot, if you had known the truly deplorable state of affairs which prevailed when we arrived here three years ago! The military took charge, you know, after Governor Hunter departed. One of the first things my husband did was to remove the monopoly in the rum trade from the grasp of those puffed-up officers of the Corps. – Do you know, Mr Leigh Perrot, they used to sell the spirits they purchased for a clear profit of *five hundred percent*!'

She paused as a white-gloved hand bearing a carafe refilled Mr Leigh Perrot's wineglass. 'At the time my husband took office,' she continued, 'the convicts refused to work in what they call their own time – that is, after their assigned duties are fulfilled – for any other form of payment besides rum . . . by which name they designate any form of spirit, the more fiery the better! But now Mr King is to have a brewery built at Parramatta, and is encouraging the farmers to plant barley; soon, we hope, there will be plenty of good honest beer for our thirsty colonists. Who knows, perhaps in time, *beer* may supersede their craving for rum!'

Mr Leigh Perrot nodded sympathetically as he stretched forth his hand to raise his glass of claret to his lips; then, rather to his relief, he was claimed for a more lighthearted interchange by pretty Mrs Campbell, whereupon Mrs King transferred her attention to the imposing-looking gentleman seated at her left.

Now almost sixty years of age, Richard Bowyer Atkins, the improbable Judge-Advocate of the Colony, had somehow managed to retain the impression of a commanding presence, which lent him a spurious air of dignity in the law court and upon such formal occasions as this vice-regal dinner party. On closer inspection, his features revealed the signs of a life dedicated to dissipation and debauchery. Now, though he sat upright in his chair, he did not deceive his hostess. He had, she knew, been quite drunk when he arrived; very soon he would be dead drunk. – Well, Mrs King consoled herself, at least she need make no real effort to converse with him. She had placed him next to Mr Harris (much to the latter's disgust) because she knew she could rely upon the surgeon to deal with the Judge-Advocate when the latter finally slipped beneath the table . . . *after* the ladies had left the dining room, she prayed. It was Mr Harris, she recalled, who had described the life led by the Judge-

Advocate as 'worse than a Dog's', and his dwelling as 'a perfect pigstye'.

Josepha King sighed as she took a helping of rabbit fricassee and admitted to herself a rare criticism of her husband. Somehow, in spite of the fact that Richard Atkins had left England as a disgraced debtor, he had contrived to impress (or hoodwink) three successive Governors of New South Wales: Arthur Phillip; John Hunter; and finally her own dear King. Yes – 'twas her own dear King who actually established this creature in his high position. Oh, she could guess how Mr Atkins must have harped on his distinguished connexions at home, hinted at influence from high places which could be brought to bear . . . men, alas, could be so gullible! Her private protests to her husband had been unavailing. 'There is no other person in the Colony at all equal to the office,' Mr King had told her. 'We must simply overlook his – ah – inebriate habits. Simply overlook them.' If only that were all they must overlook! The Governor's lady shuddered, not caring to dwell upon unsavoury details relating to the Judge-Advocate's notorious penchant for very young females.

The military officers, she had to admit, had summed up Mr Atkins better. What was it Captain McArthur had called him? Ah yes – 'a public cheater living in the most boundless dissipation'. Aptly phrased. Colonel Paterson, too, had censured the man out of hand, describing him as possessing every degrading vice as well as a total want of gentlemanly principle! Strong words, but well deserved – oh, well deserved indeed. A man's private life, she thought, might perhaps be considered his own affair, however regrettable it were, if his public duty was beyond reproach. But apart from all else, Atkins' knowledge and practice of the law was, to say the least, incompetent. He relied heavily on his chief clerk, a convict with pretensions to legal lore. God help those unfortunates who appeared before the Judge-Advocate! Many was the death sentence he had pronounced when he was in his cups. – At least, his hostess consoled herself, there was no danger of his making an appearance at the ball this evening. He might be able to sit upright still, but by now she very much doubted his ability to stand. It would be the usual story: Mr Harris to the rescue, and two servants detailed to decant the Judge-Advocate into his carriage . . .

Safely removed (by Mrs King's careful design) from this judicial monster of depravity, Miss Austen was listening to Mr Flinders relate the tale of his voyage along the northern coastline of the continent in the *Investigator*, from which he had just returned.

'. . . and so, after charting the Gulf of Carpentaria, we reached Torres Strait . . . only to discover that *Investigator's* timbers were by now quite rotten . . . so we were forced to cut short the survey and return, springing leaks all the way!' He described his considerable exploits in a remarkably unassuming and seemingly lighthearted manner, but it was nonetheless quite clear that his work of surveying and charting the coastline was a consuming passion. The trials of his recent expedition, Jane thought, would amply explain his emaciated appearance. '*Carpentaria*', she repeated to herself: why, that name had an echo of *Gulliver's Travels* about it!

'And if I know you, Flinders,' Mr Wentworth remarked, 'you won't be satisfied until you have found another ship to complete the survey – or is *Investigator* capable of being patched up?'

Matthew Flinders shook his head. 'Not a hope of it: poor old girl, her seafaring days are finished. She has done good service. But I am indeed planning to set off again as soon as possible – but to *England*, D'Arcy: the Governor has instructed me to find a new ship there and sail her back without delay.'

'So you will be reunited with your Ann at last – I am happy for you!' Mr Wentworth declared.

Mr Flinders returned to Miss Austen. 'Ann – that is to say, my wife – hoped very much to accompany me to the Colony two years ago, when I was first appointed here. We were married just four months before I left. But it was –' he paused significantly '– thought better she should remain in England.'

He did not expatiate upon those events which had conspired to cheat the newly married couple of their hope. In fact, his bride had lived secretly aboard *Investigator* while her young husband awaited orders to sail. They had quite assumed that she would accompany him on the voyage . . . but one unlucky day, an officious visitor from the Admiralty, inspecting the ship in dock, had caught sight of Ann Flinders sitting in her husband's cabin with her bonnet off, clearly in residence on board. He had reported the fact to Flinders' patron, Sir Joseph Banks.

Whereupon Sir Joseph, who firmly believed that discipline on board ship was bound to suffer when the Captain's wife was aboard, had given Flinders the option of either sailing alone to the Antipodes, or else relinquishing his commission as Surveyor to the Colony. Poor Flinders, torn between two passions, had after considerable soul-searching left his gentle Ann behind.

'We shall be together within a twelvemonth, please God!' he exclaimed joyously – and then, as he saw the shadow of a private sorrow cross D'Arcy Wentworth's face, he in his turn felt compassion for his friend. D'Arcy's close companion of many years, the mother of his sons, had died two years ago. 'Twas common knowledge, of course, that D'Arcy Wentworth never lacked female consolation, but Matthew Flinders knew full well that his Catherine had occupied the first place in his heart.

There was a delicate pause, during which Jane Austen accurately divined unspoken sadness of a personal nature. She, too, had caught that fleeting glimpse of melancholy upon Mr Wentworth's handsome features.

Then, from across the table, William Chapman's carefree voice rang out, just as a dish heaped with meat patties encased in crisp golden pastry was proffered her, held by an anonymous pair of white-gloved hands.

'I say, Miss Austen! The Governor's meat patties are famous – you must try them!' The young Secretary's face was flushed with wine. 'And pray take a little catsup to accompany them – Mrs King's tomato catsup is the best in Sydney!'

As Jane helped herself to a couple of the patties, he went on cheerfully: 'We have not always feasted like this, you know. – Why, not so long ago, we sat at this very table eating bow-wow pie!'

'Bow-wow pie,' Jane repeated, as though it were a riddle. Surely he could not mean –

Mr Wentworth smiled as he observed her perplexity. 'A few years ago, Miss Austen, before sufficient crops had been grown to supply our needs, we were all put on very short rations indeed. As I recall, His Excellency issued an edict that anyone invited to dine at this table should provide their own bread –'

'All except Mrs McArthur!' William Chapman interjected.

'All except Mrs McArthur,' Mr Wentworth agreed gravely. 'His Excellency made her the sole exception. – Well, Miss Austen,' he continued, 'to accompany the bread we brought, we were once or twice served a pie made from the native dog. 'Twas quite a tasty dish.'

'I see,' she said, toying doubtfully with the patty on her plate.

'But I can assure you,' Mr Wentworth went on, 'these excellent patties contain nothing but good wholesome mutton.'

Jane smiled. 'I take your word for it, sir. *Bow-wow pie* . . . for an instant I imagined that to be one of the – the *cant* phrases used by the servant who has been assigned to us. I confess, I find her language singularly diverting.'

'Aha!' D'Arcy Wentworth's blue eyes twinkled. 'I may claim to be something of an expert in cant, Miss Austen! I am a magistrate, you know, and it is essential to know something of cant if one is to comprehend half of what is uttered before the bench. Flash or cant – it is all one, the vocabulary used by the *Family*.'

'The *Family?* – Pray enlighten me, sir,' Jane begged him.

'All those who get their living by dishonest means, Miss Austen, upon the *cross*. – As opposed to the *square* practices followed by honest folk such as ourselves – all fair and upright!'

'I see you have formed a favourable impression of my character, sir,' Jane answered with a hint of coquetry. 'You evidently consider me to be – let me see, what was it Ellen said the other day? Ah yes, a square *covess*!'

'To the nines, Miss Austen!' Mr Wentworth responded enthusiastically. 'But,' he went on in a tone of exaggerated conspiracy, 'perhaps we should *cheese it*, lest we be considered "half-flash and half-foolish", as the Family say of those who like to air a mere smattering of cant, and pretend to a knowledge of low life they do not in truth possess.'

Jane glanced at him demurely. 'I should not care to be thus designated, Mr Wentworth; by all means, let us *stow it!*'

A knowledge of low life which he did not in truth possess? – Catching the gist of that exchange, even while he turned to attend to Mrs Palmer upon his right, Matthew Flinders raised an eyebrow. D'Arcy Wentworth was an artful codger, to be sure! Doubtless those rumours of D'Arcy's notorious exploits when he was a student in the London hospitals would not yet have reached Miss Austen's innocent ear. A magistrate he might be now, and a most distinguished citizen of New South Wales to boot, but *then* . . . Ah well, doubtless she would not remain in ignorance very long; there were always plenty of people eager to spread gossip and calumny. A very good way to avoid it, Matthew Flinders had found, was to put to sea as often as possible.

Mrs Palmer, meanwhile, was speaking in her languid voice of the new farming methods her husband had introduced at his Hawkesbury estate. ' . . . reduced the number of labourers we employ from around forty to a mere fifteen or so,' she was saying. 'And all by following the new theories – rotating the crops and letting some paddocks lie fallow, for example . . .'

As always, Flinders found himself fascinated, not so much by the matter of Susan Palmer's speech, as the manner of it, those long-drawn vowels that marked the fact she had been born and raised in another colony. Or rather, a *former* colony, he corrected himself: one must remember to speak of America correctly.

Mrs Palmer, in fact, belonged to a loyalist Virginian family; she had met her husband when he was serving as a naval officer in the American War. They were a popular and handsome couple; their residence, at 'Palmer's Cove', was one of the smartest in the Colony, and not unlike one of the elegant plantation houses built along the James River, in Virginia. Jack Palmer had quitted the Navy several years ago and was now a very wealthy private citizen. Susan Palmer's two sisters had also settled here – it was her youngest sister, Sophie, who had married Mr Robert Campbell.

All this had been made known to Mrs Leigh Perrot and her niece during a morning call at the Patersons'; and Elizabeth Paterson had also divulged, with some amusement, the scandalized reaction of some Sydney matrons when Susan Palmer had produced an addition to her family only last year. At forty-one, her childbearing days might reasonably have been considered over. ' 'Twas pronounced positively indecent!' Mrs Paterson declared.

'It seems to me,' Aunt Perrot had remarked as she and Jane returned home from this call, 'that Sydney outdoes Bath for gossip.' Then she had frowned and said: 'I think, my dear Jane, we should again make use of that clever stratagem you proposed when we were at sea; let us acquaint one of these garrulous colonial ladies with the *facts* concerning my unfortunate experience of two years ago. Else, gracious heavens, who knows what rumours might fly about! They will have me destined for the Female Factory before I know where I am!' They had lost no time in following this plan, with the same satisfactory results they had obtained on board the *Jason*.

Tonight, more than one speculative glance had been directed towards Susan Palmer's loosely draped gown . . . and speculation swelled to certainty in several matronly minds when, after dinner, the Palmers made their adieux to the Kings; they were not staying for the ball.

As soon as the cloth was drawn, Mrs King shepherded the ladies from the room, leaving the gentlemen to their port. The Palmers were not the only ones to leave directly after the dinner: Mrs Paterson departed to return to her convalescent husband; and the Judge-Advocate was perforce driven off to his 'stye'. Mr Harris reluctantly attended to the discreet obsequies of that dead-drunken gentleman after he finally keeled over, supervising the two impassive convict footmen who bore out to his carriage the man whose jurisdiction could spell life or death to such as themselves should they again transgress the law.

Seventeen

THERE WAS THE crunch of wheels on gravel as one after another, sometimes inelegantly jostling for place, equipages of various shapes and sizes drew up before the portico of Government House to deposit a new batch of guests, intent upon enjoying themselves at the vice-regal ball. For some, perhaps, enjoyment was not the main intention: there were a number who hoped to obtain a private word in the Governor's ear – or, failing that, in the ear of the Governor's lady; Josepha King was often known as her husband's 'Under Secretary'. Several of those carriages were as smart as any you might see upon the streets of London or Bath; but the horseflesh between their shafts was often in sad contrast to the shining paintwork and cushioned seats of those showy barouches, tandems, gigs and four-wheeled chaises.

Jane Austen, waiting amidst a knot of other ladies in the long drawing room, where the floor had been polished up and chalked to a fine slippery surface for the dancing to come, caught sight of Lieutenant Watson among the new arrivals. She observed how his face lit up when he spied her there, and gave an inward sigh, even as their glance met and a smile of acknowledgement curved her lips. Why did she attract such very young admirers, she wondered, thinking inevitably of Harris Bigg-Wither, whose eyes had held just such a spaniel-like expression of devotion.

Gazing upon the scene before her, she reflected that these new guests seemed noticeably to change the tenor of the evening, to create a different ambience. They conversed more loudly, were inclined to laugh somewhat immoderately, and altogether showed a quite noticeable lack of refinement and formality, compared with those who had dined at the Governor's table. It soon dawned upon Miss Austen and the Leigh Perrots that most of these later arrivals were in fact emancipists: former convicts who had served their sentences and were now translated into prosperous and presumably respectable citizens. The sentences of many felons who had arrived with the First Fleet of transports would, indeed, have expired more than a decade since. Well, it was evident that some, at least, had made good use of their ten years of freedom. Governor King was fond of declaring that the Government in England had not intended the prisoners to be consigned to oblivion and disgrace for ever. There seemed little fear of that where the present company was concerned.

'A remarkable metamorphosis,' James Leigh Perrot remarked at Jane's elbow. It seemed that his thoughts coincided with her own. He essayed a joke – 'From convict grub to emancipated moth!' – as he indicated the new arrivals being drawn towards the throng already clustered beneath the great glittering chandelier.

For darkness had now descended, with that suddenness to which they had grown accustomed: there was no subtle, lingering twilight here. Lanterns illuminated the night outside, and light shone forth from every window of the house.

Mrs King emerged from the throng with three of her guests in train; she came over to the Leigh Perrots and Miss Austen and introduced to them a Mr and Mrs Reibey – the latter a striking and extraordinarily self-assured young woman, stylishly attired in a gown of shot-silk blue-green taffeta – and a Mr Simeon Lord. He, like the Reibeys, was engaged in trade, they learned, and it emerged that he was about to become a near neighbour of the Governor, for he was building an ambitious residence close to the Tank Stream bridge.

'You will put us quite out of countenance with your *three* storeys, Mr Lord,' Mrs King chaffed him, at which that tall young man merely smiled and bowed.

Such a gathering of Kings and Lords! Jane Austen thought; she wondered if the wordless Mr Lord were one of those persons whose ploy was to maintain an enigmatic silence in company, and thus acquire a reputation for wisdom and discretion, whether deserved or not.

Mrs King swept off to other guests, and the Reibeys and Mr Lord began to talk amongst themselves in what Aunt Perrot considered an ill-bred manner; from what she could hear of their conversation, it appeared to centre exclusively upon the subject of commerce and profits. Her disapproval increased as she noted that Mrs Reibey seemed to hold as many opinions and to express herself with as much vigour as her male companions.

Then Mr Campbell bore down upon them. 'Have you met the Savages?' he asked.

For a wild moment Jane Austen imagined he must mean the *Aborigines*; the Savages, however, proved to be a tame naval couple lately arrived in the Colony, who followed meekly in Mr Campbell's wake.

'Mr Savage is our new assistant surgeon,' Mr Campbell informed them. 'He has been telling me of his intention to introduce the system of inoculation for the cow pocks here, as a safeguard against the small pocks. – I must confess that when I was in England, I was surprised to discover how widespread the practice has become.'

'Dr Jenner – as you know, it was he who made this great new discovery of such universal benefit to mankind – is of the opinion that *one* inoculation with the cow pocks variole will provide lifelong protection,' Mr Savage pronounced, warming to his subject. 'However, since the practice was introduced but four years ago, this can scarcely be proven yet.'

Mrs Leigh Perrot sighed. How tedious this talk of cow pocks was! Really, one could not imagine a more unlikely conversation for a ballroom. She gazed about in a disdainful manner. How insupportable it would be to pass many evenings in this manner – in such society! The insipidity and yet the noise; the nothingness and yet the self-importance of all these people!

Jane Austen, too, glanced idly about the room. She watched smiling acquaintances greet one another . . . she saw the hopeful, bored, guarded or self-revealing expressions of those who stood about alone . . . the inscrutable faces of the convict servants hastening to and fro. So many faces . . . quite a number of them, she observed, pitted with those telltale pocks. And *they*, she thought with a shiver, were the survivors of the disease.

At this point, all conversation was overlaid by the strains of the musicians striking up, and the ball was opened in the time-honoured manner, with the Governor and his Lady taking the floor in a stately minuet. Some robust contre-dances followed; these included Sir Roger de Coverley, now considered so *passé* in the best circles at home. As that old familiar tune was heard, Aunt Perrot glanced towards her niece and raised her eyebrows in a supercilious and disparaging manner; for her part, Jane thought it rather charming to hear the old refrain once more.

Much to her satisfaction, Miss Austen was sought as a partner for every dance, and was generous enough to grant three to Lieutenant Watson. She danced twice with the amiable William Chapman, once with Surgeon Harris (he, she thought, seemed agreeable enough), and once with Mr Flinders. She even took the floor with Captain Bunker, who, like many bulky men, proved surprisingly light upon his feet once he entered the dance. But it was most delightful of all to be sought out by Mr D'Arcy Wentworth, who, late in the evening, partnered her to the lantern-hung verandah for refreshments following the cotillion they had danced together. As they sat chatting lightheartedly, the musicians took up their instruments and to everyone's amazement launched into the tantalizing strains of one of the new *valses*. A gasp ran round the assembly . . . a *valse*, at Government House! Aunt Perrot's eyebrows ascended to their highest arc, this time to signify a very different reaction. She had not thought such a modern craze would already have come *here*! The Governor and his Lady again led the floor, as if to impress the vice-regal seal of approval upon the lilting tune; and, forsaking fruit punch and cheese-cakes, Miss Austen and Mr Wentworth returned to watch as other dancers gradually joined in. The Reibeys were the cynosure of every eye as they twirled over the gleaming floor, Mrs Reibey's gown swirling in iridescent kingfisher colours beneath the great chandelier.

'*Lypochrysops ignata*,' James Leigh Perrot murmured to himself from another corner of the room. A butterfly of the night . . . for sure, *she* was no moth!

'A remarkable woman, Mary Reibey, quite remarkable,' Mr Wentworth remarked in a tone of warm admiration. 'Remind me to tell you her extraordinary history sometime, Miss Austen. We do not usually speak of the – ah – recent past, here in the Colony. For obvious reasons: we have far too many secrets to keep dark, too many skeletons rattling in our cupboards! Our concentration, on the whole, is strictly upon the present and the future. But Mrs Reibey's circumstances were especially noteworthy . . .'

It was agreeable, Jane thought, to suppose that she and Mr Wentworth might have the opportunity to meet again . . . Then that intriguing gentleman turned to her, smiling provocatively. 'Do you dare to dance the *valse*, Miss Austen?'

'I – I believe I can muster up sufficient courage, sir!' Jane responded gaily; whereupon she found herself drawn upon his arm into that graceful, spinning, rather shocking dance. One of Mr Wentworth's gloved hands actually touched her waist while they circled the floor, and the other lightly clasped her fingertips. It was the most delightful sensation in the world. Jane herself was a naturally graceful dancer; moreover, she had carefully studied Mrs Reibey's steps during those first few moments; consequently, she was not ashamed of her own execution of the *valse*.

Jane's entry into the dance did not escape the notice of her aunt, as she sat chatting to little Mrs Savage. Mrs Leigh Perrot was displeased. The *valse* – such a vulgar dance! And Mr Wentworth . . . what exactly were his origins, she wondered. Jane so clearly taking delight in his company . . . no, she did not approve at all. She had just been telling Mrs Savage of their decision to remove to Parramatta for the remainder of their sojourn in the Colony.

'Mr Perrot has formed the opinion that his nature observations and butterfly hunting may be best conducted from Parramatta,' she told Mrs Savage, her gaze wandering across the room to watch her niece's progress. 'We hope to make the journey next week. Mr Chapman is to arrange accommodation for us.'

Mrs Savage's bright, birdlike eyes followed her gaze. 'Is not that your niece dancing with Mr Wentworth?' she asked ingenuously. 'How well they perform the *valse*! Such a gay dance –' She looked about a little wistfully to see if she could locate her husband. He was talking to Mr Harris in a far corner of the room, she observed, doubtless discussing symptoms and cures *ad infinitum* . . . 'They say that Mr Wentworth is the richest man in the Colony,' she continued artlessly. 'He came here as assistant surgeon, you know, the same post that my husband holds now, and served on Norfolk Island for a time. They say . . . but there, I do not believe half the things I have heard spoken of Mr Wentworth!'

'Indeed?' Mrs Leigh Perrot remarked encouragingly; and was profoundly disappointed when she realized Mrs Savage clearly intended to say no more upon the subject. No matter: she would make it her business to discover from other quarters what mysterious *things* were spoken of Mr D'Arcy Wentworth.

It was too soon for the eager and energetic, but high time for yawning chaperones and the stiff-legged, when the musicians put away their instruments at last. Carriages and chaises bore off the company; the lamps were extinguished; and the sentry with his musket returned to patrol the verandah, which a little while before had been the scene of refreshment and flirtation, and, for those who mingled their pleasure with commercial affairs, some profitable talk of business. Silence and darkness lay now upon Sydney town.

Within Government House, in an upstairs chamber behind the curtains of the vice-regal bed, Josepha King lay sleepily recalling haphazard aspects of the evening. In time, she mused, the breach with the Patersons must surely be healed . . . their friendship went back so many years, right to the time when they were all newly wed, and Mr King took up his appointment as Lieutenant-Governor of Norfolk Island . . . The mutton patties had been well up to standard, every last one consumed . . . and they had run out of catsup: she must instruct the housekeeper to prepare a fresh supply . . . Matthew Flinders had looked worn out, and so very thin – she must provide some hearty meals for him . . . how satisfactory to think he would soon be reunited with his wife! The Judge-Advocate . . . but no, she would not dwell upon that monster; 'twas a sure way to sleeplessness! The tune of the *valse* (had it been too daring to introduce it?) came into her mind, and she could not repress a little chuckle as she remembered one particular vignette.

'I do believe,' she said softly, addressing the recumbent figure that lay beside her, 'that D'Arcy Wentworth is halfway to making another of his conquests. Did you not see him almost sweep Miss Austen off her feet in the *valse*?'

A half-snore and an incoherent mumble was all the response she obtained.

'Of course, it would never do,' she continued musingly, 'besides, I am sure Miss Austen is much too sensible . . . but her aunt did hint of some disappointment her niece had suffered, and – well, would it not be pleasant if during her stay in the Colony, a harmless flirtation with Mr Wentworth could help her to forget it? She seems such an amiable young woman.'

Eighteen

U PON THE LEIGH PERROTS' removal from Sydney the
following week, there was a decision to be made: should
they travel to Parramatta by water or by road? The distance was
much the same either way, with the saving of a mere three miles
by land. In the end they decided upon the road; as Aunt Perrot
remarked; to be upon dry land still seemed a blessing after all
those months at sea. Besides, they had been warned that the
boat service was not reliable.

The evening preceding their departure they visited the Patersons to take wine. It was their first encounter with the Colonel,
who appeared to be more out of spirits than ailing in body.
However, he brightened when James Leigh Perrot engaged him
in conversation: it transpired the two men shared an equal
passion for natural history.

Mrs Paterson, cheerful, bustling soul that she was, drew the
ladies towards the fire; the room was pervaded by the spicy,
fragrant aroma of some native wood. Aunt Perrot was surprised
to see a fire lit – surely a needless extravagance, she thought.
The weather simply did not warrant it – she herself had resisted
every hint of Ellen's that a fire might be lit in their own cottage
. . . As Jane Austen spread her hands towards the pleasant blaze,
she was grateful for the warmth; she had heard her aunt pour
scorn on Ellen's well meaning suggestions with a wry sense of
familiarity: how often had she shivered at the Leigh Perrots'
house in Bath during a chilly English autumn!

'So you are off to Rose Hill,' said Mrs Paterson. '– Oh, pray
excuse me, I will give it the old name: I should say, Parramatta.

We called it Rose Hill in the old days, you know, but Governor Phillip was always eager to use the native names –'

'But Rose Hill is such a charming name,' Aunt Perrot said. Far preferable to the outlandish *Parramatta*, she thought. 'Roses are quite my favourite flowers.'

Mrs Paterson smiled. 'Perhaps it conjures up for you a picture of wild roses rambling everywhere – that, alas, is not the way of it. The settlement was first named for Mr Rose, Treasurer to the Navy – a very important individual, I am sure you will agree. 'Twas a prudent choice, I daresay!'

Mrs Leigh Perrot pursed her lips, feeling slightly foolish.

'There *are* native roses that grow there,' Mrs Patterson went on, 'that is to say, roses of a sort – quite pretty little flowers. And there are rosy little parrots we call Rose Hillers.'

Aunt Perrot thought nostalgically of the rose garden at Scarlets: the fat-petalled cushions of her damask roses; the pale, delicate China rose; the profusion of pink moss roses which she used to cut for the drawing room . . . why, just thinking of them, she could almost smell the glorious scent of the musk rose, her favourite of all.

'I am quite sure you will find Parramatta more agreeable, altogether less dusty and disreputable than Sydney,' Mrs Paterson went on. 'And I daresay your husband will be able to pursue his observations to his heart's content.' She spoke in a soft Scottish accent, with a delightful rolling of the 'r's' in Parramatta. She glanced across the room to where the two gentlemen sat deep in earnest conversation. 'The Colonel is a very keen naturalist, you know. As a young man he made several explorations in Africa, and even wrote an account of his journeys and all about the Hottentots.' She gave a little laugh, but only half in jest, as Jane Austen was quick to perceive. 'I sometimes think he would rather have devoted his life to fauna and flora than the Army – to the kangaru and the flannel flower, rather than redcoats and muskets!' She dropped her tone to a confiding murmur: 'Though he himself would vehemently deny that.' She sighed. 'He supervises the gardener who was sent out here by Sir Joseph Banks to collect the flora of the Colony. A Mr Caley . . . rather a *lady's man* . . . there has been some trouble . . . However, he appears to be a first-rate botanist, and his garden at Parramatta is a sight to behold. Dear me, Mr Paterson has sent so many specimens back to Sir Joseph Banks: not only plants, but rocks, insects —'

'Insects!' Aunt Perrot pounced upon the word with the agility of a grasshopper. 'Pray tell me, Mrs Paterson, are there as many cockroaches in Parramatta as exist here? Perrot tells me they are harmless, but I confess I find them quite disgusting, and so much larger than the English variety. They are enormous! And they are everywhere!'

Jane Austen completely shared her aunt's revulsion to the ubiquitous cockroach. — Why, only this evening she had opened her sea-trunk to take out her warmest pelisse, and three or four of the creatures, so hard and shiny and seemingly malevolent, had jumped out and scuttled off, to lurk evilly in some dark corner.

'Och, you will soon discover that all manner of insects are an everyday occurrence here,' was Mrs Paterson's blithe response. 'There are the wretched flies which plague us throughout the warm months . . . huge hairy spiders which crawl into the house . . . the crickets with their infernal din . . . hornets . . . swarms of beetles . . . and of course the dear, harmless little skinks!'

'You have omitted the mosquitoes, my dear,' Colonel Paterson remarked mildly, overhearing this catalogue of plagues.

'The mosquitoes!' his wife exclaimed. 'When *they* are at their height, we sleep beneath bed-nets, just as we used to do in India when we were stationed there.' Tactfully, she forbore to mention fleas. Fleas were everybody's personal problem.

Aunt and niece shuddered alike at this parade of wild life; clearly there was to be no escape from cockroaches at Parramatta. And what in the world were *skinks*, they each wondered privately. Better, perhaps, not to inquire . . .

But there were other things besides mere insects. Miss Austen devoutly hoped that in Parramatta there might be less evidence of the worst horrors of the penal system . . . the chain-gangs, for example, that toiled up and down Brickfield Hill each day; twelve wretches to each gang, all clad in yellow garments festooned with arrows and yoked to a cart loaded with bricks and tiles. She always averted her gaze from their staring eyes and straining limbs. Sometimes, she had heard, one or other of them would simply drop dead. Then there were the floggings . . . mercifully unobserved, but horrible to hear recounted. Ellen was always eager to pass on news of a flogging: the exact number of lashes, whether the prisoner had collapsed at the triangle . . . But worst of all, when one passed by the stone prison wall in Sergeant Major's Row, it was impossible to avoid noticing the bodies dangling from the gallows in the yard within . . . each victim 'executed agreeably to his sentence', as the official jargon so elegantly expressed it. As for walking along Pitt's Row, that street was scarcely more salubrious than Brickfield Hill, filled as it was with low taverns and gradually petering out into a line of squalid huts inhabited by Cyprians of the lowest sort. (Miss Austen had in fact ventured into Pitt's Row by accident.)

And yet, she had to admit, Sydney Town was not *all* chain-gangs, gallows, rum and prostitutes. She had purchased Chinese fans intended for Cassandra, Martha, her mother and Mary from a very pleasant little shop in Chapel Row; and she had greatly enjoyed visiting the Campbells' exotic garden down by the Wharf, with its camellias and peonies and those famous strutting peacocks which Mr Campbell had procured from India. And always, of course, there was the splendid spectacle of the harbour, glimpsed from a score of different aspects: blue, sparkling water beneath a clear azure sky. It certainly made a difference to one's spirits when the sky was always clear and blue and high – in striking contrast to the lowering clouds of England, and that incessant speculation concerning the likelihood of rain.

Just three days ago, Mr Flinders had kindly escorted her to Flagstaff Hill, some distance beyond the Hospital in the area known as 'The Rocks', where flimsy timber cabins were perched precariously on flinty outcrops sprouting ferns, and goats and bare-footed children climbed nimbly along the narrow tracks. On top of Flagstaff Hill, close by a windmill where a line of farmers had stood waiting their turn to grind corn, they had looked across to the line of distant hills, the abrupt western boundary of the Colony . . .

'I have seen the famous Blue Mountains at last, Mrs Paterson,' Jane said now, sipping her glass of wine. 'And no one could fail to understand why they are designated *blue*! But how tantalizing it is to be ignorant of what lies beyond them! Mr Flinders told me the Aborigines believe a mighty spirit dwells there, who hurls down thunder and lightning or sends a burning wind and flooding rain when he is angry.'

At this juncture a little maidservant appeared bearing plates of shortbread and seed cake, which she handed round timidly.

'Many of our own people are just as superstitious in their own way,' Elizabeth Paterson said. '– Hold the plate level, Mary, or you will tip the shortbread on the floor. There is a widespread belief that a race of Chinamen lives beyond the mountains. Some folk will even solemnly inform you that this continent is joined to Asia! – Hold *both* plates level, Mary: now the seed cake is in peril.'

Colonel Paterson came over and rescued the plate of short-bread from Mary's uncertain grasp. 'Countless wretches,' he observed in his pleasing lowland burr, 'must have attempted to escape to China, and perished on the way. Mr King was quick to issue a proclamation refuting this misconception, but the old tale dies hard. I suppose,' he added thoughtfully, 'it has an element of desperate *hope* about it . . . 'twas a tale oft repeated on the transports of the First Fleet.'

'Mr Paterson has seen more of the mountains than most of us,' their hostess remarked. 'An expedition which he led to try to find a way through was the very first attempt of its kind – was it not, my dear?'

A reminiscent smile lit the Colonel's tired features. 'Ah, that was back in the good old days,' he said wistfully. ' 'Twas when Major Grose was Commander of the Corps and acting Governor. We discovered the river which is named for him – it flows into the Hawkesbury. But we were soon forced to turn back; the going was too hard.'

'And what of the other attempts?' James Leigh Perrot asked.

'Well, there was George Bass' essay: he took along all manner of rock-scaling equipment, but it did not help him much – he did not get very far at all. You really cannot imagine, sir, what those jagged peaks and steep-sided valleys are like, so densely over-grown with thick bush. Mr Barrallier has come closest to success – he set out last year.' The Colonel smiled ironically. 'Mr King was pleased to bestow a grand title upon his attempt: 'twas called the "Embassy to the King of the Mountains"! His Excellency provided Mr Barrallier with a letter of credence – doubtless intended for the chief of any tribe which might inhabit there. His party advanced a good hundred miles, but was prevented from going farther by a huge waterfall. And so the "Ambassador" returned to Sydney with his credentials intact!'

'The barrier will surely be crossed one day,' Elizabeth Paterson said comfortably, observing with satisfaction that every piece of shortbread, made with her own hands from a family recipe, had been eaten.

'One day,' the Colonel agreed. 'Meanwhile,' he added with a heavy sigh, 'there is more than enough to concern and occupy us *this* side of the mountains . . . more than enough.'

It was disheartening to find Colonel Paterson quite so dispirited, and difficult to conceive that he had until recently been in full command of this rugged garrison.

'Mr Flinders spoke of the attempt made by Mr Bass,' Jane Austen recalled; indeed, he had spoken of Mr Bass with singular regard.

James Leigh Perrot repeated the name as though he had caught a familiar echo. 'Bass . . .' he murmured. 'Would that be the same Bass who published a paper on the anatomy of the waumbat? I should be eager to discuss it with him.'

Colonel Paterson nodded. 'Mr Bass,' he said a trifle drily, 'has also explored the anatomy of our coastline, and proved that a strait separates the mainland from Van Diemen's Land. But I fear, sir, you have missed the opportunity to make his acquaintance by several months: he sailed in February upon a trading voyage to South America, after which I believe he intends to return to England.'

Mr Leigh Perrot looked disappointed. 'I recall he also investigated the feeding habits of the black swan, and the behaviour of the white-capped albatross —'

'Poor Mr Bass,' Elizabeth Paterson broke in. 'He had to leave his wife in England to come here – they had just been married. That was two years ago. I know he longs to be with her – he hopes to profit by his trading voyage, and return home with a fortune.'

This had a curiously familiar ring to Miss Austen. 'How very like Mr Flinders' experience that sounds! What a pair of sad, romantic tales!' she exclaimed.

'We should receive word of George Bass soon,' the Colonel said. 'If ever a man deserves to profit from his enterprise, he does. They are a splendid pair, he and Flinders, a credit to the

Navy.' He seemed to have regained some of his lost spirits and smiled quite cheerfully at Jane. 'You talk of romantic tales, Miss Austen . . . Curiously enough, 'twas a romantic tale which first attracted Matthew Flinders to the notion of a sea-going career . . . a tale by Mr Daniel Defoe.'

'*Robinson Crusoe*', Jane exclaimed – yes, 'twas clear enough such a tale might well impress a young boy, and persuade him to go to sea.

'Precisely so, Miss Austen. We are fortunate to have in Mr Flinders such a very able explorer and surveyor,' the Colonel pronounced.

Mindful of the journey they were to take tomorrow, Mrs Leigh Perrot soon rose to take leave. 'We are to rattle to Parramatta by coach,' she said. 'I hear the road is hilly and the surface leaves much to be desired.'

'A real bone-shaking trip,' Mrs Paterson agreed cheerfully. 'And is Ellen going with you?'

'She is,' Mrs Leigh Perrot replied without enthusiasm. 'Still, if we were to dispense with her services, I daresay we might be landed with someone worse.' She thought longingly of the well-trained menials she was used to ordering about at home. She particularly missed Evans, whose self-effacing manner had concealed the quiet efficiency with which she ensured no tape or button ever went missing, no stocking remained undarned.

'We shall see our friends the Strongbows in Parramatta,' Jane Austen said eagerly. What importance short-lived acquaintanceship assumed in this sparsely populated settlement, she reflected. And yet, they had shared all those months at sea together. In truth, they had probably seen more of one another than one did of many of those old friends at home. But then, of course, it was the passage of time, the continuing observation of gradual change and development, which created depth of friendship, not mere frequency of meeting. 'The Strongbows intended to stay at Parramatta before taking up land in the Hawkesbury district,' she told Mrs Paterson. '– The *Oxbury*, as Ellen insists on calling it! I hope the twins are prospering,' she added, turning to her aunt. 'Rebecca will have her hands full, I daresay.'

'I wish you well in your observations, sir,' the Colonel told James Leigh Perrot. 'Be sure to make the acquaintance of the Lewins in Parramatta. John Lewin is an artist and a keen naturalist . . . his wife, too, is an artist, I believe.'

'Mrs Lewin's chief interest in the line of natural history pertains to *homo sapiens*,' Mrs Paterson told Aunt Perrot dryly. 'She excelled herself when Monsieur Baudin put into Sydney Cove, by making a double conquest of *both* the artists attached to his expedition.'

The Colonel cleared his throat. 'However that may be, my dear, I believe Mr Leigh Perrot will find he has much in common with Mr Lewin, who is presently compiling a Natural History of the lepidopterous insects of New South Wales.'

James Leigh Perrot blinked with interest. 'I thank you for that intelligence, sir! Lewin . . .' he muttered to himself. 'Lewin . . . ah yes, I have it! 'Twas a Lewin who compiled *The Birds of Great Britain*, a splendid work –'

'That was John Lewin's father,' the Colonel informed him.

Aunt Perrot did not care to hang about the threshold. 'Come, Perrot,' she urged. 'Leave off this talk of butterflies and birds. Think of the journey ahead of us.'

Upon their return to their cottage – a short walk skirting the parade ground of the Barracks – Ellen informed them that someone had called during their absence. Mrs Leigh Perrot was a trifle dismayed to learn who that caller was.

'Mr Wentworth, ma'am – a lovely man!' Ellen told her. 'Them's lucky what are assigned ter work fer 'im – 'e left this fer you, sir,' she added, handing a folded paper to her master.

Mrs Leigh Perrot watched her husband open the note with some misgiving.

' "Having learned from Mrs King – travelling to Parramatta – beg you will take the opportunity to visit Homebush along the way – offer some refreshment . . ." ' James Leigh Perrot skimmed the few sentences aloud. ' "Am returning there this evening – shall hope to see you, together with your esteemed lady and Miss Jane Austen – I remain, Sir, etcetera . . ." ' He handed the note to his wife, and Jane caught sight of the bold signature: D'Arcy Wentworth. 'Twas a signature worthy of a buccaneer, she thought!

'A civil gesture,' her uncle remarked mildly. 'I daresay we shall be glad of some refreshment along the way.'

His wife sighed. 'I do not see how we may very well avoid calling upon Mr Wentworth without seeming discourteous,' she assented unwillingly, 'since it was from Mrs King he learned of our departure, and since he has been to the trouble of leaving this note.' Then she added, largely for her niece's benefit, 'I have made a few inquiries concerning Mr Wentworth, and I find that he is nobody; nothing to do with the Strafford family – a mere distant cousin of Lord Fitzwilliam, it seems –'

'Such considerations, Aunt, do not count for as much here in the Colony, I believe,' Jane ventured, impelled to attempt a defence of Mr Wentworth. She was aware of the dislike her aunt had conceived for him. 'I have heard that Mr Wentworth is much respected as a magistrate,' she added.

'And I have been told by more than one informant that Mr Wentworth is the richest man in the Colony,' James Leigh Perrot stated unequivocally.

Mrs Leigh Perrot compressed her lips, then opened them to say: 'In this place money certainly appears to command more respect than rank. Mr Wentworth is also a great friend to the emancipists, it would appear.' She did not care, especially with Ellen still hovering there, to reveal what else she had heard concerning D'Arcy Wentworth: talk of a convict consort, a host of illegitimate children . . . and here was her own niece, not content with having made a spectacle of herself at the Governor's ball by dancing with such a man, defending him as a respected citizen.

The next instant Ellen astounded them by saying: 'There's plenty who tell as 'ow Mr W was on the high toby rig afore he come 'ere an' that by rights 'e should 'a bin below decks in the transport what brought 'im ter Sydney, 'stead of lording it as an officer on the top deck. But,' she added, quite taking any sting from her assertion. ' 'e's a rank plummy gent for all that.'

'The – er – *high toby rig*?' Mrs Leigh Perrot repeated, frowning. That particular expression had not been aired at the Scadding table. 'What do you mean, Ellen?'

'I means, missus, 'e were a scampsman – a highwayman!'

'Ellen!' her mistress was scandalized. 'How dare you speak so of your betters – be off this instant!'

The sullen look she wore so often descended upon Ellen's face as she slunk off to the back quarters, muttering beneath her breath. 'My betters! So sez her nabs – but 'twere jest by a fluke Mister W weren't done fer a scamp, that I know fer a *fact*!'

Jane Austen's complexion was heightened a little as she took up her candle and went to her room. She found the prospect of seeing Mr Wentworth again distinctly agreeable, she could not deny it. As she snuggled into her bed and blew out the candle, she smiled at Ellen's fanciful assertion. A highwayman indeed! Absurd. And yet – it was not absolutely beyond the bounds of possibility to imagine D'Arcy Wentworth's piercing blue eyes behind a mask, above a brace of pistols . . .

Westward to Parramatta . . . the four-wheeled closed chaise, drawn by two horses, in which the Leigh Perrots, their niece, their servant and their luggage were conveyed, jolted and jarred along that dusty, rutted, undulating route, and in the event, Mrs Leigh Perrot found herself anticipating their halt at Homebush with a sense of relief.

Once past the cow paddocks, pig-pens and smallholdings that clustered on the outskirts of Sydney town, they were in the wild bush, surrounded by unfamiliar grey-green trees. There was the tang of eucalyptus in their nostrils, and unfamiliar birdsong in their ears. Pink-and-grey galahs, yellow-crested cockatoos, the kookaburra with its maniac laugh, unseen bell-birds whose chinking call could be heard even above the noise of carriage wheels and horses' harness: all these, as well as many other vociferous feathered creatures flew and flitted, perched and swooped along the way, all eagerly observed and commented upon by James Leigh Perrot, who spent half the journey with head and shoulders thrust out of the carriage window.

Each time they ascended a rise and obtained a view of the country beyond, Jane Austen expected to see a fresh, a different prospect. Her expectation remained unfulfilled: this was not little England, with its quick variety; this was a landscape on the largest scale, offering a similar impression for mile after mile; any significant change of scene was so gradual as to be almost imperceptible.

Ellen was perched upon the box-seat beside the driver, whom she found a disappointingly silent fellow. He was a swarthy man, yet not unhandsome, a gypsy transported for selling stolen painted ponies at country horse fairs – a common practice of his people as they travelled from one parish to another. Possessing an inborn gift for handling horses, Jem Merrilees found his convict employment, first as a groom, then as a coachman, quite congenial; moreover, having lived his former life as a virtual outcast, a member of a tribe always on the move, his sense of displacement and exile in this far southern land was not so keenly felt as it might be by others who had known more settled lives in England.

Inside the chaise, swaying upon the shabby cushions, Jane was intrigued to observe her aunt's jaw in constant motion: she resembled nothing so much as a disdainful camel chewing the cud. Perhaps she had the tooth-ache, Jane thought, and was holding a clove in her mouth to bring relief. As the carriage turned off the road to enter Mr Wentworth's property, and began its progress along a drive bordered on either side by tall casuarina trees, Aunt Perrot raised a handkerchief to her lips, discreetly removed whatever she had been chewing and threw it from the window. Catching her niece's eye, a little confusion showed on her face.

'Ah, Jane, I daresay you wonder ... the whaling captain – Captain Bunker, you know, who was at the Governor's dinner, sent along this – this *chewing* substance to replace my peppermints. I find it not unpleasing; it resembles a soft toffee, and is flavoured with mint. But it does not adhere to one's teeth the way toffee does. The most remarkable thing about it, however, is that it does not melt. The flavour endures for a long time – one piece has lasted me all the way from Sydney. You must try some later on. Captain Bunker warned me on no account to swallow it; it has an elastic quality he told me, and could wrap itself around one's innards. He tells me 'tis much favoured by the sailors on his whaling boats. It originated, if you please, with the Indians in America, who obtain the substance from some tree. The sap – sappy something, I forget the name.'

'I think, my dear, you must mean the wild sapodilla or naseberry tree,' her husband interjected helpfully. 'A large evergreen.'

Aunt Perrot smiled fondly at her spouse. 'I am sure that is what I mean, my love.'

At that moment they drew up before the porch of Homebush House, a large, rambling dwelling which had been added to at various times to accommodate the growing needs of its occupants. And there to greet them was Mr Wentworth himself, wearing a smart silver-buttoned jacket and buff-coloured nankeen breeches which showed off his shapely calves.

'Welcome, welcome to Homebush!' he cried, striding forward to open the carriage door before Gypsy Jem had time to jump down and attend to that office. 'Dear ladies – Mr Leigh Perrot, sir – I am delighted to see you here.' And, having handed Aunt Perrot and Miss Jane Austen out of the carriage in a most gallant manner, he then stretched up a hand to Ellen and helped her to descend. There was a distressing flash of naked pink thigh as Ellen leapt down, her petticoats awry.

Uncle, aunt and niece were ushered into a large dining room, where a luncheon of cold meats awaited them, spread upon a long cedar table adorned with a veritable cornucopia of fruits. Smiling maidservants bustled to and fro with flasks of wine – the first contented-looking servants Jane had yet seen, she thought; they formed a striking contrast to the impassive footmen at Government House, and their own sulky Ellen. Clearly, it was no penance to be assigned to Mr Wentworth's household! The whole atmosphere was one of warmth and friendliness, with a degree of informality. In a curious way, it reminded Jane of the Rectory at Steventon in the old days.

There was the sound of children's laughter and running feet in the background; she caught sight of several boys and girls of various ages passing to and fro along the wide verandah that ran around the main part of the house. Although there was no mistress of this establishment to greet the travellers, a pleasant-looking, thirtyish woman whom Mr Wentworth addressed as 'Anne' appeared to be in charge of the servants and the children: she must be his housekeeper, Jane surmised.

Mr Wentworth sat in a high-backed chair at the head of the table – every inch the master of his domain, Jane thought. Presently he beckoned to two boys, aged about twelve and seven, who had appeared in the doorway.

'Allow me to present my sons, William and D'Arcy,' he said with fatherly pride. 'They are shortly to journey to England to obtain the benefit of a liberal education: as yet we are not able to provide suitable schooling here for those destined to become the future leaders of the Colony.'

The two boys were unmistakably the sons of their handsome father – though William, as Jane observed, had a slight cast in his left eye. They bowed and shook hands like little gentlemen, responded in correct, stilted phrases to a few ceremonious remarks from the Leigh Perrots, and were then released to rejoin their siblings outside; Jane spied them kicking off their shoes the moment they left the room. It was, she reminded herself, an irregular household: so many children, and none conceived in wedlock. And yet it was all so singularly harmonious . . .

Mrs Leigh Perrot had considerably more difficulty in adjusting to the irregular circumstances of her host; indeed, she experienced distinct embarrassment when the two boys were introduced, even though she knew their father had legally adopted them and given them his name. Casting about for a safe topic of conversation, her gaze fell upon the richly carved cedar sideboard. 'You have a very fine display of silver, Mr Wentworth,' she remarked stiffly.

'Some family pieces, madam,' he informed her casually. 'That silver and this seal' – he touched a fine cornelian set in gold that dangled from his fob – 'were my sole inheritance. My grandfather, the last of the family to inhabit our castle in Ireland, dissipated his fortune entirely, and my father was forced to enter business in County Armagh. – To be precise, ma'am' – here Mr Wentworth's blue eyes twinkled – 'he became the landlord of an hostelry. However,' he continued, striking a spark of pride, 'when I went to England to study surgery and walk the London hospitals, I saw a good deal of my kinsman Lord Fitzwilliam; he did not consider our fallen fortunes an impediment to friendship. Indeed, he and I still correspond – I have even conveyed to him a number of animals and birds for his estates.' At this point he turned to address Mr Leigh Perrot particularly. 'I first sent Lord Fitzwilliam an emu, sir, then a pair of black swans – one of which died, alas; next, as I recall, a pair of curious opossums; and most recently, a waumbat.'

Jane had a brief vision of a solitary swan, plumaged in perpetual mourning, afloat upon some far-distant lake. This catalogue of creatures reminded her of the old rhyme which began with a partridge in a pear tree . . . She was intrigued that Mr D'Arcy Wentworth, champion of the emancipists, should so obviously desire to draw his aristocratic connexion to their notice.

James Leigh Perrot nodded. 'It is quite remarkable how these native creatures are able to survive, even flourish, in England's much harsher climate. His Majesty has a herd of kangaru at Richmond, you know, and I believe the Earl of Salisbury keeps a pair of dingoes at Hatfield House. At Blenheim . . . the Duke of Marlborough . . . some great gliders –' his voice tailed off, leaving mere Lord Fitzwilliam quite eclipsed in such superior company.

Mr Wentworth smiled. 'And doubtless you are aware, sir, that a platypus was sent to Napoleon Bonaparte last year – a paradoxical token of the Peace, *n'est-ce pas*? I gather 'twas not very graciously received: his highness the First Consul made it known that he would have preferred a pair of kangaru to hop about the park at St Cloud. Perhaps he wished to emulate the King across *La Manche*!'

Mrs Leigh Perrot uttered a 'hmph' of patriotic displeasure. 'Scarcely a republican desire,' she commented.

'I rather doubt, ma'am, whether Bonaparte is a republican at heart.' Mr Wentworth took up a bunch of luscious purple grapes. 'Pray try some of these,' he urged. 'There is a perfect bloom upon the skins this year. Or perhaps you would prefer some figs – or apricots. Surely,' he went on, 'we have had ample proof in recent years that Bonaparte's main desire is undoubtedly the building of an empire.'

'And do you imagine he might be promoted to Emperor, Mr Wentworth?' Jane exclaimed, peeling an apricot with a little silver knife. 'How – how very Roman it would sound.'

'I believe he may promote himself to Emperor, Miss Austen,' Mr Wentworth replied, handing her a cluster of those delicious grapes.

'We assume the Peace still holds,' Mr Leigh Perrot put in. ' 'twas a fragile truce . . . if war has broken out again, I suppose it may be months before we shall hear of it. We are so far away –'

'One benefit to me from the Peace has been that I was able to arrange for a French sire to be sent out to my stable,' Mr Wentworth told them. 'I have a great interest in breeding racehorses. We already hold several meetings in the Colony. – Perhaps you would care to view my stables?'

'To me, sir, horses are merely the means of getting from one place to another,' James Leigh Perrot told him, by way of declining the invitation for himself. 'All I ask is that they have four sound legs and will not cast a shoe.'

'I should be most interested,' Jane averred; a tour of the stables seemed to present a splendid opportunity to talk *à deux* with Mr Wentworth – for surely her aunt would remain behind to keep her uncle company.

It so happened, however, that Jane Leigh Perrot had a considerable interest in horseflesh herself; she was an enthusiastic horsewoman, and was just about to inform Mr Wentworth of this fact, and join her niece in acceptance of his offer, when – she could not quite determine how it came about – she somehow found herself and Perrot being ushered out to view the gardens by the smiling housekeeper, while D'Arcy Wentworth and Miss Austen strolled off in the opposite direction. She had an uneasy feeling that she had been outmanoeuvred. 'I have never known Jane to take an interest in *horses* before,' she remarked to her husband in a somewhat peevish voice.

Entering the cobbled stableyard, Jane gave the satin-coated mares and geldings a rather perfunctory inspection.

D'Arcy Wentworth stopped at the stall where his prized French stallion was kept, and gazed in possessive admiration upon that splendid animal. 'I have called my beauty *Amitié*, since 'twas the Peace which brought him to me,' he told Miss Austen.

'I trust he will bring you luck,' she answered. 'Pray tell me, sir, why did you call your property *Homebush*?' Most wealthy colonists, she had noticed, chose to give their houses and estates names which carried an association with the land they had left behind.

Her companion shrugged. ' 'Twas one of those names which seem to turn up of their own accord. It is my home – it lies in the bush.'

Jane nodded at this pragmatic answer, and said thoughtfully: 'Yes, you *are* at home here; I sense that this is where you feel you belong. – In this Colony, this continent, this hemisphere, I mean.' She gave him a delightful smile. 'Of all those whom we have met so far, few seem to me truly content to be here. There are one or two – Mr Campbell certainly; the Palmers, I believe ... but so many others are hankering to go home, to be elsewhere. They talk constantly of the people, places, things they have left behind – it is almost as though they feel they have dropped out of life itself while they are here! Or, if they are not so positively desiring to leave, they are not absolutely desiring to stay, either: they seem to exist in a limbo of indecision, whether to stay or go.'

'That is perspicacious of you, Miss Austen; I do indeed feel this to be my home. I have no thought to return to live in England – or Ireland. But I assure you, there are many more of us who feel this way than you imagine. I suspect you have not had the opportunity to meet many of our humbler free settlers and emancipists, especially the latter, for whom this land unequivocally represents their future life. Few of them have either the desire or the means to return whence they came. I would wish,' Mr Wentworth continued, with a tinge of sadness in his voice, 'that some who chose to leave the Colony had stayed. Will Balmain, for example – a fellow surgeon and one of the truest friends a man could wish for. There were others . . . and now it seems certain George Bass will return to England. So I must part from another friend. Distance can be a cruel tyrant, Miss Austen.' He sighed then. 'I daresay that some who have gone might have chosen to stay had there been less dissension in the Colony. For myself, I do my best to remain outside all those tedious quarrels and disputes.' Then, with a determined change of mood, he smiled and said, 'If you would care to hear a truly unique name for a house, and the reason for it, I can tell you of one. Surgeon Harris intends to christen his residence "Ultimo" '.

'*Ultima Thule* . . . the end of the earth?' Jane hazarded.

'Nothing so poetic,' her companion assured her. 'Though in time I daresay it may become a modern myth. This is the way of it. – A few months ago, John Harris found himself in severe disfavour with his Commanding Officer – 'twas all caused by one of those ceaseless disputes between the Governor and the military. Even though he is a member of the Corps, Mr Harris is a staunch ally of the Governor, you know. I won't weary you with the details – suffice it to say that in the end, Harris found himself threatened with a court martial. However, in drawing up the charge, the half-educated felon assigned as a clerk made a stupid – or perhaps I had rather say a lucky – error. Instead of writing down "the 19th *instanter*" as the date of Mr Harris' alleged offence, he wrote "the 19th *ultimo*". Result: the charge was quashed, and we are to have Ultimo House to celebrate the fact!'

Jane laughed, and watched as Mr Wentworth entered a stall to inspect a chestnut gelding, running his hands expertly over one foreleg. 'I have hopes of this animal,' he told her. 'I had to chastise young William this morning – he galloped it around the home paddock without seeking my permission first, the scamp! – However, it seems no harm was done to you, my beauty,' he added, stroking the creature's nose affectionately. He was, Jane realized, secretly delighted by his son's boldness.

The escapade served to remind him of something else. 'Did I not promise, on the first and last occasion on which we met, to relate to you the tale of Molly Heydock – Mary Reibey, as she has since become?'

'I believe you did,' Jane answered, recalling that beautiful yet determined-looking young matron who had shone amidst the throng at the Governor's ball.

'Well then, Miss Austen, imagine if you please a vagabond boy, thirteen years of age, apprehended when attempting to sell a stolen horse: a brood mare, no less, worth a small fortune. This said boy is brought to trial and sentenced to death – which sentence is commuted to transportation. 'Tis a bold, rude boy who answers his accusers with spirit.' Mr Wentworth gentled the chestnut as he continued: 'And so this young vagabond is taken aboard a vessel bound for these Antipodes and, according to established custom, is forcibly stripped of his clothes and sluiced down before the ship weighs anchor. Upon which *he* is discovered to be a female – and a comely lass at that!'

'A well contrived plot, sir,' Jane observed approvingly. ' 'Tis almost worthy of a novel – though I daresay some critics would complain 'twas too contrived. But pray continue: you must explain the reason for such an impersonation, and tell how the metamorphosis from vagabond boy to the dazzling Mistress Reibey came about. For I deduce that to be the kernel of your story.'

'I believe I may satisfy both those demands,' Mr Wentworth responded, smiling. 'The boy's name was given as "James Borrow" at the trial: quite an apt *nom de guerre*, do you not think? But once the impersonation was revealed, *she* was put in skirts again, and it soon became evident she must belong to a family of some pretensions to breeding and education. She said her name was Molly Heydock.' He paused then. 'I do not wish to betray a confidence, Miss Austen, but I believe you to be one of those rare females upon whose discretion one may depend.'

Jane inclined her head, acknowledging the truth of this compliment to herself, if not to the rest of her sex.

'Well then, *in confidence*, Mary Reibey has told me herself that both her parents died when she was twelve years old, whereupon she was placed in the care of her grandmother and other relatives, who soon began to neglect and mistreat her. Being a high-spirited and wilful girl, 'twas then she ran away, assuming a boy's identity to give herself some measure of protection and a greater freedom. And so she fell in with sundry thieves and vagabonds of the King's highway.' There was a curious twist to his mouth as he uttered these last words. 'She arrived here – oh, ten years ago, and was assigned as nursemaid to Major Grose's family.'

Then he smiled, his blue eyes crinkling. 'There is yet another element to the story, Miss Austen. For upon the transport coming out, our heroine met her hero, Tom Reibey. He was employed by the East India Company in those days, and had taken passage *en route* to India in that same vessel. Off he went to Calcutta, but two years later he returned to settle here – and to marry Molly Heydock. There's a fine romantic twist for ye!' But his tone was ironic, as though, Jane thought, romance was something he had long ceased to believe in.

'Ever since,' the storyteller concluded, 'the pair of them have prospered mightily, first farming on the Hawkesbury, then setting up in business at Sydney. And now,' he said, 'you may perhaps understand my admiration for that lady.' He left the stall and rejoined Miss Austen in the cobbled courtyard.

'As I have not made the acquaintance of the lady for myself, *my* admiration must be for the excellent construction of your tale, sir,' Jane remarked. 'With hindsight, I suppose one might say 'twas a fortunate circumstance which led to the transportation of that vagabond boy: I daresay it saved your heroine from worse evil. To say nothing of her meeting with the hero!' She sighed. 'To counterbalance her story, I suppose there must be scores of less happy histories.' Her thoughts turned to Rebecca Ashcroft, falsely accused, by her own account, of the theft of a coral brooch. 'Do you think, Mr Wentworth, there are many miscarriages of justice?'

He shrugged. 'There are certainly plenty of convicts who protest their innocence and prate a plausible tale of wrongful arrest. As a magistrate, I am used to hearing just about every excuse a man – or woman – may devise. But,' he added with a wry smile, 'the miscarrying of justice may go the other way, you know, and a guilty party be let off scot-free, as the saying goes.' He nodded to himself. 'I have known of such a case.'

Now they were retracing their steps back to the house, and as they passed beneath an archway entwined with winter-flowering jasmine, so sweetly scented, Mr Wentworth said suddenly: 'I have heard that your good aunt was herself falsely accused of purloining goods from a shop, brought to trial and acquitted.'

'Oh,' said Jane, 'that is a great secret and only known to half the Colony.'

'One must admire her for seeing the business through,' he said, smiling. 'I daresay she could have bought off her accusers had she chosen to – 'tis a well-known ploy, and nine out of ten ladies in her situation would have done so.'

'I admire her for it too,' Jane told him. 'Sometimes I am apt to feel a little impatient with my aunt's opinions, but then I remind myself of what she has endured and try to be more forbearing.'

'Of course, by the time a tale comes full circle here, it is usually embellished beyond recognition,' Mr Wentworth told her ruefully.

Such was the pleasant ambience engendered by their *tête-à-tête* that Jane felt it on the tip of her tongue to relate the ridiculous remark Ellen had made about Mr Wentworth himself being a *high toby man* . . . but at that very instant they were interrupted by Aunt Perrot's imperious summons.

'Oh, there you are! We should be off this moment – the chaise is ready to start off.'

Whereupon, after taking a civil but scarcely effusive farewell of their host, Mrs Leigh Perrot led the way to the carriage, where Gypsy Jem was already seated upon the box, reins gathered up. She stepped inside and settled herself against the dusty cushions, followed by her husband.

'Goodbye, Miss Austen – we will see each other in Parramatta before too long, I trust,' Mr Wentworth said, taking Jane's hand.

Ellen was hovering behind him – a beaming Ellen, singularly transformed by her pleasant visit to the kitchen quarters of this friendly household. To her delight, Mr Wentworth hoisted her up to her place alongside the driver's seat (there was another startling glimpse of bare pink flesh) and then Jem turned the horses' heads towards the Parramatta road. He had indulged in a tankard of rum in the tack room, and for the remainder of their journey Ellen found him almost overly loquacious, in contrast to his former silence. In addition she had frequently to admonish him to keep his hands upon the reins.

'An irregular household,' Aunt Perrot pronounced once they had joined the westward road again. 'Most unusual. All those children. – Dear me, how the carriage sways! Do you imagine the driver can have been drinking?'

'I believe,' Jane said with what her aunt would doubtless consider a certain lack of decorum, 'that quite a number of gentlemen in the Colony have found irregular consolation for their single state, and fathered children whom they have then legally adopted. Governor King himself –' She gave a rather mischievous smile.

'My dear Jane, you have been listening to salacious gossip!' Aunt Perrot exclaimed. 'I do not consider it fit that a young woman such as yourself –'

At this point her husband felt obliged to enter the conversation. 'Ahem, my dear – the visit passed off well, I think. And by his own account, Mr Wentworth appears quite well connected. Lord Fitzwilliam – his family castle –'

'Oh, pish,' Mrs Leigh Perrot said in her most dismissive manner. 'Those Irish baronets are two a penny; and every family in Ireland lives in what they are pleased to call a *castle* – usually 'tis nothing more than a big, draughty old house reeking of turf fires.' She looked quite affronted.

Jane sought to restore harmony. 'I do believe I should like to try a piece of Captain Bunker's mint toffee, Aunt,' she said meekly; upon which Aunt Perrot, somewhat mollified, and satisfied, moreover, that she had pronounced the last word upon the subject of Mr D'Arcy Wentworth, produced a little square of that substance, which Jane placed in her mouth.

'Take care you do not swallow it,' she warned her niece.

Her husband then professed his willingness to try it as well – and for the rest of the journey, they all three sat within the carriage, jaws working ruminatively, as they dwelt upon their separate and disparate thoughts. Jane pondered on the romantic story of Mary Reibey, and the refrain of an old rhyme ran through her head: 'If wishes were horses then beggars would ride. Put beggars on horseback and then – woe betide!'

Nineteen

THE MOVE TO Parramatta was definitely for the best. Their new, shingle-roofed, single-storeyed house on the western road was superior to the cottage they had occupied at Sydney, and further distinguished by an orange tree growing in the little garden at the front.

'Marmalade!' Aunt Perrot declared as soon as she clapped eyes on the tree. 'I daresay one may concoct marmalade from oranges as well as quinces.' And she resolved to set about instructing Ellen in the mystery of its making.

'A pity there will not be time for a batch of orange wine to ferment,' Jane remarked. It had been their favourite brew at Steventon.

There was less evidence of the military here in Parramatta – those red and white galloots, as Ellen called them; and the chain gangs they encountered were engaged chiefly in agricultural toil. The Female Factory, both penitentiary for wrongdoers and workplace for women not assigned to other service (their manufacture was the rough cloth that fashioned convict garments), was situated a discreet distance from the town, across a bridge that spanned the river. It was possible to take agreeable walks in Parramatta, undisturbed by the more grossly distressing sights of Sydney. And, unlike Sydney, this settlement had not been plucked clean of every tree: as a result, there was a softening effect of light and shade along its roads and pathways. There were a number of quite reasonable shops, and, inevitably, a fair sprinkling of taverns – the most picturesque being The Red Cow, set in a green garden with a picket fence. And on Sundays, the Leigh Perrots and Miss Austen dutifully attended the new church of St John, where the oldest tombstone in the graveyard had been set up a mere decade ago.

James Leigh Perrot was heart-content to wander the banks of the Hawkesbury, notebook in hand, watching the teeming birdlife and seeking out specimens of flora. Sometimes he went farther afield, to Seven Hills or Toongabbie and towards Green Hills, in search of larger fauna in the thick scrub: kangaru, wallaby, bandicoot or waumbat. His success in discovering the secret place of the platypus, the underground lair of the waumbat, was due to the fact that he acquired a willing companion and helper, a native boy about eight years old, himself an object of natural wonder with his dark skin, slender limbs, liquid eyes and engaging grin.

Bingami was an orphan of one of the tribes, now broken and scattered, which had inhabited the banks of the Hawkesbury before the advent of the European. Intensely curious, he had watched one day as the white man, notebook in hand, strolled through the bush, stooping occasionally to peer at a plant. He saw to his amazement that the white man had two pairs of eyes; he would use both pairs when he wrote something in his notebook, but pushed one pair on to his forehead when he looked into the distance. Now and then he would pluck some plant or branch and put it in a dilly bag slung from one shoulder. He seemed to be food gathering, and Bingami was puzzled that his women did not do that for him. He knew that in the white man's camp, this old one lived in the place where the tree of sweet juicy fruit grew; often at night a small black shadow would flit into that garden and take as many oranges as could be carried in two hands cupped together. The old one had three women, Bingami had discovered.

At length, having ascertained that this white man did not carry a fire-spitting stick like the one which had thrown death at his father, Bingami found courage to approach him; and when James managed to convey that he merely wished to collect specimens, edible or inedible as they might be, Bingami quite simply attached himself to him to assist in this strange endeavour. They made a strange pair, the staid English gentleman uprooted from the formal parkland at Scarlets and the smooth pavements of Bath, and the Aboriginal boy torn from his tribal way of life in the wild bush; yet they soon formed a companionable bond, curiously resembling that of grandfather and grandson. In time, Bingami took up his residence in a lean-to shelter at the back of the Leigh Perrots' cottage. He gathered kindling for Ellen, and presently acquired a tame magpie, a stalwart black-and-white creature with a rapacious eye, a sharp beak and a mellifluous yodelling call. This bird became the guardian of the orange-tree; it would make low, disconcerting swoops upon ladies' bonnets and gentlemen's hats, or else peck at the ankles of visitors as they made their way to the front door.

The pursuit of the butterfly, James Leigh Perrot's true passion, must await the passing of winter and the metamorphosis of chrysalis into butterfly . . . Meanwhile, he acquired a goodly collection of plant specimens which his niece diligently helped to press, recording the name, if it were known, beneath each one. Sometimes Bingami would supply a name in his own language; guessing at the possible spelling, Jane would write that down as well. It seemed, James Perrot realized, as though the Aborigines named only those plants or trees which were of use for food or shelter or to make fire. A primitive, practical use of language. Some of the native flowers Jane thought delightful, and she attempted a few paintings . . . the strange spider flowers, for example, the red and grey grevilleas, and the yellow-gold mimosa with its feathery leaves and sharp, peppery scent. From earliest days the colonists had used the supple branches of the mimosa to build their simplest dwellings, intertwining them with mud in the immemorial process of wattling and daubing – and so this lovely plant had acquired the common name of 'wattle'. It occurred to Jane that, naming the mimosa in this way, the pragmatic colonists had followed the same practice as Bingami's people.

Mrs Leigh Perrot surprised both her husband and her niece by reviving a pastime she had much enjoyed during her youth. She would hire a mare from the livery stable attached to the blacksmith's forge and go riding at least thrice a week. The exercise was beneficial both to her liver and her disposition.

Ellen had acquired a persistent admirer in Gypsy Jem, who came regularly from Sydney to court her; as a result her sullen demeanour seemed to melt away. Aunt Perrot was under no illusion as to what transpired in the back room of the cottage when Jem came visiting, but was prepared to overlook such goings on if the result was this improved version of Ellen. Furthermore, upon encountering Mrs Leigh Perrot one morning mounted on her mare, Jem had the good sense to compliment her horsewomanship, which made her incline quite kindly towards him, gypsy and felon though he was.

As for Jane Austen, for some time now she had looked forward to making the acquaintance of Mrs McArthur, that Elizabeth McArthur whose name graced the farm in Parramatta which was her home, and which she now supervised during her husband's prolonged absence in England. So uniformly admiring was every comment Jane had heard expressed regarding Mrs McArthur that she had almost made up her mind to mislike the lady before ever she set eyes upon her. In the event, however, she discovered in Elizabeth McArthur a charming, intelligent woman in her mid-thirties, with whom she felt sure she could have struck up a true and lasting friendship, had time permitted.

Elizabeth Farm, built ten years ago, was a low brick dwelling surrounded by a pleasant garden of fruit trees and native shrubs, and having a hundred acres of arable and grazing land. The garden sloped down to a creek, and the bricks that had built the house, each stamped with its convict arrow, had been made from clay dug out of the creek banks. The whole house, indeed, had been conjured and constructed out of the natural materials around it. Sturdy ironbarks had been felled to supply its timbers; the roof was made of swamp-oak shingles; inside, local cedar, resembling rich mahogany, had been used for doors and skirting-boards and furniture. It was a house that would grow through the years; already the McArthurs had added elegant curved annexes to the two large rooms on either side of the central hallway.

Jane and Elizabeth – they soon progressed to first-name terms – would often sit on the stone-flagged verandah overlooking the garden, while three-year-old William, youngest of the McArthur children, played under the apple trees, his mamma keeping a watchful eye upon him. Sometimes the sound of music would float out to the verandah from the room where one or other of Elizabeth's two younger daughters, Mary and Emmeline, sat practising the piano.

Jane admired the calm competence displayed by Elizabeth

McArthur in running the farm and ordering its convict work-force as well as attending to her husband's varied business affairs while he was away. Her devotion to her husband was quite remarkable; she appeared serenely confident of his genius, and consequently of his superiority not only to herself but to the world in general. She was quite dedicated to his chief ambition, the introduction of the wool industry to the Colony through the breeding of merino sheep.

During her time at Sydney, Jane had heard so many unfavour-able opinions of Captain McArthur that, meeting his loyal wife, she wished she might also have had the opportunity to make the acquaintance of that controversial gentleman himself, and form her own opinion of his character. It was hard to reconcile the impressions of him which she had received from Mr Campbell, from the Kings and Patersons, among others, with Elizabeth McArthur's uxorious pride. Just the other day, Governor King had referred to Captain McArthur in the strongest terms imaginable, and his words were soon repeated throughout the Colony. His Excellency had now received the unwelcome news of the Captain's favourable reception in England, where his court martial appeared to be indefinitely deferred. 'Experience has convinced every man in this Colony,' the Governor had declared with choler, 'that there are no resources which art, cunning, impudence and a pair of basilisk eyes can afford that he does not put in practice to obtain any point he undertakes. – And now, by God, he has obtained the favour of Lord Camden!'

Simply to judge from what she knew of Captain McArthur's actions – the grievous wound he had given Colonel Paterson in that fateful duel appeared the most extreme example – it seemed clear to Jane that he must be an ambitious, impatient, ruthless man, both impudent and imprudent. As for that grand scheme to introduce the wool industry, was that to be ascribed to a vision of prosperity for New South Wales, or to per-sonal aggrandizement? – A mixture of motives, she suspected shrewdly, as in most human endeavour.

'My husband is so impulsive. He cannot compromise – he is nobody's "obedient servant".' – That was the very nearest to a criticism of her husband that Elizabeth McArthur voiced to Jane Austen. But was there not one simple explanation for her unshakable devotion to this man? He was her husband, she had borne his children; their destiny was irrevocably entwined. It seemed theirs was a love match which had endured; and when love is admitted as a factor in any argument, the most irrational conclusions may be happily arrived at. Yet clearly Elizabeth McArthur was far from being a mere complaisant and dutiful wife. On the contrary, she was a high-spirited woman of considerable accomplishment who had won her own leading place in this little society.

'You cannot imagine, my dear Jane,' she declared one afternoon, 'how I longed for congenial female company when we first came to the Colony, thirteen years ago. I had not one female friend I could unbend to, or to whom I could converse with any satisfaction to myself.' She sighed. 'I was absolutely delighted when the Patersons and the Kings arrived all those years ago. Elizabeth Paterson is so very amiable and intelligent, and Josepha King' – she hesitated slightly – 'is possessed of a great share of good nature and frankness.' She glanced across the garden to see what William was up to. 'William! You are not to go down to the creek. Come here, sir! – As you must know,' she continued with a sorrowful note in her voice, 'those friendships have been grievously disrupted by recent events. – *Interrupted*, I prefer to say; I feel sure that once the gentlemen have resolved their present difficulties, we three ladies will resume our former close companionship. – *William!* Come down from that tree!'

Jane was much struck by Elizabeth's refusal to despair at the present unhappy situation concerning her husband and Mr King. If female persuasion and good sense could do anything to heal that breach, she felt sure Elizabeth would do her utmost to achieve it. And then, as the mother went to lift down her son from the olive tree, her thoughts turned to her sister and to Martha Lloyd, her own two closest female companions. Yes, she decided, even had she herself attained the most amiable husband, the most ardent lover in the world, her need of female companionship would surely have been the same.

Elizabeth administered a not very stern rebuke to William and sent him off to play with his spinning-top. 'He is such a rascal,' she said fondly. 'Oh, I have so often wished there were doting grandparents here to help bring up my children! I have missed my own family so very much over the years. They live in Cornwall – our family has inhabited the same old farmhouse for several generations.' She sighed. 'My mother was almost heart-broken when she learned of our decision to come here, after we were married. But I told her that if we must be distant from each other, 'twas much the same whether I were two hundred or far more than as many thousand miles away. I reminded her that the same Providence watches over us here as there and the same sun shines upon us both —'

'With more powerful effect here, however!' Jane put in lightly.

Elizabeth smiled. 'That little speech to my mamma was made before ever I experienced the full strength of the Antipodean sun!'

Thoughts of her home led Elizabeth to further reminiscences. 'When Mr McArthur first appeared upon the scene, my father did not consider him at all suitable as a future son-in-law,' she told Jane with engaging candour. ' 'Twas not for any social inequality,' she added hastily, wondering if Miss Austen had heard the rumour that her husband was once apprenticed to a stays-maker (someone had unkindly nicknamed him 'Jack Bodice', she had been told). 'Mr McArthur's father was a Scottish gentleman who fought at Culloden alongside his seven brothers,' she said firmly. 'He was the sole survivor of them all, and escaped to live in the West Indies, then returned to settle in Plymouth and married there. So my husband belongs to the West Country, too.' She shook her head. 'No, my father thought that Mr McArthur's manner when he came courting me was too proud and haughty for the humble fortune and expectations that would, it seemed, be our lot.'

'Fathers are apt to believe no suitor is worthy of their daughters,' Jane commented.

Elizabeth gave a little grimace. 'I daresay you are right in many instances; however, *I* was considered shamefully indolent and inactive by my family. They were forever scolding me! No, Jane — I offer in myself an example of the fact that it is not always, with all our wise foreseeings, those marriages which promise most or least happiness that prove in their result such as our family or friends may predict. Few of my friends, I am certain, thought when I married that either Mr McArthur or myself had taken a prudent step.' She paused to look about her and then spread out her arms in an all-embracing gesture that took in her pleasant house, the many acres round about, the fruitful garden that lay before them. 'Yet see how bountifully Providence has dealt with us!' she cried.

Another day they wandered through the orchard picking some of the apple crop. The winter sunshine was warm, caressing.

'Is this not a garden of Eden?' Elizabeth said, laughing and holding out a rosy apple. 'See, we have the apple – the snake too, I fear – and so much else besides! I cannot truly say that I am homesick for England. How could I be unhappy here? I pine for my husband, of course – but to feel that we have such a part to play in this new land: that, I think, is a privilege that comes to few. Oh, you should hear my husband upon the future for the Colony which he envisages! Sometimes I wonder how one lifetime may accomplish it all, and almost fear he must harbour some delusion of immortality! Consider all this' – she swept her arm about the orchard, the apple, almond, apricot and pear trees – 'here is one of the finest climates in the world. The necessaries of life are abundant, the soil fruitful –' Then she shook her head and dropped her arm to her side. 'There is only one circumstance that could possibly induce me to wish for a change, and that is the difficulty of educating our children, and having to send them away to England. Both my two eldest sons and my daughter Elizabeth went with my husband, you know. It is so hard to be parted from them, and for them to be parted from us. Poor little John! When he bade me farewell he scarce shed a tear, not realizing what this parting meant – alas, I hear he has shed many since. And yet the alternative would be to entrust their education to the tuition of some emancipated convict gentleman, or uneducated clerk – unthinkable!'

Jane recalled her own experience of being sent away to school: she and Cassandra had gone first to Oxford for a few months, to receive lessons there, but Jane herself had nearly died of a putrid fever, and they had immediately been fetched home by their anxious parents. Then they had gone to the Abbey school at Reading, a superior academy for young ladies. She spoke of this, whereupon Elizabeth McArthur exclaimed: 'So – you are one of these modern, educated women!'

'Oh! I scrambled into a little education, without any danger of becoming a prodigy, I do assure you!' Jane replied lightly. 'In truth, I learned far more from my father and from his library than ever I did at school.'

Elizabeth smiled. 'When I first came here, there was such a lack of companionship and I was at such loose ends that I set myself to study astronomy, under the tutorship of Mr Dawes – 'twas he who designed the observatory in Sydney – then botany . . . and music as well. I blush to think of my attempts to understand the intricacies of astronomy; botany I found more within my abilities – and 'twas not long before I could play "God Save the King" on the piano!' She smiled. 'After that – well, along came the children, and now there is scarce time to accomplish all that must be done within each day! I marvel now to think that ever I found time hanging upon my hands.'

Jane remarked that Elizabeth's passionate appreciation of this land, and her sentiments concerning its future, seemed to echo the feelings expressed by Mr Campbell . . . and Mr D'Arcy Wentworth. When she mentioned Mr Wentworth's name, Elizabeth gave a very womanly and comprehending smile. 'Ah, the charming Mr Wentworth,' she responded with an affectionate yet guarded note in her voice. 'I have yet to meet the female who can resist him.' She added casually, 'When you stopped at Homebush, I daresay you met a woman there – Anne Lawes?'

'Why yes, there was someone,' Jane answered. 'I heard him call her "Anne". I took her to be his housekeeper.' Even as she said this, she realized perfectly the plain truth of the matter; she hoped she had successfully concealed her schoolgirlish confusion.

Elizabeth gave a light laugh, which was, however, quite without malice, and placed her rosy apple in the basket that lay at their feet. 'His *concubine*, my dear Jane,' she said unequivocally '– that is the official term coined in the Colonial Office for a convict mistress. Quaint, is it not? Mr Wentworth has broken many hearts in his time, but prefers to remain apart from holy matrimony.' She shrugged. 'It appears that Anne Lawes – a decent enough soul – has now succeeded his late lamented Catherine.'

'Indeed,' Jane commented impartially. What did it matter, she asked herself, how many *concubines* D'Arcy Wentworth might take unto himself? She attempted a suitably lighthearted response. 'You will scarcely believe this,' she told Elizabeth, 'but Ellen, our servant, solemnly assured us before we visited

Homebush that Mr Wentworth had been a highwayman – a high toby man, in her parlance!'

To her considerable surprise, a small and slightly awkward silence ensued, until, attempting an equal lightheartedness, Elizabeth said: 'Oh, as to Mr Wentworth's mysterious past, *he* is the only person who could possibly explain that. But,' she added significantly, 'it might be better not to ask him. There is an unwritten rule here, you know: never to inquire too strictly into anyone's former life! It could so often prove embarrassing . . . as though one had asked a frog to recall the tadpole –'

'– or a butterfly the caterpillar,' Jane suggested with a smile. It was a simile nearer home.

Upon which they resumed their fruit picking, while the infant William, unobserved, sank his small teeth into his third apple.

There was a pleasant reunion in Parramatta with the Strongbows. Their twin sons, now most usually referred to as Zeke and Jos, were thriving. Rebecca, too, seemed content in her role of nursemaid. Her bright, fresh young looks had, it seemed, attracted the respectful attention of a young soldier, Harry Rogers, scarcely more than a lad himself. Emma Strongbow told Miss Jane Austen and Mrs Leigh Perrot that she permitted Rebecca to walk home with Harry from church each Sunday; their attachment, she said, had flourished quite amazingly between church porch and garden gate.

'I should like your advice, Mrs Leigh Perrot,' she said earnestly. 'Do you think I should allow these two young people to meet more often? I am aware of my responsibility for Rebecca's moral welfare.'

On this occasion the ladies were sitting in the garden of the Strongbows' cottage. The twins had been set down upon a blanket on the grass, while Rebecca herself attended to some laundry.

Aunt Perrot, who allowed Ellen a laxity she would never dreamed of permitting amongst her servants at home, thought briefly of the squeals and rustlings that emanated from the back room when Gypsy Jem came courting. 'The moral welfare of one's female servants is of the utmost importance,' she pronounced; and had the grace to drop her glance from Emma

Strongbow's clear inquiring gaze. 'Especially,' she added, 'in such an immoral atmosphere as this. I would be in favour of *retarding* the relationship as much as possible . . .'

Hanging linen up to dry, Rebecca overheard this exchange. 'The old cow!' she thought furiously, glowering in the direction of that nice Miss Austen's stuck-up old aunt.

On another occasion, when Jane had gone alone to visit at the Strongbows' cottage, she learned from Rebecca herself that she was persevering with her reading. She told Miss Austen that she used to take the weekly *Gazette*, once her employers had finished with it, to some quiet corner and pore over its columns, laboriously tracing the lines with her forefinger.

The *Sydney Gazette and Advertiser* had come into circulation just this year. Circumscribed and censored as it was, each issue was nonetheless eagerly awaited by the colonists. Mr King had appointed an educated convict called George Howe, a West Indian formerly known by the name of 'Happy George', who had once worked on the London *Times*, to produce this newspaper. He was known in official jargon as 'the Government Printer'. The first issue had opened with a plain indication of the close watch to be kept by Authority over its columns, lest any subversive or scurrilous matter should appear: 'We open no channel to Political Discussion or Personal Animadversion' it stated uncompromisingly. Howe's office was a ramshackle shed behind Government House; here he sorted out the news, official announcements, shipping notes and advertisements which he had collected, wrote them up, then went to the Governor's Secretary to present his copy for inspection and approval. Returning to his shed, he would crank up the press and turn out the finished copies.

'But for some terrible long words I ain't never heard before I c'n manage it quite fair,' Rebecca told Jane proudly. 'I c'n read all them 'vertisements what folk put in to buy and sell goods – I like 'em the best!'

Jane smiled and thought perhaps she agreed with this preference. She recalled reading one such advertisement in the latest issue which had inevitably reminded her of Mary, her sister-in-law . . . 'To be disposed of by Private Contract,' it had stated, 'a capital English Mangle, in all respects as good as new.'

'I saw as 'ow Mister Harris 'ad 'vertised for a book of his what 'ad gone missing,' Rebecca said.

'I daresay he loaned it to a friend,' Jane said lightly. 'People are notoriously apt to forget to return the books they borrow.'

Rebecca gave her a shrewd look. 'Oh, a gentleman may *forget* to return a book. For common folk, 'tis called *thieving*.'

Jane sighed. How could she rebuke Rebecca for impudence, when the girl spoke out of her own unfortunate experience? Then her thoughts turned to Surgeon Harris. She imagined him turning the pages of his books as he sat in his little parlour, which was neat and shining as a new pin.

Mr Harris had built a gentleman's cottage on land close to Elizabeth Farm – just a brief stroll, in fact, from Mrs McArthur's garden. The surgeon's duties were divided between Sydney and Parramatta: he was in attendance at Parramatta on Tuesdays and Saturdays, and usually spent Sunday there as well. Jane had visited his pretty little house with Elizabeth McArthur; and while they spent a pleasant hour, he had come to some conclusions about her. Indeed, he had appraised Miss Austen with a faint gleam of honourable speculation. For John Harris was as yet unmarried. She was, he thought, a pleasing young – well, youngish – woman; her clear hazel eyes sparkled with intelligence. But he knew that Miss Austen would never be content to stay in this sun-drenched Colony. She belonged indisputably to that other, misty English world of subtle lights and shades. She was alien to this place; and had she by some amazing chance elected to remain, she would always appear so. He could not explain to himself exactly why he should be so certain of this; it was scarcely a scientific conviction. It was just that after any length of time in the Colony, one seemed to acquire an instinct as to who would adapt to life here and who would not ... related, somehow, to the instinctive knowledge of which plants or trees introduced from other lands were likely to put down their roots and thrive, and which would droop, decline, and wither.

There was always some building work being carried out in the vicinity of Elizabeth Farm, and a saw-pit was situated a little distance from the house. Here, two convicts wielded the huge double-handled saw that cut the ironbark logs into roof beams and floor joists. A rough platform was erected above the pit; on this one man stood while the other worked below, standing in the pit itself. The log would be laid across the pit, and the two convicts then worked together, pushing and pulling the great saw up and down in a vertical motion until it was sawn through.

It was unfortunate, as it turned out, that Jane, together with her aunt and uncle, should have accepted Elizabeth McArthur's invitation to accompany her on a tour of her property the very day that Nathaniel Benson had been assigned to the saw-pit. Convicts of very strong physique were notoriously few: so many were men of puny build from city slum or village hovel, rickety, consumptive, syphilitic, their health further undermined by the long passage to the Colony. The McArthurs' overseer would not normally have chosen Nat Benson, a wizened forty-year-old, to work in the saw-pit, but during the last few days a sudden wintry wind had caused an outbreak of coughs and colds. The convict quarters were filled with rheumy eyes, running noses and graveyard coughs; and Nat was one of the least affected. The upper sawyer was known as 'the Pug'; he was a strong enough fellow, a former prize-fighter, in fact; his felony had been to fall into a blind rage and throttle a man to death in a tavern brawl. The Pug was used to the saw-pit, but not to such a weakling as Nat Benson at the other end of the great saw. The work had gone slowly all day, with no rhythm to the sawing: it was a case of a quick stroke down and a painfully delayed upward haul.

As Mrs McArthur and her visitors drew near, a new log had just been hauled up and laid across the pit. The Pug shouted down to Nat: 'Come on now, make an effort, man! Here's the Missus come to watch us split this log!' And with a dash of showmanship left over from his prize-fighting days, he spat on both hands, then clove down with a mighty thrust. Nat's chest was already bursting, his arms and shoulders in agony, his hands blistered from the ceaseless effort of pulling and pushing from below. He looked up to catch the Pug's words, and the latter's sudden sweep down caught him by surprise; he had relaxed his grip upon the saw handle, and now the great blade, lacking the force from below which would have helped it to bite into the new log, slipped over the curved surface, swung out at an angle, and its wicked sharklike teeth slashed into Nat's upturned face and clove across his upper body, slicing through his neck so that his head dangled grotesquely from his still standing trunk. His dreadful scream was cut off short in a bubbling cry as his life's blood spurted out and he went down into the sawdust.

Although neither Elizabeth McArthur nor her visitors could actually see into the pit from where they stood, it was all too evident that some ghastly accident had occurred. The Pug stood gazing down at that hideous scarlet sodden thing below him, then turned aside to retch and vomit. Shaking from the proximity of such immediate disaster, Jane Leigh Perrot and her niece allowed James to urge them away from that place; they retreated quickly towards the house. But Elizabeth McArthur walked to the edge of the saw-pit, looked down, then gathered up her skirts and ran to summon help, leaving the Pug at the scene of this, his second unpremeditated murder.

Even Surgeon Harris, inured as he was to the sight of violent death, blenched when, summoned to write a death certificate for Nat Benson, he saw that mutilated corpse lying upon the window shutter on which it had been brought back to the convict quarters. Benson looked as though he were the victim of some inept executioner who had failed to cleave head from body in a single sweep.

Had John Harris been present when the accident occurred, his previous philosophizing upon the ability of some, the inability of others, to adapt to raw colonial life, would surely have been supported. Jane Austen's immediate reaction had been to retreat from a scene in which she had no place, and with which she had no desire to be associated. But Elizabeth McArthur had coped with the emergency, and unhesitatingly shouldered her responsibility within the scheme of a lifestyle she had accepted completely. It was indeed a striking demonstration of his theory.

Twenty

THE STRONGBOWS WERE still living at Parramatta while
Daniel completed arrangements to occupy a grant of land
farther up the Hawkesbury, well past the Green Hills. Here he
planned to graze cattle and some sheep: not the aristocratic
merinos so dear to John McArthur, but, as he had earlier
decided, good fat lambs for the butcher's block. He planned to
build a sturdy house from the local stone – but first, he would
erect a temporary timber dwelling, as commodious as possible
for his family. He seemed to himself to have travelled as far in
time and circumstance as in mere distance: the young husband
who had embarked upon the *Jason* was now a father and
provider. He was quietly confident that in time, his Antipodean
property would surpass his elder brother's inheritance, the
Devon farm. For the moment, his sole anxiety concerned the
natives. There had been several attacks upon settlers in the
countryside farther out, and thefts of sheep, pigs and grain were
common. Two settlers had been killed last month in native
raids. Should he expose Emma and his sons to such danger?
Would it be prudent for them to remain in Parramatta until he
was well established?

He found an opportunity to air his anxiety at a social gathering one evening at the Lewins' – That same John Lewin who,
together with his artistic wife, was busy working on the *Natural
History of Lepidopterous Insects of New South Wales*.

James Leigh Perrot had already made the acqaintance of the
Lewins. He had also met the gardener-botanist, George Caley,
who was often at the Lewins' when James called there. Mr Caley

was especially interested, it transpired, in the eucalyptus, of which there appeared to be many varieties. He was not an easy man to converse with; he had no fund of small talk; but once launched into a discourse concerning his beloved plants, he would wax eloquent indeed, and quite drown out all other speakers with his voice, which had the flat accent of the English midlands. He had studied, he told Mr Leigh Perrot proudly, at both the Manchester School of Botanists and at Kew.

James could not help observing that Mr Caley seemed remarkably attached to Mrs Lewin; he was always bringing her nosegays of flowers, which she would accept with quite exaggerated pleasure. She made drawings of the plants Mr Caley collected to send to his famous patron; doubtless, Mr Leigh Perrot thought, this was the reason for their friendly association.

The Lewins were a dissimilar pair. The husband was a thoughtful, rather vague-mannered man of considered speech. It was quite surprising to learn that he had recently made a dangerous expedition to Otaheite which ended in shipwreck; as a result, he had found himself in the midst of a bloody civil war amongst the natives.

Anna Lewin, in striking contrast, was a loquacious lady with soulful, heavy-lidded eyes and a husky voice. She had a habit of reaching out to touch the person she happened to be conversing with, stroking a coat sleeve or perhaps lightly grasping her interlocutor's hand. An artistic lady; he should not be startled by her forthcoming style, James Leigh Perrot told himself.

This evening, both the Leigh Perrots and their niece were bidden to the Lewins', as well as Emma and Daniel Strongbow, Mr Harris, and one other guest, a sad-eyed gentleman of middle age, dressed in shabby black.

Mrs Lewin was wearing a flowing, embroidered garment, Moorish in effect, with a head-dress *à la turque* twisted around her head. She glided towards Jane Austen, both hands outstretched in greeting, and fixed her guest with her great eyes. Her manner of conversing was intense, her voice low-pitched, so that one was obliged to incline towards her in order to hear what she was saying. A faint scent of musk seemed to emanate from her presence.

'Dear Miss Austen, I am vastly amazed that you should have

chosen to come to this place of your own free will and inclination' – these were almost her first words to Jane. 'I think I may confidently say that it is the very last place in the world I should choose to visit for pleasure. – *I*, of course, accompanied my husband here, and had no choice in the matter. Though I should not positively say I *accompanied* Mr Lewin, for that was not the case. We had secured a cabin on the *Buffalo*, in '98 – I went ahead of my husband, who had gone to bid farewell to his father. The time came for the ship to sail – but Mr Lewin did not arrive! My dear, doting, unpunctual husband actually *missed* the ship's sailing, Miss Austen! Happily the Johnsons were on board – the former chaplain to the Colony, you know – and he and his wife befriended me. And Captain Raven was so very kind . . .' her white-lidded eyes looked down and her voice trailed off.

Jane was left unaware of the fact that shortly after Anna Lewin's arrival in Sydney, she had been involved in an unsavoury court case, an action for slander, as a result of that voyage. She was said to have conducted herself improperly with Hugh Mackin, the second mate of the *Buffalo*: she was reported to have been repeatedly in Mackin's cabin after dark, and he was said to have 'kissed her with all the freedom and familiarity of a husband'. The case had meandered on for months, to the delight of Sydney's scandalmongers, until it was ended by the arrival of John Lewin himself, who had gallantly demonstrated his faith in his wife by entering the case as joint plaintiff. Finally the verdict had gone against their accuser.

'But clearly,' Jane observed now, 'Mr Lewin did arrive here later.'

'Oh, he sailed shortly after me, on the *Minerva*,' Mrs Lewin said carelessly. She sighed deeply, at last releasing Jane's hands, which she had grasped with all the intimacy of a few moments' acquaintance. Suddenly she exclaimed: 'Oh, how I miss the artistic life I knew in England! Salons – exhibitions – that cultured circle in which we moved!'

Her words recalled for Jane the concentric society of Bath, where everyone spoke of moving in a circle – it might be *this* circle or *that* circle, but it must always be the *right* circle: to which prevalence of rotatory motion, she supposed, might be attributed the giddiness and false steps of so many.

'This is a barbarous place in which to find oneself, Miss

Austen,' Mrs Lewin continued in an exhausted manner, 'quite without art, music, literature – for me the absolute *necessities* of life, I do assure you! A place *barren* of culture.' Her eyes widened in a positive agony of deprivation. 'Oh, if you conceive the suffering inflicted upon a creature of my sensibilities, to be severed from all artistic intercourse!' She raised her eyes dramatically, then lowered her gaze to meet Jane Austen's calm regard. 'But I can tell, Miss Austen, that my strong artistic feeling, my creative impulse, my craving for the brilliant gatherings of salon and studio are not readily comprehended by you. How could they be? You live at Bath, I understand, doubtless immersed in the social round . . . But we artists, *we* are different to the rest of the world.'

Jane could but shake her head, quite at a loss to fathom the depths of Mrs Lewin's sensibilities. 'I daresay,' she remarked coolly, 'that in time the Colony will nurture its own painters, musicians, poets –'

'You speak of poetry!' Mrs Lewin intoned dramatically. 'Pray tell me where a poet would find inspiration *here*. Is he to write sonnets to – to whales, canzonets to kangarus, madrigals to prime merinos?' She paused for breath and added on a dying note: 'Dirges to black swans?'

Just then that sad-eyed shabby gentleman who alone amongst the company was unknown to Miss Austen happened to draw near them. Mrs Lewin's hand darted out, quick as a lizard's tongue, to rest upon his threadbare sleeve.

'But,' she declared huskily, 'who am I to speak of the poetic art when our very own exponent of the muse is here? Allow me to present the poet of Parramatta, Miss Austen – Mr Joseph Crabtree. Mr Crabtree is acquainted with Mr Wordsworth and several other of the Lake Poets.'

Mr Crabtree bowed with a flourish, in the old-fashioned manner, and gave a nervous, deprecatory smile. 'Dear madam,' he told Mrs Lewin, 'you are too kind thus to apostrophize me.' He must have caught the gist of Mrs Lewin's impassioned speech as he approached them, for he went on to say: 'It is my conviction, dear ladies, that poetic inspiration dwells all around us wherever we may be. A sudden intimation of immortality – every common thing viewed in a celestial light – indeed, the poet's eye may discern beauty in the humblest, meanest circumstance or the lowliest creature – even in a cockroach!'

'And pray, have you composed an ode to the cockroach, Mr Crabtree?' Jane inquired innocently; but there was a certain devilish glint in her eye which Cassandra would have recognized.

The poet cleared his throat. 'I did not mean my words to be taken too literally,' he asserted uncomfortably.

'Mr Crabtree has composed two splendid poems about another insect,' Mrs Lewin murmured. 'The butterfly!'

'Not the same butterfly,' Mr Crabtree was careful to explain. 'The poems in question were composed upon two occasions, about two different species, while I was staying at Grasmere a few years ago, with Mr Wordsworth and his sister – I daresay you may have heard of Mr Wordsworth, a fellow poet?' He gave a pedantic little cough. 'Indeed, upon hearing the description of both insects, which I was able to give him from memory, Mr Lewin expressed the opinion that one was in fact a *moth*. I may very well change the title of that verse – I would not wish to be accused of *practising a deception*.'

Was there not something a little strange, even a hint of wildness in the way Mr Crabtree spoke those last three words? Upon Mr Harris coming up at that moment and engaging the poet's attention, Mrs Lewin drew Jane aside and said softly: 'Poor Mr Crabtree. He was transported here for forging an uncle's will, and has never surmounted the disgrace, though his sentence expired some time ago.' – Then, turning back, she said throatily: 'We are depending upon you to recite to us later in the evening, Mr Crabtree. Your two butterfly verses would serve us admirably.'

'Dear Madam, you are my Calliope,' the poet responded gallantly.

Jane Austen's heart sank a little; she was not an admirer of the so-called Lakeland School of poetry, and it seemed more than likely that Mr Crabtree was one of its disciples.

Mr Leigh Perrot and Mr Lewin, meanwhile, had become engrossed in a discussion of that extraordinary theory recently propounded in quasi-scientific circles: that the earth had two creators, one for each hemisphere.

'If it were true,' Mr Lewin declared, 'then certainly it would seem as though one creator were doing his best to copy the other. There is so much here that is like – and yet unlike – what is familiar to us in the northern hemisphere. 'Tis tempting to give such creatures and plants the same name. But in truth the koola, the native bear, is *not* a bear . . . the marsupial opossum is *not* the same as the American opossum . . . the Banksia rose is *not* a rose . . .'

At this point, a supper of ham patties, cakes and negus was brought in, and the company cheerfully broke off their several conversations to settle upon chairs and enjoy the repast.

Surgeon Harris sat beside Mrs Leigh Perrot and Emma Strongbow. 'I was most impressed, ma'am,' he told Aunt Perrot, 'upon the last occasion we met, by your niece's knowledge of inoculation for the cow pocks.'

Mrs Leigh Perrot nodded rather distantly. She recalled very well that unsuitable conversation at the Governor's ball. 'Jane's grandfather upon her father's side was a surgeon, I believe,' she said coldly. 'Perhaps some interest in medicine has been passed down to her. – On her *mother*'s side, of course – that is, my husband's sister – she is closely connected with the Leighs of Stoneleigh Abbey: a highly respected family.'

Mr Harris gave a wry smile and blotted pastry crumbs from his mouth with his napkin; Mrs Leigh Perrot had made her opinion of the social standing of a mere surgeon very clear.

'I will bring Zeke and Jos to be inoculated before we settle in the countryside,' Emma Strongbow said eagerly. ' 'Twill not be long now before our house is built –'

Mr Harris, however, shook his head. 'I fear the vaccine Mr Savage brought here has not proved effective – the inoculations he conducted did not take,' he said. 'We must wait for a more effective strain to reach us.'

Daniel Strongbow, who had overheard his wife's remark, broke off a conversation with Mr Crabtree to say: 'I cannot help but wonder if I am doing the right thing by my family by taking them into the countryside. Perhaps 'twould be best if they were to wait here awhile, till I be properly settled. The natives do seem to pose a threat to safety – at the very least, to peace of mind.'

'You must be thinking of those two settlers at Richmond who were killed a short while ago,' Mr Lewin said. 'In my opinion, both would be alive still, had they treated the native

222

with some measure of respect.'

Mr Harris nodded his agreement. 'I believe the men concerned had slaughtered several natives for trespassing on their land in order to seek food.' He sighed. 'They might have done better to consider that every piece of land we clear takes away a portion of the native hunting grounds. Those "trespassers" were very likely starving.'

'Quite right, Harris,' Mr Lewin approved. 'The Aborigine, it seems, is doomed to struggle vainly to try to hold on to what was his before we took it as ours. How is he to feed himself now that he may no longer hunt or gather food in what was his tribal territory? Is it not an injustice that he should be accused of trespassing upon land which has been taken from him?' He had begun to sound quite passionate; now he paused and added quietly: 'Mr King has put on record that he considers the Aborigines to be the real proprietors of the soil.'

'My husband and Mr Caley both hold considerable regard for the Aborigines,' Mrs Lewin remarked to the company in general. 'Mr Lewin has executed some very fine native like-nesses, and Mr Caley has several Aborigines who help to maintain his garden –'

Mrs Leigh Perrot was quite struck by the way in which Mrs Lewin spoke of her husband and the gardener in the same breath. 'I find Bingami, the little native boy who accompanies Perrot upon his excursions, to be quite acceptable,' she said. (It was as though she spoke of a pet dog.) 'But I could not abide the sight of all those natives who hang about the streets of Sydney – idle, drunken creatures aping the manners of their betters –'

'Yet where are they to go, those natives, what are they to do when their tribal life has been destroyed by the European settlement?' John Lewin asked. 'What will become of Bingami when he reaches manhood? – Perhaps, madam, you would be willing to take him back with you to England?'

Mrs Leigh Perrot cast upon him a look of alarm; that was exactly the sort of harebrained scheme to appeal to her husband! She sent up a fervent private prayer that the notion would not take root in his mind.

'Could – could not the natives be recruited into the Army?' Emma Strongbow suggested impulsively, with an eager expression upon her clear young face, '– As scouts or trackers, perhaps?

I have heard they are wonderfully clever at finding their way through the bush. If ever a child is lost, their help is sought immediately.' She could not repress a shiver at the very thought of one of her darling twins lost in the wild bush.

Mr Lewin nodded. 'Their prowess in that direction has been chiefly used to hunt down escaped convicts. There has indeed been talk of forming a native company within the Corps, Mrs Strongbow, but I do not know whether anything will come of it. I cannot exactly envisage Aboriginal detachments on the lines of the Indian Sepoys. But such expedient and small solutions will not, I think, solve the large problem.' He added sadly: 'It seems we are fated either to fear the Aborigine, or to despise him.' He glanced towards his wife. 'Mrs Lewin made reference to my portraits of Aborigines; I am bound to say I find their physiognomy compatible with a high degree of intelligence.'

'But – they are such primitives!' Aunt Perrot exclaimed.

'To be primitive does not denote a lack of intelligence, madam,' Mr Harris said firmly. 'Nor, oddly enough, a lack of sophistication – it would appear that some of the Aboriginal tribal rites and customs are complicated in the extreme. Primitivism merely indicates a lack of civilization.'

'Merely!' Aunt Perrot echoed sarcastically.

Jane Austen decided to deflect the current of the conversation. 'It is strange, is it not, that we are able to designate the inhabitants of this land only as *natives* or *Aborigines* – words which might describe the primitive inhabitants of any country. Yet in India, or Africa, for example, we know the native people as Indians, as Africans . . .'

'Well, it would seem ludicrous in the extreme to call them New South Welshmen!' Mr Harris broke in heartily. 'Perhaps we might call them – Great Southlanders? Or – New Hollanders?'

'Mr Flinders once suggested a name for this great continent: *Australia.* – An abbreviation, one presumes, of *Terra Australis.* The Spanish originally coined the name. Sir Joseph Banks, I believe, did not approve: he called it a miserable dog-latin name.'

Australia . . . each person in that room tried out the word upon their tongue, as though they were sampling wine from a glass. It seemed an odd sort of name, to be sure.

'In that case,' said Jane, 'the natives would be . . . Australans. Or perhaps . . . *Australians.*'

'How very confusing,' her aunt remarked. 'Everyone would suppose you were talking about *Austrians.*'

'Well,' Daniel Strongbow deduced finally, 'it seems that so long as I treat the Aborigine with a measure of generosity, my family and property will be safe. It certainly would not occur to me to slaughter the natives – unless it were in self-defence.' He uttered a short, mirthless laugh. 'I have heard of shepherds here – convicted, if you please, for stealing sheep, but now become their zealous guardians – who have shot Aborigines out of hand for attempting to emulate their own crime! The wheel of fortune gone full circle – or turned upside-down, if you prefer it!'

The supper things were cleared away, and the guests were now ushered into another room and invited to view examples of the Lewins' collection of Lepidoptera.

'How beautiful they are!' Emma Strongbow's gaze roved across the fragile, iridescent creatures impaled within the drawers of a mahogany cabinet.

'The *buttor-fleoge,*' Jane remarked, suddenly recalling a summer day of childhood in the garden at Steventon, bowling her hoop along the strawberry walk and watching plain English cabbage-whites alight upon the bushes. '– 'Twas known thus to our ancestors, I was once told.' It was her gentle-mannered father who had said that. She felt a little stab of homesickness.

Daniel Strongbow remarked, rather surprisingly: ' 'Twould be best called the *flutterby*, to my way of thinking. *Butterfly* makes no sense that I can understand.'

Mr Lewin displayed some of his paintings. They were exquisite, showing the larva and chrysalid as well as the butterfly or moth. Jane marvelled at the meticulous detail. 'The drawings are by my husband,' Anna Lewin told her. 'When they are printed, they will be the first engravings ever made in New South Wales. *My* part in them is to colour in, like a child in a copy-book.'

James Leigh Perrot found his interest in the specimens less than it might have been if he had not been turning over in his mind that suggestion concerning Bingami which had been so casually flung out by John Lewin. To take the boy to England! The notion had indeed settled in a crevice of his mind, as his wife had feared it might.

Mrs Lewin threw up her hands suddenly. 'This,' she said dramatically, 'is the moment for Mr Crabtree to recite his poems. One should always await the right moment – just as a poet awaits his inspiration.'

So they resumed their chairs in the little parlour, and Mr Crabtree, impaled by their expectant glances, took some sheets of paper from a pocket of his shabby black coat. He cleared his throat nervously and began to read:

> 'Oh! pleasant, pleasant were the days,
> The time, when, in our childish plays,
> My sister Emmeline and I
> Together chased the butterfly!'

He paused to explain: 'Emmeline was my youngest sister. We lived in Yorkshire, and often roamed the moors together.'

He coughed again and resumed:

> 'A very hunter did I rush
> Upon the prey: – with leaps and springs
> I followed on from brake to bush;
> But she, God love her! feared to brush
> The dust from off its wings.'

He stopped speaking, and after a little pause, to ascertain that the poem was finished, polite murmurs of appreciation broke out, which Mr Crabtree acknowledged with his old-fashioned bow. Jane found it singularly difficult to imagine Mr Crabtree as a boy, leaping and springing across the moors. His verse style did indeed remind her of those rather tiresome Lakeland poets . . . Such a *striving* for artlessness . . .

'The second poem,' Mr Crabtree said diffidently, 'I originally called "To a Butterfly", but when I described to Mr Lewin how the creature was poised upon the flower with it wings outspread, he told me it might in fact have been a moth. Unfortunately, to effect a change in the interests of accuracy would, I fear, upset my scansion. I shall therefore read the work as I wrote it.'

'Oh, by all means let it remain a butterfly, Mr Crabapple,'

Aunt Perrot said. 'I cannot abide moths. Nasty, useless creatures, always getting singed in the candle flame and eating one's clothes.'

'The Aborigine designates both butterfly and moth by the same name,' Mr Lewin volunteered. '*Pilyilye*. Is that word of any use to you, Crabtree?'

The poet silently mouthed a few lines to himself, evidently substituting *pilyilye* for 'butterfly', then shook his head. 'Alas, while "moth" is too brief a word, the other has one syllable too many. – No, I shall read the poem as it stands.'

Again the clearing of the throat. Then:

> 'I've watched you now a full half-hour,
> Self-poised upon that yellow flower;
> And, little Butterfly!

(at this point he looked up at his audience apologetically)

> indeed
> I know not if you sleep or feed.
> How motionless! and then
> What joy awaits you, when the breeze
> Hath found you out among the trees,
> And calls you forth again!'

'Capital, capital!' Daniel Strongbow exclaimed, relieved to find that Mr Crabtree wrote such short poems; then, to his dismay, he realized there was a second verse to follow. He looked down in some embarrassment at his large, capable, sunburned hands as the poet went on:

> 'This plot of orchard-ground is ours;
> My trees they are, my Sister's flowers;

(I refer now to my eldest sister, Annabel,' Mr Crabtree explained.)

> 'Here rest your wings when they are weary;
> Here lodge as in a sanctuary!'

Jane Austen frowned at this rhyme.

The poet continued:

> 'Come often to us, fear no wrong;
> Sit near us on the bough!
> We'll talk of sunshine and of song,
> And summer days, when we were young;
> Sweet childish days, that were as long
> As twenty days are now.'

Mr Crabtree's audience was embarrassed to observe that as he reached the final lines, his faded eyes were filled with overflowing tears. He brought out a torn handkerchief and wept into it silently, not even making the pretence of blowing his nose. Only his hostess was not in the least dismayed; perhaps, in her opinion, it was only proper that poets should weep.

This recitation, with its lachrymose ending, brought the evening to a close, and as the Leigh Perrots and their niece strolled home, the lanthorn held high by James to light their way over the rough ground, Jane Austen found herself recalling Anna Lewin's somewhat arrogant assumption that *she* could never comprehend the creative impulse . . . She had experienced a wry amusement at the time; but now the recollection turned her thoughts to a different tack. It was so long since she had last sat down to write, had felt her own 'creative impulse' – pretentious phrase! – alive within her – though never, thank heaven, with that feverish intensity suggested by Anna Lewin. Simply to sit down, serenely, pen in hand – to think, recollect, make use of stored up observation and of imagination, experiment with dialogue, delineate character – and, by these means, persevere in the relating of a story: yes, that was what she hoped to do again someday . . . and, in the process, to experience a curiously satisfying and agreeable sensation of achievement.

Stepping carefully around a puddle (it had rained a good deal recently), Jane smiled to herself as she thought of her first attempt at a novel: *Lady Susan*. The adventures of her other *Susan*, innocent, impressionable young Susan, first at Bath and then at Northanger Abbey, had turned out much more satisfactorily: it had been such fun to mock those delicious, terrifying Gothic tales from the Circulating Library! – She had, she remembered suddenly, been busy writing this story the very day her uncle had come to Steventon with the news of her aunt's sad predicament. But what came next? After *Susan*, she had fully intended to revise the manuscript of *First Impressions*, but the removal from Steventon to Bath had quite precluded any chance of doing so; and then – then had come the fatal visit to the seaside. Jane took a deep breath of the night air. It almost seemed as though Mr Fordwick's untimely death had signalled the demise of her creative endeavour – *that* surely, was a better word than 'impulse' or inspiration . . . inspiration was a treacherous fish, too slippery to grasp. Perhaps, she thought, the whole range of human emotions: love, hope disappointment, despair, used the same fount of energy as that creative endeavour; perhaps her own resources were exhausted. But in her heart she could not really believe this. One day she would surely sit down again to write . . .

James, as he held high the lanthorn, fixed his thoughts on Bingami, imagining him at Scarlets, beneath the oak trees, or marvelling at the city sights of Bath. 'A high degree of intelligence', John Lewin had said . . . His thoughts continued ambitiously: why should not the boy have the benefit of schooling, and become as proficient in Latin and Greek as he was in the ways of the waumbat and the platypus?

Aunt Perrot's musings as she followed the path of the lanthorn were more mundane. How freckled Emma Strongbow's complexion had become she thought disparagingly. Freckles were really so very disgusting. If she put her mind to it, perhaps she could recall that excellent recipe for lemon and cucumber cream, a sovereign remedy for blemishes. What a very strange evening it had been to be sure, with that trying Mr Harris and the shabby little poet, Mr Crabapple . . .

As James Leigh Perrot held open their cottage gate, his wife felt a sudden homesick longing for green baize card tables, delicious sweetmeats in silver dishes, amusing gossip . . . and no talk of convicts, cow pocks, sheep or Aborigines! The orange tree, as they passed it, was fragrant in the night air; but oh, how she yearned for the dear damp smell of a wet pavement in Bath!

On Lammas Day, the congregation at St John's Church watched the Reverend Samuel Marsden bless a pile of loaves baked at the

Female Factory especially for this service. Afterwards, they were to be distributed to the deserving, if any could be found worthy of that description. Ox-like in strength, ruddy of complexion, he stood with huge hands upraised, expatiating upon the significance of this festival of purity and thanksgiving, and reminding those assembled souls that the Colony had all but succumbed to starvation only a short while ago. A blaze of golden wattle decorated the altar, causing a couple of susceptible choirboys to sneeze uncontrollably, and glossy fishbone ferns were arranged below the pulpit.

Lammas Day in mid-winter instead of at high summer . . . how strange that seemed to the three English visitors sitting upright upon the rude, uncomfortable benches that furnished the body of the church. It would be some time before proper pews could be installed: there were more important – that is to say, more pressing – demands of a secular nature upon the skills of carpenters and joiners. Jane Austen saw the Strongbows seated across the narrow aisle, and Rebecca looking demure in a grey pleated bonnet. And there was Elizabeth McArthur with young William and her daughters – she and Jane exchanged brief churchlike smiles as their glances met – the Lewins – Mr Caley, the gardener . . . shabby, poetic Mr Crabtree . . . Mr Harris, spending this Sunday in Parramatta . . . and upon the front bench sat Mrs Marsden, devoted helpmeet of her husband, with her two children beside her . . .

At the back of the church, emanating an unholy odour of neglected linen and unwashed bodies, the convict section of the congregation sat in surly silence. The Sabbath was the one day of the week they were free to dedicate wholly to pleasure, sport, or the serious business of getting and spending on their own account. Their weekday task-work lasted from dawn to mid-afternoon: how should a man (or woman) profit for himself when this precious time that they could call their own, their darg, was squandered in church muster, listening to the Reverend Samuel Marsden's ravings about sin, repentance and salvation? – The flogging parson, they called him. In his *alter ego* as Magistrate, he was notoriously ready to use the cat-o'-nine-tails upon the flesh of wrongdoers, to persuade their souls towards repentance.

They could not know, those sullen convicts, how that same

flogging parson chastised himself unsparingly within the pages of his daily journal, how often he almost despaired of bringing salvation to his wayward flock. *Nothing is impossible with God*, he wrote with furious determination, *or one might conclude that a person might preach to all Eternity to such men without doing them the least good.* Upon his knees he prayed ceaselessly: *May my little love be increased, my weak faith strengthened, and hope confirmed.*

The members of the New South Wales Corps garrisoned at Parramatta, sitting there in their red and yellow ranks, were inclined to share the resentful attitude of the convicts towards church muster. Among their number was young Harry Rogers, who strained to catch a glimpse of his Rebecca's face beneath her pleated bonnet, anticipating the delights of their walk from church to cottage after the morning service. He had enlisted in the New South Wales Corps – the Condemned Corps, the Rum Corps, folk might call it what they pleased – with the simple ambition to see this new land, coupled with a shrewd notion (like Daniel Strongbow, he came of farming stock) that he might settle there and make himself comfortable. Now he saw great possibilities in the Hawkesbury district for a young soldier who had served his time. And Rebecca, he had quite decided upon it, was the girl to share his life. She had told him the whole wretched story of how she had been falsely accused of stealing that coral brooch. He had implicit faith in her innocence, and was indignant to think of the wrong she had endured. Rebecca was no thief, he would stake his life on it!

As the morning service proceeded, Jane Austen noticed that her aunt's jaws were moving in that gentle, constant motion which denoted her continuing addiction to Captain Bunker's confection. She knew that Gypsy Jem had brought a fresh supply from Sydney last week. She was pleased her aunt had discovered an adequate substitute for her peppermints, but this new habit did give rise to one unhappy circumstance: because the substance was not to be swallowed, it had to be disposed of, and Aunt Perrot had fallen into the unpleasing habit of placing the little chewed-up wads where she imagined, mistakenly, no one else would discover them . . . beneath the table ledge, on the underside of a chair . . . once Jane had stepped upon a piece, and found it almost impossible to clean the stickiness off her best nankeen boots.

James Leigh Perrot, who had lately felt a twinge of his familiar enemy the gout (colonial hospitality was generous and the claret freely flowed), knelt with difficulty to pray upon the straw-filled hassock, levering himself up again with grimaces of pain. What a confounded lot of bobbing up and down this churchgoing entailed, he thought; and thankfully subsided upon the bench to listen to the First Lesson. A man could at least be sure of a few moments' respite while it was being read.

This Sunday, a new assistant chaplain, recently appointed (Jane seemed to recollect Mrs King speaking of him), was making his first appearance at St John's. As she joined in singing one of the stirring Wesleyan hymns favoured by Mr Marsden, she was vaguely aware of this clergyman approaching the lectern to read the Lesson ... a tall figure, black-bearded, drawing his cassock about him as he came from the choir stall. A ripple of interest stirred the congregation, and several genteel spinsters gazed at him speculatively. The new assistant chaplain was known to be unmarried.

The First Lesson was from the twenty-seventh chapter of the Book of Proverbs; it contained several verses strikingly appropriate to this diverse and exiled congregation; but then, as Jane Austen reflected, Proverbs was positively crammed with strikingly appropriate verses for practically any situation. Such a useful source of sermons, too! She would try to guess which verse was most likely to be taken up by Mr Marsden when, later, he thundered from the pulpit ...

'Boast not thyself of tomorrow: for thou knowest not what a day may bring forth –'

That voice! She felt as though she had been struck by lightning ... as though a bolt of lightning had jolted her very being.

'Open rebuke is better than secret love: Faithful are the wounds of a friend; but the kisses of an enemy are deceitful –'

That mellifluous timbre, that reassuring intonation, the words so clearly spoken, each sentence given exactly its right quality ... She closed her eyes as painful recollection pierced her heart. It was so extraordinarily like *his* voice, that dear, remembered voice which she had first heard in the Circulating Library at Sidmouth!

'As a bird that wandereth from her nest, so is a man that

wandereth from his place –'

And now her eyes snapped open wide to gaze in shocked, disbelieving consternation, dismayed amazement, unutterable bewilderment towards the man who stood at the lectern. For surely it *was* his voice, the voice of Elliot Fordwick, which now filled her ears! It could not be. Impossible. And yet – her heart beat violently, her skin seemed to tighten and grow clammy; with both gloved hands she gripped the edge of the bench on which she sat.

'As in water face answereth to face, so the heart of man to man –'

The curate's face was half-concealed by that bushy beard; he wore spectacles and his skin was sunburnt. Mr Fordwick had been clean-shaven and very pale; he had not worn spectacles. But both were tall and dark-haired . . . She peered desperately, regretting her shortsightedness as never before.

'Be thou diligent to know the state of thy flocks, and look well to thy herds –'

The astonishing aptness of this verse quite passed Jane by as the curate reverently closed the Bible. 'Here endeth the First Lesson,' he intoned. Before he turned away to resume his place, he removed those steel-rimmed spectacles, and finally, oh yes, beyond all doubt (but also, it seemed, beyond all reason) Jane Austen discerned behind that beard, that dark complexion, the unmistakable features of the man she had loved and lost. *It was Elliot Fordwick.* But how . . . why . . . what was he doing here, *alive*?

A frightful pang swept through her body; the colour slowly drained from her face; a wave of nausea assailed her . . . For the second time in her life Jane Austen fainted, crumpling neatly upon the straw-filled hassocks.

With her uncle and aunt supporting her, and Mr Lewin stepping forward with kind concern to lend extra assistance, she was taken half-conscious past the rows of respectable citizens, gawping convicts and side-glancing soldiery into the open air outside, and sat limply upon a low stone wall, inhaling the *sal volatile* which Aunt Perrot produced from her reticule.

'. . . not usually given to faints or fits,' she dimly heard that lady assuring Mr Lewin. 'All those smelly convicts – insufficient air – enough to make anyone feel faint!' Upon which she removed Jane's bonnet and proceeded to fan her vigorously with it.

Jane made a determined effort and, though pale as ashes, emerged sufficiently from her state of shock to pronounce her imminent recovery, dissuade Mr Lewin from fetching a carriage, and protest that the walk home in the fresh air would be the most effective restorative of all. And so, bareheaded, and craving with heart and soul the solitary peace of her own tiny room, where she might attempt to collect her thoughts and make some sense out of this extraordinary event, she rose and, in the solicitous company of her aunt and uncle, slowly returned to their cottage on the western road.

Meanwhile, the church service at St John's proceeded through prayers, hymn, Second Lesson, church offering, sermon and the final Benediction. Mr Marsden took as his text: 'Boast not thyself of tomorrow: for thou knowest not what a day may bring forth'; it afforded him plentiful scope for suitable chastisement and passionate exhortation towards repentance and salvation.

As he pounded the ledge of the pulpit with his great fist, his new curate quelled an instinctive aversion to the proselytizing style of his superior, and reverted to his own thoughts. On the whole, he felt quite satisfied with his first service in Parramatta. Nothing untoward had occurred – save the little incident of a lady fainting and being helped outside. But that was really quite unremarkable: ladies were often known to faint in church. – Yes, all things considered, Mr Elliot Fordwick felt quite confident that he had made a wise decision to come to this far distant corner of the world, away from bitter memories, from awkward circumstances, from reproaches and recriminations. A clean break, a fresh beginning in a new land with nothing to remind him of the past . . . and of that sweet direction his life *might* have taken. He felt no qualm of doubt: in the circumstances it had been the only possible course to take. His gaze roved over the weary, vacuous, resentful and occasionally vicious faces of the felons; the bored soldiery; fidgeting children; pert young ladies in their Sunday finery; sober matrons; stolid farmers. These were his people now, and this his place.

Twenty-One

AFTER A DAY and a night spent in tormented thought, Jane found herself quite unable to unravel the maze of fantastic speculation which Elliot Fordwick's astonishing reappearance induced in her mind. He had arisen from the dead like Lazarus, a reincarnation which had quite overturned the equilibrium of her existence. She felt as if she were now inhabiting a surreal world; it was totally irrational; she did not care for it at all.

She had absolutely no intention of confiding in her aunt, or her uncle. Though Jane Austen and Jane Leigh Perrot had now passed upwards of six months in each other's company, their association was scarcely more truly intimate than it had ever been; as for her uncle, she had no wish to disturb their kindly, stable relationship by presenting him with an emotional dilemma which he would doubtless find dismaying. As if the whole extraordinary circumstance were not sufficiently demoralizing in its effect upon her own feelings, there were a number of other factors involved. Unfortunately, her aunt was well acquainted with Mr Fordwick's name and the details of his ill-fated courtship; in spite of her singular inability to recollect names correctly (Jane knew that the poet of Parramatta would forever remain a Crabapple in her aunt's mind), she was more likely to recall the name of Elliot Fordwick, since it had been connected to a family matter. Then there were their new friends and acquaintances to consider – Elizabeth McArthur, the Strongbows, Mr Harris, the Patersons, the Kings ... even D'Arcy Wentworth! Jane eschewed the thought that her ill-starred romance and its extraordinary aftermath might become the subject of colonial gossip.

Most of all, she dreaded the chance of a sudden, unheralded encounter with Mr Fordwick. The Colony contained such a very small society; it was scarcely possible to avoid seeing anybody for very long. Her fainting fit provided an excuse to keep to the house for several days, and to cry off a supper party at the Strongbows' – but she could not hide indoors for the remainder of their sojourn here. Sooner or later, Mr Fordwick must hear of the three English visitors staying at Parramatta: Mr and Mrs Leigh Perrot, of Bath, and their niece, Miss Jane Austen.

One of these factors was resolved when her aunt and uncle returned from the Strongbows' party. In the course of conversation, it appeared, mention had been made of the new assistant chaplain, whose name, Mrs Leigh Perrot stated unequivocally, was 'Mr Penberthy'. Surely even Aunt Perrot could not disremember a name to that extent, could not metamorphose 'Fordwick' into 'Penberthy'!

'Are you sure he is called Penberthy?' Jane asked. (Did not that name stir some recollection in her mind?)

'I am quite positive,' her aunt asserted. 'Penberthy: yes, indeed. That is his name. I particularly noted it, because there is an old Lady Penberthy who lives in Berkshire – but I daresay he is no relation to her.' She went on to speak of other matters, of how grateful Mrs Strongbow had been to receive the gift of face cream she had taken her, concocted from cucumbers and lemons grown at Elizabeth Farm. 'Those detestable freckles will soon fade,' Aunt Perrot prophesied.

Jane did not give a fig for Emma Strongbow's freckles. *Why, oh why had Mr Fordwick changed his name?*, she asked herself. Although this curious news lifted one anxiety from her mind, it also served to deepen her bewilderment. That night, as she lay sleepless, full moonlight streaming through her little window, that elusive half-recollection which earlier had stirred in her mind was captured and held. *Penberthy!* – He was the Oxford friend Mr Fordwick had spoken of, a fellow clergyman, but of Evangelical persuasion . . . Yet still nothing was explained. It all remained as much of a mystery as ever. Jane sighed and fell at last into fitful slumber.

Two days later, a convict lad from Elizabeth Farm brought over a note. Elizabeth McArthur invited Jane to visit the Farm the next afternoon ... trusted she was recovered from her indisposition ... and wrote that Mr Penberthy, the new assistant chaplain, would also be joining them. She wished to discuss with him the possibility of opening a Sunday School for the children at Parramatta ... Jane's advice upon the subject would be invaluable ...

Here, in Elizabeth's neat handwriting, opportunity was offered for Jane to seek clarification and enlightenment of everything that was now incomprehensible and obscure. By accepting this invitation, she would see Elliot Fordwick again, come face to face with him ... Her heart began to beat rapidly, but not with that delightful sense of expectancy she used to feel before each time they met at Sidmouth. There could be nothing delightful to anticipate where this encounter was concerned; yet she knew she must force herself to accomplish it.

'I will give you a note to take back to your mistress,' she told the lad. He drew one hand across his runny nose and waited.

She scribbled her acceptance, signed it, and then, pen poised, stayed her hand. She assumed *he* did not yet know of her presence here; she decided she must attempt to give *Mr Penberthy* some forewarning of their meeting. To some extent she thought to spare him a shock such as she herself had sustained; but she also wished to obviate, in Elizabeth McArthur's presence, the obvious amazement which a totally unexpected encounter would engender on his part. It was, of course, quite possible that Elizabeth might already have told him she would be there; but to make sure she added as a postscript: *I believe, by the way, that I once met Mr Penberthy on a previous occasion during a visit to Devonshire – he may recall my name. J.A.*

She waved the paper in the air to dry the ink, then folded it and gave it to the boy to take back with him. She watched him run off, pursued by the fierce magpie, that faithful guardian of their orange tree. There – it was done; now she must await tomorrow's meeting with as much equanimity as she could muster.

Bingami had been absent from the settlement for several days. This was not an unusual circumstance: he had been known to 'go walkabout' before, and had always returned after a short absence, bearing some unusual object which he would present to James Leigh Perrot, an offering to his adopted grandfather:

strange white flowers whose petals had the soft consistency of flannel; a little green tree frog; and, once, a seashell which glittered with rainbow hues of scarlet, green and gold, all overlaid with an iridescent, silvery sheen.

'How very singular,' James Leigh Perrot had remarked, turning the pretty object to catch the light. 'It is, I believe, a sea shell overlaid with *opal* . . . but how or where Bingami can have come across it, who can tell?' He had given the shell to Jane, who put it in the box where she kept her few pieces of jewellery; it nestled next to the topaz cross her brother Charles had given her.

Bingami chose this very afternoon to return to Parramatta; and at dusk the boy came to James, holding out a little lumpy parcel tied in a piece of cloth. Mr Leigh Perrot was standing in the garden beside the orange tree, looking out for bats. Flocks of them were often to be observed at night; their squealing and quarrelling filled the air as they camped in the great trees by the river.

'*Melalla*,' Bingami said, his dark eyes shining, a wide grin on his face as he waited for the old one to open the parcel.

'What have we here?' James Leigh Perrot mused aloud, taking the parcel and opening it a little cautiously – he had not forgotten the green frog.

But nothing stirred or writhed inside the cloth. There were just four rough, jagged stones, each about the size of a walnut. Mystified, James examined them. Then he rubbed the largest with part of the rag it had been tied in. It gleamed dully.

'*Wakalta*,' Bingami said eagerly, jabbing the stone with a thin forefinger. He searched for a suitable word out of the limited vocabulary he had picked up from the white man. 'Bright shine,' he said, 'like – like moon.'

'I wonder,' James Leigh Perrot said softly, his mind seized by fantastic speculation. 'Can it be . . . *gold*?'

'Luckee!' Bingami exclaimed; and taking the stones back from James, he threw them in the air and caught them one after another, like a juggler.

'Where did you find these, Bingami?' James asked. He took them back again, solemnly laid them on the ground, walked a short distance away, then returned and made a pantomime of suddenly discovering them. He shaded his eyes with one hand and looked all around. 'Where, Bingami, *where*?'

238

His actions delighted Bingami, who erupted into joyful laughter. '*Warara*,' he said at last, 'long way.' And in his turn he began to mime a steep climbing action.

James looked away from the boy, across to the distant line of mountains, that blue curtain, hanging in heavy folds, which stood between them and the setting sun. It was a magnificent sunset: scarlet and green and gold . . . an opal-coloured sky. Had Bingami been across the mountains? Did he and others of his nimble-footed people know of a secret way through to the other side? Surely that was not such an impossibility . . . and, if these shining stones were nugs of gold, were there more of them over there, perhaps lying on the surface of the ground, just waiting to be picked up? He trembled at the notion. Gold? What would men not do to gain it? He thought of the old alchemists who practised the Egyptian art . . . of El Dorado . . . of the golden treasure of Montezuma . . . Beyond that ancient barrier of rock, did a great golden fortune await pick and shovel – or simply a keen eye and a pair of empty hands?

When the lamp was lit that night, and as his wife and niece sat sewing, James Leigh Perrot laid aside the *Gazette* and drew up his chair to join them at the table. There was a strange, excited, almost conspiratorial air about him.

'What is it, Perrot?' his wife asked, busy with a three-cornered tear in one sleeve of her riding habit. She had caught it on a prickly bush beyond Toongabbie.

'I have made – that is to say, I *believe* I have made – an astonishing discovery,' James Leigh Perrot announced portentously.

His wife looked up in surprise tinged with mild alarm: these were strong words from her mild-mannered husband. Doubtless he imagined he had made a first sighting of some plant or insect. She prepared herself to feign suitable interest. Jane Austen, whose thoughts as she darned a stocking were totally preoccupied with the enigma of Mr Fordwick-Penberthy, gazed at her uncle in alarm: was it possible he had discovered her secret?

'Where is Ellen?' James asked in a low voice. 'It is vital she should hear no word of what I am about to divulge. Any rumour of my information could set the Colony by its ears.'

Aunt Perrot stared at her husband. 'Really, Perrot, there is no need to whisper. What is all this about? As for Ellen, she has gone out to look for a black cat.'

'A black cat?' Husband and niece both looked at her inquiringly.

'Have you not noticed the stye on her eye? It makes her appear even plainer than usual,' Aunt Perrot sniffed. 'She is convinced the only way to cure it is to rub the tail of a black cat across her eyelid.'

James relaxed somewhat. 'In that case, I may show you these – stones, which Bingami brought me today, without fear of being either observed or overheard.' Whereupon he tumbled the four walnut-sized pebbles upon the table.

Both ladies put aside their work and inspected the dull yellow chunks of rock. They were quite mystified.

'I have reason to believe these are nuggets of gold,' James informed them in a tone of suppressed excitement.

'Husband! You don't say so!'

Jane observed how her aunt's eyes gleamed suddenly as she gazed upon the stones. 'Where did Bingami find them?' she asked her uncle.

'Beyond the Blue Mountains – that is my supposition,' he replied.

Exclamation was succeeded by conjecture following this further significant announcement.

'A new El Dorado!' Jane Leigh Perrot exclaimed. 'Riches beyond our dreams –'

'A way through the mountains!' Jane Austen murmured. 'The whole continent open to exploration –'

'Clearly,' James said at last, bringing both ladies firmly down to earth, 'the Authorities must be informed.'

'You mean – Governor King?' his wife inquired with a hint of reluctance. 'Yes, I suppose so.'

'But of course Mr King must be informed!' Jane Austen said unhesitatingly. 'If such riches lie on – or in – the ground in any quantity – why, a whole new era begins for this Colony!'

At that moment they heard the back door slam. Ellen was back. Jane went into the kitchen, where she found Ellen in a high good humour, raking the fire and cutting thick slices of bread.

'I ain't forgotten yer toasted cheese, Miss,' Ellen told her. 'I'll have it ready in two ticks.'

Toasted cheese was Jane's favourite supper dish. She smiled at Ellen. 'Did you find a black cat?'

Ellen beamed. 'Lor', Miss, I found a prize moggie with a great bush of a tail – I swep' it over my face three times fer luck! 'Twas a cat what belonged to the Reverend Marsden, I b'lieve.'

Jane could not help smiling at this demonstration of superstition combined with religion in perfect faith! *The parson's cat is an ambivalent cat*, she thought, remembering the old nursery game.

Two people sat on the verandah at Elizabeth Farm. As Jane drew near, having made a slow and tremulous progress towards Rose Hill, she recognized Elizabeth's pale-blue gown . . . the other figure was garbed in clerical black. A third chair stood empty, awaiting her arrival.

'Dear Jane!' Elizabeth greeted her. 'It is so good to see you out and about again. I was just telling Mr Penberthy that you believe you have encountered one another on a former occasion – in Devonshire, I think you said. – Mr Penberthy, Miss Jane Austen –'

There was all the small flurry of arrival, of returning Elizabeth McArthur's welcome, assuring her of health restored – then, procrastination no longer possible, she must perforce turn to acknowledge that introduction, to look at 'Mr Penberthy', to utter a greeting, however incoherent it might sound.

She forced her eyes to meet his gaze – and saw immediately that he was every bit as nervous as she was herself.

'Mr – Penberthy,' she said quietly, with the merest pause between title and name, and just a shadow of irony in her pronunciation.

'Miss Austen,' he responded in a voice that held some hint of deep emotion and, if she were not mistaken, a sense of enormous relief. Surely he had not imagined she would *denounce* him? 'This is indeed a – surprise. I was quite astonished when Mrs McArthur told me who would be joining us this afternoon – I never expected to find *you* here in the Colony –'

'I might say the same thing to you, sir,' Jane replied stiffly. 'Indeed, my astonishment might, I think, reasonably be held to be considerably greater than your own.'

Elizabeth McArthur was a little puzzled as she beheld this meeting of former acquaintances. Jane seemed quite strained in manner, she thought, unlike her usual lively self. Perhaps, she conjectured, Mr Penberthy was someone she had cordially disliked upon their previous meeting . . . though in truth he seemed an agreeable and intelligent gentleman, an asset, so far as she could judge, to colonial society. Jane's lack of spirits and grave expression must be attributed to her recent indisposition, she decided.

Now she turned to Jane. 'Mr Penberthy has just given me sad news of the Marsdens. Their infant son, but two months old, was scalded by a kettle of boiling water tipping over him two days ago, and the poor little mite has died. He was their only boy, you know.'

Jane bowed her head. 'There can be no news more dismal than the death of a little child,' she said sadly.

'Which leads us to the subject we have met to discuss,' Elizabeth went on briskly. 'Children. The possibility of starting up a Sunday School . . .'

The neutral ground of this discussion occupied them for some time, providing a useful interlude in which Jane was able to accustom herself, however uneasily, to the proximity of Elliot Fordwick — she could not think of him as 'Mr Penberthy'. Glancing at him covertly, she seemed to observe a subtle change in his appearance from the image she had retained in memory. It was more than superficial alteration wrought by a beard and a sunbrowned complexion: a certain refinement of feature, an indefinable assurance of integrity seemed, somehow, to have been lost. And his manner — it was as though he were acting a part — as, indeed he was, she reminded herself. Oh, *why* had this once loved stranger cast himself in the role of Penberthy? What could have induced such dissimulation, such deceit?

Eventually Elizabeth announced her intention of going indoors to fetch a tea tray. Alarmed at the idea of being left alone with Mr Fordwick-Penberthy, Jane half-rose from her chair; but Elizabeth declined her eager offer of assistance; she had perforce to remain with him upon the verandah, striving to retain her fragile composure.

It was he who spoke first, in a low, agonized voice. 'It is *you*!

Who would have thought we were destined to see one another again *here* – oh, Jane!' He groaned, and cast a look of bitter despair upon the woman he had loved and lost, and who, against all odds – against reason itself, it seemed, had suddenly appeared to shatter the make-believe world he had assembled around himself. Who would ever had imagined that *she*, of all people, would appear in the Antipodes!

'*Your* presence in this place or any other is quite incomprehensible to me,' Jane told him in a subdued yet agitated voice. She had been quite startled by his use of her first name. ' I – mourned you as one dead, departed for ever from my life – from life itself! Can you begin to imagine my sensations upon discovering you to be alive – and masquerading under a false name?'

He clasped his forehead with one hand, closing his eyes against the cruel reality of the moment. 'Will you allow me to explain – to attempt an explanation – to tell you why I have acted in this manner? I cannot seek to excuse my conduct; not for one instant do I expect you to condone it; but I should like you to know the reasons for it.'

Jane bowed her head. 'I have come here today prepared to listen to whatever you may wish to say,' she assented bleakly.

He rose then and gazed across the garden, beyond the orchard towards the creek. 'Let us walk a little,' he suggested. 'We will be more private – I shall find it easier to unburden myself to you if we are walking side by side.'

If he does not have to meet my gaze, Jane thought. 'Very well,' she said. Together they went into the garden, stolling slowly down towards Clay Creek; and finally Jane Austen heard the strange and sorry story of what had befallen Elliot Fordwick after their last meeting upon the beach at Sidmouth.

'At the time we parted,' he told her, 'I intended – it was indeed my firm intention – to come soon to Bath, to – to ask you, dear, dear Jane, to be my wife.' He paused, sighed heavily, and then continued: 'There was but one possible impediment to this resolve . . . A Mrs Repton and her daughter, who lived within my Surrey parish, had shown me singular attention when I was first appointed there as curate. They were acquainted with my patron, Lord Eaglemont, who had, indeed, provided me with a letter of introduction to Mrs Repton. I went repeatedly to their house – far too often, as I realized too late – but I was lonely, and there was always a cheerful fire in their pleasant parlour, and a glass of wine. Mrs Repton was a widow, Louisa her only child – scarcely a child, however: she was nineteen when I first met her. A very plain young woman.'

He fell silent for a moment, recalling with a shudder the attentive Mrs Repton and her daughter. – The mother, with her sharp features and jetty ringlets that bobbed beneath her widow's cap; and plain Louisa. For she was indeed a poor unfortunate Louisa, a solid, stodgy girl without two words of sensible conversation, with no mind of her own, incessantly prodded, pushed and propelled into his orbit by her mamma.

'It was not long,' he told Jane, 'before Mrs Repton's continual invitations, and the gradual assumption on her part that I would wish to spend every spare moment in the company of her daughter and herself, began to cause me considerable irritation. One circumstance I found particularly distasteful: Miss Repton would contrive to bob up in the vicinity of my favourite walks. Just when I was congratulating myself upon achieving a solitary stroll through the coppice or across the common, even on the coldest days, there she would be, with a red nose and watering eyes, shivering in the freezing wind and waiting for me to assist her over a stile.'

Jane glanced at her companion sidelong. 'You are not the first unattached clergyman, I think, to attract the attentions of a scheming mother on behalf of a plain daughter. Surely it was not impossible to extricate yourself from a relationship which was becoming more intimate than you wished it to be?'

'You might well think so. The world might assume it to be so. But I found, to my dismay, that Mrs Repton had been dropping hints about the parish, intimating to her neighbours that there was an – an *understanding* between Louisa and myself. At last the situation became quite untenable; the whole parish, I verily believe, was confidently expecting the banns to be called!' He passed a hand across his brow, then held aside a springy branch projecting into her path, so that Jane might pass by.

'It was at that stage,' he went on, 'that I decided I must go away for a while, take a short holiday. I thought that perhaps, when I returned, the situation might have changed – some other more eligible bachelor might have appeared on the scene, and all

Mrs Repton's formidable tactics of assault be directed towards another.'

'And so – you came to Sidmouth,' Jane said.

'I came to Sidmouth and met you,' he said, uttering a sigh of infinite grief for that departed joy. 'Oh Jane, I solemnly declare that those were the happiest days I ever spent.'

In spite of herself, in spite of the change, the alteration she discerned in this man to whom she had once vouchsafed her tenderest feelings, she too was swept by an unbearable sadness, a nostalgia for that brief vanished time of happiness. 'And then,' she prompted in a low voice, 'you returned to Surrey –'

He nodded. 'I returned, quite determined to break off that undesired association with the Reptons; if need be, to make a clean break. I had the promise of the parish in Sussex and I thought – I deluded myself – that I could escape from Surrey and take you to Sussex as my bride!'

'You *deluded* yourself, sir?'

'Yes! I was a fool not to have seen before how the land lay . . . Upon my return, I did not call upon the Reptons. I made a point of avoiding their company. There was a ball at the local Assembly Rooms shortly after I returned – I attended it in a party got up by other acquaintances. Oh, the Reptons were there, you may be sure, but I ignored them, I did not ask Louisa for a single dance.'

Jane could not suppress a fleeting nod of sympathy towards poor, plain Miss Repton; doubtless she had wilted all through the evening, a wallflower among the chaperones . . .

'The next day,' he continued, 'the folly of my actions was soon made plain to me. I received a note from Mrs Repton, coolly worded, desiring me to call upon her. I could not very well decline to do so, and I prepared myself for a painful interview, to settle the whole business once and for all. Mrs Repton was alone in the parlour when I called. She came straight to the point and reproached me in bitter terms for my callous behaviour towards her daughter, when, as she had the temerity to assert, "all the world" knew of the understanding between Louisa and myself! I protested that though the *world* might be aware of such a circumstance, *I* had no knowledge of it – upon which she turned vindictive. She reminded me of her friendship with Lord Eaglemont and hinted that a word from her would remove all hope of my securing the living I desired in Sussex. She told me that Lord Eaglemont himself looked forward to hearing of a happy union between Miss Repton and myself!' – Oh, I had not the slightest doubt that she spoke in earnest. I knew Lord Eaglemont to be a weak man, easily swayed by the opinions of others. It was clear enough that unless I consented to marry Miss Repton, the Sussex parish would be granted to another.'

At this point they emerged from the orchard to stand directly above the narrow creek beyond the garden. Water birds darted amongst the reeds; it was a calm, Arcadian scene, in striking contrast to the sorry tale unfolding.

(Behind them, on the verandah of Elizabeth Farm, Mrs McArthur was considerably surprised to find her guests had vanished: she stood holding the tea tray, wondering where they could have got to.)

And now Mr Fordwick-Penberthy delineated the dilemma that had faced him at this juncture: 'Unless I married Miss Repton, I had no hope of securing the Sussex living . . . but without that living, I could never ask you to marry me. As a mere curate, my income was not sufficient to maintain a wife and family in a proper manner. I could not approach your father to ask for your hand in marriage without a decent living to support my request.'

Jane watched a little brown bird alight upon the water with a graceful skimming motion. She could make no response; she could not refute those prudent words. A life of genteel poverty and everyday deprivation would very soon, she suspected, have served to dilute their affection for each other.

'I assume that since you have now come to New South Wales, you did in fact refuse to marry Miss Repton, and thereby forefeited the parish in Sussex,' she observed. Still he had not explained his change of name, she thought.

'I did indeed inform Mrs Repton, in words that allowed for no misunderstanding, that I could never marry her daughter, whatever the consequences might be.' (And at that point, as he recalled, he had seemed to hear a stifled shriek outside the door and the silken rustle of a skirt . . .) 'Apart from my natural disinclination towards poor Louisa, *your* image, Jane, was fresh and clear and glowing in my heart, my mind, my soul.' He turned to look at her with such a long, tormented gaze that at last she felt obliged to lower her eyes and study the ground.

' "Then be assured I shall write to Lord Eaglemont without delay, and you will never go to Sussex," Mrs Repton answered me angrily; upon which I took my leave, vowing that I would never enter that house again. I spent a few days musing upon my unhappy fate, when I suddenly received an urgent summons from my friend Penberthy, my college friend – we were at Oxford together.'

'I recall your speaking of him,' Jane murmured.

'Alas, poor Penberthy! I travelled without delay to London, where I found him upon his deathbed. A consumption of the lungs held him in a remorseless grip, and within a short time he expired. Like me, he had no family – not even a brother, as in my case. Poor Penberthy had been quite alone in the world, the disease from which he died having carried off his parents and all his siblings. After his funeral, at which I was the sole mourner, I studied his effects, and discovered he had made arrangements to travel to this Colony to take up the appointment of assistant chaplain to Mr Samuel Marsden.' And now Mr Fordwick bowed his head as he confessed to the deception he had practised in order to escape from his intolerable situation. He had deliberately decided to slough off his own identity, and take upon himself the name of Penberthy, and all that went with it.

'Penberthy was a bearded man – and so I grew this beard. He professed Evangelism – I became a fervent follower of that persuasion. I studied the notes he had made, and the letters he had received concerning his new appointment. He had, I gathered, never met Mr Marsden; on that score, therefore, I was perfectly safe from detection. Arrangements had been made for him to embark upon the *Titan*, bound for Port Jackson – and, in due course, I took passage in that vessel, arriving here a few weeks ago.'

Jane recoiled from the deception inherent in this bold manoeuvre. 'That was not an honourable deed,' she told him unhesitatingly. 'Rather, it was the – the action of an opportunist!'

'I do not admire myself for what I did,' he told her. 'If our actions make us what we are, this is what I have become.'

'And the letter you wrote to Bath –' Jane said.

'That was the most shameful thing of all,' he acknowledged ruefully. 'Indeed, I wrote *two* letters: one to your father purporting to be from my brother Frederick; the other to Frederick, purporting to be from Penberthy. They were similar in content. Penberthy asserted I had drowned. And so, having induced both you and my brother – the only two beings in the world for whom I felt a tender sentiment – to believe that I had died, I was free to come here and enter into a new life.'

'A false life!' Jane averred. 'It is impossible to condone what you have done, sir. Nor will you ever be free of your own conscience. I have heard you out, as you requested. I could not imagine a more reprehensible affair. To sacrifice your good name, your religious principles, for the sake of expediency, and to escape a situation you could not face –' She could say no more. Her words all but choked her. To recall the emotional distress, the anguish she had squandered upon this man! How he had duped them all – her father, mother, Cassandra – into mourning for his death!

'In a sense I *have* died,' he said quietly. 'I have lost my name, my self-respect –' he hesitated ' – and you. My sole endeavour now will be to offer whatever comfort I may provide to the miserable souls that will be placed in my care. I am to go to Norfolk Island shortly, to take up my duties there. I trust I shall never cast a slur upon the honourable name of Penberthy – he was a good, honest, faithful soul.'

Norfolk Island! The worst of all penal colonies, where the most recalcitrant convicts were sent! Jane shuddered. Then she said: 'Many of the unhappy inhabitants of the Colony have been transported here for crimes of a far lesser cunning than you have practised in this deception – I despise you, sir!' And she turned from him to walk back to the house and make a hasty adieu to a somewhat mystified Elizabeth McArthur. She desired never to see this man again.

Twenty-Two

THE CLOCK IN the ante-room to the Governor's office gave loud emphasis to the passing minutes. The relentless swing of the pendulum formed a counterpoint to the dry scratching of a goose quill upon paper as the Governor's clerk, a pleasant-looking young man with curly brown hair, occupied himself with lists of merchandise. From time to time this industrious fellow looked across to the visitor from Parramatta who had arrived without notice this September morning, requesting an urgent appointment with His Excellency. A quiet-looking, elderly gentleman who could not quite conceal an unmistakable air of suppressed excitement beneath his patient exterior.

James Leigh Perrot had been awaiting the Governor's pleasure almost two hours (and in the manner of elderly gentlemen had felt obliged to make a couple of visits to the necessary house). The clerk had given him copies of the *Gazette* to help pass the time. The latest number was straight from Mr Howe's printing press; the ink, not yet dry, had smudged his chamois gloves. By now he had finished with both news and advertisements, and had ingested sundry assorted facts. Matthew Flinders had sailed for England on the tenth of August in the *Porpoise* . . . the body of one Constable Luker had been found near Back Row, 'a breathless corpse, shockingly mangled' . . . Mr S. Lord had received a new consignment of goods which included Green Tea, Bengal soap, worsted pantaloons and plated cutlery . . . the first female from the Orphanage to graduate to marriage had become the wife of a baker at Parramatta . . .

There was only one item which absolutely compelled James

Leigh Perrot's interest. He read it avidly:

An animal, known to the natives as a Koola, is in His Excellency's possession. When taken it had two Pups, one of which died a few days since. This creature is somewhat larger than the Waumbat, and although it might at first appearance be thought much to resemble it, nevertheless differs from that animal. The fore and hind legs are about of an equal length, having five sharp talons at each end of the extremities, with which it must have climbed the highest trees with much facility. The fur that covers it is soft and fine, and of a mixed grey colour; the ears are short and open; the graveness of the visage, which differs little in colour from the back, would seem to indicate a more than ordinary portion of animal sagacity; and the teeth resemble those of a rabbit. The surviving Pup generally clings to the back of the mother, or is caressed with a serenity that appears peculiarly character-istic; it has a false belly like the opossum, and its food consists solely of gum leaves, in the choice of which it is excessively nice.

Perhaps, he thought, he would have the chance to view this creature before he returned to Parramatta . . .

In truth, Mr Leigh Perrot was quite content simply to sit upon his chair and contemplate the momentous news which he had come to impart to the Governor of New South Wales. *Gold!* – It was a discovery which must surely raise this shabby, down-at-heel, convenient penitentiary of a Colony to the forefront of Britain's proud possessions. This late-come, dishevelled, neglected child must soon become the golden apple of her Mother's eye! Now she would hold her head high in the com-pany of her siblings . . . the Indies, with their bouquets of nutmeg, cinnamon, cloves, peppercorns – those precious grains of paradise; or India, with her glittering treasures of emeralds and rubies . . . No longer would intelligence of this far south land lie buried beneath preoccupation with the French war (if, indeed, that war had been resumed, as seemed most likely, for the Peace of Amiens had been a flimsy enough armistice in all conscience) . . . Here would rise the latter-day El Dorado!

And what benefits there would be for the Colony itself, James reflected happily; how the burden of administration would be eased! New South Wales, as he had so often been told since his arrival here, had from its earliest days laboured under shortages and privations. It was something of a miracle, he reflected, that it had survived at all. He recalled those tales of near-starvation and despair, compounded by the disastrous Hawkesbury floods of recent memory, which had been related to him: tales recollected today against the comfort of a full belly and an assured harvest, but still with a residue of horror. The abyss, once glimpsed, was not easily forgotten.

It was Governor King himself who had informed him that no money whatsoever had been provided for the new Colony when the First Fleet sailed, let alone a stock of bullion with which to mint new coins. The small amount of coin minted in England, scarcely sufficient to supply the motherland herself, was cited as the reason for this omission; certain cynics, however, maintained that the venture of that First Fleet had never been expected to succeed; that England had cast her undesired humanity upon the oceans as though she were emptying a slop bucket. Those eleven ships filled with wretched felons, bound for an empty, unprofitable landfall – had Mother England really cared what happened to them once they disappeared over the horizon?

Whatever the way of it, until four years ago the only English money in circulation here (apart from receipts issued by the Commissary for goods supplied to government stores, and promissory notes which passed from hand to hand as a sort of paper currency) consisted of whatever coins had been brought in the purses and pockets of administrators, soldiers, convicts and – latterly – free settlers. Other coins arrived with ships which called at Port Jackson: rupees, pagodas and mohurs from India, johannas from Portugal, dollars from Spain . . . all were used and accepted. In '99, however, the home government had at last been pleased to furnish a supply of copper pence, to a total of five hundred and fifty pounds, and the following year a further quantity of halfpennies and farthings to the value of six hundred and fifty pounds. – Scarcely an embarrassment of largesse, but by then war had broken out, and Mr Pitt was hard-pressed to finance the expensive business of killing and maiming. Governor King had cried up the face value of these coins, promoting the coppers to twice their English value. He decreed a shilling to be worth one and eightpence, a guinea one pound two shillings. To the Spanish dollar, most numerous of the foreign coins in circulation, he gave the denomination of five shillings.

Spanish dollars were familiar currency everywhere – the Leigh Perrots were quite familiar with them in England – but they had found it difficult to accustom themselves to English coins which had a different value to that they knew at home. Mrs Leigh Perrot, in particular, was apt to become quite agitated over any transaction she conducted; moreover, her recent unfortunate experience had bred in her an unshakable distrust of all shopkeepers. The notion – agreeable enough – that twopence was worth *fourpence* in the Colony, was quite offset by the unpalatable realization that what *twopence* would have bought in England, in fact cost fourpence here.

Shifting on his chair, which had become very hard indeed by this time, James spared a fond thought for his wife. Dearest Jane! His discovery had excited her considerably; she had even surmised that a grateful government might well honour him on account of it . . . with a knighthood, perhaps, or possibly some higher ennoblement. – Sir James Leigh Perrot? Lord Perrot of Parramatta? But Aunt Perrot had frowned when her niece, with a grave expression, had suggested this; Perrot of Hare Hatch, in the County of Berkshire, sounded much more desirable, in her opinion.

James had come to Sydney yesterday by boat, along the Parramatta river – a pleasant trip, with reliable departures and arrivals now that the Governor had changed the timetables. He had stayed the night with the Patersons, telling them merely that he had a business appointment. He had been tempted to share with them the secret of the four golden walnuts, but it was a temptation he resisted; his portentous news must in the first instance be for His Excellency's ear alone. Every now and then he touched those hard lumps nestling in his pocket, to assure himself he had not fallen victim to some nimble-fingered thief as he walked through Sydney's streets. There was, of course, the chance – remote, James felt in his bones – that the nugs were not gold . . . but this possibility he relegated to the back of his mind.

During his long wait this morning, two other visitors had

252

been received by the Governor. First William Chapman had appeared, carrying a stack of books and documents; he had greeted James and inquired politely after Mrs Leigh Perrot and Miss Jane Austen, albeit with a somewhat preoccupied air, as though his mind were weighed down with worries as heavy as the books he carried. He had remained in the Governor's office for almost an hour, emerging with a look of increased anxiety on his face. James, noting this, thought with renewed satisfaction of the good tidings he was bringing to this hard-pressed administration.

He had expected to be summoned into the Governor's presence when Chapman bustled out; but at that juncture a woman had entered the ante-room. She looked to be in her forties, dark-haired, tolerably good-looking and neatly dressed. She bore the unmistakable stamp of an emancipated felon; it was evident in her nervous address to the clerk (to whom she was obviously no stranger) and in a certain subservience of manner. It was clear she was expected: the clerk had taken her straight into the inner sanctum. Her reappearance, however, was remarkably prompt, her interview concluded in a few moments. As she stood again in the doorway, James overheard the Governor's voice from within the room saying a little testily: ' . . . in the new year, I daresay, but not now, not now.'

The clerk ushered her out – reflecting, as he did so, that this was the third time Mistress Rourke had petitioned the Governor for a pardon for her husband. He shook his head: it was a mad world, this, and no mistake – years ago, as Ann Inett, this same Mistress Rourke had given birth to the Governor's two sons . . . now, married to a convict, she came seeking a pardon from their father. It was not so much the pardon itself she craved, the clerk shrewdly surmised, as the land grants which would accompany it: twenty acres for Patrick Rourke himself, and ten for each of his children.

Another few moments, and then – 'His Excellency will see you now, sir' – and at last James Leigh Perrot was shown into the gubernatorial presence.

'Vaux!' – Before turning to greet Mr Leigh Perrot, the Governor summoned his clerk peremptorily. 'If Mistress Rourke calls again upon that matter, do not make another appointment for her, d'ye hear.'

'Very well, sir,' James Vaux closed the door softly and returned to his desk. He was curious to know what matter had brought Mr Leigh Perrot here – it must surely be of some import for him to have waited so long – but if Mr King once caught him listening at the keyhole, he knew it would be the end of this cushy job – and the chance of those extra profits which came with it.

Those extra profits . . . James Vaux, whose education had encompassed a little Latin, less Greek and much knowledge of the underworld, had been transported for seven years for stealing an India wipe, a silk handkerchief, value elevenpence: just one instance of many another petty theft in his career. His industry this morning, remarked so approvingly by James Leigh Perrot, was chiefly devoted to his own interest. Over the last few months he had evolved a system of falsifying the lists for the commissary, obtaining extra goods over and above those ordered by official decree, and selling them for his own gain. This system depended upon two factors: the Governor's habit of scrawling his initials upon documents, rather than appending his full signature, and Vaux's ability to forge those three letters – P. G. K. Now his grey eyes gleamed as he bent to his task. *10 lbs nails*, he wrote carefully, *2 shovels*, *4 hand-saws* . . . and then, against the entry: *P. G. K.* Before the year was out, Vaux's enterprise was to take him from goose quill to hard labour in double irons: Philip Gidley King was not half so obtuse as his clerk imagined him to be.

James seated himself upon a chair before the Governor's desk, and His Excellency looked at him over the rims of his spectacles; it was very clear his mind was occupied with urgent matters.

'Mr Leigh Perrot? You have been waiting some time – I am extremely pressed today.' There was no expression of pleasure in meeting again this English visitor. He removed his spectacles and polished them with a handkerchief. Then – perhaps he felt he had sounded too abrupt – he took up a letter lying on his desk. 'Mr Chapman delivered distressing news this morning, sir, distressing news. Mr Flinders has just returned to Sydney: the *Porpoise*, his command – his late command – lies wrecked upon a coral reef, and the *Cato*, travelling in company with her, is lost as well, broken in pieces –'

James made an appropriate sound of consternation and dismay.

'Mr Flinders sets out the unhappy circumstances in this letter. There is no prospect of the *Porpoise* being saved – crew, officers and passengers of both ships, eighty men all told, are now existing upon a sandbank two hundred miles north-east of Sandy Cape, with sufficient provisions and water taken from the *Porpoise* to last them three months. Mr Flinders travelled over seven hundred miles back here in a six-oared cutter – a quite prodigious journey. We have been making arrangements to send immediate relief . . . Mr Flinders will probably continue his journey to England in the schooner *Cumberland* . . .'

The Governor returned the letter to his desk, glancing at Matthew Flinders' final paragraph. It was typical of that fine officer, he thought approvingly, that he should have taken pains to absolve the master of the *Cato* from any blame for the loss of that ship – and that he should have penned this intelligence immediately upon his landing in Sydney after such an arduous journey.

This unexpected setback had taken precedence today over all the Governor's many other anxieties . . . the increasing rate of petty misdemeanours in the Colony; the frightful murder of Constable Luker; his constant apprehension that more trouble might arise from the convicts at the government farm on Castle Hill. Fifteen of them had broken out in February and gone upon the rampage; they had been captured and hanged every one, but still the Governor felt uneasy. There were too many hotheads at Castle Hill.

'And what may I do for you, sir?' he asked Mr Leigh Perrot at last.

For answer, James brought forth the nugs of gold and solemnly set them upon the leather top of Mr King's desk. The four rough stones gleamed dully alongside Mr Flinders' letter.

'I believe these to be gold, sir,' he pronounced with an air of modest triumph.

The Governor's response was extraordinary. 'Gold, sir?' he said in a weary tone. 'Oh yes, I daresay it is very likely, very likely indeed.' And he sighed heavily.

'But – you do not seem surprised, sir.' – Indeed, the surprise was all on James Leigh Perrot's part.

'No, Mr Leigh Perrot, I am not surprised. Not at all surprised.' Mr King leaned back in his chair and made a steeple of his fingertips. 'I have to tell you, sir, that you are not the first – by no means the first – to have made this – this great discovery.' His matter-of-fact tone quite belied the hyperbole of those two words. 'And I dare swear,' the Governor added, 'that most of the discoverers do not come to me!' He spared a wry smile for his visitor. 'I respect your integrity, sir, in so doing.'

James was quite confused. This was far from the reception he had envisaged. 'But I thought –'

'I can imagine what you thought, sir, and I only wish it could be true: that the discovery of gold within the Colony would solve all our problems – provide a universal panacea for all our woes: was that not it? Was that what you envisaged?'

'Indeed, I did venture to suppose –'

'Allow me to inform you, sir, that the reverse would be the case – quite the reverse!'

Whereupon, to James' astonishment, the Governor got up and took a copy of the Bible from his bookshelf. Adjusting his spectacles, he found the place he sought and read aloud: ' ". . . they that will be rich fall into temptation and a snare, and into many foolish and hurtful lusts, which drown men in destruction and perdition. For the love of money is the root of all evil . . ." ' He fixed James with a piercing eye. 'Destruction and perdition, sir, destruction and perdition: *that* would be the inevitable result if gold were to be found here in any quantity. Men would set sail for these shores from the four corners of the earth – from England, Ireland, China, India, America . . . they would overrun and overturn our Colony; anarchy and chaos would result.'

'But – could not the Administration control – nay, prevent such a flood of gold seekers rushing here?' James besought him, clinging to the last vestige of his dream.

'No, sir, the Administration could not. – That is to say, I very much doubt it, sir, I very much doubt it. We have enough trouble maintaining order as it is.' The Governor's thoughts returned to the convicts at Castle Hill. 'Besides all those who would flock here from elsewhere, how should we restrain men and women within the Colony from tearing up the ground to seek their fortunes, neglecting all other duties, deserting their masters, their families . . .' Mr King shook his head, reflecting privately that the members of the New South Wales Corps would be among the first deserters. 'The Gold Corps': doubtless that would be their new soubriquet in such a case!

The Governor's eloquent prognostication of the dire results of the discovery of gold being publicly made known was finally persuasive. James' optimistic conclusions swayed – toppled – and fell. He felt like a schoolboy who had misconstrued a vital word in his Latin parsing.

Mr King replaced the Bible, returned to his desk, and spoke in a milder tone. 'I do not doubt, Mr Leigh Perrot, that gold indeed exists within this land, possibly – nay, probably – in large quantity. And there may well come a time when it may be taken from the ground without fear of such anarchy. But I do not think that will come to pass in our time.' He weighed the four pieces of gold in his hand. 'Why, sir, do you supposed the name "New Guinea" was coined over three centuries ago, for what was then thought to be the northern extremity of this continent?'

Feeling more like a schoolboy than ever, James stammered: 'I – I presume 'twas named after Guinea – that coastal region of West Africa.'

'Precisely! Guinea – the Gold Coast . . . Ghana, the land of gold – I do not need to remind you, sir, that England coined her first guineas out of gold imported from that coast.' The Governor continued his history lesson. 'The great Venetian traveller, Marco Polo, was sent by Kublai Khan with a fleet of ships from China to the Persian Gulf, and in the course of that voyage, he described a country which he called Lochac – a great mainland, wild and mountainous – where, he said, gold was abundant to a degree scarcely credible.'

'Lochac,' James repeated. 'Was that –'

'What else, sir, could it have been but this Great South Land?'

James said humbly: ' 'Twas an Aboriginal boy who brought these nugs to me –'

'Ah!' the Governor exclaimed. 'We know that certain native tribes of the north formerly exchanged gold for the products of traders from the Moluccas –'

'But I do not believe that Bingami realized –'

'And then there were the Dutch, sir, the Dutch,' Mr King

continued relentlessly. 'Two hundred years ago they explored the Gulf of Carpentaria and returned to Holland laden with gold. Which is the reason they always attached the utmost importance to this continent, which they were the first to discover and attempt to colonize – indubitably, sir, the first. *They* knew the riches it contained – and went to great lengths thereafter to prevent other nations from forming settlements here.'

'But failed in that objective,' James remarked smugly.

'Indeed,' Governor King agreed with a genial smile.

'And from your previous remarks, sir, I gather others have found pieces of gold since the Colony was founded?'

'Rumours of gold have always circulated amongst the convicts,' Governor King replied. 'Why, in the very first year of settlement, a rogue called Daley produced a stone which he declared was gold; he had the impudence to demand his freedom, as well as money, in return for revealing the place where he had found it! He was, of course, promptly *ordered* to reveal the place upon pain of punishment – whereupon he led an officer and some soldiers a pretty dance into the bush, then slipped away. He was captured and flogged, and finally confessed that he had filed down a buckle made of some yellow metal, mixed it with gold particles rubbed off a guinea piece, and blended this mixture with clay. Whereupon he was flogged again. 'Twas the end of his gold-mining aspirations.'

James smiled. 'An ingenious rogue.'

'Not the first, nor the last,' Mr King remarked enigmatically – and reminded himself of his growing suspicion of his clerk James Vaux. He feared it was well founded – a pity, for the fellow was a likable young rascal. 'A number of convicts are said to have found gold, and disposed of it for gain,' he continued. ' 'Tis my own belief that our El Dorado – assuming it exists – must lie beyond the Blue Mountains.'

James recalled Bingami's mime of climbing movements. 'I wonder –' he mused. When Bingami went walkabout, did he indeed scale that formidable mountain barrier?

The Governor became brisk. 'Well, well, Mr Leigh Perrot, this is all very interesting, very interesting indeed, but it does not advance the disposal of today's tasks.' He picked up the golden pieces and handed them to his visitor. 'I do not wish to know about these – these stones you have discovered, sir. And,' he added meaningfully, 'I trust you will keep the discovery to yourself.' As an afterthought he added: 'Mr William Moreton, next door to The Ship Before the Wind in Pitt's Row, is a reliable goldsmith and a discreet fellow.'

James stood to take his leave; Vaux, summoned by the Governor, held open the door for him.

'Ah – Your Excellency – there is just one other thing,' James said, pausing on the threshold.

'Yes, yes, what is it?' the Governor uttered, with an abrupt return to the testy manner with which he had first received Mr Leigh Perrot.

'I was reading in the *Gazette*, sir, that you have in your possession one of the tree-climbing animals which I believe the natives call – er – *koolas*. Would it be possible to see it?'

'Mr Vaux,' the Governor said in a tone of strained patience, 'kindly conduct Mr Leigh Perrot to the corner of the garden where the koola is kept. – Good day to you, sir,' he added firmly, lowering his gaze to the documents on his desk and cutting off his visitor's expression of gratitude.

A moment later, after James Vaux had left to show Mr Leigh Perrot the koola's enclosure, the Governor seized this opportunity to enter the ante-room and examine his clerk's ledger. His forefinger traced his own initials down the page: P. G. K. . . . P. G. K. . . . and stopped beside one entry. *This* P. G. K. was not his . . . but he could not deny that the rascal showed a fair hand in forgery.

James Leigh Perrot's viewing of the koola afforded him much consolation for the shipwreck of his gold speculation. He even attempted a sketch of the animal in his pocket-book. A pity his niece had not been there, he thought: she would have achieved a better likeness.

Afterwards he visited Mr Moreton the goldsmith, and had the small satisfaction of being assured that his stones were indeed pure gold. Mr Moreton evinced no surprise and asked no questions; it seemed clear enough that he had handled such stones before. James decided against selling the gold; he would look upon it as a curious keepsake. The next day he took the eleven o'clock boat to Parramatta, and came home to break his disappointing news to his two Janes, who had eagerly awaited his return.

A first-hand description of the koola did not offer any consolation to his wife when she learned how the Governor had received her husband's news. She bestowed a very cursory glance upon James' sketch of the creature. 'It seems to me,' she remarked acidly, 'that Mr King allows the everyday management of the Colony to obscure his larger vision. Anarchy and chaos indeed!' – she almost snorted. 'Why, if need be, a whole regiment could be imported from England to secure law and order. I simply do not understand, Perrot, an attitude which professes to regard riches and profit as liabilities!'

James shrugged and spread his hands. 'The Governor is adamant, my dear, that the quest for gold must be reserved for some future time.'

'And meanwhile the Colony's development is retarded for lack of funds! – Why, Mrs Marsden (poor soul, she feels the loss of her babe severely) was telling me only yesterday that the completion of St John's must wait upon the building of the new windmill here, for lack of sufficient resources.'

'A question of grinding the flour for our daily bread, rather than praying for it,' Jane observed.

To Jane, her uncle's return with news of a koola (she was kind enough to show more interest in his artistic impression of the animal), rather than the gratifying response of ineffable gratitude he had expected from the Governor, irresistibly reminded her of the old nursery story of that simple fellow who set out to buy a cow, and came home with a lump of melting butter on top of his head . . .

'I wish you to have one of these gold pieces, Jane,' James told his niece. 'It will be a souvenir of our visit to the Antipodes.'

A generous gesture indeed: such was Aunt Perrot's opinion. 'You should have it made into an ornament to wear upon a neck chain,' she told Jane.

Jane held the piece of gold in her hand. 'Twas surely a very tangible souvenir of the Antipodes . . . yet she had many more intangible keepsakes, of greater worth, locked in her heart and mind. – Impressions, characters, mannerisms, conversations . . . all of which she hoped to review and perhaps put to use with her pen before too long. Following her final encounter with Mr Fordwick (who now, as she had ascertained, had left for Norfolk Island), Miss Austen had discovered within herself a quite unexpected sense of liberation. The ultimate conclusion of that ill-fated romance seemed to have changed her thinking habits; now she felt quite free to turn her thoughts to other subjects. And chief among those was her writing. She was quite impatient now to settle down to the revision of *First Impressions*; not only that, but once again she experienced that familiar and pleasing sensation which had been absent for too long, of new characters, fresh ideas, another plot being manufactured in her mind.

James related more details of his visit – and Jane was distressed to learn of Mr Flinders' shipwreck. She recalled the conversation with that modest young officer which she had enjoyed on the evening of the Governor's ball. Now, resuming his journey to England on another ship, it would be longer still before he was reunited with his young wife . . .

Talk of the *Cumberland* sailing for England aroused Jane Leigh Perrot's homesickness. Surely her dear Perrot would soon have had enough of this tedious grey-green country with its outlandish animals and plants? Warm, very warm spring days were now upon them (spring in September! – the seasons turned upside-down) and he must, of course, await the butterflies. Any day now she hoped to see clouds, swarms, hosts of butterflies so that Perrot might have his fill of them! No Antipodean butterfly now folded within its cocoon could have been more eager to emerge than Jane Leigh Perrot was to see it in flight. For then, then at last they might all return to civilization.

Twenty-Three

In September the peach grounds were a gently swaying sea of blossom, and the standing crops of grain, encouraged by good rains earlier in the year, promised a splendid harvest. Now indeed butterflies abounded. James Leigh Perrot, armed with net and killing bottle, pursued them indefatigably: whites and yellows, browns and nymphs, blues, coppers and hairstreaks . . . a gay and lavish variety of species, flashing and darting in the bright sunshine. And always he hoped to find that butterfly hitherto unsighted and unrecorded, that new species with which his name might be associated in perpetuity . . . an ambition which, to his credit, meant far more to him than any notion of ennoblement arising from the mere discovery of gold.

Sometimes Jane Austen, alike armed with a butterfly net, would accompany her uncle and Bingami on these excursions. She was impressed by the fanatic zeal with which her mild-mannered uncle would stalk and seize his prey, wielding his net as though it were a lance, trapping the fragile flutterer triumphantly, and then transferring it into the killing bottle with its lethal atmosphere of potassium cyanide. She observed that before her uncle placed the insect in the bottle, he gave its thorax a sharp pinch, whereupon it became motionless. This stunned it, he informed her, and prevented damage to the wings which might be caused by thrashing death throes inside the bottle.

It was Bingami who first drew Mr Leigh Perrot's attention to the curious life-cycle of one Antipodean butterfly. The Aborigine conducted James to a black wattle bush, and, crouching beneath it, carefully smoothed away a little heap of debris, to reveal a crowd of ants surrounding a cluster of caterpillars. At first, James assumed that the ants were attacking the larvae, but on closer observation he realized this was not the case: caterpillars and ants, strange as it might seem, appeared to be engaged in some co-operative activity. Over a period of weeks he made a particular study of this strange phenomenon; it was, he found, the Bright Copper, *Paralucia aurifer*, which laid its eggs on the black wattle. The ants then emerged to cover the eggs with debris, forming a sort of byre, and, when the caterpillars hatched, guided them towards the succulent foliage. Once the larvae had eaten their fill, the ants took them back to the byre – a process repeated many times. The Lewins, James soon found, had made their own observation of this process. John Lewin's representation of *Paralucia aurifer* was complete in every detail, including the bright blue line on its hindwing. It was John Lewin's opinion that the reason for the ants' devoted care was their craving for a secretion exuded upon the backs of their charges; they appeared to feed upon the caterpillars, yet did not harm them. Eventually the caterpillars pupated in the byre, the butterfly emerged, crawled quickly to the light, then spread its coppery wings and flew away.

Visiting Elizabeth Farm one day with her uncle and aunt, Jane drew her uncle's attention to a golden butterfly which had alighted on the grape vine which trailed over the verandah.

'*Vanessa itea*,' her uncle announced, peering at it. 'It has a liking for fermented juices.'

Elizabeth McArthur gave a little peal of laughter. 'A drunken butterfly, Mr Leigh Perrot! I do not think His Excellency would approve of that proclivity!'

Jane Austen smiled. 'You make it sound quite human, Elizabeth. Do you not think the poor butterfly has undergone sufficient metamorphosis already?'

'Perhaps 'twould be better the other way around,' Elizabeth conceded. 'Man is a dull creature compared with these painted insects, is he not? – But perhaps *he* had best metamorphose into a moth.'

'Oh, he might do quite well as one of the Browns, I think,' James Leigh Perrot ventured. '*Heteronympha banksia*, for instance – or else the Common Brown, the first butterfly to be collected here . . . *Heteronympha merope.*'

Such fanciful notions disturbed Aunt Perrot's pragmatism. 'A human being is a human being, a butterfly a butterfly: it is absurd to attempt a correspondence between the two,' she pronounced firmly.

'May not a little absurdity be allowed on occasion, Aunt?' Jane asked her. ' 'Tis good for the soul, I have heard.'

'I never wish to be absurd,' Mrs Leigh Perrot replied. 'My soul survives very well without absurdity, I do assure you.'

This flat statement left Jane with an almost unbearable longing for just ten – no, even a mere five minutes' fizzy conversation with Cassandra, so that they might air their mutual delight in all things ridiculous, ludicrous, absurd. Vain wish!

One afternoon, emerging from the front door of their cottage, James spied a large and showy butterfly upon the orange tree, now bursting with wax-petalled, sweet-scented blossom. It was a swallowtail – yes, definitely a swallowtail, with that unmistakable elongation to the hindwings . . . '*Papilio anactus,*' James murmured to himself, a Dingy Swallowtail . . . surely a most inappropriate name! – But none of these, not the Bright Copper nor the *Vanessa itea* nor the Dingy Swallowtail, represented that unknown species he yearned to discover . . .

The notion which had been planted in James Leigh Perrot's mind at the Lewins' supper party, that Bingami might return to England with them, had, as Jane Leigh Perrot feared it might, flourished exceedingly. At breakfast one morning – it was now the first week of October and spring was slipping imperceptibly into summer – he finally decided to broach the subject. For once Ellen had not burnt the toast, and a good-humoured mood prevailed over the breakfast table. Jane Austen was reading aloud from last Sunday's *Gazette*: the item she had selected scarcely fitted the description of breakfast entertainment, since it concerned the attempted hanging of a man convicted, tried, and condemned to death for the murder of Constable Luker: one Joseph Samuels.

' "Samuels devoted the last awful minute allowed him to the most earnest and fervent prayer," ' Jane read in her clear, mellifluous voice. ' "At length the signal was given and the cart drove from under him, but by the concussion the suspending cord was separated about the centre, and the culprit fell to the ground –" '

'And so I presume they had to hang him all over again,' her aunt remarked, taking another slice of toast. 'This marmalade is excellent: I believe I quite prefer it to quince.'

' "The cart returned," ' Jane continued, ' "and the criminal was supported on each side until another rope was applied; he was launched off, but the line unrove and continued to slip until the legs of the sufferer trailed along the ground, the body being only half suspended . . ." '

'Quite extraordinary!' remarked her uncle.

'Third time lucky, I would hope,' his wife remarked, pouring him another cup of coffee.

' "All that beheld were moved at his protracted suffering; nor did some hesitate to declare that the invisible hand of Providence was at work –" '

'What nonsense!' Aunt Perrot declared. ' 'Twas a rotten rope, for sure.'

' "To every appearance lifeless," ' Jane continued imperturbably, ' "the body was now raised and supported on men's shoulders while the executioners prepared anew the work of death. The body was gently lowered, but when left alone again fell prostrate to the earth, this rope having also snapped short, close to the neck." '

'Great heavens!' James was quite gripped by the macabre drama.

' "Compassion could no longer bear restraint –" '

'Cannot you give us the meat of it, niece, without our having to follow every tedious word written there?' Aunt Perrot interrupted.

Jane rapidly ran her eyes over the remainder of the printed text. 'To paraphrase the events, then: a furious outcry came from the crowd – the Provost-Marshal galloped off to acquaint Governor King with the astonishing events. Half an hour later, reprieve arrived – the wretched half-strangled Samuels was taken off to the gaol, followed by a cheering mob. – Oh, and it says that later in the day, one of the ropes which had been used was tested in the gaol, being suspended from a beam with seven weights, each of fifty-six pounds, hanging from it. The three strands of the rope were then cut in turn – but the third strand alone was sufficient to support the whole weight. So it seems, Aunt, 'twas not rotten after all.'

'Let us hope,' Aunt Perrot said piously, 'that the wretch's grateful remembrance of such a fortuitous escape will direct his future courses!'

As Jane laid aside the paper, James seized his opportunity. 'Ahem – talking of future courses, my dear,' he said to his wife, 'I have been giving a good deal of thought to Bingami's future. The boy appears singularly attached to our little family; it seems almost unkind to leave him here when we depart –'

'Perrot!' His wife's exclamation caused James to spill a little coffee into his saucer. 'Are you about to propose that we should take Bingami home with us?'

'Yes, my dear,' he asserted mildly. 'That is exactly my proposal. He will not be the first Aborigine to visit England. There was Bennelong . . .'

'And look at Bennelong now! Several of our acquaintances took particular pains to point him out to me when we were at Sydney: he has become nothing but a violent and savage drunkard. In my opinion, husband, Admiral Phillip did Bennelong no service by taking him off to England.

'Bennelong was a grown man when he sailed to England; Bingami is still a child,' James answered with sweet reasonableness. 'I thought he might serve as gardener's boy at Scarlets, perhaps in time become under-gardener – one day, who knows, head gardener! Old Isaac would take him in hand, show him the way things are done . . . Bingami knows a good deal about the native plants and trees, and I should like to attempt a plantation of native flora –'

'If he were set to work in the hot-houses, I daresay he would not shiver so much in our English winter,' Jane Austen put in lightly.

'It is not a frivolous matter, Jane,' her aunt said reprovingly. 'Your uncle is proposing to uproot the boy, half-wild as he is, from one side of the world to the other. Heaven knows what the result might be!'

'I have a genuine concern for the boy's welfare,' James Leigh Perrot said with quiet dignity. 'I believe he would fit in with our way of life at Scarlets very well, and grow up a proper Englishman. He has been extremely useful to me here, and,' he concluded quite firmly, 'it pleases me to reward him by taking in hand his future development.'

Jane Leigh Perrot shrugged. She knew very well that once her husband had settled upon a course of action, it was a waste of effort to attempt to change his decision. – As for Jane Austen, she was quite fascinated to observe how mild, reasonable discourse was able to overcome shrill, prejudiced objection.

'Well then, the boy will need suitable wearing apparel,' her aunt said in a resigned tone of voice. 'And a less outlandish name would be desirable . . . we might call him Benjamin.'

'By all means, my dear,' her husband acquiesced, happy to humour her suggestion now that his main object was achieved. 'I will endeavour to explain to Bing . . . ah, to *Benjamin* the future that lies before him.'

What a place this Colony was for the manufacture of new names and identities, Jane Austen thought . . . First Mr Fordwick was metamorphosed into Mr Penberthy, and now Bingami the Aborigine was to become Benjamin the gardener's boy! And just how, she wondered, would her uncle contrive to inform Bingami-Benjamin about the extraordinary adventure he was to undertake?

The following Sunday was the hottest October day the inhabitants of Parramatta could recall. A scorching west-north-westerly wind blasted in, sweeping a minor dust-storm across the cleared ground and blighting fields and orchards. At the end of morning service, Mr Marsden's flock emerged into a temperature of ninety-two degrees and hurried away to slake their prodigious thirsts, perspiring profusely beneath their hot, tight clothing, and looking apprehensively upon their farming lands. Elizabeth McArthur arrived home to find her peach trees devastated, the ground littered with unripe fruit. All around the Hawkesbury the standing grain was withered, and disconsolate clusters of sheep sought the shade beneath the few trees which had been left upright in their pastures. It seemed ironical indeed that Mr Marsden should have chosen as his text that morning those uplifting words from Isaiah: 'Then Judgement shall dwell in the wilderness, and righteousness remain in the fruitful field. And the work of righteousness shall be peace; and the effect of righteousness quietness and assurance for ever . . . the desert shall rejoice, and blossom as the rose. It shall blossom abundantly, and rejoice even with joy and singing.'

But there was precious little joy in Parramatta today.

The Leigh Perrots and their niece sat uncomfortably in their cottage, dismayed at the sudden savage change of weather.

'If this is a foretaste of what we may expect throughout the summer —' Jane Leigh Perrot moaned, leaving her sentence unfinished.

The prospect alarmed them all. This morning, realizing that they were in for a hot day, Aunt Perrot had flung open all the windows, refusing to heed Ellen's advice that she should close them in order to keep the cottage reasonably cool. When the unpleasant wind sprang up, the windows were closed straightway, but by that time the damage was done: the cottage had become as hot and airless as a baker's oven.

Jane Austen felt her clothes sticking to her; her hair was damp against her brow. It seemed impossible to do anything but sit and sip tepid lemon water. She slipped her feet out of her shoes, and observed that her aunt had done the same. They fanned themselves until their wrists were tired. Then, at half-past one, the wind veered right round to the south-south-east, and in a mere ten minutes the temperature fell by twenty degrees. Ellen came rushing in to fling the windows wide open, and a cool, cleansing breeze invaded the room.

'This is impossible! We shall catch our deaths of colds!' Aunt Perrot declared, going to fetch a shawl. A shawl! So short a time ago she would have eschewed the very idea of a shawl to comfort her shoulders.

' 'Tis a cool change,' Ellen told them, standing by the open window, hands on her hips.

Jane saw the dark half-circles of perspiration that stained her gown beneath the armpits, and realized that all this while, Ellen had been preparing their dinner over the hot stove.

'Now you'll feel more like gettin' stuck into yer roast chicken,' Ellen said. She turned to address Mr Leigh Perrot. 'That Bingami's here with summat to show yer, sir.'

James nodded. 'He may come in, Ellen.'

She bustled out. 'Go into the master then, yer young varmint!' they heard her call. It was her custom to address the Aborigine boy in this fashion; there was no animosity in her words.

Bingami came into the room, with something precious gently clasped in his thin brown hands. '*Pilyilye*,' he said, his dark eyes glowing and a wide white grin spreading across his face.

'*Butterfly*, Bingami? This is scarcely a day for butterflies, poor things. They must have been scorched out of existence.'

With infinite care Bingami opened the cage of his slender fingers to reveal the butterfly he had found crawling on the ground, one he had never seen before. He had rescued it an instant before his tame magpie could snap it up. It was clearly exhausted, if not dead already . . . James was perhaps mistaken in thinking that he detected a faint quiver of movement. He gazed upon it with mounting excitement and bade Bingami put it on the table. Then, fetching his enlarging glass, he examined it minutely. It was a large butterfly, a skipper . . . its wings were black, with yellow spots. It was a male and – he peered more closely through the glass – what was this? Impossible! Something never heard of before in the annals of lepidoptery! This butterfly appeared to own that attribute which hitherto he had supposed to belong solely to the moth . . . a *frenulum*! Yes, it was beyond doubt: there, protruding at the base of the hindwing, were those unmistakable bristles which in flight would be gripped beneath the forewing by a membranous hook: a hook and eye, in fact, devised by nature. The flight of both butterflies and moths depended upon hindwing and forewing closing together to act as one. In butterflies – all butterflies save this one, it would seem – this was achieved by a generous overlapping of the base of the hindwing beneath the forewing. Moths, on the other hand, were equipped with the frenulum to provide the same result. The existence of a frenulum, therefore, had always – until now – provided part of the definition of a moth.

Until now . . . For James Leigh Perrot was quite certain that this black and yellow butterfly (he guessed it to be a skipper of the subfamily *Pyrginae*) had never been described by any other naturalist. This, in fact, seemed beyond doubt to be that hitherto unknown species he had sought so earnestly. Furthermore – James almost trembled as he realized this – it was not solely a new species: it was a butterfly which by its unique anatomy might provide a connecting link between every butterfly and every moth! James' thoughts grew incoherent. This was definitely matter for publication . . . perhaps an address to the

Linnean Society . . . certainly a letter to Sir Joseph Banks . . . But one thing was quite certain: whatever name was chosen for this butterfly, it would be designated *perrotsia!*

Bingami was disturbed to see moisture oozing from the eyes of his adopted grandfather. *'Pilyilye* not good?' he asked anxiously.

'It is an excellent butterfly, Bingami,' James Leigh Perrot replied, smiling happily even as those tears of joy which he could not suppress coursed down his cheeks.

Everything must be put aside while Ellen served their dinner: at mealtimes this convict maid-of-all-work assumed the time-honoured tyranny of every cook. 'The chicken and meself – we was roasted both!' she declared, putting down the dish for the master to carve, and taking away her helping to eat in the kitchen.

James had moved the butterfly on to a small table by the window, and as they toyed with the food on their plates, his wife and niece expressed delight in his discovery. Aunt Perrot's delight was in fact twofold: not only did she sincerely rejoice for her husband; surely, she thought, now that his dearest ambition was realized at last, they might seriously think of returning home. No other vessel had come from England all the time they had been in the Colony – but a ship must arrive before long, and depart again homeward. Her dearest ambition was that they should depart with it, and leave this unpredictable place where winds blew hot one moment and cold the next.

James' thoughts, as he ate absent-mindedly, were concerned with the phrasing of his description of the butterfly. He must be sure to take accurate measurements . . .

Suddenly Aunt Perrot gave a little scream and half-rose in her chair.

'What is it, Aunt?' – alarmed, her niece imagined a bone had lodged in her throat.

'Quick! Before it escapes – oh, too late, too late!' Aunt Perrot cried. 'Oh Perrot, oh best and dearest husband!'

She did not need to explain further: facing the window from her place at table, she had seen that butterfly, which they had assumed to be dead, crawl upon the open windowpane – and following her horror-struck gaze, her husband and niece turned just in time to see the insect poised there for a second before it

270

fluttered out into the world. It was gone!

James Leigh Perrot rushed outside – but there was no sign of it. It had vanished completely. His happiness was in a single instant changed to dismal dismay: a change as sudden as the weather of that strange October day.

John Lewin listened carefully to Mr Leigh Perrot's description of his marvellous butterfly, but it was clear he was not convinced of the accuracy of that gentleman's observation.

'A *frenulum*, you say?' He frowned. 'Upon a *butterfly*?' His tone was distinctly sceptical.

Nothing could be proved: the butterfly was gone. For a while the atmosphere within the cottage on the western road was redolent of bitter loss – it was almost as though someone had died. Perhaps, Jane Austen thought, they should all have assumed black crêpe. But the human being is a resilient creature: and there was this consolation: for the rest of his life, James Leigh Perrot would savour the priceless satisfaction of having glimpsed that unique insect which appeared to embody a correlation between butterfly and moth.

Twenty-Four

SUMMER HAD COME early this year. The weather became steadily hotter, more humid and – to the English visitors – more unbearable. They learned to shun the sunshine and seek the shade, and during the day the ladies never walked abroad without their parasols.

'I have no wish to appear as dark as a gypsy when we return home,' Aunt Perrot declared. 'Just look at Ellen – she has become as swarthy as Jem Merrilees!'

'Since they are to become man and wife, perhaps it is fitting they should match each other,' Jane commented.

For Ellen had announced that she and Gypsy Jem were to marry in the new year. 'I never thought to see meself an autem mort – I mean, a married woman, miss,' Ellen confided to Jane. 'As fer Jem, he says he never would've believed 'e'd walk into the parson's mousetrap! But – well, we've a mind ter settle down. We're due to get our tickets nex' year, the both of us, an' Jem 'as plans to start up a stable wiv nags fer hire – 'e's got a bit o' money put by.' Her homely, sunburned features assumed an almost coy expression. 'To tell you the truth, miss – I'm nuts about my Jem. 'Twas a real bit o' luck, me comin' ter Parramatta wiv you, fer that was the cause of our meeting, if you 'member –'

Jane did remember; and the recollection of that day, and their visit to Homebush, inevitably brought Mr Wentworth to mind. She hoped there might be an opportunity to meet him once again before they left the Colony . . .

During the past few weeks, James Leigh Perrot had tried to

explain to Bingami that he would be going with them across the sea to a distant land, but he was not at all sure the boy understood the concept.

'*Warara warara* – Bingami go long, long way,' the boy said, echoing James' words. But how could he have any real notion of the new life which James Leigh Perrot planned for him?

Mrs Leigh Perrot instructed the shopkeeper, Mr Hassall, to fit out Bingami with a suit of clothes; much to the Aborigine's bemusement, he was taken to the shop one day, and there, under James' supervision, he tried on a pair of worsted breeches, shoes and stockings, and a shirt and coat complete with shiny buttons. When he stood before Mr Hassall's looking-glass, it was the first time he had ever seen himself reflected completely, from his dark curly head to his long, almost prehensile toes, now encased in those hard, heavy buckled shoes. He moved nearer the glass and extended one arm until his hand touched the hand of the boy who looked back at him in the mirror: a black boy, hidden in the white man's clothing. He did not need to glance behind the glass to find out whether another boy stood there; he knew it was himself he saw . . . and yet, it was not himself.

James had expected Bingami to be puzzled, possibly amused, perhaps to show pleasure when he saw himself in his new clothes: he had certainly not anticipated the strange, disoriented, even fearful expression which entered the boy's eyes. The next instant, Bingami began to divest himself of those clothes with almost desperate haste: riving at the shiny buttons, he tore off the coat – flung the shirt over his head – wriggled out of the breeches – cast off the shoes and peeled the stockings from his legs . . . and, with a final fleeting glance in the mirror to reassure himself of his true existence, and clad only in the faded scrap of cotton which was his customary single garment, he fled outside. He did not reappear for several days following this incident; James even imagined he might have disappeared for good this time (Aunt Perrot devoutly hoped this might indeed prove so), but at length the boy returned, bringing with him a piece of bark folded into the shape of a cup and filled with delicious honey plundered from a nest of native bees . . . as a peace offering, perhaps.

Aunt Perrot put the new garments carefully away. 'I only hope they will still fit Benjamin when the time comes for our departure,' she remarked, managing to stifle her disapproval of the whole undertaking. 'Children have a disconcerting habit of outgrowing their clothes.'

Their departure . . . It was now tacitly understood that this should take place as soon as it might be arranged – That was to say, whenever the next vessel should arrive from England and prepare for a return voyage. A tactful approach by letter to Government House had elicited official sanction for this proposal; two poop deck cabins would be available for Mr and Mrs Leigh Perrot and Miss Austen. James recalled that Mr David Collins – Lieutenant-Governor Collins, to accord him his proper title – had expected to set sail from England in April to establish the new settlement at Port Phillip: it seemed a foregone conclusion that his ship, having called at Port Phillip, would continue on to Port Jackson. Each week they scanned the *Gazette* for news of that or any other ship.

On one occasion, a picnic on the river bank organized by Mrs McArthur – a pleasant *al fresco* affair offering a cool retreat on a hot day – Aunt Perrot quizzed Mr Harris about the likelihood of a vessel arriving in the near future. As usual, the surgeon was spending the weekend in Parramatta; he had carried the picnic hamper filled with the inevitable mutton pies, sweet tomatoes from the McArthur garden and succulent peaches from the McArthur orchard – rare survivors of a blighted crop – as well as other viands and a bottle or two of wine which had been cooled in the river. Mr Harris, Aunt Perrot reasoned, was in close touch with the administration in Sydney; he might have advance news of a ship.

But to her disappointment he shook his head. 'I am as much in the dark upon the subject as yourself, madam,' he answered her. 'The first intelligence of the event will be the signal on Flagstaff Hill, in Sydney: from there it will be relayed with all speed by semaphore to Parramatta.' He was reclining on the grass between Mrs Leigh Perrot and Miss Jane Austen, who both sat on canvas stools, shaded by parasols and further sheltered from the sun by the foliage overhead.

He looked up at the younger woman. 'You are extremely anxious for your complexion, Miss Austen,' he said teasingly. 'I am of the opinion that a *little* sun-browning affords a useful protective colouring for this climate.' He observed her olive-tinted complexion with a professional eye. She need not fear the sun as much as her pink-and-white sisters. A darker complexion, he thought to himself, seemed more in keeping with this dry, brown, ancient land of faded greys and greens. His thoughts wandered naturally towards miscegenation . . . there were numbers of half-Aboriginal children wandering the streets of Sydney. Wretched mites! For them, the common plight of the Eurasian, disowned and outcast by both their worlds, was compounded by the dilemma that faced every Aborigine: how to survive under the imposition of an alien, modern way of life upon their prehistoric existence.

Jane Austen looked down at the surgeon, answering him in a tone that matched his own. 'All is not vanity, Mr Harris, as the preacher sayeth. A parasol discourages the flies, you know, as well as sunburn and freckles.'

'Ah, I grant you the nuisance of the flies, Miss Austen,' Mr Harris responded – and waved a hand across his face even as he spoke. 'Curious to relate, no one seems to know whether they are indigenous to this land or not. Some maintain they were brought here clinging to our sailors' backs.'

'I suppose we should be thankful there are none of those plaguey English wasps to annoy us here,' Miss Austen declared forthrightly. 'They would at this moment be hovering assiduously over Mrs McArthur's excellent treacle tart!' As she spoke, she helped herself to a slice of that same tart, being offered with solemn importance to all the picnickers by young William McArthur.

John Harris looked at her curiously. In some indefinable manner, he thought, Miss Jane Austen had changed. Her manner was more assured; she appeared content in herself. If he had had to phrase his feeling precisely, he would have said she seemed to have become . . . her own woman. He looked away, plucked a blade of grass and chewed it thoughtfully. How singular, he thought, the life of a spinster lady. To know the needs, but never to experience the shared delights of the flesh . . . to guard her health, preserve her complexion – be it pink-and-white, olive or magnolia; to dress with care, be accomplished, charming, sprightly in conversation – for what end? To be her own woman? Was that a truly satisfying existence? He looked up into the leafy canopy above and closed his eyes against a shaft of sunlight. The human being, he thought, was a complex creature. Man alone, it seemed, killed others of his own kind; and civilized gentleman, by his unnatural mores and from mere worldly considerations, could condemn the most delightful females of his own species to an unfulfilled and empty existence. Why should this be so? Even while he acknowledged that he himself, *ipso facto*, connived at this scheme of things, Mr Harris felt a sudden impotent spurt of anger. Miss Jane Austen should now be a contented wife with little children clustering about her, instead of sitting there alone beneath her parasol, preserving her complexion and her virginity.

And yet — had he not just marked her as content? To reverse his interior argument completely: did such smooth-complexioned spinsters have the best of it, perhaps? Happy marriages were few enough; far too many women were worn out by childbearing before their middle years, become drudges to autocratic husbands and demanding offspring, victims of the prolapsed uterus, of cancers, miscarriages, stillborn babes . . . it happened so very often that they died before their fortieth year, those wives and mothers, the happy ones as well as the resigned and miserable. Whereupon their husbands promptly got themselves new young wives and a second family. Life, John Harris reflected, was not very well designed for ladies.

Could he have known it, this reversed argument of his was one which Jane Austen herself was coming more and more to appreciate as she neared her thirtieth year. Next month she would be twenty-eight. Surely a confirmed spinster! But that prospect, which had once seemed so vastly undesirable (and did so still to her brother James, she knew), she now felt quite capable of accepting as her future lot.

As for that eligible bachelor, Mr Harris, he fully intended to marry soon himself, to beget children, and to attain a serene domestic harmony. He thought he knew what qualities he required in a wife; indeed, could tick them off as though he were ordering supplies for his medicine chest: an amiable disposition; a robust constitution; a sense of humour; resourcefulness; intelligence, of course . . . He discarded the blade of grass he had been chewing and looked directly across to where Elizabeth McArthur sat on the ground, her voluminous paisley cotton skirt spread about her in graceful folds, playing cat's cradle with young William. *That* admirable lady possessed all those qualities and more. And that, he realized – yet did not realize exactly the depth of his feelings – was what he required: a second Elizabeth McArthur! But there was no other version of her; she was unique. And she was the wife of the ambitious, erratic, scheming, overbearing John McArthur. Just once, John Harris had been present when Captain McArthur had fallen into one of his terrible rages. He had thought then that he showed signs of madness, that he would need to be restrained – until, with a tremendous effort, the man had got control of himself again. Perhaps Captain McArthur *was* mad: his enterprise, energy and determination to succeed were certainly supra-normal. And he had a disconcerting lack of humour. One thing, however, seemed beyond dispute: he adored his wife. – Well, doubtless the 'hero of the fleece', as Governor King liked to call McArthur in his most disparaging tones, would hasten back as soon as he could manage it – bringing, John Harris feared, more trouble and dissension in his wake.

At that moment Elizabeth McArthur looked up and, seeing the surgeon's pensive gaze fixed in her direction, smiled at him. 'A penny for your thoughts, Mr Harris!' she called gaily.

He met her gaze and shook his head. 'I assure you Mrs McArthur, they are not worth a farthing,' he said, with a hint of melancholy in his voice.

It was shortly after this picnic party, on the fifteenth of November, to be exact, that an American ship, the brig *Wertha Ann*, out of New York and bound for China, dropped anchor at Port Jackson. She had left New York on the seventeenth of July, and carried American newspapers which contained the news that hostilities had broken out again last May between Great Britain and the French Republic.

James Leigh Perrot read out this news from the latest copy of the *Gazette*, and Jane Austen's thoughts flew at once to her brother Henry and his wife . . . had he and Eliza been trapped in France? Did they now languish there as enemy aliens? She could not bear to speculate.

Aunt Perrot was singularly unsympathetic when Jane voiced her fears. 'That was a foolish undertaking, I said so at the time 'twas first mooted. How could Eliza hope to profit from it? A run-down château – half her late husband's family guillotined, I daresay – a quite pointless expedition.'

'Eliza may have wished to provide for a memorial to the Comte and to renew her acquaintanceship with the dowager Comtesse, if she is still alive,' Jane suggested, not really caring to hear her cousin spoken of in this dismissive manner. For sure, Eliza could be provoking at times, but she was always gay and merry.

'Possibly,' Aunt Perrot said in a tone of scepticism. She had never approved of that little minx Eliza Hancock . . . Madame la Comtesse de Feuillide . . . plain Eliza Austen as she was now, she reflected with unkind satisfaction.

More unsettling still – and a prospect they viewed with united dread – was the report that Bonaparte, as soon as war was declared, had uttered threats of an immediate descent upon England.

'Invasion!' Aunt Perrot exclaimed, shuddering. 'And here are we, at the other side of the world, when such dreadful danger threatens everyone and everything belonging to us!'

Jane tried to voice reassurance. 'Depend upon it, very strong defensive measures will have been taken to meet the threat,' she said, recalling her brother Frank and the force of Sea-Fencibles he had recruited at Ramsgate. But in her heart she felt as her aunt did; she longed to stride in one bound the vast distance that separated her from her family and everything she knew and loved.

'May . . . why, that was six months ago!' Aunt Perrot realized. '*Anything* might have happened, and we none the wiser –'

They looked at one another in fearful conjecture. Frightful tableaux presented themselves: French infantrymen landing upon English beaches, marching through villages and towns . . . battles in the green countryside, the roll of drums, the trumpet call, noise of cannon . . . rape and pillage, fields and orchards despoiled. It was unthinkable – and yet it was not beyond the bounds of possibility.

James tried to calm their mutual apprehension by reducing speculation to the most mundane level. 'I daresay the Admiral may wish to relinquish his lease of Scarlets; it is most likely he will have been recalled to active service.'

His wife seized gratefully upon this thought. 'We shall need to come to some agreement about terms in that case,' she said practically. But immediately her mind fell once again into a wild surmise. Perhaps Scarlets was now the headquarters for some French marshal disposing his troops about the Berkshire countryside . . . Their town house would likely be commandeered as well – unless, of course, Bath was held as a stronghold of resistance against the invader . . .

There was no way to assuage their fears, no comfort to be gained from any source, not a soul in the Colony who had more knowledge of events than they themselves possessed. They learned later that the intelligence in the American newspapers had been reprinted from English sources. They thirsted for first-hand news.

'The vessel intended for Port Phillip must arrive soon,' James Leigh Perrot said, determined to maintain a shred of optimism. 'But then,' he realized suddenly, 'if it left England in April, as Mr Collins expected, that would have been *before* hostilities were resumed –'

'And so we shall be none the wiser when and if it does arrive,' his niece remarked soberly.

'We might as well be living upon another planet,' Aunt Perrot declared fretfully, 'so completely divorced as we are from events in the real world. I am heartily tired of reading about the petty disputes here that pass for *news*: who has been chopping down timber that belongs to another, or throwing refuse into the Tank Stream . . . It is all such stuff – sometimes relieved, of course, by the unsavoury account of some gruesome murder or robbery! As for the political entanglements and goings-on, why, if anyone so much as mentions that wretched duel between Captain McArthur and Colonel Paterson once more, I shall positively *explode!*'

Then, on the twenty-seventh of November, the *Ocean* arrived at Port Jackson, having sailed from England as a supply ship for the settlement at Port Phillip. Lieutenant-Governor Collins had, they heard, reached Port Phillip a little ahead of the *Ocean*, travelling in the transport *Calcutta* with over two hundred convicts, a small military establishment, and two free settlers. The *Ocean* brought English newspapers, official documents – and correspondence from home.

When James Leigh Perrot went to the Post Office in Parramatta to fetch that week's issue of the *Gazette*, he found there a budget of letters awaiting his collection. The exiles were wonderfully recruited to receive these: there were several closely-written papers from family and friends addressed to each of them. No matter that these had been dispatched little more than a month following their own departure from England: even though the news they contained was by now quite out of date and doubtless superseded by a score of more recent happenings, a multitude of altered circumstances, it was still a splendid restorative to feel in touch once more with friends, cousins, parents, sister, brothers . . . with the *world*, as Aunt Perrot would have it.

They opened their papers avidly, quickly scanning the crowded, criss-crossed lines, first catching the gist of the communication to make sure that no dire piece of news was contained within it; then they began each one again from the beginning, reading in a more leisurely manner, savouring every phrase. From time to time their silent, individual absorption would be broken by an exclamation, marked by a raised eyebrow or appreciative smile. And every now and then one of them could not resist throwing out some morsel of intelligence.

'The Admiral reports that all is well at Scarlets, my dear,' James reported. 'He has had Isaac returf the upper lawn –'

'Lady Bridges tells me cambric bonnets are a good deal worn this season . . . salmon is three shillings and fourpence a pound . . . her cook paid a *shilling* for a cucumber!' Aunt Perrot sounded a good deal more scandalized by this information than ever she did over murder and mayhem in Sydney town.

'Here is a letter from Henry,' Jane said, 'written just before he and Eliza were to depart for France . . . He says they went to see the Kangaru billed at the Lyceum in the Strand, where the new gas lighting has been installed. 'Twas the price of Lady Bridge's cucumber, Aunt, to view the Kangaru, and 'twas billed as "the unparalleled animal from the Southern Hemisphere". The gas lighting was extraordinarily bright, Henry says.'

'Gas,' her aunt observed disparagingly. 'Nasty explosive stuff. The idea will never catch on. People are far too sensible to risk being blown to smithereens each time they light a lamp.'

Jane forbore to point out that having once been blown to smithereens, it would scarcely be possible to repeat the process.

'I wonder,' James said musingly, 'if we should consider taking a pair of breeding kangaru back with us to run – or perhaps I should say hop – in the park at Scarlets?' He bent to the perusal of his letters once more, and did not see the fond, despairing glance bestowed upon him by his wife. Were they to be encumbered by two kangaru as well as the Aboriginal boy upon their homeward journey?

There was silence for a while: then, reading her letter from Cassandra, Jane could not withhold a sudden quick, incredulous intake of breath. For she had just become the possessor of a quite unexpected and astonishing piece of news. Cassandra wrote:

My father desires you to know that he forwarded the manuscript of *Susan* to Messrs Crosby & Cox, Publishers, which he says was an action undertaken with yr consent, given before you left England – Well, my dear, clever Sister, the Half of that Company which is Mr Crosby has very promptly and civilly replied that he is much taken with yr Novel and intends to publish it shortly. He is already drawing up an Advertisement! – Is not this the best news you have ever received in a Letter? My father (who would, by the bye, have written to you himself, had he not been called to Winchester to attend to some business) desires you to know further, that Mr Crosby offered the Sum of ten pounds for the manuscript on account of Revenue accruing from its Publication, and in yr absence, he agreed to this Payment, which he considers reasonable in view of the fact that other Sums will be forthcoming. We are agog to see yr Novel in print, and can scarce refrain from giving loud Advertisements of the Book ourselves. (Though, you may be sure, we are maintaining an amazing discretion concerning the Lady Author in our Family.) Our most earnest wish is that you will return in time for its Publication. – I am determined we shall haunt the Library in Milsom Street together, and stand beneath the chandelier to hear every body's opinion of it and their notions of who that Lady may be!

Uncle Perrot looked up when he heard Jane's gasp of surprise. 'Not unwelcome news, niece, I trust?'

She answered him in a little confusion. 'Oh no, Uncle, it is

281

merely that – that Cassandra tells me of an – an unexpected event.' She smiled. 'Nothing of great significance. It cannot be compared with a Declaration of War.'

He nodded genially. Young ladies' letters, he knew, were full of parties and dancing partners; doubtless Cassandra had related news of some flirtation . . .

If her family was able to maintain an amazing discretion concerning the publication of her novel, Jane reflected, surely she could do the same. It was not that she positively did not wish her uncle and aunt to know of it – they must hear of it in time – but she guessed that her aunt, if she were to learn of it now, would not be able to refrain from broadcasting the news throughout the Colony. And in that case, Jane thought with a shudder, she herself would no doubt become a seven days' wonder, the object of inquisitive stares and impertinent remarks, placed in a position not very dissimilar to that of the koola, or the platypus, or that other 'unparalleled animal from the Southern Hemisphere'!

She laid down the letter and allowed the unexpected intelligence to permeate her consciousness. She experienced a pleasant glowing sensation – with, nonetheless, an undercurrent of trepidation. She recalled very well giving her consent to her father's suggestion that he might send *Susan* to a publisher, but she had not imagined he would act so quickly. She had rather thought that he would probably await her return. *Susan* . . . to be published! To be advertised – subscribed – placed upon library shelves – to lie on parlour tables – to be pored over, and opinions pronounced! Up to this point, her family were all the critics of her work she had ever known. But now, would those grave literary journals, the *Quarterly Review*, the *Critical Review*, the *Monthly Review*, the *British Critic* and all the rest take notice of this new novel 'By a Lady'? She felt herself draw back from the thought, yet incline towards it at the same time; surely an untenable position. If she were to be a published novelist, then she must be prepared to meet professional criticism. And then – ten pounds! Why, that was half her total yearly allowance!

At this point her aunt's voice broke into her reverie. 'Such a very full paper,' Mrs Leigh Perrot remarked as she laid aside Lady Bridges' letter. 'And yet it contains a very little matter.

She has such an *amplifying* style –'

'Perhaps,' Jane suggested, 'Lady Bridges is mindful of Dr Johnson's axiom – that a *short* letter to a distant friend is in the nature of an insult, like that of a slight bow or cursory salutation.'

Aunt Perrot sniffed. 'Oh, I daresay, but I for one would rather read less and learn more.'

Jane suppressed a smile as she recalled a conversation she herself had written between her heroine Susan and her hero Mr Tilney, pertaining to the usual style of letter-writing among young women. 'Faultless,' Henry pronounced, 'except in three particulars – a general deficiency of subject, a total inattention to stops, and a very frequent ignorance of grammar.'

Her attention was finally diverted from *Susan* when her aunt looked up from her next letter. It was from her cousin, Mountague Cholmeley.

'Well, Jane,' she said, 'you were correct, it seems, in surmising plans would be well prepared to meet the invasion threat. The Peace was still holding when my cousin wrote this, but he says that plans have long been laid for that contingency.

'The Government and the King, it appears, would advance to meet Bonaparte; the Queen and the Princesses find refuge in the country; the Stock Exchange close down, all bank books be stowed in the Tower . . . and the Treasure taken out of London, escorted by the Volunteers –'

' 'Tis well no French man-o'-war took the *Ocean* captive when she was carrying your cousin's letter,' James observed with a chuckle. 'For sure such intelligence would have been signalled straight to Paris! I daresay, my dear, there are a hundred such rumours floating about.'

Aunt Perrot looked a little affronted by her husband's dismissive tone. She glanced at him sharply and did not vouchsafe any further items of interest from that letter.

James, meanwhile, had finished with his correspondence and taken up the *Gazette*, which this week contained full details of the Declaration of War, together with a Proclamation from the Governor. He read aloud: ' "On the 17th of May orders were dispatched from the Admiralty to the Commanding Officers of all His Majesty's ships of war, authorising them to CAPTURE, SINK, BURN, and DESTROY, the ships and vessels belonging to the Republic of France." '

The immediate reason for the resumption of hostilities, it seemed, was England's refusal to evacuate the island of Malta.

'And quite right too,' James commented. 'Malta is vital to our defence of the Mediterranean. Depend upon it, Bonaparte has designs on Egypt and India . . . we must never relinquish Malta.'

Jane thought of Frank, doubtless on active service once more in the Mediterranean, and of Charles: what were *Endymion*'s sailing orders, she wondered.

'It is as well we were not aware of the outbreak of war while we were on the high seas,' James observed. 'We should have been watching for a French sail to appear above the horizon every moment.'

'But, my dear Perrot,' his wife predicted, 'we shall be watching for the enemy every moment of our voyage back.'

Fears for the future may always be deferred, however; for the present, they were all three wonderfully reassured by the correspondence they had received — not so much for what it contained, as for its very arrival and presence here. To peruse papers from England seemed to reinforce their own identity, which this alien landscape and their unusual way of life had, during these last few months, threatened in some way to obscure. Now they felt restored . . . having, as it were, received written confirmation that they did indeed occupy their own ordained places elsewhere in the world. Even their fearful speculation concerning the invasion subsided. Those French infantrymen of fevered imagination seemed to retreat from England's countryside, march back from town and village, retire across those pebbled English beaches, return across the sea to France.

During the following week, the Governor published a General Notice:

In Consequence of the Declaration of War between Great Britain and France . . . however improbable the Attack of the Enemy may be considered in this remote part of the Globe, yet His Excellency the Commander in Chief deeming it necessary to cause proper Persons to be trained to the Experience of the Cannon, Field-Pieces, etc., the Free Inhabitants of Sydney (in any case of eventual Emergency from the Enemy's Attack) willing to contribute their Aid to the Defence of the Colony, will give their Names in to His Honour the Lieutenant-Governor during the present week.

'Hmn,' James commented when he learned of this. 'I suppose the free inhabitants can scarcely be press-ganged into defending the Colony alongside the military. I daresay,' he added, 'the citizens of Sydney are very glad the new Battery at George's Head has been completed.'

His wife recalled the first occasion on which she and her niece had visited Government House in Sydney. 'What, I wonder,' she remarked, 'is one to think now of Monsieur Baudin's high-minded disclaimer of territorial ambition, so admired by Mrs King?'

It was the sort of question to which there was no answer.

Twenty-Five

ONE TUESDAY, THE official thermometer at Parramatta registered 119° in the air and 93° in the shade.

'Sydney must be quite unbearable in this heat,' Aunt Perrot declared, and Jane thought of the dust, the pigs tethered along the Tank Stream, the piles of refuse, the toiling convict gangs, the sweating soldiery in their high-necked uniforms of lobster-red. Unbearable indeed!

Possibly the Governor's lady shared this opinion, for that same week the vice-regal entourage arrived at Parramatta to take up residence for a time. Soon a note was delivered from Government House at nearby Rose Hill to the cottage on the western road. It was addressed to Mrs Leigh Perrot, and contained a double invitation.

Mrs King wrote that she had learned of Mrs Leigh Perrot's penchant for taking exercise on horseback. The haughty Englishwoman on her hired hack, dressed in a neat riding habit with a hat upswept at one side and fastened by a curling feather, was by now a familiar sight in the Hawkesbury countryside. Bare-legged farmers in their smocks and kangaru caps and the grey-clad convicts of the road-gangs would turn to stare at the lady as she cantered by, reminding them of a world left far behind: of pink-coated huntsmen riding to hounds, of mantraps sprung in coppices where pheasants ran and gamekeepers lay in wait. Mrs King wondered if Mrs Leigh Perrot would care to join a horseback expedition to the Cow Pasture Plains planned for that week, the object of which was for His Excellency to ascertain the number of wild cattle which roamed there. Mrs

King understood that neither Mr Leigh Perrot nor Miss Austen shared Mrs Leigh Perrot's enthusiasm for riding, but if her husband could spare her for this excursion, he might rest assured she would have the protection of several gentlemen of the Colony who would be of their party, besides the Governor himself. It would, Mrs King emphasized, be quite an adventurous undertaking; the Cow Pastures lay some thirty miles from Parramatta, and they would need to camp overnight at the Nepean River and return the following day.

The second invitation seemed quite tame by comparison; it requested the pleasure of the company of the Leigh Perrots and Miss Austen at a garden party to be held at Government House, Parramatta, during Christmas week.

Whatever other faults might be ascribed to Jane Leigh Perrot, no one could have called her a faintheart (save, perhaps, when threatened by mountainous waves); and the hint of adventure contained in Mrs King's first invitation brought an intrepid sparkle to her eye.

'It is such a pity you take no particular pleasure in riding, Perrot,' she told her husband regretfully. 'And you, Jane dear,' she added, 'have scarcely had the opportunity to become an accomplished horsewoman. – I was surprised by the interest you evinced in viewing Mr Wentworth's stable. Your brother James is the only one of your family who has an eye for a horse, I believe.'

'I think all my brothers have always enjoyed riding,' Jane said, determined the honours of horsemanship should not lie solely with James. She smiled. 'I well recall Frank's first pony, a bright chestnut he called Squirrel . . . why, he and Neddy and Jemmy used to hunt on any pony they could find when they were small – even a donkey would do! My mother made a hunting jacket for Frank out of her old scarlet riding-habit – he was so proud of it! Really, I think Frank was the keenest rider of all. I believe James' enthusiasm for riding has been somewhat dampened ever since his fall. – As for myself, I cheerfully confess I always prefer a good long walk to a canter on horseback.'

'Ah, yes, poor James, that wretched fall – so inconvenient,' her aunt said abstractedly; but whose she considered the greater inconvenience occasioned by that accident, her own or her nephew's, was difficult to determine.

'You have my blessing to join this little adventure, my dear,' James Leigh Perrot told his wife. 'I almost envy you the opportunity to spend a night in the wild bush. But take care, my love – I do not quite like the sound of those wild cattle –'

'Pish, Perrot!' his wife responded lightly. 'A few stray cows and bulls – there can be very little danger when one is mounted on a horse.'

So it was that on the appointed afternoon, Mrs Leigh Perrot ambled towards Rose Hill upon the half-bred hack into which, in the few months gone by, she had managed to instil a modicum of the higher equestrian art. As she rode along the approach to Government House, that pleasant building with its agreeable air of simple elegance, there was a flash of green, red, yellow, blue and a flight of rainbow-plumaged parrots burst from a tree, bent upon raiding the well-stocked vegetable garden planted on either side of the driveway. A party of some half-dozen was assembled in the stableyard, where both their Excellencies greeted her most affably. There was an atmosphere of holiday, as though the viewing of the wild cattle were but an excuse for this excursion.

Mr King was already mounted. He beamed at her. 'Dear madam – we are delighted you are able to join our party, delighted – it is too long, too long since we have met.' He made no reference, of course, to his meeting with her husband in September; it was tacitly understood that the subject of gold was not to be spoken of again.

The other gentlemen present were Surgeon Savage, whom Mrs Leigh Perrot recalled meeting previously; Major Foveaux, the Lieutenant-Governor of Norfolk Island, recently come to the mainland to seek a cure for his asthma; Captain Piper, a military officer; and Mr Garnham Blaxell, who held the position of Deputy Commissary. Major Foveaux was very corpulent and, on account of his affliction, given to wheezing. Aunt Perrot could forgive his wheezes; but she shuddered to see a man who could allow his figure to deteriorate so. She had always held the opinion that a fat man was a much more distressing sight than a plump woman, especially as gentlemen's clothing allowed no opportunity to conceal a portly stomach or bulging thighs. She sat upright in her saddle, aware of the fact that her own well-preserved figure appeared to excellent advantage upon a horse, and averted her eyes from the Major's tightly strained scarlet tunic and dewlapped face. The gossip of the Colony had it that Foveaux was the son of a French cook in the employ of an English aristocrat, and that his rapid elevation within the Corps – from mere Lieutenant to Lieutenant-Governor in a scant twelve years – was due to influential patronage.

Captain Piper, in pleasing contrast, was a younger and much more attractive man, affable in the extreme. Mrs Leigh Perrot's spirits rose considerably when he chose to ride alongside Mrs King and herself as they set out. She considered it quite gallant of the Captain, when he might have ridden with the Governor at the head of their party. She did not realize that Captain Piper was in fact glad to avoid the Governor's attention at this time, having incurred his displeasure over that infamous duel, in which he had inadvisedly acted as Captain McArthur's second. Captain Piper's partial reinstatement in vice-regal favour was very recent, and entirely due to Mrs King's intercession; he had always been a firm favourite with the Governor's lady. She had easily forgiven his imprudent behaviour, knowing him for a generous, amusing, rather naïve individual, readily persuaded by others more scheming than himself. At all events, his company made their journey pleasant and lighthearted as they left the road and penetrated the trackless bush westward towards the Nepean river.

Mr Blaxell was a dark, restless-looking man who sat his mount badly. He kept close to Mr King, clearly anxious to secure his ear. Doubtless to promote his own welfare, Mrs Leigh Perrot thought: for no good reason, she did not like the look of Mr Blaxell.

A welcome breeze was generated by their progress. The dry air was redolent of the sharp fragrance of crushed foliage as the horses trampled through the undergrowth. The ladies wore nets over their faces to protect them from those irritating little black flies that swarmed everywhere. Above every other sound – the whirr and clap of birds' wings, the alarm notes of their calls – came the insistent, cataphonic shrilling of a million cicadas.

Captain Piper was assiduous in clearing aside overhanging branches which threatened to impede their progress. Once they startled a group of kangaru dozing in the shade, which bounded away in alarm.

'Just look at those fine fellers!' the Captain exclaimed enthusiastically. 'They are real goers!' A sudden notion seized hold of his mind, and in his engaging manner he instantly imparted it to his companions. 'Why should we not hunt the kangaru to cheer up the sportin' life of the Colony!' he exclaimed. ' 'Pon my word, I can just imagine it – ridin' to hounds in our pink coats, the whippers-in, the sweet sound of the huntin' horn – yes, I'll wager the kangaru would give us a good run for our money!' His eyes gleamed as he spoke.

'Well,' Mrs Leigh Perrot acknowledged, smiling at such eager enthusiasm, 'if something did come of your idea, Captain Piper, 'twould not be so very different from the way fox hunting began.' She saw Mrs King's look of inquiry, and elaborated for her benefit. 'The Beaufort, as I heard it from my father, were on the scent of a deer one day – oh, a good forty years ago, it must have been – near Badminton, when suddenly a fox put up from covert, just as our kangaru did a few moments since, took to the open, and gave the field such a capital and sporting run that from that time onward hounds were steadied from deer and encouraged to fox.'

'I shall canvass the notion about Sydney,' Captain Piper declared. 'The tailors would welcome it for sure – there would be several dozen orders for huntin' pink, I shouldn't wonder!' He smiled with delight, still in the grip of his enthusiasm. 'I think I might ride up and have a word with Foveaux about it – excuse me for a moment, ladies' – and the next moment he urged his mount forward to catch up with the Major.

The two ladies, exchanging middle-aged smiles at such exuberance, saw him evidently explaining his scheme to the bulky Major, who sat stolidly in his saddle, and did not display any noticeably enthusiastic response.

'And if I know our gallant Captain, *his* pink coat would fit the most snugly of any huntsman's on the field,' Mrs King predicted, smiling indulgently. 'They call him the Beau Brummel of Botany Bay, you know –'

She stopped short as they suddenly saw Major Foveaux's horse rear up, almost unseating its portly rider, who clung somewhat inelegantly to its neck in his effort to prevent a fall.

Mrs King realized almost immediately what had happened. 'Snake!' she hissed. 'No need for alarm, I assure you – a common enough occurrence –'

Mrs Leigh Perrot valiantly endeavoured not to feel alarm; but she could not help recoiling when she spied that monstrous brown snake rapidly making for the undergrowth.

'Tally ho!' Captain Piper called as he made after this new quarry. He had drawn his sword – it glittered in the sunlight – and now, leaning down perilously from his saddle at an acute angle, he dealt the snake a fatal blow just behind its head, using the flat of his slender blade. The reptile lay in thrashing, glistening coils, the sinuous symmetry of its gliding muscles destroyed upon the instant.

'Demme, sir, why didn't you slash off its head with the cutting edge of your toasting fork!' roared the Major.

Captain Piper's eyebrows rose. 'There are ladies present, sir: this is by far the cleaner way of execution,' he replied.

Major Foveaux wheezed incoherently. Meanwhile, the Governor had wheeled back on his horse and now addressed the Captain in ironic terms. 'A bold swordstroke, sir – and more to be commended than *one* such stroke we know of, when you, sir, the hero of the snakeskin, defended another gallant captain, the hero of the fleece!'

The other gentlemen exchanged glances; Garnham Blaxell sniggered audibly; and Captain Piper trotted back to the two ladies in some confusion.

'Will I never shake off His Excellency's displeasure?' he muttered disconsolately to Mrs King.

'Oh come, Captain – don't despair. 'Twill all come right in time,' she answered consolingly. In truth, she felt much as Mrs Leigh Perrot did concerning that wretched duel. What an inordinate influence it had had upon the life of their little world!

By way of diversion she began to tell Mrs Leigh Perrot how the wild cattle came to be in that remote area across the Nepean. 'They are humped cattle, you know,' she said, 'brought from the Cape with the First Fleet of transports. Soon after settlement, four cows and two bulls broke loose and escaped – 'twas a grievous loss in those desperate days of near-starvation. 'Twas thought the beasts had perished, but a few years ago, an exploration party discovered them west of the Nepean, grazing upon the river flats. By then they had grown to some sixty head, but had, of course, become quite wild, and could not be led back to the settlement like tame beasts.' She bent forward to pat her horse's neck as they passed by the snake, still writhing in its death throes. 'Mr King is of the opinion they must number several hundred head by now; he is anxious for them to be recovered for domestic use.'

It did not seem necessary, she thought, to explain that her husband regarded these cattle as his own property. The original strayed beasts had belonged to Arthur Phillip, who, after he left the Colony, had cheerfully granted ownership in their descendants to Philip Gidley King.

'Several hundred head!' Mrs Leigh Perrot exclaimed. 'I had no idea there would be so many. And *humped*, you say –' Did that mean they were like Highland cattle, she wondered, great shaggy beasts? She began to think the concern her husband had expressed might perhaps be justified.

It was not Captain Piper's way to remain despondent for long. 'Talkin' of snakes,' he exclaimed, 'have you heard of the plan that repulsive idiot Hayes has in mind to deter any of the wrigglers from comin' on to his property? – He proposes to put up a grand mansion on the land he bought earlier this year – he paid a hundred pounds, you know, for a hundred acres . . . He says he will call his estate Vaucluse, after some place in France.'

Mrs King enlightened her companion. 'Captain Piper is speaking of Sir Henry Brown Hayes, an Irish knight brought here for the abduction of an heiress. A shameful deed. He is in fact a widower, with several grown children.'

'He is a repulsive and odious feller and the fortune at stake was a cool twenty thousand,' the irrepressible Captain Piper put in.

'The young woman was rescued, I believe – her reputation ruined, of course.' Mrs King sighed. 'At all events, Sir Henry came here last year, served six months' imprisonment upon arrival, and now, as you have heard, is to become a colonial gentleman living in some style. – But what of his plan concerning snakes, Captain? I have not heard of that.'

'Well, it seems the feller is convinced that if he surrounds his dwelling by a ditch filled in with turf imported from ould Ireland, 'twill keep the reptiles at a safe distance!' Whereupon he put his hands together in a steeple and raised his eyes to heaven. 'The blessed Saint Patrick, as you will remember, ma'am, having chased all snakes away from that Emerald Isle. – Did you ever hear such nonsense?'

They all laughed heartily – and Major Foveaux, hearing the merriment behind him, cursed the sensation which had come upon him, as of an iron band encircling his chest and constricting his very breath. He was very far from feeling merry. Wheezing, he loosened his high collar. There seemed to be no cure for this damned asthma. Coming to the mainland had not helped one whit; perhaps he should follow Mr Savage's advice and try a sea voyage, a visit home . . . in which case someone else could have the dubious pleasure of taking over the administration of the Island prison. He was tired enough of those hard-case Norfolk convicts, God knew: and of the criticisms which had been levelled against him, just because he had sold off a few female felons to some of the settlers there! Why, even the new chaplain recently come to the Island – the Reverend Penberthy – had seen fit to admonish him in the course of a private conversation!

A trooper and two assigned servants had preceded the party to the point about midway along the Nepean River where they were to camp overnight. Tents had been set up, a campfire lit, and a picket line prepared for the horses. The Nepean was a short river, rising on the uplands and flowing north as far as the confluence of the Grose river with the Hawkesbury. It was upon the farther bank of the Nepean that the Cow Pastures lay.

The brief twilight of that summer day soon faded into darkness as the sun went down the sky in a glory of gold and crimson. How they had gaped at these magnificent sunsets when they first came to the Colony, Jane Leigh Perrot thought. They were a commonplace wonder now. A little later, she savoured the unique experience of sitting around a campfire, eating charred mutton chops and potatoes roasted in the ashes, and drinking good burgundy from the vice-regal cellar. They might, she felt, have been in the midst of some wartime manoeuvre – an impression heightened by the gentlemen's uniforms. But in such a case, neither she nor the Governor's lady would have been part of the company. The thoughts of Mrs King herself seemed to be running on similar lines, for now that lady leaned forward in the firelight to say: 'Do you imagine, Mrs Leigh Perrot, that you and I might be described as *camp followers*?' – a

293

jocular remark which drew much mirth from the gentlemen.

The Governor announced they must be up by first light (*camp followers*, he decreed, were exempt from this order) so that they might come upon the cattle unawares. But before they turned in for an early night, he insisted upon recounting one of those humorous anecdotes he enjoyed so much.

' 'Twas told me by Mr Harris last week,' he said, 'that a stranger in Sydney town came upon a certain person standing at the Wharf — I will not divulge to which country that person belonged: suffice to say that his speech was in a rich brogue — and asked him the following question: "Where are Mann's Rooms, my fine fellow?" — desiring, no doubt, to sup there and taste their famous turtle soup.' — At this point the Governor himself affected a rich brogue. ' "Why, as to that, sorr," this sagacious person answered, "Why, as to that . . . *they're in his house*, sorr!" ' — Whereupon His Excellency burst into uproarious laughter, thoroughly appreciating his own tale. 'I have told George Howe to put that in the *Gazette*,' the Governor said. ' "Put it in the paper, George," I told him —" 'twill liven up your columns!" '

Mr Blaxell, who had drunk deep of the burgundy, gave a somewhat inebriated guffaw; but Major Foveaux yawned behind his hand. 'Another of these Irish jokes,' he murmured to Mr Savage. 'One hears nothing else in Sydney these days.'

Jane Leigh Perrot found that she was glad of Mrs King's presence as she lay upon a stretcher in the tent the two ladies shared. The night seemed to close in about them. A flap of the tent opening was pinned back to admit air, and in the triangle of black velvet sky which it revealed, a cluster of stars shone brilliantly. There were strange rustlings from the bush; they heard the dreary monotonous pipe of the pallid cuckoo, the familiar hooting of an owl, and once the quickly arrested scream of some small creature become the victim of an unknown predator. Far away a dingo howled — a long-drawn, eerie call which ended in a subsiding growl. 'Twas the call of a native dog who had once belonged to a tribe and lived with men, but now, like the Aborigines themselves, was lost and homeless. There were other, more comforting sounds: for a while, the murmur of masculine voices as some of their companions lingered at the campfire — the occasional jingle of harness and stamp of horses' hooves; and, for a few moments, a low, melodious strain of music as the trooper passed down the picket line, whistling a strangely appealing air.

'Do you know that tune?' Jane Leigh Perrot whispered to her companion in the dark. 'It has a haunting quality.'

The other listened for a moment, then answered sleepily: ' 'Tis the marching song of a Kentish regiment, if I mistake not . . . 'tis called – 'tis called "The Bold Fusilier".'

The gentlemen rose at daybreak, according to plan, and lost no time in crossing the river. Splashing through the shallow water and emerging on to the pastures on the farther side, they soon came upon several groups of cattle – sleek, well nourished beasts in good fettle. In the half-light they lowed and bellowed at the approach of horses and men, and lumbered off into the distance. Having estimated the number at this first encounter, the Governor and his party returned to breakfast at the camp. They planned to ford the Nepean at several places and explore different areas of the river flats, to obtain as accurate an estimate of the total herd as possible.

'And are our two *camp followers* to join our explorations?' His Excellency inquired, in a high good humour.

'We certainly do not intend to be left behind,' Mrs King replied with spirit – and both she and Mrs Leigh Perrot joined each subsequent fording of the river, proudly proclaiming themselves the first and only ladies to have crossed the Nepean.

There was one untoward incident, when a bull of more bellicose persuasion than its fellows held its ground before the horseman who advanced towards him, lowering its horns in menace and pawing the ground. That horseman happened to be none other than the Governor himself, and Mrs King cried out in alarm. The massive beast was clearly intent upon charging her husband with those wicked horns. But His Excellency soon showed of what stuff he was made. Refusing to retreat, he wheeled his horse out of the path of the ferocious charge at the last instant, and gave the creature a resounding thwack across the nose with his riding crop.

'Bravo, sir! A very matador!' Captain Piper called, as Mrs King closed her eyes in relief.

The tally of cattle mounted well beyond expectation: there

must be over a thousand beasts, they estimated.

'And all descended from four cows and two bulls,' Major Foveaux remarked. ' 'Tis indeed a great begetting.'

Moreover, as Mr Blaxell was quick to point out, there seemed to be a good proportion of cows to bulls; the Governor had feared there might be a great excess of bulls: it was a strange fact that during the first few years of settlement, male creatures had far outnumbered females.

Mr King's good humour persisted as, shortly after noon, they recrossed the river for the last time, and set out to retrace the route to Parramatta. In the way of most journeys of return, it seemed shorter and swifter than the outward trip.

At the entrance to Government House, Jane Leigh Perrot bade farewell to the rest of the party. 'I would not have missed the excursion for the world!' she assured Mrs King. 'Not for all the tea in China!' – Upon which she turned towards the western road, eager to relate her adventure in the wild bush to those who had stayed at home.

Jane Austen's birthday fell in mid-December. She had always wished it could have been in the other half of the year: as a child, to have the excitement of a birthday with the joys of Christmas tripping on its heels had seemed a satiety of good things. 'I am twenty-nine,' she said aloud, upon waking to a shaft of sunshine in her little whitewashed room, and a mocking chorus of kookaburras perched in a tree outside. 'Most definitely "on the wrong side of twenty-five", as people say!'

'Sweet pretty creature! Sweet pretty creature!' a willy wagtail chirruped, as though in consolation.

Last year, she had wakened to frost patterns on the window-pane and a collar of snow upon the sill . . . Cassandra had picked a bunch of delicate, green-tinted snowdrops to give her . . . and she had suffered from chilblains!

The day brought unexpected pleasures: at breakfast, her aunt produced a brief letter and a small copy of Cowper's poems which Cassandra had pressed upon her before they left Bath, with the injunction to keep both secret until today. Delightful surprise! Opening the book at random, Jane anticipated the happy pleasure of renewing acquaintance with her favourite poet . . . ah, here was a stanza which Cassandra had lightly marked in pencil. It was from the poem entitled 'Human Frailty' –

> But oars alone can ne'er prevail
> To reach the distant coast;
> The breath of heaven must swell the sail
> Or all the toil is lost –

It had been a fitting godspeed for their long voyage, Jane thought: a voyage they would soon embark upon once more. At last their homeward passage was assured: cabins had been allotted to Mr and Mrs Leigh Perrot and Miss Austen on board His Majesty's transport *Calcutta*, lately arrived at Port Jackson from Port Phillip and due to sail for England early in March.

Her aunt had proposed as a birthday celebration one of the little card parties they had given occasionally in their modest cottage; the Strongbows, Elizabeth McArthur, Mr Harris and the Savages had come from time to time to play whist and cribbage and partake of wine and cake. But Jane preferred there should be no public announcement of her birthday, and so the notion was dropped. Elizabeth McArthur, however, learned of it somehow, and sent round a bouquet composed of native flowers: scarlet and yellow Christmas bells, a few fragrant love flowers, some sweet-scented purple boronia, and the gorgeous red waratah, all twined about with sprays of perfumed doubah.

Jane decided the bouquet was worthy of a painting. 'It shall be my birthday occupation,' she decided. 'For sure the flowers will all be wilted by tomorrow – I shall preserve their memory.'

There was one more surprise: her uncle handed her a little package which revealed a slender gold necklace, prettily worked. 'You may recall niece, that a little while ago you gave me your nug of gold for safe-keeping. I took the liberty of instructing a goldsmith in Sydney to turn it into a necklace for you –'

Jane was overcome by her uncle's kind thought. 'When I wear this necklace I shall always think of you,' she said, 'and feel how very kind you were. I shall wear it to the party at Government House.' And she gave him an affectionate kiss.

And so the birthday passed in flower painting and poetry reading, and for dinner Ellen produced a creditable roast fowl, with Jane's favourite cheese-cakes to follow. Jane was quite pleased with her finished painting: next day, it glowed freshly upon the paper while the bouquet itself drooped and faded in the vase.

As the year drew to a close, new difficulties had beset Governor King; the carefree expedition to the Cow Pastures had been a welcome interlude amidst mounting worries. While Mrs King remained at Parramatta, His Excellency travelled back and forth to Sydney to attend to business.

Lieutenant-Governor Collins had sent a letter from Port Phillip by the *Ocean* to report that he had halted unloading their supplies, as the site chosen for a landing, towards the end of the peninsula, had proved very disappointing. He suggested the project be abandoned, at least for the time being, and that instead he should remove across the Bass Strait to join Lieutenant Bowen in Van Diemen's Land. (Back in September, Mr Bowen had established a settlement on the Derwent river, at Risdon. It had already been announced in the *Gazette* that this was to be renamed in honour of Lord Hobart, Secretary of State for War and the Colonies.) Mr King had agreed to Mr Collins' suggestion, and had decided to send Captain Bunker to help him. – Nothing, he thought, ever seemed to go according to plan or turn out successfully for poor David Collins.

There was further dismaying news from Matthew Flinders: sailing aboard the *Cumberland*, he had hailed a passing ship bound for Port Jackson to report that that schooner, too, was unfit to continue the long voyage to England. Accordingly, he intended to put into Mauritius to effect repairs. He should just about be making landfall there now, the Governor reckoned. The island was, of course, a French possession: Flinders would still be unaware, perhaps, that war had broken out again. It was to be hoped he would be granted as courteous a reception there as Captain Baudin had received in Sydney . . . Mr Flinders, the Governor thought gloomily, was scarcely more fortunate in his undertakings than Mr Collins.

And alas, poor Baudin! Just now, news had arrived of his untimely death upon Mauritius three months ago. *La Géographe* had put in there after she left Port Jackson; now she was sailing back to France without her Captain. Mrs King had been most terribly distressed to learn of his death.

It seemed they must mourn another, too. The Governor sighed heavily. There was still no word of Mr Bass or the *Venus* – 'twas over a year now since he sailed off for South America. The inevitable conclusion must be that the *Venus* had foundered. Poor George Bass. He had gone to seek his fortune, but had lost his life instead, vanishing without trace . . .

Then there was the continuing threat of an uprising within the Colony from the Irish convicts . . . the Governor felt sure the odious Sir Henry Brown Hayes had a finger in that pie.

On a lesser plane, but giving rise to considerable irritation and inconvenience, Mr King had finally been forced to confront his clerk, Vaux, with evidence of his thefts from the Commissariat. The rogue was now at the Coal River settlement, hewing black diamonds. 'Twas a damned nuisance: the villain wrote a neat hand and was better educated than most. The new clerk was a ham-fisted idiot who made a blot upon every page. Dammit, the Governor thought, he missed Vaux's impudent face!

Above all, Mr King longed to receive news of his recall to England. It was months now since he had requested to be relieved of his office and allowed to return home. He was not well, and this hot summer, one of the worst on record, did not help matters. But it seemed that Lord Hobart was preoccupied by the War and had little attention to spare for the Colony . . .

His Excellency's depression dampened his wife's spirits, and thus it was a rather glum looking vice-regal couple who stood to welcome their guests to the garden party at Government House, Parramatta, in Christmas week. Even the weather conspired against enjoyment: it was excessively humid, and distant clouds seemed to portend a storm. But still the sun shone down remorselessly. They needed rain – but not today! A large marquee had been set up in the parkland beyond the house; here liveried footmen served warm champagne and fruit cup from huge silver bowls. A military band was stationed at a discreet distance, playing patriotic marches. Perspiration soaked the players as the sun beat down upon their shining instruments.

The Leigh Perrots and Miss Austen arrived rather late, on account of Aunt Perrot having to immerse her feet for a full half-hour in cold water before she was able to fit on to her feet the blue slippers which exactly matched her silk gown. Even now, her feet were still swollen with heat and she suffered for her vanity as she strolled about greeting acquaintances with a set smile upon her face. Jane Austen wore a simple tamboured muslin with a yellow trimming; there were roses of yellow silk upon her bonnet. The gold necklace her uncle had given her was clasped about her neck. She looked quite cool and fresh, even if she did not feel it. She deplored the way this dreadful climate kept her in a continual state of inelegance.

It seemed that everyone they knew was there; Jane was astonished, as she gazed about, to realize just how many acquaintances they had made during their short sojourn here. Besides those who resided in Parramatta – Elizabeth McArthur, the Strongbows, Lewins, Marsdens and the rest, the Patersons had come up from Sydney, together with the Palmers, Campbells, Savages, and several others besides, including Captain and Mrs Abbott, lately based on Norfolk Island, and now returned to the mainland, where Captain Abbott had taken command of the military detachment at Parramatta.

While her aunt and uncle exchanged pleasantries with the Patersons, Jane accepted a glass of champagne from a tray proffered by a footman, content for the moment to stand by herself and observe the throng. At such moments her thoughts were apt to stray to that vague outline of a new story which had come into her mind . . . it would, she had decided, be a salutary change to choose a more ordinary setting than any she had used before. The Bennet family, whose fortunes she had related in *First Impressions*, were not so very grand, to be sure (their way of life, indeed, curiously resembled that of a certain Rectory family at Steventon); but this time she wished her heroine to be less affluent still. There would, she had thought, be three sisters, all young and all unmarried. One should be called Penelope (her aunt so often talked of her cousin Penelope: 'twas a name which appealed to Jane). Their father was to be an ailing gentleman in straitened circumstances, unable to provide for his daughters. They should do their own washing and eat their meals off a tray. She had not yet worked out the plot in any detail, but it was to rest upon the uncomfortable realization of all three sisters that 'twas thoroughly undesirable to grow old and be poor and laughed at as old maids. As for their family name – why, it should be Watson!

Recalling this, she looked about for her young military admirer, but failed to see him anywhere.

'Are you searching for someone, Miss Austen? Am I to hope it is perhaps myself, that you desire to gaze upon my manly presence and listen to my scintillating conversation?'

Only Mr Harris could tease her in this manner – indeed, she thought suddenly, he was the nearest to a brother she had known since she left England.

'For sure, sir!' she responded with a smile. 'Whom else should I seek so anxiously? Unless – unless it was Lieutenant Watson, who, I must confess, I do not usually need to seek out.'

Mr Harris shook his head in mock sorrow. 'Ah, there you must remain disappointed, I fear. The young Lieutenant has been assigned to oversee the training of those stalwart volunteers who are to defend us from the predatory French. Even now, I daresay, he is demonstrating which end of the musket to point at the enemy and the proper use of flint and primer – and all the time uttering a thousand curses to himself that he is denied *your* company at this garden party.'

He raised his glass to salute her before he sipped his champagne, and Jane exclaimed when he saw his hands, which were neatly swathed in bandages.

'What misfortune has befallen you, sir?' she asked.

'What do you imagine, Miss Austen? – The bite of an ungrateful patient – an argument with a carving knife? – No, I must tell the truth: they are a little burnt.'

Another voice broke in. 'He is a modest fellow, my dear young lady, and since he will never tell the tale himself, I shall relate it for him!' – Captain Piper had joined them, and Mr Harris quickly introduced him to Miss Austen. The Captain bowed. 'I had the pleasure of accompanying your aunt, when we visited the Cow Pastures,' he told her. 'But as for my friend Harris here – why, Miss Austen, he merely saved Sydney town from burning to a cinder some days ago! Henceforth he shall be known as Harris, the Hero of the Fire!'

Jane's eyes sparkled as she demanded to hear the heroic tale.

'Know then,' Captain Piper said, 'that the fire started in a bakehouse on Back Row East (there is an historic precedent – 'twas a burnt loaf, you may remember, which began the Great Fire of London). It soon spread to Chapel Row, then shifted

north, fanned by a strong wind.' He struck a dramatic attitude.
'The conflagration was at its height, all seemed lost, the only
hope was for every citizen to rush down to the harbour and
immerse themselves alongside the sharks, while goods and
property and all they held dear were consumed in the fierce
flames . . . But then, hot-footed to the rescue came Surgeon
Harris, who took charge – caused buckets of water to be filled,
then emptied, then filled again . . . organized a valiant team of
fire-fighters . . . in short, he saved the day!'

'In the course of which valiant action my hands suffered a few
blisters,' John Harris said, looking a trifle embarrassed. 'I simply
happened to be on the spot to take charge – anyone would have
done the same.' He was clearly determined to change the
subject. 'Is it not splendid to see Colonel Paterson at large
again?' He looked across to where the Patersons were chatting
to the Kings, seemingly in the greatest amity. 'He is resuming
all his duties – his wound is quite healed –' He stopped, recalling
too late the part Captain Piper had played in that notorious duel.

'*Touché!*' the Captain admitted ruefully. 'I sometimes think,
Harris, that wretched affair will haunt me for the rest of my
days.'

At that moment he was claimed for conversation by Major
Foveaux, who had now definitely decided to return to England,
and was making use of this gathering to canvass likely can-
didates to succeed him at Norfolk Island. He then intended to
put their names forward to His Excellency. 'Ah, a word with ye,
Piper,' he said now . . .

'Captain Piper acted as Captain McArthur's second in that
wretched duel,' Mr Harris told Jane Austen. 'I spoke before I
thought!'

The next moment their attention was caught by a loud
altercation. Looking round, Jane saw two gentlemen in furious
argument: Mr Marsden and Mr Caley. Why, she wondered,
should the churchman and the gardener disagree so violently?

'– I warn you, sir, that if I catch him again, I shall *shoot* him!'
Mr Marsden was shouting, beside himself with rage.

The threat sounded quite desperate to Jane, but to her surprise, Mr Harris laughed and shrugged. 'It is only the Reverend
Marsden going on about his precious rabbits – Caley's dog must
have got at them again. It happens every few months; and then,

tragedy of tragedies, there is no rabbit pie for the Marsden household!'

Jane was relieved there was not to be another duel. She had often seen Mr Caley's dog, a scruffy ginger and white mongrel with keen amber eyes. It usually accompanied its master along the street; once Bingami's magpie had chased it from their front garden. The argument was eventually abandoned upon Mrs King approaching the two combatants, saying something which made them both laugh in spite of their quarrel, and sending them off in different directions.

Then Emma Strongbow approached Miss Austen, twirling a frilled parasol. Not one freckle was to be spied upon her pretty face – a circumstance which must delight Aunt Perrot, Jane thought.

'Dear Emma,' she said, genuinely pleased to see her. In their brief colonial history, the Strongbows ranked amongst their oldest friends. 'How are the twins? What news of Rebecca?'

'Oh, the boys flourish. Zeke is a little angel, but Jos . . .' Emma Strongbow bit her lip and sighed. 'He is so wayward at times. I sometimes wonder whether that dreadful woman, Bet Hawkins, could have curdled his disposition with her milk . . . I hear, by the way, that she has been sent to the Female Factory for disorderly behaviour.'

'Perhaps Jos is cutting another tooth,' Jane suggested practically. 'It really must be such a painful process, as bad as any toothache we experience in later life.'

'I daresay you are right. It has been so hot, too – I feel that perhaps the babes would be happier without their woollens. Yet I dare not risk them catching a chill . . . Oh, I should not talk in such a fashion about my own darling child! – As for Rebecca, she is well and happy, and still keeping company with her soldier boy. Mr Strongbow has promised she shall have a cow to milk when we move to the farm – 'twill not be long now, the house is almost completed. If only you were not leaving us, Jane – I should so like you to have been our first house guest!'

'I should have liked that too,' Jane answered. 'But I am homesick, Emma.' She gazed outside at the parched parkland. 'I yearn for an English view – English verdure, seen under a brightly shining sun whose rays are not the least bit oppressive.'

The Leigh Perrots, the Palmers and the Campbells were

303

grouped beneath a stand of she-oaks, discussing the likely future of Parramatta. Mrs King had led Mr Marsden over to them; he stood a little apart, still fuming a little over Mr Caley's dog.

'I predict,' Mr Campbell was saying confidently, thumbs hooked into the lapels of his pale lavender coat, 'that Parramatta, having missed adoption as the seat of government for New South Wales, will become a fashionable resort – the Richmond, the Versailles, the Barrackpore of Sydney, whence folk will come to refresh themselves and enjoy restful scenery combined with elegant and delightful pleasures.'

' 'Tis just the right distance from the capital,' Mr Palmer agreed. 'Neither too far away nor too near. A half-day's journey in a fast chaise.' He thought a trifle smugly of his own smart equipage, curricle-hung and embodying the latest improvements.

'I find it an agreeable retreat,' Mr Leigh Perrot put in. 'It has an air of quiet dignity compared to Sydney.'

'What is your opinion, Mr Marsden?' Susan Palmer asked in her soft Virginian drawl. She avoided catching her sister's eye: Susan Palmer and Sophie Campbell, as close as Jane and Cassandra Austen, could both predict very well the likely tenor of Mr Marsden's reply.

'My opinion, madam,' growled the clergyman, 'is that Parramatta is a sink of iniquity. I know it as the scene of everything immoral and profane. But I labour unceasingly in the Lord's vineyard to draw souls to His grace.'

'Mr Caley's dog has much to answer for,' Sophie murmured in her sister's ear delightedly.

Jane wandered out from the marquee, intending to rejoin her aunt and uncle. She saw them in the distance, and began to make her way across to the cluster of she-oaks. But halfway there she realized this course would bring her face to face with Mrs Lewin. That lady, her head swathed in a gauzy turban, was engaged in soulful conversation with Mr Crabtree, her devoted follower. It was far too hot and sticky, Jane decided, to endure artistic pratings and mediocre versifying. She swerved from her path and found a blessed retreat: an archway led to a dim bower shaded by an ornamental vine. There was a stone bench and she sank down upon it thankfully.

'Miss Austen! I had hopes you would be here –'

She started at the sound of that well remembered voice with its faint Irish accent; in truth it was a voice she had half-hoped to hear all the long afternoon. Mr D'Arcy Wentworth was standing at the far end of the bower. He came towards her, a look of pleasure on his handsome face.

'I had intended we should meet before this,' he said, 'but I have had several pressing business matters to attend to during the past weeks. These left me little time for enjoyment. And now, alas, I hear you are to depart from us by the next ship to England. I am sorry we cannot keep you here.'

'I am not like you – I do not belong here,' Jane told him quietly. 'I yearn for England – for my family.' It was strange, she thought, how they seemed to have a continuing conversation, D'Arcy Wentworth and herself. And then, with some amazement as she heard her own words, she told him: 'I too have – business to attend to.'

D'Arcy Wentworth looked surprised. 'Business, Miss Austen? Pray, what would that be?' He was plainly intrigued.

'I – I write novels, sir. One of them is to be published before long.' She stopped, suddenly confused. 'I – I prefer not to speak of this in general. I – I cannot think why I have mentioned it to you. – Pray excuse me.' She felt herself stammering like a schoolgirl.

'I shall respect your confidence, believe me. – One is to be published, you say? I am impressed. I shall hope to read it one day. But – I knew it!' He smiled suddenly, and an infinite warmth of spirit, a great kindness, seemed to flow out from him and touch her very soul. 'I knew there was something more to you, Miss Austen, than a charming presence, a nice sense of wit, and an ability to dance the *valse* so well!'

Jane coloured up. 'I do not quite know how to express it, sir, but if I did not possess the desire to write, I should feel an – an emptiness of spirit.'

Jane was aware that she was talking to Mr Wentworth as she had not talked before to anyone – not even to Elliot Fordwick, during their brief, doomed courtship.

At that moment, the rain suddenly came down. There were no preliminary, spattering drops, no warning drizzle: water simply bucketed from the heavens all at once, in a veritable deluge. Nor was there any hope of dashing through that downpour into the house or back to the marquee for shelter; they must simply sit it out here. The trailing vine above them provided tolerable protection.

'Rain at last!' D'Arcy Wentworth said thankfully.

'Imagine saying that in England,' Jane replied; and they both broke into laughter, and suddenly felt quite at ease with each other once again.

'Well, Miss Austen, since we are marooned here for the duration of this downpour, I think I should reciprocate the confidence you have given me.' He gave a secret smile. 'I cannot tell what rumours you may have heard of my life before I came here, so many years ago. But I should like you to hear the truth of that matter from my own lips.' He paused, seeming to expect a response.

Jane hesitated. 'I have heard a little . . . that is to say . . .' Finally she decided to reveal the astonishing assertion voiced by Ellen Bowden. 'I have heard,' she said crisply, 'that you were once a high toby man – a highwayman!' Her expression seemed to indicate the obvious absurdity of this.

Mr Wentworth regarded her quite gravely and inclined his head. 'A shocking notion indeed,' he remarked soberly.

And there and then, while the rain sluiced down in torrents to soak into the parched and thirsty earth, D'Arcy Wentworth embarked upon the story of his early life.

'As I believe I had occasion to remark the day you visited at Homebush,' he began, 'my paternal grandfather quite dissipated our family fortunes, and as a result my father never gained his inheritance of our ancestral seat, Fyanstown Castle, in County Meath. We are an Anglo-Irish family, Miss Austen,' he added proudly, 'descended from a certain Robert de Wentworth of Wentworth Woodhouse, in Yorkshire, who flourished in the thirteenth century. Some say our lineage goes back further – to Reginald, a French noble who invaded England with William the Conqueror. However that may be, my father in his reduced circumstances became a humble innkeeper in Country Armagh. I was the sixth of his eight children, and 'twas made abundantly clear to me, as soon as I was able to understand such matters, that I must make my own way in the world.'

'Just as my brothers have,' Jane told him. 'The Church and the Navy have claimed three of them. Henry, my fourth brother, is –

is –' How exactly to describe Henry's profession? 'He is engaged in business at present,' she ended lamely.

'I regret to say that none of the gentlemanly professions – Church, Army, Navy, or the Law – appealed to me, Miss Austen. As for business – I have, of course, long since become a man of considerable busyness, but matters of property and profit were far from my mind in those carefree days. No, I settled upon a more lowly occupation: I aspired to study medicine. I was apprenticed to a Doctor Patton, and hoped, through family connexions, to secure an appointment with the East India Company.' He smiled, and shook his head as though in wonderment at the unexpected turnings in his life. 'I fully expected to travel to India and practise my chosen profession there: never, in my wildest flights of fancy, did I imagine I should spend the greater part of my life in a yet more distant land!' He sighed, but not with regret for India – rather for all the mislaid dreams of youth. 'I enjoyed my apprenticeship to that good man, and was besides an Ensign in the Irish Volunteers. That was an apprenticeship of another sort; my service brought me in contact with men from every stratum of society, from tradesmen to baronets.' And now there was a faraway look in his eye as he reviewed in memory the rollcall of his fellow Volunteers.

'Well now,' he went on briskly, 'there came the time when I crossed the Irish Sea to go to London and walk the great hospitals there.' He turned his full gaze upon his listener, and his face seemed to regain a strangely youthful look as he recalled those scenes of his young manhood. 'And 'twas there, my dear Miss Austen, that I fell into trouble . . . yes, in that wicked, beguiling city of London.'

Jane smiled. 'Dr Johnson has said that when a man is tired of London, he is tired of life –'

Mr Wentworth finished the quotation for her: ' "– for there is in London all that life can afford!" Ah, how true that seemed to me, a young man "towering in the confidence of twenty-one", as the good Doctor has said elsewhere! My cousin Lord Fitzwilliam was the unwitting cause of my downfall. He introduced me to the fast society in which he mingled, the ton of London town. He did not realize just how penniless his poor relation from old Ireland was! The gaming table was our passion – night after night we played for high stakes. Soon I was deep in debt, but too

307

proud to admit my predicament to those careless companions.'

'And what happened, sir? Were you flung into the Fleet?'

'The Debtors' prison? Not I!' D'Arcy Wentworth laughed in a daredevil fashion. 'No, Miss Austen, I became two people.'

'Two people?' Jane looked properly mystified.

'Quite simply, I divided myself in half, Miss Austen. One half of me remained what I already was, a young Anglo-Irish gentleman of good connexions, walking the hospitals. The other half became a most reprehensible fellow – a Mr Fitzroy, who occupied a sleazy lodging in the Seven Dials, whither he repaired whenever it became imperative he should recoup his gaming losses.'

Jane took in her breath sharply. 'The Seven Dials!' she repeated; it was as though she said 'the gateway to Hell'! Unfamiliar as she was with London, she yet knew the unsavoury reputation of that teeming ghetto of narrow winding alleys and tottering houses close by St Giles, notorious as the haunt of villains, rogues and ruffians. Why, 'twas said that an honest man entering there would in five minutes have the shirt snatched from his back.

'Mr Fitzroy was a bad lot, I regret to say,' Mr Wentworth said cheerfully. 'Not at all the sort of person you or I would wish to give the time of day to, Miss Austen. He was, as you must surely have guessed already, none other than that highwayman of whom your Ellen spoke, that high toby man with a brace of pistols to strike terror into harmless wayfarers, a black cloak to melt into the darkness, and a mask to cover his blue eyes!'

And now, as those same blue eyes pierced her own with a quite unrepentant gaze, Jane drew back from him a little on the bench they shared. 'I – I have not been at such close quarters with a highwayman before,' she said.

'Oh, never fear,' he told her. 'Mr Fitzroy has been dead and gone these many, many years – and Mr Wentworth is here to protect you from his ghost!'

Somewhat at a loss, she uttered a short, incredulous laugh. 'Sir, this is a truly amazing tale.' She thought of their first meeting, around the Governor's dinner table: it seemed clear enough now that D'Arcy Wentworth's knowledge of the flash language and 'The Family' had not been wholly acquired by presiding upon the magistrates' bench, as he had suggested.

'Unlike the histories you write, Miss Austen,' he continued, 'my tale is true, every word of it. And yet, I would not have you think that Mr Fitzroy was a violent or murthering character. I very much doubt, for instance, if his pistols were even loaded when he went off upon his – adventures. What can I say in the fellow's favour? I do believe, now I think on it, he had some notion of robbing the rich to give to the poor. Students of medicine are often inclined to wild behaviour, you know, before they turn into sage and sober surgeons and physicians –'

'Let us not mince matters, sir' – but Jane's curving lips belied her uncompromising words – 'Mr Fitzroy was a rogue!'

'Ah yes, I fear 'twas so.' Mr Wentworth shook his head. 'I cannot contradict you. In truth, he did deserve your fullest disapprobation. A dreadful fellow, quite on the cross, without a single square virtue to commend him!' He fell silent for a moment. Was he recalling certain nights at the dark of the moon, and Mr Fitzroy lurking in the shadow of a great tree beside the London road? 'At all events,' he went on, resuming his cheerful tone, 'you will be pleased to hear that eventually he was apprehended and charged with highway robbery, not once but thrice, and brought before a judge at the Old Bailey.'

Jane looked puzzled. No one had ever suggested D'Arcy Wentworth had been transported.

'But he was not convicted. – You see, 'twas strange, but none of the witnesses called by the prosecution could ever recognize the dreadful Mr Fitzroy of the Seven Dials, when young Mr Wentworth of Guy's Hospital stood before them in the dock. They could not prove 'twas the same person – thought there might be some similarity, but would not swear to it – and for want of proof positive, the prisoner was perforce acquitted . . . three times, as I have said. But on his third appearance at the Old Bailey – 'twas in '89, about this same season of the year – he was let off upon the clear understanding that he would take passage as assistant surgeon in the next fleet for Botany Bay. When this assurance was obtained, he was forthwith discharged, and subsequently set sail in the *Neptune*. – And that, my dear Miss Austen, is how Mr D'Arcy Wentworth came to New South Wales and was subsequently sent on duty to Norfolk Island – and has remained here ever since. As for Mr Fitzroy, all that remained of him – two pistols, a cloak, a mask – was left behind in England!'

He stopped speaking and looked at his companion cannily, as though gauging her reaction to this extraordinary confidence. What did he expect? Shock – horror – disdain? Jane slowly turned her head from side to side, thoroughly bemused. At last she said coolly: 'If that was devised as the plot for a novel, sir, I daresay 'twould be considered too far-fetched by half.'

He said: 'If 'twere a novel, 'tis clear enough who was the hero and who the villain, is that not so?'

'As clear as day,' Jane returned swiftly. 'Mr D'Arcy Wentworth is hero and villain both.'

'In that case he has much in common with almost everyone outside the pages of a novel.' He paused, contemplating her thoughtfully. 'But not you, I think. You are heroine through and through. I see nothing of the villainess in *you*.'

'I have lived a comfortable and relatively secluded life,' Jane told him. 'There has been little in it to tempt me from – from what Mr Marsden, I daresay, would call the Path of Righteousness.'

'A straight and narrow way. Mine has been a broad, twisting road by comparison.' He looked quizzical. 'It may be that Mr Fitzroy has had a greater influence over me than I have ever realized. Had I not made his acquaintance, I am sure my life would have followed a vastly different course. I should perhaps be living in some pleasant English house, having returned from India, together with a wife and family . . . and I daresay, Miss Jane Austen,' he concluded quietly, 'that my wife would very likely have been a lady like yourself.'

Jane lowered her gaze and turned aside her head for a moment. Then she said: 'Idle speculation upon what might have been is a singularly empty exercise, as any man of business should be the first to know.'

He smiled at that and rose to his feet. 'See, the rain is clearing. – Perhaps, Miss Austen, you will put one of my selves into a novel someday?'

She got up as well, brushing a slight dampness from her skirt. Indeed the rain had almost ceased; the sun was shining through. She peered up at the sky. 'There should be a rainbow, I think. – Yes, I might very well use your name, Mr Wentworth – perhaps twice over, dividing you again. There could also be a Mr Darcy, could there not? Mr Darcy . . . yes, I find that a pleasing name. I give you fair warning, sir, it is a likely thing to happen. I most often use the names of relatives and acquaintances in my stories – I think perhaps it helps me to a firmer belief in the characters I invent. – For instance, when I return home, I intend to revise a novel I wrote a little while ago, and I have it in mind to rechristen my heroine *Elizabeth*, after my friend Mrs Mc-Arthur. I so admire her sagacity and taste – I do believe I will compliment her by re-naming my heroine after her!'

'You have my free permission to use both my names – and Mr Fitzroy's, too, for the matter of that. I shall keep a lookout for your Mr Wentworth – and your Mr Darcy.' He looked at her for a moment, and when he spoke again it was in a different, more serious tone. 'I have a special favour to ask of you, Miss Austen.'

'If it is in my power, and *on the square*, Mr Wentworth, I shall be happy to acquiesce to it.'

He maintained his solemn expression. 'My two sons, D'Arcy and William, whom you met at Homebush, are also to travel to England on the *Calcutta*, to obtain their schooling. I should be so very much obliged to you, Miss Austen, if you would perhaps keep a watching brief over them, as they say in legal parlance. I should be most happy to think your benevolent influence was extended over them.'

'I shall look forward to executing that commission, Mr Wentworth. And as I have four brothers, you may deduce that my qualifications for acceptance are well founded in experience.'

At last he smiled once more. 'I would imagine that yours must have been a notably fortunate and felicitous family, Miss Austen.' Upon which he offered her his arm, and they ventured out to join the other damp survivors of the garden party, who had hastily sought shelter in the marquee. As a result it had become very overcrowded and extremely stuffy.

Aunt Perrot, pushing out to obtain fresh air, frowned to herself as she saw her niece approach on Mr Wentworth's arm.

'We are going home directly,' she told Jane. 'Perrot must put his feet in a mustard bath as soon as we get in. He became quite drenched in the downpour. We were wet through before we reached the tent –'

Indeed, Mrs Leigh Perrot did appear slightly bedraggled, and her blue satin slippers were soaked and ruined by trudging over the wet grass. Most of the guests were in a similar case. Mrs Lewin's turban, Jane noticed, was damp and deflated, and sat sadly drooping to one side of her head.

The musicians, who had dashed into the stables with their instruments, now emerged to play once more; they began a lively tune that helped to retrieve something of the party atmosphere.

'This climate!' Aunt Perrot exclaimed in extreme umbrage; it was, of course, exactly what she was used to saying so frequently in England.

Mr Wentworth insisted upon taking the Leigh Perrots and Miss Austen back to their cottage in his carriage; as they trotted down the western road, to Jane's delight she saw there was indeed a rainbow in the sky, a great soaring riband of colours, fast fading as she looked. Doubtless, she thought with an inward smile, Mr Crabtree would seize upon it as the subject for a poem.

Twenty-Six

CHRISTMAS BENEATH THE blazing eye of the omnipotent Australian sun was both familiar and strange. Good tidings of great joy to all mankind were proclaimed from the pulpit at St John's, while on the surrounding hills, felonious shepherds kept watch over sheep grazing in parched pastures beside diminished creeks. There were carol singers and mince pies, and a Twelfth Night party at Elizabeth Farm, in rooms decorated with gaudy wilting crimson flowers and trails of native greenery instead of glistening holly and sly mistletoe; and the old rituals of snapdragon, charades and blind man's bluff were performed on that hot January evening.

One day early in the new year, Ellen Bowden washed her hair (a rare event), dried it in the sun, then put on a muslin gown given to her by Miss Austen, tied about her waist a blue sash she had got from an itinerant pedlar, and walked to church to wed Jem Merrilees.

'Oh, sir, I be all of a twitters,' she coyly confessed to James Leigh Perrot, who escorted her to church; and glancing at her face, he was amazed to perceive the remnant of a lost innocence upon her features. Jane Leigh Perrot gave Ellen her own cameo brooch as a wedding gift; it was pinned to Ellen's muslin bosom as she took her vows. 'She has had her eye on it for long enough,' Aunt Perrot observed shrewdly. 'I would rather give it to her than find it missing once we were at sea.'

Both Jem and Ellen had received free pardons, and were to set up in married life in a wattle-and-daub cottage at the other end of Parramatta. Jem hoped in time to start his hackney stable; for the present, he continued his employment as a driver, and it was arranged that Ellen should come each day to attend to household chores in the Leigh Perrots' cottage until the visitors departed. She would bake their mutton dry and overcook their cabbage to the last. Neither Ellen nor Jem, Jane Austen mused, would ever see again those green hedgerows of England entwined with dog-roses and honeysuckle, nor the smelly bustling streets of London; but who was to say that the savage, antiquated English law had not served them a good turn when it delivered them to this scorched landscape of grey-green foliage and dusty cart tracks?

In January, the vice-regal entourage returned to Sydney, and there a New Year's ball was held for the Commander and officers of the *Calcutta*, that ship in which the Leigh Perrots and Miss Austen were soon to embark. They did not attend the ball. 'We shall see more than enough of the *Calcutta* and its officers by the time we reach England,' Aunt Perrot prophesied. The threat of French attack upon the seas loomed nearer now; the fully armed *Calcutta* seemed to offer reassurance.

Towards the end of that month, a whaler, the *Ferret*, arrived from America with more English newspapers, having set sail in late August. The news was eagerly devoured. England had not, after all, been invaded; but the *Times* still carried scaremonger reports: the countryside near Boulogne was white with the tents of the French army; Bonaparte had erected a stone column on a hill above the town, which afforded a clear view of the English coast . . .

Finally, they learned that the *Calcutta* would sail in the second week of March. It was decided they should repair to Sydney during the first week of that month, and well ahead of their departure from Parramatta their sea trunks were dragged out and repacked. Mrs Leigh Perrot was assiduous to obtain a remedy for seasickness; Mr Harris provided a receipt, but could not guarantee its infallibility. She also procured a new supply of Captain Bunker's everlasting toffee. They would be staying with the Patersons in Sydney while they waited to embark.

There were a number of farewell visits to make in Parramatta, and messages and commissions were showered upon the departing travellers, varying from a velvet bonnet for Mrs Marsden ('Nothing *very extreme*, you know, but fashionable withal,' she exhorted Mrs Leigh Perrot) to an olive-press to be ordered for Elizabeth Farm; from heartfelt remembrances to be delivered from Rebecca Ashcroft to her family, to the safe-conduct of a number of John Lewin's impressions of the Lepidoptera of New South Wales, for delivery to a London engraver. 'We shall have eighteen *moths* to look after in our cabin, my love,' James Leigh Perrot told his wife.

Jane Austen parted from Elizabeth McArthur and Emma Strongbow with a real sense of regret; it was unlikely in the extreme that they would ever meet again, she thought.

Mr Leigh Perrot composed a gracious letter of appreciation for the many kindnesses they had received within the Colony; he intended it for publication in the *Gazette* after they had sailed, and posted it in the contributions box outside the Government stores. (Months later, upon receiving from Mrs Strongbow a copy of the issue in which his sentiments were printed, he was somewhat chagrined to discover they had been merely paraphrased thus: 'A stranger has remarked, that old English hospitality expands itself throughout the Colony. In Sydney, he says, he was entertained with ceremonious politeness; in Parramatta, with friendly affability.')

His own collections of impaled butterflies and pressed flowers were carefully secured for transportation to another hemisphere, together with several growing plants destined for the hot-houses at Scarlets. Furthermore, with the help of Mr Caley, two kangarus, a male and female, had been obtained. These, as Jane Leigh Perrot had regretfully anticipated, were destined for the park at Scarlets. Until they sailed, the marsupials were to be confined in the garden enclosure at Government House in Sydney, by kind permission of His Excellency.

'They will present a fine spectacle, basking beneath the oaks,' James asserted confidently. 'And they will help Bingami to feel less strange amid his new surroundings,' he added hopefully.

'And how, pray, are the animals to *bask* in winter, when the park is covered by snow?' his wife asked tartly. But she did not press the point. So far as she was concerned, her husband might make an Antipodean Noah's Ark of the *Calcutta* if he wished, just so long as it bore them home safely and speedily.

A few days before they left Parramatta, the serviceable suit of clothes and buckled shoes were brought out and held up against

Bingami to ascertain whether he had outgrown them. (He had not, being as skinny as when he and James had first encountered one another.) Bingami himself was greatly relieved when they took the clothes away again; he had thought they were going to encase his own smooth skin inside that rough, hairy skin of coat and breeches, and put those weights with their shiny buckles upon his feet once more.

James Leigh Perrot asked his niece to try by some means to impress upon the Aboriginal boy just what their plans for his future were: he did not believe his own efforts in that direction had been fully understood by Bingami. Jane hit upon the notion of drawing a series of cartoons. The first showed Bingami as he was now, standing amid the bush, with a kookaburra perched on a branch above his head. The second showed him wearing his new clothes. Next came their departure for Sydney by coach, Bingami seated next to Jem upon the driving seat. Here was their entry on to the ship, together with the kangarus . . . ruefully, Jane realized that neither of her sailor brothers would have passed as remotely seaworthy her depiction of His Majesty's ship *Calcutta*. Now she drew the ship again, upon a wide expanse of sea, and tried to indicate its long, long journey by showing the waxing and waning of many moons – at which Bingami nodded wisely. Next came the arrival in England; and finally she drew Bingami engaged in gardening at her uncle's country house.

Bingami's disconcerting response to all this artistic industry was to grin widely, pull his hair, and rub one foot against the back of his other leg as he stood watching the progress of her pencil upon the paper. Jane had the uneasy feeling that he regarded the whole essay as no more than a fairy tale.

A fairy tale it proved to be. There was a full moon, golden as mimosa, yellow as a Gloucester cheese, the night before they left for Sydney. As Bingami lay upon a heap of sacks in the lean-to shed behind the cottage, he heard out of the night that call he knew above all others . . . the hooting cry of the little owl which in the language of his people was known by his own name: *Bingami. Mo-poke, mo-poke!* The owl was Bingami: he was the owl. And, as he heeded the clear insistence of that call – *mo-poke, mo-poke!* – he wondered what he was doing here, why he had lingered so long in this white man's camp. He remembered that his own place lay far apart from these strangers in his land. Silently he left his sleeping quarters and slipped away into the bush, one small shadow among greater shadows . . . The pair of kangaru might or might not survive that journey to another world, but Bingami was not destined to become Ben the gardener's boy, to hoe vegetables and rake the gravel paths of an English country house.

In the morning, when it was discovered Bingami had gone, James Leigh Perrot shook his head sorrowfully; but his wife heaved a sigh of heartfelt relief, and told Jem to give away the serviceable suit of clothes and buckled shoes to some deserving white-skinned lad. And so, with Jem taking up the reins, they set off in the shabby coach once more, along the rutted road to Sydney, waving farewell to a little crowd of wellwishers.

The Patersons welcomed them with Scottish hospitality, and the Colonel viewed with almost fanatic interest James Leigh Perrot's collections and John Lewin's paintings. He listened sympathetically to the tragic tale of the butterfly which had escaped, and to James' theory that it had seemed to indicate a link between butterfly and moth. The Patersons, it transpired, were themselves to leave Sydney in May: the Colonel had been appointed to take charge of a new settlement at Port Dalrymple, in Van Diemen's Land.

'They say Van Diemen's Land is very picturesque,' Elizabeth Paterson observed bravely; 'but I confess, when travellers set off for home, it always sets me yearning for a glimpse of Edinburgh.'

Another ship, the *Rose*, had recently dropped anchor at Port Jackson on her way from America to China. An officer of the Marines had taken passage on her, having sailed from London to Boston: and having advertised himself as a courier, he brought a batch of English mail to the Colony, which included one or two letters for the Leigh Perrots and Miss Austen. James Leigh Perrot was gratified to learn from his stockbroker that the investment he had made to recoup past losses had prospered in his absence. And Mr Edgeworth, his neighbour at Scarlets, wrote to tell him that he had offered to put that semaphore system which he and James had devised together at the disposal of the military, in the event of an invasion.

Miss Austen received intelligence both heartening on the one hand and distressing on the other. With thankful relief she learned from her brother Henry that he and Eliza had managed to slip safely out of France after the Peace was broken. 'Orders were issued by the French Government to detain all English travellers,' Henry wrote; 'and quite a large number of Visitors who took advantage of the Peace must languish now in France as *détenus*. But Eliza gave such a good Account of herself at the several Post-houses as we fled to the coast (whilst I malingered as a Speechless invalid coughing into my cravat) that she was quite taken to be a Frenchwoman, and so we made our Excape.'

But Cassandra's letter contained the depressing news that their mother had suffered a quite serious illness, though she was now mending. (That, of course, was five months ago . . . she might have suffered a relapse. Jane firmly turned her thoughts aside from further unhappy speculation.) Jane's return, Cassandra declared, would doubtless complete their mother's convalescence. 'We plan a visit to Lyme before the year is out, together with Henry and Eliza. Pray return in time to join us!' She had copied out an amusing verse which Mrs Austen had composed, and Jane felt more cheerful when she read this. It was entitled 'Dialogue between Death and Mrs A:'

'Says Death, "I've been trying these three weeks and more
To seize an old Madam here at Number Four,
Yet I still try in vain, tho' she's turned of three score;
To what is my ill success owing?"

' "I'll tell you, old Fellow, if you cannot guess
To what you're indebted for your ill success –
To the prayers of my husband, whose love I possess,
To the care of my daughter, whom Heaven will bless,
To the skill and attention of Bowen." '

' . . . Mr Bowen,' Cassandra wrote, 'has proved himself a very skilled and attentive medical adviser.' Perhaps ominously, her letter contained no news of *Susan*, save to say that the man of affairs employed by Henry in his London offices had been deputed to deal further with Mr Crosby; pessimistically, Jane wondered whether this meant that the publication of her novel had been abandoned . . .

The news concerning her mother was an additional incentive to return home; and now it was with profound satisfaction they learned that the sailing date for the *Calcutta* was definitely fixed for the fifteenth of March.

Sydney seemed positively to bustle with activity after the seclusion of Parramatta. The tall masts of the *Calcutta* dominated the wharfside, and the sight of that brave vessel was a heartening assurance of their eventual return to everything they knew and held dear. There would be one very significant difference between their outward and homeward journeys: the *Calcutta* would, of course, carry no convicts back to England. Her erstwhile convict quarters had been cleansed and sweetened. But while this promised relief from the tensions engendered in sharing the transportation of human outcasts, that other constant anxiety would accompany them: the danger of encountering a French man-o'-war.

Meanwhile, a much nearer danger presented itself just eleven days before the *Calcutta* sailed. The fourth of March, a Sunday, the Leigh Perrots and Miss Austen spent quietly, paying an afternoon call – a formal leavetake – upon the Governor's lady. Josepha King received them in that same small parlour where they had sat during their first visit, some nine months ago. Mrs King was as friendly as ever, but Jane Austen thought she seemed a trifle distracted, as though her mind were upon other matters. As they exchanged compliments, Mr Chapman appeared to wish the travellers godspeed and a safe passage.

'Pray rest assured that I am personally attending to the embarkation of the kangarus,' he told Mr Leigh Perrot. – He, too, Jane thought, appeared somewhat distrait.

That very night, well after the Patersons and their guests had retired to bed, there came a thunderous knocking at the house door: rudely aroused from sleep, the inmates awoke to an awareness of extraordinary events afoot. Bells tolled; trumpets sounded; they heard the tramping of soldiers mustered for duty, orders barked across the barracks square close by, the rumbling of cart wheels . . . all the commotion of a settlement suddenly called upon to defend itself.

What was it? Had a French Fleet suddenly swept into Sydney Cove? By the time the Leigh Perrots and their niece had dressed in haste and, with a peculiar sense of urgency, joined Mrs

Paterson in the parlour, the Colonel had left the house to take command of the assembling forces. The Paterson's servant appeared, sleazy with sleep, and was bidden to prepare tea.

'The Irish convicts at Castle Hill have risen,' Elizabeth Paterson told them, white-faced yet calm. 'The news has just reached Sydney from Parramatta. Colonel Paterson is mustering our defences here in case the rebels march on Sydney: the regular troops are being joined by the volunteers of the Loyal Association, and Captain Woodriff is to bring a hundred and fifty officers and seamen from the *Calcutta*.' She swallowed, and, recollecting her husband's exhortation not to alarm their visitors unduly, said with as much assurance as she could manage: 'There is no cause for any grave apprehension. Major Johnstone is marching to Parramatta with a body of soldiers, and Captain Abbott is mustering the defences there. 'Tis said the Governor himself is riding to join them – the rebellion will soon be dealt with, you may be sure.'

Mrs Paterson's three guests maintained the demeanour to be expected of English gentlefolk suddenly placed under threat. But troubled feelings lay beneath their impassive expressions and studied calm. How dreadful, James Leigh Perrot thought, if his desire to see the Colony were finally to result in tragedy overtaking his wife, his niece and himself! As Jane Léigh Perrot sipped her tea, she thought how ironic, how cruel a stroke of fate it would be if this rebellion were to succeed – just one week before they sailed for home! As for Jane Austen, she could not help conjuring up in her mind's eye ghastly scenes such as those reported by eye-witnesses of the Terror in France.

'It must be much worse for all our friends in Parramatta,' Elizabeth Paterson said quietly; and together they joined in a prayer for their safety.

Mrs Paterson found it helped to busy herself with little tasks; she fetched the brandy decanter for Mr Leigh Perrot, then wound the carriage clock upon the mantelshelf. It was now an hour past midnight.

'We have expected an attempt at rebellion sooner or later,' she said. 'Mr King has never concealed his distrust of the Irish convicts set to work on the Government farm at Castle Hill. A great many of them are political prisoners and some are priests . . . together with the rest of the Irish felons in the Colony, they belong to an illegal association formed in Governor Hunter's time: they call themselves the United Irishmen. Well, now our expectation has been fulfilled. Lieutenant Hobby brought the news of the uprising straight to the Governor, then came to rouse my husband. It seems that upwards of two hundred convicts assembled, rang the alarm, set the big house at Castle Hill on fire, and then dispersed to search for arms. Their leader is a man called Cunningham – 'tis said his plan is to gather more convicts to his cause throughout the countryside, arm them, take Parramatta, then march on Sydney to seize the ships in the harbour. One of their number turned informer, apparently, and apprised Captain Abbott of this –'

Aunt Perrot visualized the *Calcutta* in rebel hands and closed her eyes briefly. 'But two hundred is not such a very large number,' she said hopefully.

Elizabeth Paterson lowered her gaze; she did not disclose the fact that her husband had said the rebels apparently expected to gain a full thousand followers from the Hawkesbury and Parramatta districts as they marched.

Speculation was exhausted as time dragged by; after three or four hours, when there was no sign of a rebel army approaching Sydney, they repaired to their beds once more, dozing fitfully and rising again to face a morning of rumour and counter-rumour.

There were other visitors in the house when the Leigh Perrots and Miss Austen came into breakfast. To their amazement, they saw Mrs McArthur, Mrs Marsden and Mrs Abbott seated there, looking tired and anxious.

'I hoped we might meet again some day, but did not imagine 'twould be so soon, nor in such inauspicious circumstances,' Elizabeth McArthur greeted them. 'We left Parramatta by boat about eleven last night –'

' – together with my husband and our children,' Mrs Marsden added. ' 'Twas thought Mr Marsden would be sought out as a prime victim of the rebels' fury, since he is a magistrate.'

That was not the whole reason, as everyone in the room except the English visitors were aware: three years ago, when there had been other trouble with the Irish, Mr Marsden had had a young Irishman called Galvin flogged within an inch of his life: his compatriots had not forgotten that.

'The alarm was first brought to us by a settler at Seven Hills,' Mrs Abbott said; 'then, just before we left, a constable who had managed to escape from Castle Hill reached Parramatta, and told us the rebels were but a short distance away –'

'They were as close as the Parkgate,' Mrs Marsden added shrilly, 'but for some reason, thank God, they did not advance –'

'We were extremely relieved when we arrived here to learn that a relief force was already on its way from Sydney,' Mrs McArthur continued. 'I feel sure the situation will be brought under control in a very short time –'

Suddenly poor Mrs Marsden almost broke down. 'Oh! pray excuse me,' she quavered. 'You can have no idea what a dreadful night it was, what we have suffered in our minds – oh! if only another clergyman would arrive to replace Mr Marsden, so that we might return to England! It is shocking to live in a place where one is in continual fear –'

'A good sleep is what we all need,' Mrs Abbott said briskly. She turned to pat Mrs Marsden's arm reassuringly. 'Come, Eliza, your spirits will soon be restored, and all this will be forgotten, as if it were no more than a bad dream.'

And soon after, the three ladies left, presenting a brave front as they stepped into the street, to be gawped at by all the loiterers at large upon this unusual day.

It was all over by the evening. They soon learned what had transpired. Major Johnstone had reached Parramatta at first light, where he divided his force and himself led one party to Toongabbie, where the rebels, their number now swelled to four hundred, and armed with a strange array of weapons – pikes and pitchforks, pistols, cutlasses and bayonets – had taken up their stand on Vinegar Hill. He advanced towards the hill with about twenty soldiers and a dozen armed settlers, and made three attempts to parley with the rebel leaders. The third time, he and his trooper rode up to face Cunningham and the other leader, Johnson. 'What is it you want?' the Major demanded of Cunningham. 'Death or liberty!' Cunningham answered him; whereupon the Major clapped his pistol to the rebel's head and ordered him to surrender – while his trooper did the same to Johnson. At this, firing broke out on both sides, and the undisciplined rebel force soon broke and fled in disarray. The official tally was fifteen rebels killed and six or seven wounded, with many prisoners taken. At first it was thought Cunningham was dead, but later in the day he was seized at Green Hills, and was hanged immediately. The Governor, who had ridden through the night to Parramatta, issued a proclamation of martial law in all the western districts.

It was learned that the rebels' failure to enter Parramatta that night hinged upon a breakdown in communication with their leader: the signal for them to enter at the Parkgate was to have been the firing of Elizabeth Farm, which would have drawn the soldiers from the Barracks. The rebels would then have taken over the Barracks, seizing all arms and ammunition. But Cunningham's order to this effect had never been received.

There was general relief and a sense of escape from some fearful fate. The last days which the Leigh Perrots and Miss Jane Austen spent in the Colony were darkened by the punishment of the rebels. Eight more were hanged in chains, two being strung up in Sydney. Others received floggings of as many as five hundred lashes; fifty were sent to labour at the Coal River.

Governor King, hastily penning an account of this first rebellion ever to break out within the Colony, for dispatch to London by the *Calcutta*, wrote: 'I deeply lament the necessity imposed on me of directing the execution of those selected from upwards of two hundred taken with arms in their hands and who had a most active part in those transactions.' Although Mr King was of the opinion that the numbers of the rebels might have increased to more than two thousand – being the number of Irish in the Colony – if they had had time to gain more recruits to their dastardly cause, he did in truth feel considerable compassion for the majority of those deluded fools. 'It is my belief,' he wrote to Lord Hobart in London, 'that some very artful, designing wretches, above the common class of these deluded people, are deeply implicated.' His suspicion fell strongly upon the Irish knight, Sir Henry Brown Hayes . . . and he was not altogether convinced that the French were not involved in some manner. A certain François Girault, a Frenchman plying the trade of a pedlar, had been apprehended and was under strong suspicion of having secretly aided and abetted the revolt, spreading revolutionary dissension and discontent. Inflammatory pamphlets which he distributed to the convicts at Castle Hill had laid beneath the ribands in his tray. He was to be deported on the *Calcutta*; nothing more could be done with him; he had been sufficiently ingenious to avoid open detection, and so escaped condign punishment.

'A spy!' Mrs Leigh Perrot exclaimed when she heard of his activities. 'Depend on it, a French spy!' Then she frowned. 'I do believe 'twas the same pedlar who coaxed Ellen into buying that blue ribbon for her wedding dress – I remember now, Ellen said he spoke in a foreign voice!'

On Thursday 15th March, the three travellers at last embarked upon the *Calcutta* to be welcomed aboard by Captain Woodriff. It was a fine day, with a breeze which augured well for their departure. Each wooden inlet, each little island of that splendid natural harbour was clearly defined; their last sight of New South Wales would be indelibly engraved upon their memory.

Just as the obliging Mr Chapman had been present at the wharf to greet them upon their arrival, so now he was there to see them off – having first attended to the welfare of the kangarus. The refugees from Parramatta had by now returned there; martial law had been lifted some days ago, and the Governor had taken pains to assure everyone that nothing but the appearance of a foreign enemy – a remote prospect – would lead to a renewal of trouble. Jane Austen had repeated her reluctant leavetake of Elizabeth McArthur, and there had been a wistful longing in Mrs Marsden's eye as she contemplated their journey home to England. The Patersons accompanied them on board – it would not be long before they themselves sailed for Van Diemen's Land.

The ship was carrying home a detachment of marines whose term of duty had expired, as well as several invalids, and a few emancipated convicts whose circumstances permitted them to return to the motherland which had cast them off. The passengers quartered on the poop deck, along with the Leigh Perrot party, included a pale-lipped, coughing officer of the Corps who did not look as though he would live to see the farther shore; a rich emancipist returning to drum up business for himself in London; and a complaining, childless military wife who could not abide to remain in Sydney a moment longer. Her husband, Jane observed, seeing them together on the deck, appeared to bid her farewell with mixed emotions of sorrow, exasperation and relief. Throughout the voyage her fellow passengers were destined to listen to this unhappy lady inveighing against the iniquities and boredom of the Colony. Major Foveaux, who had now definitely decided to return to England, had hoped to sail by the *Calcutta*, but had not been able to wind up his affairs in time. – Captain Piper, meanwhile, had gone to Norfolk Island as Lieutenant-Governor in his stead.

There was one other gentleman they knew, who had brought on board his two sons, to travel to England in Captain Woodriff's care: Mr D'Arcy Wentworth. While Colonel Paterson helped Mr Leigh Perrot to dispose his growing plants about his cabin in the most advantageous positions, and Mrs Paterson condoled with Mrs Leigh Perrot upon her pessimistic premonition of seasickness, Mr Wentworth and Miss Austen exchanged a few words. Young D'Arcy and William were already eagerly exploring the ship.

'So finally we bid goodbye to each other, Miss Austen,' Mr Wentworth said, holding her gloved hand in a light grasp. 'Take care of my boys for me; think kindly of our little Colony; and spare a thought sometimes' – his blue eyes were lit with self-mockery – 'for a reformed highwayman.'

Jane felt an absurd pricking of tears. 'I shall do all of those things, Mr Wentworth,' she replied in a tremulous voice.

'And – shall you write of New South Wales, Miss Austen?'

She shook her head, then found her full voice again. 'People, I have discovered, are much the same everywhere,' she said. 'But as to settings and events – I believe the Colony presents too large a landscape for my modest purposes, while its events –' she broke off, thinking of the extraordinary happenings of their last days here, which had culminated in hangings, floggings and the hardest labour of the chain-gang. 'No, Mr Wentworth,' she concluded, 'let other pens dwell on guilt and misery. My talents, such as they are, must be contained within a smaller, happier framework.'

The Colony was reluctant to let them go; the ship got under way, but it proved a false start: the wind lulled suddenly and she was obliged to bring to near Garden Island. All Friday morning they rode at anchor in a limbo of having departed Port Jackson, yet still remaining there.

The delay afforded the opportunity for one more farewell,

however. At midday, a rowing-boat was observed hauling towards them across the glassy surface of the sea. Jane Austen, standing on the poop deck, saw that it contained two people: the rough, bearded oarsman and a young military officer who sat gripping both sides of the boat, as if to hasten its progress. As it approached the side of the *Calcutta*, a cockleshell beneath her bows, the young officer stood up, an action which rocked the rowboat perilously, and, cupping both hands to his mouth, hallooed those on board. Jane peered down at him. Was he a late-come passenger, she wondered. Then, suddenly, she recognized him. It was Lieutenant Watson!

'Miss – Austen!' he called, waving vigorously. 'I – had – to – say – goodbye!'

She was quite overcome by his impetuosity, and leaning over the deck rail, she blew him a heartfelt kiss for the trouble he had taken to row out this far. He, in his turn, was utterly undone by that kiss-in-air: he seemed to forget he was standing in a boat rocking upon shark-infested waters, and actually advanced a step, as it were towards her. 'I – will – never – forget – YOU!' he called ... but in that instant, the rowing-boat tipped very seriously indeed to larboard, and with a spectacular splash Lieutenant Watson fell into the sea.

While Jane looked down in just a little consternation – but mainly, it must be confessed, with irrepressible amusement – the stalwart boatman unshipped one oar and fished a very drenched young officer out of the water. Undaunted, he sat down and raised one dripping scarlet-sleeved arm in a mute and final salute, while the oarsman, without more ado, set his course back the way they had come. Jane stood blowing kisses after him in reckless abandon. It had been such a gallant farewell gesture ...

A breeze blew up in the afternoon: the *Calcutta* weighed again, and by six that evening had cleared the Heads and was received by the open sea. And as that ship began her long, lonely voyage, the sky above Sydney Cove was afire with crimson and red, shot through with deepest blue and streaked with gold ... the glorious opalescent sunset of the Antipodes.

Envoi

IT MAY BE of interest to append a few notes concerning the real-life characters of this story:

Jane Austen's novel *Susan* was not published by Richard Crosby after all; in 1816 he relinquished the manuscript (in return for the ten pounds he had paid for it) and two years later it was published posthumously by John Murray under the title *Northanger Abbey*. In 1804–5, Miss Austen began writing a new novel, now known as *The Watsons*, but abandoned it about the time of her father's death, in 1805. Mrs Austen, together with her two daughters and Martha Lloyd, who joined their household at this time (she later became the second wife of Francis Austen), then lived at Southampton for a short time, and in 1809 settled in the village of Chawton, Hampshire, in a house belonging to her son Edward Austen Knight. Here Jane Austen wrote *Mansfield Park*, *Emma* and *Persuasion*. Meanwhile, her two earlier novels *Sense and Sensibility* (originally entitled *Elinor and Marianne*) and *Pride and Prejudice* (originally called *First Impressions*) were published in 1811 and 1813 respectively. *Mansfield Park* was published in 1814, *Emma* in 1815, and her last novel, *Persuasion*, posthumously, in 1818. In 1817 she began a new novel, *Sanditon*, which remained unfinished, for about this time her health broke down. She died on 18 July 1817 – it is generally supposed of Addison's Disease, a morbid state caused by adrenal insufficiency which was first described by Thomas Addison in 1855, and for which effective treatment was not introduced until 1930.

Cassandra Austen lived on at Chawton after her mother's death in 1827, and Martha Lloyd's marriage to Francis Austen. Cassandra died in 1845 at the Francis Austens' house near Portsmouth.

Edward Austen Knight died at Godmersham in 1852, surviving his wife Elizabeth by forty-four years. She died in 1808, after the birth of their eleventh child. He did not remarry.

Francis Austen later became Admiral of the Fleet Sir Francis Austen GCB. He commanded the West Indian and North American Station, 1845–8. His first wife (Mary Gibson) died in 1823, after producing nine children, and he later married Martha Lloyd. He died in 1865. Jane Austen's other naval brother, *Charles Austen*, became a Rear-Admiral and was employed in the suppression of the Slave Trade and against Mehemet Ali. In 1850 he commanded in the East Indian and Chinese waters, and died of cholera on the Irrawaddy River in 1852. He first married Frances Palmer, who died in 1814, and then her sister Harriet.

Henry Austen's business career ended in bankruptcy in 1816, and later that year he entered the Church. He held the living of Steventon for three years following his brother James' death in 1819, and later became perpetual curate of Bentley, Hampshire. Afterwards he lived for some time in France. He died at Tunbridge Wells in 1850. His wife Eliza died in 1813, and he married a lady called Eleanor Jackson in 1820.

James Leigh Perrot died at Scarlets in March 1817. His will, made in 1811, was a bitter blow to the Austen family. On 6 April 1817, Jane Austen, her illness now increasing, wrote to her brother Charles: 'I am ashamed to say that the shock of my uncle's will brought on a relapse . . .' Everything was left to his wife for her lifetime, much of it absolutely, with a sum tied up in trust to revert to his nephew James Austen and his heirs when Jane Leigh Perrot died, at which time legacies of one thousand pounds should pass to such of James' brothers and sisters as should survive their aunt. James Leigh Perrot left nothing to his own sister, Jane Austen's mother. (He had, however, already expended the considerable sum of ten thousand pounds in rescuing Henry Austen from insolvency upon the collapse of the latter's business.) In the event, James Austen did not live to inherit; he died in 1819, and in the last year of his life his aunt Jane Leigh Perrot withdrew the annuity of one hundred pounds which her husband had given him in 1808. *Jane Leigh Perrot* died in 1835, aged ninety-two.

Philip Gidley King remained as Governor of New South Wales until 1807; he died in London the following year. His quarrel with John McArthur was patched up when the latter returned to the Colony in 1805; indeed, the McArthur family stayed with the Kings at that time at Government House in Sydney. *Mrs King* stayed in England for twenty-four years, then returned to New South Wales in 1832, where two of her daughters were settled. Her daughter Maria married Hannibal McArthur, son of John McArthur's elder brother, who had also settled in the Colony.

John McArthur returned to the Colony in 1805 and took up a large grant of land at the Cow Pastures, where he pursued his ambition to breed merino sheep. He was later to become known as the founder of Australia's wool industry. In 1808, he played a leading role in the deposing of Governor Bligh, and as a result suffered a further period of exile in England. When he returned once more, he built a large country house, Camden Park, in the Cow Pastures district. He died in 1834; *Elizabeth McArthur* survived him by sixteen years.

D'Arcy Wentworth died at Homebush in 1827. His obituary in the *Monitor* declared: 'He was a lover of freedom, a consistent steady friend of the people; a kind and liberal master; a just and humane magistrate: a steady friend and an honest man.' His son *William Charles* was his heir: in 1813, the latter was a member of the party which first succeeded in crossing the Blue Mountains. He first learned of his father's youthful exploits from a pamphlet produced in London; it was a great blow to his self-esteem. He wished to marry one of the McArthurs' daughters, but they opposed the union. Subsequently, William Charles became an ardent political champion of the Emancipist party within the Colony.

Matthew Flinders was interned on Mauritius by the French Governor of that island for six years; he finally returned to England in 1810, and died four years later.

John Harris travelled to England in 1809, and returned to New South Wales with his newly wedded wife, Eliza, in 1814 as a private settler. He died in 1838 at his property, Shane's Park, South Creek. He had no children, and arranged for the bulk of his estate to pass always to a male heir bearing the name John Harris.

Colonel William Paterson, upon his return from Van Diemen's Land, was one of three acting administrators of New South Wales following the deposing of Governor Bligh in 1808. (The other two were Johnstone and Foveaux.) He died during a voyage back to England in 1810. *Elizabeth Paterson* returned to live in England and married as her second husband Major Francis Grose, the former Commandant of the New South Wales Corps. She died in Bath in 1825.

George Caley became homesick for England and returned there in 1808, taking an Aboriginal companion with him.

John Lewin's engravings were safely conveyed to England, and his book, *Prodromus Entomology, Natural History of Lepidopterous Insects of New South Wales*, was published in London in 1805. He also produced *A Natural History of the Birds of New South Wales*, as well as thousands of drawings and watercolours. About 1808 he and his wife moved from Parramatta to Sydney, where for a short time they kept an inn, The Bunch of Grapes, and later a shop known as The Universal Warehouse. Their fortunes improved considerably when Governor Macquarie took office in 1809. Lewin also took pupils, and in the *Sydney Gazette* (6 June 1811) advertised 'his Assistance to the Youth of both Sexes in the Study of Drawing, from a Wish to render every Assistance in his Power to the Cultivation of Talent in this infant rising Colony'. He died in 1819. His widow returned to England in 1820 with their son William, born about 1810.